Harvesting Ashwood
Minnesota 2037

ALSO BY CYNTHIA KRAACK

Minnesota Cold
Winner of the Northeastern Minnesota Book Award for Best Fiction

Ashwood

Chapter One

For a decade the great gray house known as Ashwood had opened its gates for survivors of the Second Great Depression. They walked through the tall front doors carrying what remained of their life in boxes and backpacks. In its basement storerooms, they traded mismatched remnants of clothing for new pants and shirts and sturdy shoes. The kitchen set out a small meal to fill their shrunken bellies with food from the estate's greenhouses and fields. A mentoring adult walked them to a dorm where children slept in safety between clean sheets.

I was a survivor who carried my own bag through those same gates and stood in the dark outside these doors. Though the seven years since I arrived have treated me well, I could never forget the darkness of the time the city kids tagged g2d or simply D. While adults coming through our gates no longer looked as desperate, the children removed from their families and delivered to the secure haven of Ashwood claimed my heart.

A house with almost three dozen children never truly sleeps. Many of Ashwood's residents feared the dark, myself included, so dim lights punctuated its halls. Each night the adults of Ashwood took turns resting near the residence's center where a child might wander, listening for homesick tears, offering a glass of clean water, or smoothing a blanket. Unless the child was my stepdaughter, Phoebe. She called, "Mom," and I was the only one who could ease her from terror to sleep.

"I'll take care of her, David. Don't worry."

I touched my husband's arm as Phoebe's voice came through the monitor, knowing her suffering caused him deep distress. Across a cool hall I sprinted to her room. She sat upright in bed, eyes open and unseeing, mouth open, hands clawing at her blanket. I brought my arms down around her rigid body, rocking her as carefully as a package stamped fragile.

"You're okay, Phoebe. It's Mom holding you, loved one." Words flowed in the darkness, words I knew she might not hear, would not remember. But the words built a rhythm that guided my hands as I rocked long minutes until Phoebe relaxed onto my chest.

"Mom." She whispered one word, swallowed. Her little-girl voice traveled along a dry throat, sounded painful. "I'm thirsty."

I found the water glass kept next to her bed and brought it to her lips. She sipped then rested again. I put the glass down and continued rocking her until she slept.

This episode felt different to me, more unsettling. I checked our sons' room before settling in the kitchen. With no one needing my attention, I used my sleepless time to review production numbers for Ashwood's thousands of acres of fields, commercial greenhouses, and barns.

"Annie, what are you doing?" David's Midwestern-accented tenor slipped across the kitchen's metal and stone surfaces. "Come to bed. It's almost three." By the clarity of his words I knew he hadn't slept either since Phoebe's screams.

"You startled me." I saved my work, shut down the data pad. "I couldn't settle after calming Phoebe and thought the quiet might help me untangle the dairy numbers." He held out a hand, helped me to my feet. "And you should be asleep. That 6:00 a.m. transport is only three hours off."

"There'll be time for sleeping on the jet. I'd rather be awake with you." After seven years together, our steps matched as we walked, his six-foot-four stride adjusted to my five-foot-seven movement. A heavy man when we first met, David was now muscular and healthy from Ashwood's physical demands including a few hours of field work each week. "I want to talk about this trip, Anne. I think we're about to land deep in a South American conflict."

"Will you be in danger?"

"Not this time."

I heard the implication that there would be a next time. The only question was when.

"Come to bed." David held up the sheets. "We might not sleep, but I'd rather leave remembering your body by my side." In the dim room his dark hair made his face ghostly. "That was a bad spell. Is Phoebe all right?"

I settled next to him, placed my head on his shoulder. "She was sitting upright when I got to her room, eyes wide open." I waited for him to ask the next question. He didn't. "We're doing everything we can, David. It just seems like the terrors are happening more often."

HARVESTING ASHWOOD
Minnesota 2037

Cynthia Kraack

NORTH STAR PRESS OF ST. CLOUD, INC.
Saint Cloud, Minnesota

Dedication

For my family.

Copyright © 2012 Cynthia Kraack

ISBN 978-0-87839-607-8

All rights reserved.

This is a work of fiction. Names, characters, places, and incidents are the products of the author's imagination or are used fictitiously. Any resemblance to actual events or persons, living or dead, is entirely coincidental.

Cover Art: Terrence Scott.

First Edition: June 2012

Printed in the United States of America

Published by
North Star Press of St. Cloud, Inc.
P.O. Box 451
St. Cloud, Minnesota 56302

www.northstarpress.com

"I worry that the mental imbalance of Tia's family is in Phoebe's genes." He pulled me closer, the scent of his body as familiar as my own. "The Bureau of Human Capital Management's therapist didn't respond when I asked her that question."

We parented Phoebe with different expectations. He watched for signs of potential problems. I fed her creative spirit. "Tia was certainly unsure about becoming a mother. Nurse Kim handed you this little baby while Tia cried." David hadn't looked at his first wife as he accepted their daughter. "The first thing I saw was that this tiny baby had her mother's beautiful rosebud mouth."

"Her mother was crazy, Annie. You knew that."

"We didn't know that, David." This was a discussion we had had too many times. "Phoebe is just a little girl. She won't be eight for another two months."

He tapped the window coverings' control. Cut into a hill, the western residence wing overlooked the back edge of one apple orchard and an acre of oak trees. I could barely see the safety lights that illuminated Ashwood's fences.

"Let's enjoy the view of the woods." Jostling us both, he bent an arm under his head. "Forgetting the cost, our tree wind stand was a brilliant idea." I listened to his breathing, how it changed as he spoke. "Remember the snowstorm the first day we met?"

I was the Bureau's new estate matron greeting the government intelligentsia couple assigned to live at Ashwood. He was insistent about going over estate plans, and I resented his behavior. He tended to recall that day with a different set of memories.

"If we're going to be awake, tell me why you're worried about this trip to Paraguay." Maybe the lack of sleep goosed my anxiety about David's assignment.

"Because I don't know what's going on in South America. The Department of Energy has only a handful of small projects in Paraguay." He rubbed his forehead, then swiped a large hand over his face. "Things don't add up and no one will talk." I felt his chest deflate as he yawned.

"Why did you get called?"

"Damned if I know. The assignment docket calls for an adviser which doesn't jive with the project's budget."

Between the tree stand and the residence, I saw a handful of coyotes moving in a swift, graceful line from the estate's eastern fences toward the stables. They'd be disappointed unless rabbits wandered across their path. Morning security video would send someone to check our fencing. Securing Ashwood against the uninvited, whether human or wild, claimed daily priority.

"You'll be home in a week, in time for your father's birthday. The boys think it is pretty special that Grandpa Paul is turning seventy." I yawned, snuggled my body close to his. "Do you mind if we sleep? I think the night just caught up with me."

I felt his shoulder relax as my eyes shut. Heard the alarm wake him too soon, let him ease out of bed. I stayed behind until the second alarm sounded to start my day. Tile floors cooled my feet as I stood up, made me remember to tell Sarah that winter area rugs should be taken out of storage.

While he finished dressing, I washed my face and thought how the years of estate living kept us strong. David's forty-five-year-old body looked lean under his traveling suit. He wore his hair close cut, less for maintenance than to deny its thinning. Before he left our room, I ran my hand across his head and kissed his lips.

"There's nothing to worry about here. We'll be fine," I said, holding my voice steady. I kissed him again, following his lead in how long we lingered. "Take care of yourself."

Chapter Two

Waiting for coffee to finish brewing, I watched the first estate transport arrive from the Twin Cities metro area. On a muggy September morning, six men, fourteen women, twelve children, five toddlers, and three infants entered our day-labor gate. Across the acreage of Ashwood and Giant Pines, fields required threshing, cows needed milking, kitchen gardens hung heavy with ripe crops. Twice as many adults were needed for field or animal care physical labor, half as many children could be helpful with light labor around the residence, greenhouses, or gardens. The infants and babies would be a burden on our nursery.

Mothers headed toward the daycare center. All others proceeded to the harvest season dining hall. In spite of the heat, giant pots of oatmeal waited on the stove top. Family, staff, and laborers would work fueled with the same foods. I poured my only cup of brew for what appeared to be the start of a hot day.

"Good morning, Ms. Anne." Cook Jeremiah carried a bowl of fresh berries from the kitchen's east wall storage room. "Thought these would be good for the residence dining room. Field Manager Magda provided early apples for the outdoor workers."

I filched a few berries as he passed. "How is our canned goods inventory?" I knew the answer in numbers but depended on our food expert to translate jars into meals.

"We're holding our own for three, maybe four months. If I can find six workers next week, we'll push that out twelve weeks." He stirred the oatmeal. "If not, we'll use what we can of the gardens' harvest, freeze extra, and add about six weeks to the inventory."

"We'll find a way to get you that labor, Cook. If we have to pull kids from school, I'll take full responsibility." I held up a hand knowing he would protest food processing with a kitchen of child workers. "You know we have at least three women with solid kitchen experience in our day laborers under Sarah's supervision."

"Stuff works out." The nasal pitch of Jeremiah's voice combined with his Minnesota upbringing stretched out the *o* sound. "These folks must have been in line for the five o'clock transport. Not easy for the women with kids."

"Some days I regret opening up a day care center." I only half-meant my comment, but during this string of days of too many dependents accompanying less-than-experienced laborers, I worried that the estate needed to make changes. Government offices, cutting staff in deference to the growth of private sector companies, forced people unaccustomed to physical work in line for day labor opportunities in fields and factories.

I reached for real cream, poured it in my coffee. "You weren't here when we opened the center to expand the workforce from Lakeville and Burnsville. Now we attract too many city people without field or kitchen experience."

"The local transport will bring our regulars in a half hour." He washed the berries with gentle hands and shook water from the colander. "Ashwood won't lose its regulars to munitions or devices factory work."

"If we can keep pay competitive and share food production with employees, I think you'll be right, Cook." I scooped a small dish of oatmeal for myself and moistened the cereal with milk. "The only breakfast food stored in this kitchen when I arrived was oatmeal."

Jeremiah extended a small dish of berries. I balanced it on top of my coffee mug. "We've come back full circle. Lately managing Ashwood has been like building a house from sand." I made sure to smile at this young cook who would have known hunger, but not how to manage a kitchen during the early years after the *D*. "I'll take breakfast to my office. Have a good day."

I turned right as I left the kitchen, walked through the residence's original foyer, and into the glass walkway connecting our home to an office building constructed by the DOE. David mimicked its attractive fieldstone and brick exterior to warm the grim gray exterior of our home, a former government residence.

Through the glass I noticed small pieces of the stucco flaking into soil behind the landscaping shrubs. Built a decade earlier to be utilitarian, the structure proved difficult to maintain, much less beautify. David painted our tall front doors bright red, and we planted gardens of colorful flowers to mark the building as a home. While the surrounding greenhouses, fields, and stables showed prosperity, the original structure suggested the possibility of a different story. Each year the government drew back more support, and no small private business could find the kind of money needed to correct aging public work construction.

"Ms. Anne." A young resident worker approached from behind.

"Yes, Antwone?"

"There's a lady in the foods." He took a breath as if the minimally cooler air of the residence provided great relief. "She wants to meet you. A first-timer called Smithson with a boy. Not a kid used to working. I can tell them."

"How old is he?" I'd had few interactions with Antwone. His stubborn continuation of street mannerisms had grown annoying, particularly in school where he spent most of his class time showing great disinterest or even beating rhythms on a table.

"Old enough to work." Magda was the one who found two knives in the one bag Antwone brought to Ashwood. Now, the boy who needed almost three days of sleep before we could begin to acclimate him to light duty in the kitchen showed this Smithson boy no sympathy. "Maybe 'leven years old. He missin' teeth. Don't look like he lost them fighting."

"What does the woman look like?" I could tell he liked being a messenger, his scrawny chest puffed out and his hands flew in time with his words.

"White. Red-brown hair. Kind of like you." He stopped. "How old are you, Ms. Anne?"

"Why is that important?"

"She might be the same age, but I din't know what that is."

"Thank you, Antwone."

Eyebrows raised, he looked me up and down, more like a teenager than an eight-year-old who should be thinking about long division. Over a hundred children moved through Ashwood's halls in my seven years owning the estate. Maybe the same number of adults worked somewhere on the estate over the course of a year's production. None carried the possible upset of a woman and boy named Smithson.

"Tell her I'll be in the small dining room in an hour."

"Sure thing, Ms. Anne." He nodded as if testing my direction against his own sense of protocol. "What about the kid?"

"The boy is here to work?"

"Last I saw he was eating oatmeal and looking like he might puke."

"Did this woman ask for me to see both of them?"

Antwone's eyes sparkled, as if we were having a fun talk. "Can't say that. So I'll tell her that she's supposed to be with you in the small dining room in an hour. No kid." He turned, feet ready to race back to the stranger.

"Antwone."

He stopped, slightly turned, didn't say a word. For a moment I wondered why we'd finished a conversation bereft of any protocol and now I felt a need to make sure this child had some level of understanding of Bureau of Human Capital Management's expected behavior. Maybe the swagger Antwone affected each time he left the kitchen bothered me.

"You've been here four months, Antwone. You're a bright worker. But you have to remember simple protocol. Let's take your leaving from the top."

Young enough to take his worker status for granted, he turned toward me. I didn't choose to see his resentment. Living away from home and bending to government protocols were big challenges to young city kids used to making their own way while parents worked long hours. "I don't mean disrespect, Ms. Anne."

"I believe you. And I know you understand that we have to help prepare you for your next assignment." I forced a small smile, hoping to show Antwone encouragement while my thoughts flew to a woman named Smithson. "Next time you'll remember."

He bowed his head slightly and rolled his eyes. Then left without even a head tip of respect. I ignored the slight, turned, and stared out the long windowed hallway as if I could see the Smithson woman and her boy. It had been over ten years since I had seen the child.

Chapter Three

THE DOE OFFICE BUILDING HOUSED DAVID, his team of five engineers, and a research laboratory. For eight years David's spacious office had overlooked the side orchards. Only twenty months remained in his government service requirement, and then the DOE identity chip buried under his left shoulder would be removed. I hoped to catch him and talk about the Smithson woman before he left.

Instead of doing his traditional last minute clearing of his desk, David sat reading.

"Jet departure has been rescheduled for this afternoon." He looked up the moment I stepped into his office. "So I was reading an opinion piece about the challenges of returning government revenues to a tax-based system from our current fees schedules." A topic we often discussed. "You have an interesting perspective on the subject. Maybe you should write a piece." I still carried my breakfast, needed a place to set the cup and bowl down. "Something wrong? You look shaky."

Stepping into the space with his precious collections of old baseball hats, athletic team mugs, and family pictures, I put my things on his table. "There's a woman named Smithson in the day-labor group. She wants to see me."

I watched David process the Smithson name. He rubbed his right cheek, tongue moving inside his mouth in time with his hand. "You were surrogate for a couple with that name."

Retention of personal details ranked high in David's strengths. His parents now lived with us, and I briefly knew his first wife, but all the people from my past were merely names and stories. "She has a boy with her who is about the same age as the baby I delivered." We looked at each other. "Possibly not a coincidence."

"I thought they lived somewhere in the eastern United States. I wouldn't have the first idea of how to find the surrogates who carried Phoebe and Noah." He paused, perhaps wondering if he should know this detail. "You're going to see her?"

"In an hour." My head and heart tried to connect, to make sense of the conflicts this woman brought into my day.

"Aren't you curious?" David stood up, left his desk to join me.

"Of course." I extended one hand, kept the other quiet. "It's just that there have been other claims about blood ties that have been awful fakes. I'm reluctant to be put through all those emotions again."

"I know, I've watched what it takes out of you." He caught my hand. "I'd planned to wake up the kids and have a second breakfast with them, but I could join you and Ms. Smithson?"

"I'm better doing this alone. The kids will miss you. They need this time before you leave."

"I thought I'd try to calm Phoebe about the language tests." He sipped my coffee. "You got this from the kitchen."

I acknowledged his taste of the real cream with a nod. "Just remember she's only seven years old, David. The kids I taught before the depression wouldn't even know what language proficiency meant."

"Different world, Annie. And our girl is a genius." He paused, tried to smile. "You're right to remind me she's young. I'd like to see her spend more time kicking a soccer ball, but there are powerful folks with plans for her future." I heard resentment under the words although his voice lightened. "If you're sure you don't need me, I'll go eat another bowl of oatmeal, the perfect hot-day cereal. Let me help you carry these to your desk."

Alone in my office, work discipline abandoned me once I sent a communication to Magda to change our regular Tuesday morning meeting. Maybe because of our friendship, she stayed at Ashwood after completing her government assignment. Every year she absorbed more responsibility until she managed not only production in the greenhouses, fields, and orchards, but also the logistics of getting our goods to market. David's father, Paul, brought grain farming knowledge to her team.

I drank my coffee and ate the berries, but I pushed the oatmeal aside. Like my over-stimulated mind, my hands refused to quiet. On my data pad, I opened a Twin Cities' news site, forced myself to pay attention to the top ten articles. Statewide elections would be held in two months with no clear leaders among the three parties. Expanded school schedules for urban students posed problems for employers. Rumblings about the closing of a popular feeding station on the north side of St. Paul might cause parents financial problems. A volunteer guard unit departing for South America was short of its required numbers. I read nothing further than the first two paragraphs. My thoughts circled back to the Smithson woman.

I searched Bureau data about the Smithsons. At least a half dozen intellectual citizen Smithsons with East Coast residences appeared, mostly scientists or engineers. One couple stood out because they were both deceased, leaving behind two sons, one the right age.

David and I learned after Phoebe's birth that babies carried by surrogates for intellectual couples were genetically enhanced to build a future generation of even smarter employees for the country's top global products of consulting, research, engineering and policy development. We never told David's family anything about why Phoebe spoke and read three languages and displayed a brilliant understanding of advanced math or how Noah, six months younger, began reading before he was three.

The Bureau managed the educations of these two, an eerie reality David and I found unsettling. The children carried by surrogates would always be financially cared for by the government, which made me wonder about the Smithson woman's intentions.

I gave up trying to distract myself in my office and headed back to the main residence to see our kids. David sat on the beautiful wooden bench he'd built, one sleepy boy on either side. He rubbed John's back while Noah stared without focus at the morning's bright sunlight.

"Hey, it's my three favorite guys," I said as I reached out to touch the boys. "I think your grandma might like help in the garden today when you're through with school."

Neither grumbled, unlike my brother and me who at this age felt that time to play was what happened after school. David's children were required to spend a significant part of each day in educational activities. Our son walked an undefined path—not required by law to fulfill any daily labor as were the young workers of the estate, nor to complete the strict education program of his half siblings. A few months shy of John's seventh birthday, we treated him like Noah's fraternal twin instead of half brother, and kept their schedules the same.

"Mom, could we get a dog for Christmas?" Noah's sweet, high voice bounced off the hallway's slate floors before being swallowed in the tall clerestory-windowed foyer.

"It's only September, Noah. I guarantee that you'll think of other gifts you'd like by December." We had plenty of cats working in the barns and outbuildings, but domestic dogs carried some political inappropriateness from the days of the D when feeding starving people replaced feeding pets. The old grandfather clock marked the half hour. "I've got to keep moving," I said. "I love you."

Our early kitchen worker crew consisted of six children setting up breakfast under the direction of Amber, a twelve-year-old girl I would love to adopt if laws allowed. Most of our workers came from poor urban families who agreed to estate assignments to improve their children's lives. When I was living from hand to mouth during the depression I might have thought this the best choice available. In turn, we made a commitment to these parents that their children would be fed, educated, prepared for some future work, and kept safe. Ashwood hadn't ever failed on that commitment.

The Smithson woman stood looking at historical pictures of Ashwood hung on the walls of the dining room. She turned as I came in and waited for me to close the door.

"I'm Clarisse Smithson." She tipped her head, a city-person greeting. "Thank you for meeting with me." She hesitated for a second before acknowledging my position. "General Manager Hartford."

Her voice, so well modulated that I knew she was university educated, brought me back to my frustration about available day labor. Clarisse was an urban woman not used to country work. Her pants had been tailored for long legs, her shoes purchased for walking on smooth surfaces. The hands she folded on the back of a chair looked irritated after an hour of pulling weeds. A once-expensive sun hat lay on her back, held in place by leather strings. Pulling out a chair, I gestured that she should do the same. She waited for me to be seated, then sat. The morning's heat warmed the room. "What did you want to discuss?"

One of her hands inched toward her pants pocket. I wondered if she had written notes she wished to consult. I noticed a small bulge, felt cold fear at the possibility of a knife missing security detection. She drew out a handkerchief, dabbed at her chin.

"I am Gregor Smithson's only surviving adult relative." She stopped. "You are the mother of his younger son who was born in Washington, D.C., when you were in training for the matron program."

Before she could continue, I stopped her. "I am not the mother of your brother's son. I was a *surrogate* for his parents."

She cleared her throat, sat up straighter in her chair. "Gregor died earlier this year, about four months after his wife fell off the roof of their home. There are conflicting stories about why she was there." I realized she had not shared the woman's name. "Gregor's older son was born early in the depression, during my brother's first marriage. He is in a British boarding school near his mother's home."

"Tell me about your younger nephew."

"He needs a home."

"You know that I am stepmother to two gifted offspring, so I know the government establishes generous individual annuities for these kids."

She sat still, but I noticed she bit her lower lip before responding. "That's right."

I looked at her, waiting for more information. Her eyes moved around the room. "And?"

"And my ex-husband stole it. Managed to have the funds transferred to an account in South America before he fled Minnesota. I haven't heard from him in five months. The financial agency where I worked fired me when it was uncovered that he hacked my security to make the transaction. He left me nothing. That's why I brought your son here."

The story might be true, but I didn't feel comfortable. "You applied for emergency assistance for the boy?" She shook her head. "You know there is special funding?" This time she nodded.

"No one is going to trust me with access to accounts set up in his name. All I have is my apartment and a small trust fund set up by Gregor. When my nephew finishes school and his service year, he'll inherit a handsome fortune. Until then his prospects are poor."

"So put the boy in the boarding program for gifted students. Let the government take care of him."

Fidgeting, she again removed the handkerchief from her pocket. "He no longer tests well enough for the gifted schools and with one non-intellectual natural parent, he can't claim a boarding school slot. He's lost opportunities."

I wished David were here as witness. I didn't think Clarissa would tell her story the same way twice. "So why come to me?"

"There are lots of reasons. I hoped you might be able to fit me into the Ashwood business office so your son could attend the estate's exceptional school. Maybe he could even study with your husband's children and return to the gifted program."

As she spoke, her eyes focused on me, her chin steadied. "At the least, I would think you'd want to be sure your son is able to eat three meals a day and be safe. I could continue to provide a home and make sure he is educated if I had a monthly stipend. Gregor's annuity was meant to make my life more comfortable, not to support two people."

"I'd like you to stop calling this boy my son." I stumbled in my words, wondering what the Smithsons named the boy, yet holding back from asking. "You are his kin. Your brother entrusted you to care for the boy."

I thought I saw her facial features change as I spoke, not with disappointment but with anger. "Blood tests show he is not the child of Gregor's wife." Her statement stood tall in the room. "In fact, his wife was infertile. Had ovary issues. I have filed a legal request for access to your DNA. That's what I wanted you to know."

Boiling water pouring down my back could not have brought me to my feet faster than this news. "Ms. Smithson, I'm going to have you and the boy transported back to the city now. You'll both be paid for the day."

"That's it?" She asked the question with disdain. "All that reputation for building a sense of family on your estate and investing in education, and this is the way you respond to the very strong possibility that your firstborn child might not have dinner tonight?" She remained sitting. "You're a huge fraud, General Manager Hartford. Huge."

"Ms. Smithson, you're naive if you believe you are the first person to come here with this kind of story." I softened my voice in spite of the sting of her words. "It's no secret I have no remaining family, so many people have tried to pretend that we are related. Too many." I activated a page under the table for our estate security. "We have your contact information and will wait for your lawyer's documents."

A knock sounded at the door before it opened. "This is Clarissa Smithson," I told the guard who wore Ashwood's security staff uniform. "She needs transport back to the city with her nephew, who is somewhere with the child laborers. Tell the business office they should both be paid for the day, with extra funds to cover meals."

She stood and walked toward the door, but stopped. "If you want to know, his name is Andrew." Our guard stepped aside to give Clarissa Smithson room to exit.

Before the door closed, I adjusted the room's monitors to focus on the estate's business offices, where I knew the boy would be reunited with Clarissa. She did not reach out to him when he walked toward her from the kitchen gardens. Thanks to the high-definition security system installed by Ashwood's Chief Engineer Lao, I could see sun-brightened red highlights in the boy's auburn hair. From the back, Andrew looked like my brother as a boy.

Chapter Four

Seven twenty in the morning and my sense of well-being hung like a spiderweb spun on a vegetable plant's greenery. Before sharing Clarissa Smithson's story with David, I called my most trusted confidant in the Bureau, who also happened to be legal guardian to David's children.

"Reyes Milan here. How are you, Anne?"

He was the first regional Bureau official I met my first night at Ashwood. Then I called him Auditor Milan. His career had taken him to the top of our government with a fancy title, but for me he was now simply Milan. When we were through with business, we talked about our families, about our pasts.

"Clarissa Smithson cleared our early-morning laborer search today and brought a boy named Andrew with her to Ashwood." I paused. "Does the name mean anything to you?"

"You were a surrogate for Smithsons. East Coast couple, I recall."

"Clarissa demanded we meet. Supposedly her brother, Gregor Smithson, and his wife have both passed away. His older son is in England, but his younger son lives with her. She says her husband stole the boy's entire annuity, which cost her her job."

As I moved closer to the core message of Clarissa's visit, tears formed in my eyes. "She claims the baby I carried for the Smithsons is biologically my child. That Gregor's wife was infertile."

Silence on Milan's side increased my discomfort. He could hold secrets as long as the ocean held water.

I didn't tell Milan about the boy with hair like mine, just broke his silence with facts. "Clarissa wants an office job at Ashwood and an education for the boy, or enough money to support both of them in the cities. She said she has asked for access to my DNA files." Milan had to hear my voice quiver. "What can you tell me?"

Milan sounded like his physical profile—middle-aged, unremarkable, and deliberate. In my years of working with Milan, he had delivered devastating or amazing news in the same calm tones used in review of a business plan.

"You signed the uniform surrogate contract and release at the time you agreed to carry the Smithsons' baby, so legally you would be held harmless regardless of the aunt's claims." Under his words I heard implications. "I can give you the name of a good lawyer who specializes in surrogacy casework."

"Milan, what you're not saying scares me."

"In rare circumstances surrogates were impregnated with the father's sperm, not implanted with a fertilized embryo." He hesitated before finishing his statement. "The same legal agreement protects both sets of surrogates."

"How would I know what happened in that clinic?"

"If this couple still lived, probably never. The clinic would not disclose if an alternative procedure was performed. If Ms. Smithson's story about the loss of Andrew's annuity is true, support compensation is available under orphan protocol." His voice lowered and I heard his kindness. "Don't worry, Anne. I'll have answers in forty-eight hours."

"How did you know his name?" The boy's less-than-genius intellect also triggered a red flag in my mind. "She said he isn't eligible for the intellectual offspring schooling but is too bright to be successful in regular schools."

"I'm looking at his file. She may be wrong about that piece of information, but I'm not free to talk about the boy."

Someone knocked on the door.

"Thanks, Milan. I'll need to talk with David. Would you have the boy's picture in his file?"

"Anne, talk with David. I'll contact Maxim Quershi to get involved from the Bureau's legal perspective, and we'll go from there. I have to leave."

I hung up, stared at the pictures Clarissa Smithson examined earlier. I had no pictures from my first year in estate management training, when I missed my deceased family so deeply that I was grateful to be a surrogate mother for one of the intellectual elite couples. The pregnancy filled an emotional hole. The financial arrangement offered the potential that someday I could leave estate management with a nest egg to make marriage and my own family possible. I tried to remind myself of that future dream every day after the baby boy I delivered was carried off to the Smithsons.

Chapter Five

Supervisors of Ashwood's greenhouses waited to use the room. I greeted them each by name, struggling to remain calm while I absorbed Milan's news. No one stopped me in the kitchen, where kids were already beginning breakfast cleanup. I skirted the big dining room and crossed the central hall to join David, his parents, and the children, who were finishing their meal on the family patio.

Humidity tightened Phoebe's curls. No one around the table seemed bothered by the irony of eating hot, heavy grains on a hot, heavy morning. Noah and John, now fully awake and done with their breakfast, played a game that would eventually grow too loud. Phoebe laughed with her grandmother, who drank coffee in spite of the heat.

"Come sit with us, Mom." Phoebe still laughed as she sang out an invitation. "You look tired."

I touched the top of her head with my lips while I reached for a glass and the water pitcher. "The heat has me worn out already." I pulled a chair toward the table. "Maybe I'll just sit out here and let Magda and Grandpa Paul work today."

"You could help me study." Laughter left her small, round face with its rosebud mouth. "I'm scared."

David and I tried not to look at each other as her voice squeaked on the last words. I remembered Tia telling me about how her brilliant father's suicide had affected her as a child. I tried not to see her mother's excessive drive in this child. If the struggle between nature and nurture played out in our kids, maybe the four adults at the patio table could outweigh the mother who died when Phoebe was only months old.

"You'll do fine, Phoeb. You didn't have one answer wrong on the last practice test." Sitting back, I drank my water. "As much as I love your smiling faces, I need to grab your father so we can talk about important adult things."

They groaned. "Drink enough water today, Mom," John commanded as David and I stood up. "Don't get summer sick."

"I promise, John." I held up my water glass. "You should convince your grandparents to go easy on their coffee."

We left the table and entered the residence. The sounds of our children still in my ears, I thought about the Smithson boy. Did Antwone's comments suggest the boy was odd? Was he a normal youngster like our John when the clinic had promised the Smithsons a genius? Was he my son?

"Smithson claims that her sister-in-law was infertile and the boy is actually my child." An administrative staff member walked past us. "I saw him on the monitors. His hair is exactly like my family's—red highlights in brown." David stopped walking. "She wants access to my DNA data, and Milan says there's a possibility this is true. Apparently some clinics fertilized the eggs of surrogates without our knowledge."

In the long glass hallway, David placed an arm around my shoulders while we walked. Apples, nearly ready for harvest, dragged tree limbs almost to the ground just beyond the soccer field. "That's quite a disclosure," he said. "You've talked about how empty you felt after giving the baby to his parents. Wouldn't it be amazing to discover now that this child is your son? What are your legal rights?"

Classic David, at his finest in offering an orphaned kid part of our home without thinking about the bigger picture. "If he's your son, you want him to be part of our family, don't you?" His arm dropped to his side as the DOE security guard opened the office building door.

"Milan offered to research the files and have an attorney review all the contracts related to my surrogacy." David's question unnerved me. "I've been thinking about all the implications for our kids and their futures. Andrew, that's his name, might have problems."

He looked at me with surprise, eyebrows raised. "If this kid was my son, I wouldn't even ask you before putting an extra bunk bed in the boys' room." Lines across his forehead formed easily in the way a forty-five-year-old man's face ages. "We've got Phoebe's psychologist if he needs help. One more kid won't break the bank."

"David, we don't know that this isn't all a giant farce." My voice quivered, surprising me. "I need time to be sure. Time to think through what's best if this woman is telling the truth."

"And I'm telling you that you don't need to think about anyone else if the boy is yours. There's plenty of resources, and affection, to stretch over one more set of shoulders." He winked. "We have room for one kid, even if he can pick up coins with his toes like his mother." His arms settled around my shoulders. I heard his lips kiss my hair. "Now I've got to run."

By dinner we'd all be comfortable with David's absence, for that was the way we lived—he traveled the world responding to the most powerful customers of the U.S. Department of Energy and I managed the third-largest privately-held agricultural production estate in Minnesota. In my office solar sensitive blinds filtered the morning's strong sun. Thermal heating and cooling kept the main residence comfortable, but the DOE office building changed systems frequently as a lab setting for future technology. The current system worked less than perfectly against September's worst weather.

Three hours into my workday I had nothing accomplished. I pulled an old photo collection off my credenza to remember my own family that nurtured me and my first husband, Richard. How young I looked at his side before the economy collapsed.

"Anne. You look like you're deep in thought. Didn't we schedule the agricultural operations group meeting at this time?" Magda walked in to sit at her favorite place at my office table. Estate living kept both of us lean, but I thought she looked younger than her thirty-five years while I felt the approach of my thirty-ninth birthday.

"Are you okay?" Remnants of an Eastern European accent gave her deep alto voice a catlike growling quality. Her current life partner, a quiet Jamaican woman named Ena, managed installation of crop rotation in the greenhouses. Together they seemed to be organically a part of all that was green on the estate.

"I'm wishing Paul had another branch of the Regan family tree we could shake for more strong South Dakota workers." I sighed. "Seven years ago this estate had almost bare food shelves, large market obligations, and not enough laborers. Today we have prosperous businesses with high-demand products and the government ratcheting up its agricultural product requirements while it sucks up most of our workforce. I don't understand what's happening."

She shrugged at my recap of old news. With an ever-growing Bureau of Human Capital Management directing allocation of all labor, there was always pressure on estate management to provide training opportunities as well as jobs for the young and the unemployed. Unfairly, we did our best with little guarantee of retaining the people we trained if other industries had needs.

"When did all these manufacturing companies build factories around the cities?" Magda asked as she stretched. "It's not like they're making shoes or something locally useful. It's all missiles and munitions. Not at all self-sufficiency."

"This morning's first group of day laborers didn't look like the whole lot could produce more than the resources they might use." I added to her concern. "All city workers trying to put in a full day in this heat." I put the pictures down, moved from my desk to join her. "I'm worried about having enough people to finish harvest."

"You always worry about something, Anne." Magda, a true operations manager, tossed aside easy problems. "Ena's system of rotating people through time in the greenhouses and the fields minimizes heat issues. We'll be okay." She removed a pencil from her thick braid of hair. "Let's come back to this thought after we go through reports."

We drilled through planting, harvesting, and produce distribution. Paul joined us to talk about the grain harvest. His knowledge of the flat plains of southern Minnesota and South Dakota saved our crops in many situations. Forty minutes passed.

"Even field staff breaks at some point." David stood in the doorway. "I need a minute with my wife and father."

"I need to supervise a vendor arrival," Magda said as she gathered her things. "We'll talk about the day crews later." David stepped aside to let her pass, then closed the door.

Our son had David's dark eyes, his grandfather's high eyebrows, and the large hands of my father. Paul sat with his back to the estate map hung on one wall of my office while my regular chair allowed me to look out the windows.

"I received notice that this is a top-security mission to Paraguay." David closed one eye and looked at his father. "They've given me a few additional hours to clear up other project work. I'll be gone at least ten days."

"Let's not tell your mother about the security aspect." Paul spoke directly to David. "She'll think about her brother getting caught in that Afghanistan aid business and worry."

Under Paul's words, I heard a tone that suggested he wanted to protect me as well. "It's not the first time you've been in a top-security mission," I said. "Think of China and the month you spent inside Ukraine."

"I don't know what's going on in Paraguay, but it's different." David's words came out slowly as he clenched one hand and released it.

I wanted to calm him, to put my hand over his, but I knew the need for comfort was mine. David and Paul continued to talk as I watched, hearing under the conversation that there was information my husband couldn't share. I decided not to become worried unless he passed the DOE/U.S. military starred security packet to me before leaving. Those were the times I feared.

"We'll be out of communication for the entire assignment."

I groaned at David's news, anticipating Phoebe's anxiety during this kind of absence.

"With my departure time moved back we have a chance for us to speak." He gave me a "be brave" smile. "Maybe we'd better let Dad in on your visitor this morning?"

Paul sat back in his chair. I could see the worry he'd carry about David's safety in small tension lines hidden in creases above his eyebrows that didn't release once we moved to a new topic. While my husband was still attractive in his mid-forties, his father was a handsome outdoorsman with close-shaved silver hair and an easy smile. He tilted his head and raised a few fingers, cuing me to share.

Trying to be succinct, I recounted Clarissa Smithson's story and claims and Milan's response. "So, I might have a son we've never met or someone trying to draw me into caring for a surrogate who is no blood relation."

"You've been rescuing kids as long as we've known each other, Annie. Think of having your boy come home." His voice was genuine. "Shows God is still ruling the universe."

"I don't know yet that he is my son, Paul. Clarissa isn't the first adult to come here with some version of this story."

"Well, what do you think?" Paul asked. "You've got good maternal instincts. What did you feel when this boy was born?" He quirked an eyebrow upward. "And what's his name? Did you meet him?"

"Andrew."

"The warrior." Paul interrupted. "My grandfather's name. He flew bombers in World War II."

I nodded, mystified by my father-in-law's interest in this boy. "David can tell you that I find Andrew's birthday difficult each year. Does that mean I'm his mother?"

Paul reached across David to pat my hand. "If he is your son, he's a lucky boy. And I'll have another reason to be pissed as hell at the bunch of assholes who have been running this government."

"Thanks, Paul." I pulled my hand back slowly. "I appreciate your support." Their enthusiasm was governed by pure emotion, as if this child was a stray cat and not a person who could influence the entire future of our family. "Legally I have no obligation regardless of the boy's biological relationship. But if he is truly my child, I will want him here to be part of our family."

"Whatever you decide, you've got my support," David said. "I wanted Dad to know before I left."

"Until we're sure, please don't tell anyone else." Paul looked surprised. "I don't want Phoebe distracted if Andrew is not my son."

"Fair. Let's talk about Phoebe." David started us down a puzzling path. "I don't know if you heard last night, Dad. It was bad." Paul nodded to show that he and Sarah did hear Phoebe's screams.

"The psychologist visits again next week. I'm wondering if Phoebe's having more night terror because of the proficiency tests or if there's something else going on." David worried almost excessively about our children's future. "I know it's difficult to find pediatric psychologists, but this woman doesn't have my total confidence. Maybe Milan can find someone stronger?"

"That's not Milan's job, David, and Phoebe does like Dr. Wanda." Our conversation was repeated each time Dr. Wanda's visit approached. Paul looked uncomfortable being in the middle of our mild disagreement. "Let's stay with Dr. Wanda and keep Phoebe's life as calm as possible. She doesn't need to know you're on a different kind of trip." David straightened in his chair, and I rushed my next sentence. "I'll call Terrell for advice." A former member of Ashwood's team, this friend had a counseling background that could be helpful.

"How do you deal with my not being able to talk to the kids while I'm gone?" I extended a hand as if touch could ease David's anxiety.

"The language testing is early in your trip. She understands time differences and how demanding projects can be on your first days." I noticed that the time for lunch service was close. "Honey, I'd like to have lunch with the kids, so I have to leave."

"Have fun. I'm eating in my office while I do calls." We all rose. David and I hugged, me resting just a few seconds longer than usual against his chest. "I'll leave the starred packet on your desk before I leave," he said into my ear as he squeezed me tight. "I love you."

"I know. I love you, too. Take care of yourself and come back quickly." We kissed again, the starred packet setting this farewell apart. I knew the packet's contents—his will, directions for accessing DOE funds, a final video.

Paul and I walked back to the main residence, his talk about the corn, soybean, and grain harvests filling my ears. To him, Ashwood was just another big farm where rain fell or didn't fall, where bugs caused problems and machinery worked or didn't work. What kept Paul young and involved lived in our residence—his family.

"Ms. Anne, Mr. Paul." Ray, a longtime member of the agriculture day staff, waved us down as we exited the residence to walk to the Ashwood production offices. "Did you know some government agency is here to claim our combine? They got a big rig here to haul it away."

"What the hell," Paul said as he turned to me. "You saw that mail yesterday. The one about requisitioning surplus equipment for national security."

"I never thought they meant agricultural equipment." All three of us covered the ten-minute walk in five. "Did Homeland Security talk with you or Magda about this?"

Paul slowed. "I talked with a Homer Penfeller last week. Told him we didn't have anything here but farm equipment and a few used transports. I thought that was the end of the conversation. He had the complete inventory we filed with the estate's taxes."

"The Security people have a lot of paperwork with them. I tried to explain to them that this combine will be used by many of our neighbors in the next few weeks, and crops will rot in the fields if we lose it." Ray rubbed his hands together, then swabbed his forehead and neck with a pocket kerchief. "City guy obviously. Don't know his elbow from his, well, you know what I mean."

I called Ashwood's government-appointed lawyer while we walked, then placed a quick second call to our private attorney. Raima would understand the impact of losing that single piece of extremely expensive equipment for Ashwood as well as for a half dozen other estates.

"Paul, they must know we've been asked to use our equipment at a discount cost for work on federal jobs. Whatever would Homeland Security do with a farm combine? What can you do with it beyond harvesting grains?"

The black Homeland Security transport parked outside our ag office building looked out of place in this busy yet tranquil setting. Day laborers gawked at the vehicle while our regular staff looked determined to not stare. Dozens of local people depended on Ashwood for their families' financial stability as well as for services like day care and schooling.

I looked at the sky, at the sun shimmering in midday heat. "Hell of a day, isn't it?" I asked Paul or Ray or maybe myself. "Let's talk with the feds."

Chapter Six

In the early days of recovery from the big D, we all wore uniforms related to our jobs. Federal bureaucrats belonging to certain agencies were the last holdouts from that time. My challenge as I walked into the estate offices was to find the one dress detail in the group of strangers filling our office that designated their leader.

I chose the man whose small flag pin displayed gold trim. This person was either a bureaucratic hero or manager of the crew. "You look like the person in charge of these people," I said, walking toward him and extending my right arm. The feds watched my action with looks of concern. Before their leader could step back from my germ-laden hand, I stopped and dipped my head in mandatory protocol. His dipped further than mine, a sign of respect for my position as a business owner.

"You must be Matron Anne Hartford." The gold flag man advanced my way.

"Your information is old," I said, wondering what his reference to my former role signaled. "As owner of Ashwood, I carry the federal title of General Manager Hartford."

"You are an honored surrogate, a volunteer safeguarding our nation's treasured intellectual citizens."

His soliloquy, delivered with a certain robotic quality, grated on my nerves. He ignored the small gesture I made to indicate we should move into a conference room while continuing with his grandstanding.

"I am Homer Penfeller, deputy detail supervisor of requisitions for the Midwest Homeland Security sector." Straight as a steel rod, without warmth or grace, the flag-adorned man dipped his head as if sharing his name brought us both great pleasure. "I spoke with Mr. Paul Regan about a piece of machinery." He acknowledged my gesture toward the conference room by taking one step during his last words.

I walked first, then Penfeller moved in front of Paul, who hurried his own pace so that the two reached the door at the same moment. My father-in-law allowed his dislike for what this bureaucrat represented to show. Paul made a point of reaching ahead of the man to open the door, as if inviting Penfeller into the room. For his part, Penfeller turned toward the crew he'd brought to Ashwood and lifted a hand. Seven men and women moved from the outer office area toward the conference room.

"Supervisor Penfeller, this room is small. Surely we can speak without all of your staff." I rested my hands on the back of a chair as I spoke.

"Matron Anne, I have three estates to visit before the end of this workday. My staff will record our discussion." He forced a smile, eyes involuntarily blinking as the edges of his lips raised. "Time is important to all of us."

"Then perhaps I've underestimated the importance of this meeting." We all remained standing. "If you require seven people to witness talks with an estate owner, I am led to believe that this is a very serious matter. Ashwood's attorney will conference with us," I referred to my data pad, "in ten minutes."

Motioning to Paul, I walked toward the door. Penfeller did not step aside, a bureaucrat dealing with people unbound by pretentious government staff protocols. I watched how his people responded to my announcement, saw confusion in a few, stoic stares from others. Their leader might be full of hot air, but this team was on a mission.

"As a former esteemed member of the Bureau of Human Capital Management, you understand how government runs on tight schedules, Matron."

"You are wrong on many levels, sir," I replied. "Please show this entire estate the respect it has earned. You are in the offices of the private corporation I head. This building was constructed with private funds. I contract with a number of government bureaus and agencies. In my experience, I have found that only the Department of Revenue runs on a tight schedule and only when monies are due."

I almost stepped on his toes on my way to the door. "Someone will bring your team water and notify you when our attorney is ready to talk." Turning to him, I established eye contact. "Our talks will go better if you remember that I am General Manager Hartford, not a matron or surrogate or any other bureaucratic-titled employee." Once in the hall I closed the door.

Paul followed me to his office. I checked my data pad to locate the presence of listening devices before speaking. Everything read clear.

"Tell me everything you know about Penfeller's demand, Paul." Under the features of his weathered face, emotions deepened lines surrounding his lips. I loved him, but this wouldn't be our first disagreement over estate business. "We need the recording of your conversation with Penfeller before Joel joins us. I'm not leading a lawyer to the table without full disclosure."

Paul spread work-worn hands on the surface of his always clean desktop. "Anne, that citified office manager is gonna read some long-winded directive about the need of the federal government to build a secure homeland through collaborative endeavors with neighboring countries. He can't speak two sentences that make sense. I heard his spiel about four times before I told him that when he could speak simple English, we'd talk."

While I listened to Paul, I conducted a word-match search of the private information boards. Penfeller's phrase sounded like government talk for some kind of initiative. I broadened the search beyond our region to search for efforts the National Security Administration might have underway in multiple locations.

Reference points began to appear in a random scatter from California across the wide plains of Montana and Wyoming through the middle of the country, then into the rich farmland areas of Pennsylvania and New York. Almost two hundred managers of federal government estates reported large harvesting equipment requisitions. But our land and businesses were owned by Hartford, Ltd., with documentation stored in many safe harbors to protect against just this kind of event.

"It would have been helpful if you had warned me about Penfeller." Paul showed no remorse as I scolded. "Just to avoid a confrontation like this."

The feds could lay claim to the water system technology and the experimental energy recycling systems developed and owned by the Department of Energy and a seasonal vehicle storage facility on land we leased to local road maintenance agencies for equipment storage. Most of our land I owned outright. Other packets Hartford, Ltd., held in hundred-year leases. Our equipment and facilities were clear of debt.

"Anne Hartford."

Touching my earpiece, I responded to the voice of Joel Santos, our government-appointed attorney who helped us interpret the mazelike requirements of paperwork, negotiate unwieldy regulations, and create a level playing field when multiple agencies collided in their regulation of commerce, safety, education, or employment. I liked him, not what he did for a living. Past experiences earned my trust in him to be fair and honest, which was the best I hoped for in most government employees allowed near our money.

"Hello, Joel. Thanks for the quick response. We have visitors from the National Security Agency here wanting to requisition our combine before harvest is complete." I tried to remember Joel's background. "You know what a combine is, don't you?" Paul pointed to his data pad to indicate he'd located recordings of his conversation with Penfeller.

"I filed the paperwork when you purchased that equipment, Ms. Anne. You still owe my son a ride on that monster."

"Well, Paul Regan, who runs our field operations, is opening a link to taped conversations with a Homer Penfeller, who is sitting in our offices with NSA's paperwork, which supposedly will state that the United States needs our combine immediately as a matter of national security." I paused. Paul tapped his own earpiece and mouthed "Raima" as he walked away. "Please help us deal with these folks. Penfeller is acting like Ashwood is a federal estate that must answer a Washington, D.C., order."

"Interesting," Joel replied. "I can free up time."

"Look at the conversation transcripts, Joel, then we'll conference with Penfeller." I held up two fingers to Paul, knowing these final words with Joel would cost plenty on Raima's billing. "Stay available. Okay?"

"One more thing, Anne. I know this isn't a good time."

"Not really, Joel. I have another call I can't delay."

"I'll be brief." His voice rushed. "You need to know that Ashwood is on the short list of estates for the first wave of youth deployment efforts. You and I can affect the number of assigned metro youth if we get out ahead of the announcements." He stopped abruptly. "These kids are tough, Anne. You're going to want to get in front of this issue."

"First I've heard of it, Joel. Book us for a half hour this afternoon, and I'll bring my primary managers."

"Five-thirty is the only time I've got open." Dinner with the kids disappeared.

"We'll make it work. Stay flexible now for Penfeller." I hung up and tapped Raima onto video. "What's going on, Raima? Joel Santos is telling me he knows nothing about Penfeller, then dropped news of a coming youth deployment program that might drop tough metro kids onto our estate."

"Good morning, Anne." Raima's rich alto filled Paul's office. "All this and you didn't even mention the surrogate issue. Not a good day for you?"

I thought of David's departure, said nothing. When Raima and I had dinner in the city, I told her the kinds of things women share, but on the billing clock words cost money.

"Let's prioritize," I started. "We have Penfeller and his NSA crew in a conference room now, so they get first attention. Is there any possibility his agency's records show Ashwood's combine as a federal investment instead of a private asset?"

She chuckled. "Their asset management systems are notoriously antiquated, particularly when that works in their favor. Paul, can you get a copy of Penfeller's paperwork?"

"I'm on my way." Paul left.

"Even if the paperwork is built on inaccurate information, there could be a few weeks of dancing with the bureaucrats to clear up the issue, Anne. I'll assign a first-year associate to do that." She shifted in her tall desk chair. "Hasn't anyone at Ashwood been staying on top of the youth corps effort? You do know kids are going hungry in the inner city?"

She knew my answer by the way I sat back in the chair, nailed there by sudden understanding that I missed a serious stone in the roadway of small business management and might take a face plant. I extended my arms across the chair's arms, shook my head. "We've been up to the top of our heads with government-required changes in production and dealing with a shortage of labor ready to work the fields or harvest." I hoped Paul would stop for some reason and give me a minute to continue this conversation. "What have I missed?"

"Rearmament is drawing down good workers from the labor pool, which explains your daily transport crew quality." She twirled a bracelet on her lower arm, all that was left of her family heirlooms. "But there's something else going on in the metro about changing the slacker tradition of the inner-city communities. Many of those adults don't have the work tradition needed by the new factories. The current thought is that physical tasks on the estates might be a good training ground for changing attitudes in the younger generation."

"I'm seeing older people with solid working tradition get off the transports who can't put in a full day in the fields. How would we deal with kids who've spent most of their days on the streets?" The door opened. Paul placed a note in front of me. "One issue at a time. Let's get back to the combine. You should have the paperwork on your data pad. If you're available, Raima, join us and Joel in conference with Penfeller."

Paul followed me into the meeting, chased one of the NSA crew out of my chair, then tapped a second uniformed goon from his own favorite place at the table. Joel and Raima appeared on screen.

"Supervisor Penfeller, this is Attorney Joel Santos, Ashwood's federally appointed legal counsel. All documents and filings are maintained through his office." I paused. "And Counselor B. Raima serves as our private representative. Attorneys Santos and Raima have worked collaboratively on a number of issues related to the estate and Hartford, Ltd." Pausing, I looked to Penfeller to speak. He stared straight ahead at the screen. Moments passed. Penfeller cleared his throat, held out his glass, bringing one of his followers to the table's edge to grab the pitcher and pour his boss more water.

"Is there a specific requisition order for us to review?" Joel asked. Over Joel's shoulder I could see the tops of downtown St. Paul buildings. The state of Minnesota had so little influence over our daily lives that I felt like a national citizen living in this region.

"I believe you told Mr. Regan you would bring a requisition to Ashwood for a large agricultural harvesting machine." Joel looked to his data pad as if checking facts. "You are aware that this particular combine is the primary asset of Hartford AgriService, Inc., and is critical for the estate region's success in meeting government production quotas?"

The NSA representative's lips turned into a pout as he listened. He sniffed before responding. "Our agency legal experts have reviewed the revenue stream utilized in purchase of this equipment and believe the federal government in fact owns approximately fifteen percent of this combine," he pronounced the word as if he were talking about adding ingredients in a recipe. "Counsel, you are aware of exclusive funding arrangements between Hartford AgriServices and the Department of Energy?" Penfeller looked up at me, then refocused on the screens. "Under emergency requisition language in this nation's deployment codes, it is our legal position that we do not need specific documentation to remove this piece of property."

Raima, six feet, two inches of dignity and strength, rapped a data pad stylus on her desk surface. "Interesting approach. Quite clever, yet I can cite at least two dozen cases that found that argument invalid." Doubt showed in the faces of many of Penfeller's crew. Their eyes darted toward him, then back to the screen. "We do need to see your requisition before we formally respond. Isn't that correct, Counselor Santos?"

"Supervisor Penfeller, just make it visible via systems, then we can have a real discussion," Joel directed.

Penfeller repeated his frozen stare routine. As the seconds stretched, Paul gazed around the room, then raised an eyebrow my way.

"You do have a requisition?" I asked. "You didn't bring all these people here and interrupt our work without official documentation?"

The NSA agent touched his flag pin as if expecting a nanochip might spew out the necessary forms. His team shuffled. Under the table I activated a security alarm as the mood in the room changed.

"You are disloyal Americans, questioners of the agency at the center of maintaining the security of our beloved country," Penfeller said, each word shooting like corn from a silo blower. "All that you have and eat and wear come from the bounty of this great nation. I will report your acts of questioning what has been deemed necessary for preserving the peace of our land and the world. Others will know that Ashwood is not a trustworthy name."

Paul stood. I extended a hand and signaled for him to return to his chair, but this odd man had touched serious emotions in my father-in-law.

"You have no idea where you are speaking those damn insinuations, sir." Paul's voice could be heard above Penfeller's final rumbling of pseudopatriotic words. "My son lost his first wife in service to this government. My brother-in-law served in Afghanistan and lost his life. I have a son who is in the U.S. Marines, following in my footsteps. This young woman," he pointed his large weathered hand my way, "this woman feeds thousands, employs hundreds, and works like a dog to improve the lives of every child and adult who spends time at Ashwood. And as you acknowledged earlier, she made the sacrifice of being a surrogate." He pointed at Penfeller. "For all we know, you might be a thief in a fancy costume."

"Paul, enough." I knew my father-in-law could hold the floor for a significant time when driven by emotion, particularly patriotic emotion.

"Supervisor Penfeller, I'll give you fifteen minutes following this conference." Joel spoke as an attorney in serious cross-examination. "Either produce the requisition document that brought you to Ashwood or have your superiors be in contact with me with full explanation of what appears to be agency incompetency if not worse." His eyes followed Penfeller. "If I find that the paperwork is in the least out of order, you will be the first person for whom I issue summons. This is a serious matter, far beyond patriotism. Our government is here to serve and protect our citizens, not threaten or steal from them."

"We serve the same leaders, Counselor Santos." Penfeller faced the screen, watched Joel's face like a person unfamiliar with distance conference capabilities. "I assure you we have common goals."

"I'm directing you to leave Ashwood's expanded perimeter now. No waiting for transports, no parking outside the gates." Joel tapped his pencil on his desk as he spoke. "Call your workers outside the fence and tell them to back off."

Turning away from the screen, Penfeller walked from the room. With a twist of his fingers he beckoned his crew to follow. Outside the conference room, Ashwood's own security staff lined the hall to close ranks as the NSA people left the building.

Closing the door, I returned to our legal counsel. "It sounds like you uncovered something about this requisition process after my call."

"NSA is in fact rounding up various pieces of equipment from federal estates for an undisclosed military intervention." His body language suggested we move on to other issues. "Let's talk at five-thirty about the youth reassignment program." Not smiling, Joel looked at me. "Before then, follow the link I'm sending about the issue." His screen darkened.

"I've forwarded some thoughts about how Ashwood could benefit from this initiative as well as strategies for minimizing what could be extremely costly to your business." Raima grabbed the opportunity, typical of lawyers who acted as if they cared about your dollars. "You're behind the curve on this one, Anne. The first filings are due in three days, and significant analysis is required behind each part of the report. I'd make it your priority." She checked a data pad. "I've got time tomorrow at three I'll set aside to review anything your business analysts generate. Good luck."

As her screen darkened, I turned to Paul. "Why haven't we been on top of this urban deployment program?"

He looked at me as a father might, a look of empathy underneath his scold. "You've had many issues on your desk and all of Phoebe's difficulties. Magda and I tried talking about this with you last week, but bringing in the crops posed more immediate problems." He stood, squeezed my shoulder. "We'll get on it right away and have something ready for you after lunch." He winked. "You do remember lunch?"

For seven years, through births and deaths, from near financial ruin to great success, I managed this place. But now, something outside my control, somewhere in the giant of our government, put a hazy dimmer over the vision I had for Ashwood. Plentiful food grew in the greenhouses and fields, but people were hungry in the cities. We could provide work, but not find workers. I sensed forces were pulling strings on a far bigger stage, some that might threaten Ashwood, our finances and our family's security.

"Yes, I remember lunch and that I missed eating it with the kids." I stood as well. "I'll have the kitchen send something to my office and do as counsel directs."

Chapter Seven

Raima's information packet could cause riots in the wrong hands in any metropolitan area. As domestic agricultural production approached the highest level in a decade with a stable population, diplomats felt free to use food supplies as currency. Still shy of domestic capability to provide adequate food for every U.S. citizen, politicians watched this trend like mouse-starved hawks. A rumble in the media about possible domestic food shortages could send people to hording first, then to the streets. The promise of full cupboards and jobs brought the Median party to the White House. News that the promise had been brokered away could be catastrophic.

If there were dots to connect that could solve the pending crisis, I was clueless. More than clueless, I felt threatened. The government demanded the majority of what Ashwood produced to stabilize consumer markets. We sold a smaller portion privately to support our business. The rest of what we grew fed our family, workers, staff and day laborers. Ashwood attracted the best day laborers because we provided two solid meals a day instead of one. I could not control diplomats, but I would fight to keep Ashwood viable and all its people fed.

Hours before the call with Joel I brought my team together. Chief Engineer and Security Manager Lao, Head Teacher Jason, Cook Jeremiah, and Business Manager Andre arrived within minutes of each other, all looking as if they carried the heavy burdens of this unusual harvest season. Magda and Paul placed their protective hats and shirts on an empty chair. We filled our water glasses. I watched Magda and Andre silently bow their heads before taking a first sip and respected their thankfulness for this key resource.

"Thank you for changing your schedules." Andre nodded, the others continued to settle into their chairs. "We have less than two days to respond to the youth redeployment initiatives. I don't know why this critical matter slipped between the cracks of our team, but we'll talk about that another day. Right now I want us to use our time in building a defensive response."

If anyone in the room had a tendency to pointing fingers that would be Magda. If anyone on the team was usually anal about keeping everyone on task, that role fell on Andre. Magda appeared agitated, Andre bristly. I waited for either of them to protest before beginning my assessment of our situation.

"Ashwood and Giant Pines have thirty residential workers ranging in age from six to sixteen. We also employ roughly twenty community youth workers whom we feed two meals a day and educate in the estate's school." I turned on the room screens so data covered the walls—wages, meals per day served to child workers and adult laborers, educational costs analyzed by residence status of child, as well as incidental expenses like clothing, transportation, and medical care. "Andre, what is our average expense per residential worker compared to expenses of a day worker?" I asked as the data continued to build.

"Residential workers run approximately three times the expenses of a full-time day worker regardless the age of the child." His voice still carried a slight French accent from growing up in Cameroon. "We absorbed five new residential workers in the past eight months, so that pushed our housing capacity to its limit. Additional residential workers require capital investment in new dormitory spaces. We're also required by the local government to keep the estate school open to our regular day laborers' children or we'll lose funding for a half-time teacher." He waited for people to read through the data. "Jason can tell us more about the school." Ignoring that some of his peers had not been involved, Andre opened a new topic. "At least the DOE grant kids would bring a teacher and their own housing."

Puzzled faces turned to me. "We used regular business information to respond to a DOE request to house a gifted student's special school. They've bundled this program under a series of grants with handsome financials and a lot of spiffs. Because of timing, Jason, Andre, and I responded. Ashwood would have to accept up to ten students. There is lots of upside—the school is totally self-funding with positive public relations for Ashwood." Heads nodded, returned to Andre's data.

"Have you worked up the financials on the costs of building dorm space and school changes for the urban initiative?" I asked Andre. A few lines of numbers caught my attention where something about cost per meal and vendor expenses contradicted my historical understanding. "Jeremiah, something about our food costs is off. If you remove the new residential workers, these numbers have increased almost thirty-five percent in the past five months after standard inflation. With use of the kitchen garden produce. The numbers should be lower. What's going on?"

"These numbers are different from those I circulated yesterday," Andre interjected. "That can't be. I approved the final reports this morning."

With less than two hours until the call with counsel, work stopped. "We don't have time to isolate the problem, Andre." He didn't look up as I spoke. "Could we use your old projected financials and put someone onto looking at the problems in this report?"

"I need ten minutes," Andre said as he stood up. "A subset of these numbers have to be filed with our youth redeployment application, so we need to get to the bottom of the situation. Talk through other sections of the program while I'm gone."

"Here's where I'd like to focus while Andre's gone." I redirected the team, knowing a short break would draw them into production issues. "The preliminary government recommendation is that Ashwood absorb up to ten residential workers while we retain existing day laborer and worker numbers." I paused as the team took in that information. "That means adding significant expense with no assistance."

Lao, his logic and calmness always critical to our proceedings, put up his hand—a quirky habit he had never shed while sitting at the management table. I nodded toward him.

"Timing is everything. If these kids arrive for the harvest, we could use temporary quarters without a housing variance. Once harvest is complete, we do not have space, beds, or other facilities to meet Bureau of Human Capital Management domestic worker requirements. Taking on that kind of building could put jeopardize Ashwood's profitability."

Like many small businesses, we used private financing for major expenditures. The past two years Hartford, Ltd., had been totally self-sufficient and even the thought of dealing with debt management both bothered and distracted me.

"In operations, we have no capability to train that many kids." Magda looked my way and paused. I pulled out of my own thoughts to pay attention. "As we boost greenhouse growing, there's just no place for untrained young workers. I'm reading that this program will focus on older urban kids with spotty work histories. These are the ones more likely to bring knives and drugs and a whole lot of problems. Ashwood isn't set up to be some kind of attitude boot camp for troubled kids."

"I hear these kids might not be so good in school, either," Jeremiah added. "We had a cook networking session this morning. Lots of talk about this youth deployment program bringing big problems out to the country."

"Are they sending out kids who should be going to detention farms?" Paul's question quieted us. "Anyone know why these kids have spotty work histories? I hear about meaningless metro assignments like scrubbing sidewalks or sorting materials at the recycling centers. Some of these kids might be too bright to stay with that kind of work. Some might be thugs. I'd like to know more about their profiles."

"You'll be our key player if any of these kids land here, Paul. You do well with the older guys." I let the conversation rest for a few seconds, wished there was time to talk one-on-one with the team about this challenge.

"I hear three themes coming through—there are significant unfunded costs to this program as well as a negative impact on our involvement with our local community." I brought the discussion back to where we started. "Finally, even if we were assigned well-trained kids, we don't have the work, the facilities, or the resources to assure their success here." I looked around the table, saw agreement. "So how do we build our case?"

"We use the Bureau's labor ratios as a start," Magda suggested. "We point to Ashwood's past willingness to accept kids with educational needs." She shrugged, a sage manager who had learned through trial and error how to work with a wide range of young people. "We've been a friggin' pilot site for school programs since Jason arrived. No one can say this estate has walked away from helping kids."

Jason settled back in his wheeled chair. The hot weather sapped his energy. "I can work up data on how many community youth and day laborers' children will be displaced by additional residential workers. If these kids need special assistance, we'll have to push nonresident students back into community schools." He sipped at his water. "Andre can reuse the financial model we've built for other grant applications to show what our school saves community districts."

"Ms. Anne." The speaker on the table activated. "We are shutting down all data systems. We've been corrupted."

"Tell Andre to get back in here." I turned off the speaker. "Lao, do you know anything about what's going on?"

His calm face provided no visual cues. This man claimed my trust through years of protecting Ashwood and all within. "We do have a problem within our systems. I'd rather not say more."

"We have backup data?" My fingers tapped their way across my data pad, entering a privacy code for the secured server Lao maintained for my use.

"It would not be wise to open that system right now, Ms. Anne." Lao raised his voice. "Use yesterday's data tables, but do not open your secured data."

Hesitating with two digits left in my password, I looked up. Everyone looked at Lao, fascinated as he moved to his knees and then down to the floor as easily as a toddler sliding from an adult's lap. He tapped his index finger against his lips and waved his other hand as he disappeared under the table. I took the wave as a sign to continue the meeting.

"Let's pull together our report using yesterday's data as Lao recommends. If anyone has difficulties locating those numbers, talk with Andre." I stretched as I looked out a window. "Hot as hell out there again. Magda, I'm so pleased we put up tents for sun shelter and the misting station. I trust everyone's using maximum UV protection?"

"They're wearing our gear." She gazed out the same window. "Too many of these metro day laborers come with silly city sun shades and have no idea how quickly they could be burned or get sick."

"Magda, Jason, Paul, and Lao, I'd like you to join me for the five-thirty call. Jeremiah, you'll be needed in the kitchen." I reached for the water. "If anyone needs me, I'll be working at my desk the rest of the afternoon."

They filed out, Lao hanging back. "Would you have time for a walk through the orchard, Anne?" His tone told me nothing, and that alone told me he had serious information to discuss away from possible security issues within our complex. "We will have a good crop, Magda says. I have an idea about irrigation that needs your approval."

"Let me say good-bye to my husband first." He waited as I headed to David's office just in time for a hug and a kiss. "Let me walk you to the transport." His morning anxiety raised my own.

"Better if we do everything normally." David hitched his case over his shoulder and extended his free arm. "I can tell you're having a wicked day."

He pulled me close. "Take some time to think through this Smithson situation. I had one of the DOE folks do a little file searching, and I think our family would be good for Andrew." We kissed again. "No pressure, Annie."

"You're a great guy, Mr. Regan." David preferred humor when a departure might become emotional.

"That's why the DOE tells me I have to go to Paraguay."

"Seriously, take care of yourself. I love you." I backed away.

"I know." He left, waving his left hand but not turning again.

Work demanded that I be a calm wife. I return to the conference room and Lao. He directed our walk back across the courtyard to the estate's business office. Andre stood deep in discussion with staff, but Lao lifted a thumb and Andre joined us.

"Out to look at the apples?" our business manager asked.

Lao nodded. "The three of us need to discuss something now. Won't hurt for Anne to get some sunshine at the same time."

I never, never questioned Lao's intentions. From our earliest days of working together I knew he took his responsibility for watching over Ashwood as a deep commitment. With a wife and a toddler living here, he also called the estate home.

Afternoon September heat blasted my face as we left the building. Instinctively I lifted my face upward for the sun's warmth, then tilted my face back toward the ground as I reached into my pants' pocket for sunglasses. "Is this the seventh day above ninety degrees? I thought yesterday's rain might have snapped the heat."

"Back-to-back fronts from the south, Anne." Lao lifted his hat to his head from his neck, where it hung by strings. "We'll pick up hats for you and Andre at the workers' station."

My boys stood side by side next to a long table with a group out in a sorting shed. They were workers as good as any young kids. I gazed at my watch, surprised that most of the afternoon was already gone. Having missed lunch with the family, I needed to be with them for dinner even if I could only spend a few minutes at the table.

Ashwood's dusty footpaths led us to the orchards, where high tech and low tech combined to keep hungry birds out of the low-hanging trees. Weather patterns this growing season gave us potential for a record harvest of apples, pears, and raspberries. Apples provided us with a solid income and valued food resources. Pears and raspberries were luxury crops we sent to market for top money. Here, all was quiet with summer weeding and spraying completed and all the hard work now left for the sun and rain. Lao veered toward the apple stands.

"I will be quick," Lao said as we stood amid low Honeycrisp variety branches. "Andre and his staff began finding small discrepancies in Jeremiah's food accounts last quarter. We performed an internal audit and tracked issues back to the beginning of the year. Very sophisticated entry technique."

Andre interrupted. "He's been embezzling from Ashwood and directing funds toward an account in Bermuda. Significant funds."

"Why would Jeremiah do that?" I asked. "He's been the best kitchen manager we've had since Terrell left. Jason has only good things to say about his partner as a teaching assistant. I don't understand."

"It doesn't matter why a man steals," Andre responded. "We need to report him to the authorities today and have him arrested."

Bees moved through the orchard. Far ahead on the transport path I could see wavy heat rising from the crushed stone surface. "This might be one of the worst days I've had for a long time." They would not think me whiny for stating the truth. "But it does matter to me why Jeremiah would risk so much. He'll spend years in jail. A lot of years."

"He has stolen at least twice his annual wage in just nine months." Lao pulled down a branch and picked a red and gold apple. "And his partner may be the person responsible for corrupting our data files. By the time we return to the residence, we'll know if that's true." He offered the apple to me.

I shook my head. "And why didn't I know this was going on?"

"The numbers were small until recently." Distant shades of Cameroon came forward in Andre's voice. "We thought our newest analyst might be misclassifying expenses. This last quarter Jeremiah and his partner became bolder, although erratic."

"It was my decision to let the investigator take time," Lao said. "Insurance will cover most of the loss, so I didn't want to make this a big deal until we were ready to take action. We were going to tell you everything. A meeting called Outside Security Utilization is on your calendar." He rubbed the apple against his pants. "Something must have tipped Jeremiah that we were on to him and he transferred funds this morning."

Hartford, Ltd., spanned many enterprises beyond Ashwood and Giant Pines, a sister estate, so its managers operated with great autonomy. I felt uncomfortable about how that independence looked today. I had no excuses beyond complacency for letting people like Penfeller and Jeremiah mess with Ashwood. "So you called the Bureau? He is our last key government employee."

"We had no choice." Andre's voice blended with the rustling of the leaves as a hot breeze moved through the trees. "I have a meeting with him in a few minutes to go over numbers. Lao called the authorities, who are on their way." He tipped his head with respect in my direction. "You can block our action, Ms. Anne, but the cook position is too critical to the estate to not have a person we can trust."

"I have had an investigator working on the system security breach." Lao tucked the apple in a pants pocket. "This is very serious. I am nervous about Jeremiah even touching a data pad while we are out here."

"But we're at the most critical time of the year for filling Ashwood's food reserves. This morning he told me we had about three months of supplies in place." My hat felt like a band constricting my brain. "I'll have to ask Sarah to supervise a temporary replacement from the Bureau."

The men remained silent, giving me time to accept our dilemma. "Okay. Tell me what you need me to do."

"Just knock on my door at four-fifteen and come in to sign the paperwork," Andre said.

"Fine, I'll be there. What about his partner?" Tonight's dinner arrangements popped up in my mind as I tried to accept a dual betrayal.

"He'll be arrested at the same time. We'll secure their quarters while the arrests take place." Lao extended a hand toward me, an odd gesture for this self-contained man. He turned his palm up as he spoke. "If I may be the bearer of possible good news?"

"Please, Lao, please share something to rescue this day." I wondered if he knew my day began with the Smithson situation and realized how dazed I felt that on top of David's assignment.

"You know Terrell and I have remained friends throughout his travels with the DOE?" Lao never hurried his words.

"And?"

"And, because he's completed his last years of DOE projects, I took the liberty of asking him about his interest in returning to Ashwood as a privately employed manager."

"Lao, if you tell me he said yes, I may have to dance with you under these trees."

Wrapping one arm across his middle and the other behind his back, Lao bowed then straightened up, opening his arms as if for a waltz. His smile challenged the sun's brightness.

"Oh, my God." I let the words fly into the quiet while I hugged a surprised Lao. "When is he available?"

"He's on his way here from Baltimore and arrives around ten tonight." Andre, who never knew Ashwood's best cook and my closest confidant, saw me grin like a crazy woman as Lao talked. "If you want to prep him about Ashwood, he can be in your office as early as tomorrow morning."

"Should I pick him up at the jet port?"

"Anne, I think you and your family have enough going on tonight." Lao's voice gentled. "Be with them. Tomorrow will be an easier day."

Chapter Eight

THEFT, EMBEZZLEMENT, AND BRIBERY made up the bulk of estate crimes. From day laborers carrying food out under their clothes to complicated transfers of funds to private accounts, the authorities demanded immediate involvement in dealing with the accused. Local officials claimed jurisdiction over simple theft of less than five thousand dollars. State officials enforced all weapon-related issues. Fund transfers and embezzlement fell under federal control because most estates were still managed by government employees. Tight management of information about these crimes was notorious. Big government had nurtured an astounding amount of employee misbehavior.

My first night at Ashwood, Bureau authorities arrested my predecessor for stealing from the estate. On a farm where production was bountiful, child workers with the thin faces of hunger ate dinner of white fish with a small serving of vegetables night after night. Maybe greed brought Jeremiah and his partner to the same fate as Ashwood's first matron, led out in handcuffs surrounded by officials in dark-blue clothing.

Some government employees, like all the other intellectual class including David, were paid handsome incomes and lived like the upper middle class in assigned housing. Members of a slim middle class, if they were lucky, might raise their family in a two-bedroom apartment or a shared house. A small sliver of government employees lived exceptionally well. For many, jobs like those on the management team of an estate were the best this country had to offer—good pay, free housing, food, medical care, and education for their children. Military life offered the same benefits if a family was willing to accept the risks.

Unlike long-standing family farms, Ashwood existed in a quasi-government status managed by people I hired but staffed almost entirely by workers and laborers assigned through the Bureau of Human Capital Management. Jeremiah was the last senior manager I accepted on assignment from the Bureau. As I signed papers authorizing Jeremiah's release to the authorities, I was reminded of my trust in individuals paid by Hartford, Ltd.

Thanks to Sarah supervising the kitchen following Jeremiah's arrest, dinner was served without a hitch. I tried to push aside my concerns to enjoy the early meal with my family. More important than our simple entrée and salad, the love of my kids fed me. The boys sat between Paul and Sarah, with Phoebe at my side.

"Where's Dad this time?" Phoebe asked as the boys' perpetual activity stopped to allow food to travel from plates to mouths.

"South America, sweetie."

"He'll be hot there, just like us." Her fork stabbed lettuce and pea pods. "When will he call us? I want to tell him about a new way Teacher Jason showed me to study for the exam."

"Talking with Dad's going to be tough this trip. He's traveling into mountain areas, and his schedule is difficult." Our lie flowed easily. Phoebe's shoulders slumped. "I would love to hear all about it tonight. Do you want to take a walk after my call is done?"

"I need to show you in the classroom."

"Great. We'll still take a short walk." I gave her a little shoulder bump. "It's been a long day, but I have to get some fresh air with my favorite girl."

A small worry wrinkle appeared above her eyes. She leaned close. "Since Dad's not here tonight, could I sleep with you?" The pitch of her voice rose. "Please."

I knew Sarah and Paul heard Phoebe's request, waited for my response to signal if they would be on call tonight. "That sounds like a good idea. No pj party games, though. Dad and I were up early, so I'm tired."

"And I woke you up with a bad dream."

This time I put my arm around her. "True, but we have been really busy today with big problems."

An inward look, more adult than childlike, showed on her face, suggesting she didn't remember anything or had memories of the night terror that she didn't want to remember.

"Hopefully we'll both sleep well tonight." The boys ignored our conversation. Sarah and Paul sat back with their coffee cups, which reminded me of the days when sharing coffee in the kitchen gave Terrell and me time to develop a great friendship.

I wondered what Terrell would think of our little girl and realized few in our family would really remember him. "I have a big announcement." My in-laws loved good surprises as much as my kids did, and their anticipation lifted me from the day's fatigue.

"You've all heard me talk about my friend Terrell, who was Ashwood's cook when you three big kids were babies?" Phoebe and my in-laws nodded. "The really great news is that he is coming back here to take over all the estate food management. Even better, he arrives tonight."

Phoebe tilted her head. "He sang to me when I was a baby and taught me to count."

Her memory astounded me. "Absolutely, sweetie. Terrell had a beautiful voice and knew just how to rub your back when you couldn't sleep. He taught you how to walk along the wooden bench in the front hall."

"The bench Dad made." We all heard the whispery longing under her words.

"The most beautiful piece of furniture in Ashwood." I winked at her. "You kids can split my cookie because I have to go back to work." Folding my napkin next to my plate, I wanted to stay at the table until everyone was through eating, but I had no choice. "Boys, if Grandma wouldn't mind, I'd like to read with you two tonight and have Phoebe join us." I looked to Sarah. "Grandma's welcome to stick around."

"That's a date," said Noah in a fake deep voice and wicked smile. "Do I sound like Dad?"

"No," exploded from Phoebe as she rolled dark eyes. "You sound like a six-year-old."

Their laughter raised my spirits. "Don't rush, Paul. I'm heading over early to go through notes before we start." He lifted his cup to acknowledge my comment.

The sounds of their voices soon mingled with thirty other kids arriving for dinner. Unlike young workers at regular estates, ours receive a wardrobe of seasonal clothes when they joined Ashwood, so each table looked bright and unique. For most kids, six outfits and three pairs of shoes represented more hope than they had experienced in their deprived homes.

When I came to Ashwood, I assigned each worker an adult mentor, but as the number of kids passed the number of adults, we moved into a buddy system of older children accepting responsibility for new arrivals. Our management team still stepped into a surrogate parent role with these little buddy groups. We all did night patrol, listening for lonely tears or sleepless kids.

Ashwood's workers represented many economic, ethnic, and racial backgrounds. But since my first Christmas on the estate we had never absorbed a group as large as the ten proposed in the urban initiative. Every estate feared the possibility of gang issues coming into their workforce with older metro kids. From symbols buzzed into short hair to small forbidden tattoos, we inspected every new assigned worker.

On the way to the DOE building, my thoughts focused on our upcoming phone call. Sitting down, I made a list of strategies for opting out of the Bureau's new assignments. When the others arrived, the conference with Joel began.

"I'll give you an off-the-record summary of what's happened in the Minneapolis circuit this summer," Joel began. "The news you see barely covers the depth of poverty saturating the city. Kids schooled in the general education system have high testing failure rates, keeping them out of job-training programs. Their parents' wages aren't covering rising food costs, so many families are experiencing hunger. I wouldn't say we're anywhere near starvation, but officials are scrambling to get ahead of the situation."

Beyond the conference screen, I watched Ashwood outside my windows. A group of girls kicked a soccer ball in the open yard, ignoring the heat in that resilient way of youth. Phoebe's curly head bobbed in the younger girls' section. One of our patrol dogs chased sticks thrown by two boy workers sitting just beyond the girls. These kids had rounded faces, muscled arms and legs, shining hair.

"The Bureau has identified about five hundred kids for worker program assignment." Joel looked tired; maybe working beyond the typical bureaucratic end of day sapped his energy. "These new assignees are all far beyond the normal age of program initiation—most are at least twelve and a few are as old as fifteen."

"That doesn't make any sense," I interjected. "Workers enter the system when they're young so an individual development plan can be put in place to maximize the estates' schools. By their late teens, the best we can do is impact work behavior."

Paul nodded in agreement. "Sounds to me like these kids don't fit the original profile or have parents who don't like the thought of signing them into the system. Now there are issues and these kids are too young to force into factories or the military."

Bureau legal counsel remained silent. Outside the window Phoebe fell as she ran, rolled gracefully, and caught up with the small crew of girls. Not one of our workers feared for their safety within Ashwood's boundaries, which gave them the security to study, work, or chase a soccer ball. We relied on their hard physical work to keep the estate productive. They relied on us to offer a protective environment where they could learn and grow.

"Joel." I continued to watch Phoebe as I spoke. This fight was for her and my sons and all our workers. "We've run the numbers. If these assignments are made, we'll significantly downsize the number of community laborers and workers at both Ashwood and Giant Pines. There isn't enough work to support additional workers, even if they are trained." I placed one hand flat on the table and raised the other as if taking an oath. "We will lay off community workers first, all the kids working in our greenhouses and barns who are not residents. That means they'll be dumped on the local school district. A dozen kids."

Without looking in Jason's direction, I continued. "We'd also eliminate two full-time laborer positions in order to hire a full-time supervisor for the new workers. Depending on which laborers we choose, our school's enrollment will be reduced by another three or four." I saw Jason's upper body tense as he followed my logic. "That would break our county contract and affect local families financially, as well as change their kids' educational experience."

My managers became still. "Or, if it would make Ashwood less attractive as a dumping site for these assignees, I'd be willing to dismantle some part of our school program—perhaps the postsecondary preparation courses could be closed to all but students identified early as college eligible." I ignored the discomfort of my staff. "If our numbers alone are not convincing for the assignment team, would restructuring of the famous Ashwood education system help change minds?"

I knew the very idea pained Jason, who over the past years in Ashwood's school built curriculum used throughout the national estate system. Appearing to trust my direction, he nodded my way.

"If we are assigned ten underperforming older urban students, the Bureau will need to provide funding and staff resources for a remedial program," Jason offered. "We now teach with larger teacher-student ratios than the Bureau requires because of our proficiency with early learners. We do not currently have remedial curriculum or teachers."

"Anyway, Joel, what about the gifted offspring provisions of the DOE contract that allows estate schooling?" Only Jason and I had thorough knowledge of these protocols. "How do we meet requirements for preparing David's daughter and son for their long-term education if we dilute Head Teacher Jason's system?" Joel's forehead wrinkled, one eye slightly closed. "I wouldn't want to ask the DOE for permission to offer less academics for two future intellectuals."

The argument ran along a thin line—boarding schools existed for gifted teen-age offspring, but Phoebe wouldn't be eligible for admission for another five years. When Joel didn't respond, I decided to pull a second DOE contract into the discussion.

"If the negative business and community effects of assigning these workers to our estate is not convincing, Hartford, Ltd. will also apply for a hardship stipend to replace income anticipated from DOE contract 11301217 for our privately incorporated school." My office became quiet.

Counsel had been caught unaware, his face worked into a tired, neutral bureaucratic pose. He was a decent sort and in the moment I felt bad about springing the DOE contract into the conversation.

"Did you say that contract began with 1130?" He rubbed a hand over the side of his face. "One of the new gifted arrangements?"

I nodded. "Yes, we've been selected as a regional site."

"That would change everything about the urban youth assignment." Glancing at something in his office outside of our view, he was distracted. "Give me a minute," he turned away to say to someone. "DOE 1130 contracts trump regional youth assignments. I suggest this call is over. If you don't mind, I can make the last transport home if I sign off."

"Go ahead, Joel. And thank you." The screen darkened, our conference room stayed quiet. Paul raised one hand and slapped Magda's extended hand.

"Well, a dozen smart kids who need a challenging academic experience are probably a better match for this place than ten troubled urban kids," Magda said. "Trust those kids won't take jobs from local workers or laborers."

"These kids will add labor requirements." Jason picked up the details. "We'll add at least one half-time teaching professional and a chaperone/housekeeper."

The soccer girls disbanded. Phoebe looked toward the office even though one-way glass hid us from her view. I knew the day had stretched too long and covered too many rough paths. I missed David.

"It would be nice if we could help out with the urban initiative in the future," I said. "You're all good at finding opportunities. Right now I need to spend time with my kids and get some fresh air." I stood. "I almost forgot to share big news—Terrell is coming back. Tonight. Lao, please call me when he arrives." Tired faces relaxed, including mine. "Thanks everyone for pulling through a tough day."

Spontaneous happiness broke out around the table. Terrell could make that happen.

Chapter Nine

My stepdaughter absorbed physical touch like a plant draws water. She snuggled, she leaned against an arm, she sat with her hand on a friend's leg while watching movies. So we walked through the orchards in this sticky evening hand in hand, her chatting about books she wanted to read, a curious chunk of china found by one of the workers while tilling a new garden. Finally, we talked about David's current travel.

"Why now, Mom?" Anxiety built the words into a whine, her intense young personality pushing much smaller worries into bouts of near-obsessive thoughts. "I need Dad here for my proficiency tests. We had plans." She bumped her body into my arm. "Did he tell you about our plans?"

"You bet, and plans are still in place for lunch at the History Museum's restaurant." I responded slowly, swinging our hands as we walked. "I'm taking the day off. Grandpa Paul and Ms. Magda will manage here." I squeezed her small fingers. "I'm looking forward to visiting the museum with you. I know you were looking forward to being with Dad, but maybe a girls' time away could be almost as much fun."

She shook free of my hand to throw her arms around my waist. "That's the best news today." Freed of one worry, she broke loose and did her young-girl dancing step next to me. And, typical of Phoebe, she stopped midstep with another question. "About Dad's trip." Her voice, so clear, carried through the humid evening air. "It feels like you aren't telling us the whole story."

"Well, communication is quite difficult because of where he'll be based." I offered a truth buried in soft language. "In fact, I don't know if we'll talk at all while he's away, and that makes me sad."

"I thought you might be worried about that boy this morning."

The estate grapevine spread innuendo faster than facts. For a moment I wondered who heard Paul or David talking about Andrew, or if Antwone knew more than he shared in the passageway.

Ashwood ate at my hours, and sometimes emotions. What crops to grow, what animals to breed, where to buy, where to sell, forms to complete, the pressure to feed its people, make the payroll, pay the increasing taxes. And always the drive to care for the children—all those who came to be part of the estate—maybe this boy who may be my son.

"You heard something today about a boy?"

"Your surrogate boy." Phoebe no longer danced as she walked, no longer held my hand. She spoke of facts learned from estate gossip that flowed like water in a rainstorm. "Grandpa says he could be my stepbrother. It's too bad we couldn't have another girl. I've got two brothers already."

I hoped I heard acceptance of the Smithson boy and envied her ease with the whole question, realized she'd had more time in her day to think about Andrew, a possible new sibling, than I, his possible mother.

"I'm not quite ready to talk about him until I know all the facts, Phoebe. How did you hear this story?"

She walked away, bending to pick a volunteer bachelor's button growing in the orchard path. "I don't remember. Somebody was talking this morning. Then you didn't come to lunch." She handed me the flower. "Race you to the school?"

The sweet thrill of childish play still sounded in her invitation, although the pace she set suggested the competitive drive I saw in her evening soccer game with the older girls. Only my daily running kept me ahead of her as we neared the building. Inside she still moved quickly, but now with the confidence of a scholar. This was her favorite place at Ashwood, both a haven and a place of joy. An amazing student, she led me through her review drill with competence and intensity.

We left the school building before the sky turned dark, unexpectedly finding Lao and Terrell on their way to the main residence.

"Well, Ms. Anne Hartford, aren't you looking fine." Not much had changed about Terrell in the five years since he left Ashwood. He stood tall and athletic, his drooping eye a bit more closed, shaved head shining from the glow of a light hanging from the crab apple tree. "And what you have done to this place. Feels like . . . like a home."

He opened his arms and I laughed as I walked into them to be hugged to his strong chest. "That's what it is, Terrell. Welcome home." I wrapped my arms around his neck. "You're the best thing to happen to this place in many months." I stepped back, inspected him more closely, knew he was doing the same before he looked around me.

"This can't be baby Phoebe. This pretty little thing is tall like her daddy and has her mother's amazing hair." He extended a hand. "Cook Terrell. I don't know if you remember way back when we spent some time together in my kitchen."

She extended her arms, toddled from side to side, humming some old nursery tune. "I remember the song!"

"Well, I'll be. They say women never forget special men in their lives." He tipped his head her way and she curtsied in return. "I suppose your brother is just as smart as you, Ms. Phoebe."

"Which one? Noah or Adam?" A sly look crept into her smile. "Or maybe the one who may be coming?"

"Quick mind, quick tongue. I was waiting for your mom to tell me about that," Terrell murmured as he turned once more to the residence. "What did you do to my kitchen? Our morning coffee window looks like it's been bumped out and those gnarly bushes you hated are gone."

"You were right that the old floor plan wouldn't expand to keep up with food management needs." I hooked an arm through his. "About three years ago Lao and I hauled out your drawings and redesigned the whole space. I think you'll like your new domain."

We entered the residence through the workers' entrance, Terrell glancing around like a kid returned home from college and sniffing the air as a true cook would for traces of the day's meals. Amber, the only remaining child worker from his earlier stay, surprised him with a card she'd made.

"This can't be Amber so grown up. What are our friends Lana and Ladd doing?" he asked as she straightened from her bow.

"Lana's studying nursing and Ladd left college to become a marine." Her sleek dark hair still moved in its smooth bob as she tilted her head to one side. "Ms. Anne and Director David were not happy with his choice."

"They were about your age when I got here." He looked around the kitchen, his eyes moving over an elevated ledge on the giant island in the heart of the room. From where he stood he could see a row of stools stashed under the ledge. He nodded and smiled. "Hard to believe those two are launched out into the world and little Amber is my right-hand worker."

"You're lucky to have Amber—she's smart. The workers respect her direction, and she can tell good jokes." She laughed, a sweet, low sound that gave me a few minutes of easy happiness at the end of a tough day.

"If I could have a sister, I'd want one like Amber," Phoebe added, while taking Amber's hand.

"Your old rooms are available, or you might want to share a small house with Teacher Jason. The residence is noisier now than you remember." There would be time to tell him about Lana's success in school and how Ladd tossed away a scholarship for the quick money promised by a military recruiter.

"Well, at least there's no babies crying," he teased Phoebe and winked as she giggled. "I'll take my old rooms. I got a bit of arthritis in my back, so walking up that path in the winter isn't appealing." He placed his hands on one of the stainless steel countertops. "I'm gonna like being back in this kitchen."

"It's where you belong," I said. "I wish David was here." Paul and Sarah joined us. "You remember David's parents, Paul and Sarah Regan. They live with us here, and Sarah is a whiz in residence management including the kitchen. She can give you a thorough report on inventory and such tomorrow."

A stretch of annual pandemics in the past decade kept most people from shaking hands, but the long-standing residents of Ashwood, hearing of Terrell's arrival, joined us in the kitchen with hands extended, if not arms opened, to welcome him back.

John and Noah, already in their pajamas, came to my side. "This is the man who kept me healthy while all of you were babies," I said. "And made all your baby foods."

"Phoebe, these two guys will always keep you safe," Terrell said as he shook their hands. "I watched out for my sisters until they were all grown up."

"Now it's time for bed for all the Regan kids. I'm looking forward to coffee together in the morning." I gathered my three for reading and bed.

The children's rooms had eastern exposures which helped with early-morning wake-ups part of the year and provided a calm, muted end-of-day light. Bright blue quilted blankets covered the boys' bunks, the same kind of beds slept in by Ashwood's workers. Unlike bedrooms of my youth, these spaces were designed for sleeping, dressing, and storing personal items, with precious little area for playing or studying. A soccer ball, cleats, books, and a box of construction blocks littered the room's limited open space.

We walked around their messy pile without my usual reminder to pick up their stuff. On this warm night, the open window helped cool the room. I folded covers on both beds, helped settle white sheets over their shoulders.

"Where's Dad tonight?" Noah's eyes followed me as I rubbed John's back. "Does he have a bed to sleep in?"

"He's in Paraguay, sweetie." I kissed John's cheek. "That's all we know." I kissed Noah. "But you know Dad can sleep almost anywhere." They both giggled. "Good night."

As I turned off the boys' light, I felt hopeful about managing Ashwood through another possible economic downturn with Terrell, a strong strategist, at my side. It wasn't until much later that night as the moonlight showed Phoebe's small silhouette on the pillow where David should sleep, when her sweet girl smell of sunshine and homemade soap teased the air, that I returned to the original puzzle of the day, my possible son: this boy named Andrew. I knew if he was mine, I wanted him here. With David and Paul and Sarah and our kids, he would have a family. I fell asleep without thinking about what I would do if he wasn't my son. That decision could wait.

Phoebe stirred next to me about two hours after she fell asleep. She sat up, removed our cover, and swung her legs to the side of the bed.

"Honey, are you okay?" I asked, assuming she needed to use the bathroom.

She said nothing as she lowered her feet to the floor, and in the quiet of the room I heard her teeth clench, grind, and release; clench, grind, and release, An awful sound suggesting illness or fear.

"Phoebe, are you awake?" I rolled myself out of the bed as well, moving to her side with as little noise as possible.

Her eyes looked somewhere, certainly not at me and not at the wall of cabinets she faced. Raising one hand, Phoebe dragged at her hair. Teeth clenching and grinding, she moved steadily toward the wall then lurched toward a set of drawers. I worried about waking her. Willing my hands to be as gentle as handling a fragile newborn, I brought my arms around her slender body. "Shhh, sweetie, you need to wake up."

She uttered nonsense sounds in tones as guttural as a child can make.

We stood in the dark room, her nightgown damp with sweat, her body stiff in my arms, and rocked. Maybe fifteen seconds passed, maybe thirty, as I curved myself around her small rigid frame and wished I could ease away this night's terror.

When her body drooped, Phoebe groaned. "What happened?" she whispered, sounding parched.

"You had a bad dream." She leaned against my ribs, sweat dampening her nightshirt, a slight shakiness beginning. "Would you like some water or to use the bathroom?"

I had to lean close to hear her say, "I want to lie down. I'm cold."

"First, let's get you out of that damp night gown and put you in one of Dad's clean T-shirts." She lifted her arms, eased out of hers. I pulled David's shirt over her body. We returned to bed and Phoebe returned to sleep. I held her, barely dozing to keep useless watch for an emotional villain.

Chapter Ten

On a typical morning, intellectuals and their families living on estates slept hours after the laborers began their day. At Ashwood we were all early risers—adult laborers often dressed in the dark on summer mornings, with child workers eating at six-thirty or seven depending on their assignments. Before five on Wednesday morning, Terrell and I stood in the kitchen, drinking his strong signature coffee and having our first planning discussion.

"What time does your family want breakfast?" In the kitchen's strong light, I could see the subtle signs of aging in my friend's face. "Jeremiah's notes don't tell me a thing about how the Regans like to be fed." Easy slang talk disappeared as he built understanding of how the estate, far larger and more complex than when he left, now functioned.

"David and the kids usually eat in the family dining room at the same time as the later workers." I relaxed as we talked, proud of the estate. "You remember that Sarah and Paul are still farmers at heart who wake up with the sun. They make coffee in their own quarters for a little private time, and usually have breakfast in the big dining room with the early crew."

"You are aware that Ashwood's storage is down to about a seven-week supply of staples?"

The news blindsided me. "Jeremiah estimated twelve weeks."

"He may have been counting on fresh produce to stretch what's been preserved." Terrell drew out his data pad. "What's almost empty is the stuff we need to buy in the market—flour, spices, and such. Preserving the harvest won't be possible with what's in the pantry. Inflation is ratcheting up prices almost daily, so I'm preparing a large order." He leaned back against a counter. "If the estate can afford to make a small investment, we could mill our own grains. Magda and I discussed it last night, and we'll have a proposal ready in a few days."

"Jumped right in, Terrell. I thought we might relax with a cup of coffee and catch up on each other's lives this morning." I smiled, knowing we both were better in our jobs today than on our first morning in this kitchen.

"We'll have that talk with some of your mother-in-law's iced tea on the porch tonight." He straightened up and gave directions to Antwone, who carried a pile of plates with about as much concentration as a pillow might demand. "Does seem to me that there is laziness in this kitchen crew. According to Magda, my predecessor wasn't the best supervisor."

"She's right. He and I had a number of talks about making this staff more efficient and disciplined." We both watched Antwone as he slipped a breakfast bar into his pants pocket. In another part of the kitchen, Amber noticed as well and walked out of the room with the boy. "Not that I want to return to old Bureau of Human Capital Management protocol, but these kids need to know what will be expected if their training takes them to another setting." I yawned and tried to cover it with a throat clearing.

"Annie, you look tired. Thought so last night and know so this morning." The man who fed me through the first years of estate management and motherhood still paid attention to the details.

"A few nights without regular sleep are harder as I crawl toward the end of my thirties." My hands tightened around the coffee mug. "Actually, Phoebe suffers from night terrors. She's had a few rough nights. Add that to David's departure, and, yeah, I'm feeling tired."

"You know kids. Would you call Phoebe high strung?" He offered more coffee. I placed my hand over my cup.

"She's smart and caring and funny and athletic and intense about everything." Talking about my girl brought a smile.

"Like her biological mom?" He asked as if looking for clarification instead of stamping an imprint on Phoebe.

"Hard to know." I soft-pedaled back from an opinion. "I know a bit about how gifted kids are put together emotionally, and I'm not convinced she's a little Tia. But we all worry about her in a way we don't about Noah." I put down the coffee cup, tired of its warmth on what looked like another hot day. "Mostly I want her to be able to go to bed and to sleep without fear."

His nod indicated he'd heard about Phoebe's night devils. "I heard Phoebe's getting help. Anything you need from the dietary angle?"

"We have a therapist working with her, and Magda has made a few nutrition suggestions." How I wished David was here to talk over last night's sleepwalking episode. "I haven't seen that food has any impact."

"What about this Smithson boy?"

The change of subject came unexpectedly, like the last swallow of coffee that had turned cold in your cup. "Until Phoebe mentioned him last night I was under the impression that maybe four Ashwood people knew about Clarissa Smithson's visit."

"How long have you lived on estates, Annie? Nothin' stays quiet longer than a few minutes."

"Well, Clarissa Smithson isn't the first person to suggest that some young boy is the child I carried as a surrogate." I looked at his face for surprise, wasn't disappointed. "But she is the first person with all the right facts."

Magda entered the kitchen, hair curling out from under her brimmed hat, sun-protection clothing softly covering her muscular body. From her calm appearance, I assumed the day had started without problems.

"This is like a return to the good old days." She gave Terrell a hug. "If you promise you won't leave for a long time, I'll give you one of these every day." He shook his head and laughed.

"And just like the good old days, I need to get to my office," I grabbed a breakfast sandwich and left them to begin my early morning routine of reviewing market data and government reports.

One of David's DOE assistants sat outside the office building entrance. DOE personnel worked from seven in the morning through late afternoon unless they were preparing for travel with David. Jega, a tall woman whose broad shoulders suggested her role as one of my husband's bodyguards, volunteered nothing about why she stood near the iris scanner at this hour.

"Good morning, Jega. You're here early." I paused at the scanner. A small stepladder from the kitchen stood in the building's inside foyer for children's use of the DOE's security system. "Are you heading to Paraguay as well?"

"You have a visitor in your office, General Manager Hartford." She held out a small ink pad and I remembered everyone on the estate requiring access to this building being fingerprinted during the siege of Ashwood in my first days.

"This must be a rather special visitor to put the building into this mode?" Beyond the quiet hall, the sunrise pushed across fields and orchards. Some central sense of security, not defined by scanners and government agencies, shifted. "You have my prints on file."

"Please, General Manager Hartford. Protocol." Jega extended the small pad while taking my sandwich. One of our hands quivered as I pressed my thumb down. "Thank you."

I checked my thumb for the ink I knew wouldn't be there, took the sandwich back, then stood aside as she activated the office door. For all her adherence to DOE regulations, Jega always wished me a pleasant day, and I missed her solemn voice offering that simple greeting.

My office door stood open, someone with higher clearance having overridden its lock. I straightened my shoulders. Milan arose from a visitor chair, a stranger doing the same next to him.

"Anne, come in," my adviser said. His plain, middle-aged face looked old, thinning hair barely visible across his skull. He wore a dark summer suit and I wondered what time he and this second man must have awakened to dress so formally for travel out to the estates region.

"What is it? Has something happened to David?" Strange how my brain sent the words out into the room while my mind rationalized that what wasn't said out loud couldn't be true. I extended a hand to guide me to my desk, to the chair David built for me at Christmas two years, maybe three years, ago.

"Let me close the door," Milan murmured while tucking a hand around my elbow, maybe holding me upright. He directed me away from my desk, toward the stranger. "Anne, this is Grand Executive Director Lars Peterson representing the Department of Energy. He flew in overnight to talk with us about a situation in Paraguay."

Somehow we all moved to the cherry conference table. Somehow a glass of water appeared in front of me. The sun climbed higher in the sky, lights fading in the outbuildings. An ordinary day at Ashwood.

"I'm sorry to be here under these circumstances, Mrs. Regan." A name never used in our lives after our summer wedding ceremony. Protocol dictated that Hartford remained my legal name, and neither of us cared about such formalities. We were merely David and Anne, husband and wife, dad and mom, lovers.

"I've knew your husband and his first wife when they were students at MIT. He's a brilliant scientist and good human being. I've heard much about you one time when he and I traveled together. And about your children."

I shook my head, impatient with the social niceties when news about David waited behind the words. "What's happened to David?"

Milan took over from the DOE bureaucrat. "Truth is, Anne, we don't really know. You're going to hear on the news this morning that the United States has become significantly involved in a military conflict in the confluence of the borders of Paraguay, Bolivia, and Argentina." Because Milan spoke only of what needed to be said, his voice held my attention.

"A group of American personnel, including David, were caught in an ambush at the Asunción airport late last night. That's all we know."

"Who is holding them?"

"That's part of the problem." Peterson rolled his left fingers as if a pen should be held between his thumb and index finger. I tried not to watch that hand as he spoke. "We don't have all the players sorted out. Bolivia and Brazil are both suspect, but it's no secret Paraguay has been home to terrorists for decades. We just don't know."

"Let me understand. You rushed my husband, one of this country's most essential scientists, into an unstable and politically dangerous situation. He travels with a bodyguard into the cities to buy birthday presents for our kids, and you couldn't protect him getting off an airplane?" Pain fueled anger. My David, a DOE chip embedded near his shoulder in the same way we identified our cattle, missing. My husband, who was in the middle of managing a large project for the Chinese government, sent to a craphole like Paraguay. "This all makes no sense. No sense, Mr. Peterson."

No matter how much this man cared to be kind, his words were meaningless. He would travel back to his wife and family, celebrate a child's birthday, take a walk after dinner. The worst part of this day was over for Peterson. Your loved one has been in a fatal accident, your mother has terminal cancer, your home has been foreclosed. A dozen bad-news deliverers have walked through my life, all decent people charged with a lousy responsibility.

"What's being done?" The question came out demanding as I pushed to understand both the situation and the reason for David's involvement. "There must be some time line from the people who pulled this off."

"As I said, no one has claimed responsibility for the ambush." Peterson sat back.

"So what are we supposed to do?"

"Take the day, Anne," Milan suggested. "Spend it with your family. Then go back to your regular routine. Your family and Ashwood need you to stay strong."

Harvesting Ashwood Minnesota 2037

How could they understand that my strength began intertwining with David when he gave me the key to an old South Dakota house as promise of a future when we were through with government service? That my regular routine meant waking with David, making decisions with my husband, protecting the world we built together.

"This is all you know?"

Peterson shook his head, his lips pressed together, leading me to wonder what words he'd held back.

"What happens now?"

"The DOE will maintain this office into the future so you have no fear of financial instability regardless of the outcome of this situation." Peterson stopped, perhaps hearing the massive insensitivity of his bureaucratic speak. Scientists tell us the body develops pain channels that remain active long after tissue heals. A decade after losing my last relative, one strong channel flooded. I looked to Milan and saw sympathy in the set of his mouth and the seriousness of his eyes.

My old confidant moved the water glass toward me. "Have a drink, Anne. It's too early for anything stronger. I did bring light tranquilizers if that would help."

My hand sprang from the chair, not to grab for drugs but to clamp over my mouth and a primal moan. I stopped their path, swallowed, pushed out words. "I thought you were just showing up to talk about Andrew Smithson."

"There is also news about Andrew." He placed a small medicine container in my hand, closed his fingers around mine. "You were one of the surrogates impregnated with selected sperm." He paused. Too numb to protest confirmation of this long ago wrong, I merely looked at our hands. Milan continued, speaking to me in the quiet tone of a trusted friend. "Your instincts were right when you were pregnant—Andrew is your son. The DNA tests matched."

"Then he belongs here," I said. And I wondered if David didn't return, if I would look at my firstborn child and remember this day. "Don't make me deal with his aunt. I don't want any lasting entanglements with that woman."

"You would think different if you got to know her, Anne," Milan said. "In the future you and I and Clarissa Smithson will sit down together." He demanded eye contact, and I let him see the threat of tears in mine. "I'll work through the details of establishing your legal status as Andrew's mother. His guardianship will transfer to me." He made a note.

I didn't know if he moved us toward talking about guardianship intentionally, or if the conversation now slid on its own to that delicate ground. Under Bureau of Human Capital Management protocol, upon David's disappearance, Phoebe and Noah moved under Milan's legal guardianship.

"We have to talk about the children of David and Tia." He opened with gentleness. "Nothing needs to change in their day-to-day life, and I will assign a temporary waiver for you to do all the things you and David currently manage as parents. We'll monitor what happens and make decisions after more is known about David's situation." Giving my hand an unexpected squeeze before pulling his away, he continued. "Let's assume he'll be back here in good time and we don't have to discuss this further."

Peterson cleared his throat. "I'm sorry to rush us along." He frowned. "DOE has placed this building in lockdown status until David returns. Staff will continue to work here, the lab will remain open. Analyst Jega's provided us with a list of non-DOE individuals who regularly move in and out of your office, and we will set up limited access for them. Tomorrow, we'll install a partial barrier to the area beyond your office and coffee counter to secure David's work."

A wall, even temporary, in the space where David and I spent much of our working day suggested a permanence I wasn't willing to accept. I took a breath. "What that says to Ashwood's people feels rather alarming."

Milan slipped into his strange undefined role between the DOE and the Bureau of Human Capital Management to block Peterson's plan. We moved to talking about anticipated media coverage, how I would receive private updates, what the media would cover, and circulating a written statement to our staff.

I looked at my office clock and noticed it was six-fifteen. When I raised my eyes to the window, the estate's normal morning activities continued with the drive needed to grow food, raise livestock, feed people. In the near distance Lao walked with a day laborer, a kindly man from Lakeville who worked at Ashwood to provide a high-quality education for his daughter in our school. A man who frequently stopped to talk with David about sports.

"What do I tell our children?" The question cut through Peterson's placing a DOE security folder in front of me. "And his mother? Sarah lost a brother in Afghanistan twenty years ago. What do I tell Sarah?"

"If you'd like us to stay an hour or so, I'm willing to talk with whomever you choose as a representative of the DOE. We want Ashwood's people to understand there is no reason to be worried about their own security or continued operation of the estate." How could he understand that David's role at Ashwood had nothing to do with the daily business operations, that my husband gave all his work effort to the DOE? The people of Ashwood would miss the essence of my husband, the man who knew their names and their kids' plans, the farm kid who could clear brush when needed. Together David and I built an atmosphere at Ashwood estate, and that's what people would miss.

Their transport left the estate through the DOE small drive before the residence workers brushed their teeth. Except for Jega at the entrance, I stood alone in the office building. David's locked door, always an affront when he traveled, now felt threatening. Today I would be with my family to tell them the news of David's disappearance and Andrew's arrival. Tomorrow I'd focus on bringing my husband back.

Chapter Eleven

"Knock, knock." Paul pushed my office door open. "Need a friend?" One wide eyebrow, turned white by age and living under bright sun, raised into a questioning line above eyes like those of his son. Under gentle words the hint of a tremor implied that he'd seen the government's silver transport depart.

"Please." I stood by the windows as if solutions for today's problems were hidden in leaves and fields just beyond its glass. As if David might jog up the drive covered with sweat and a layer of road dust and stop in my office on his way to clean up for breakfast. "You saw the transport?"

"They were here about David?"

His hands settled on the back of a chair, fingers spread, age spots and raised veins snagging my attention. With so few urban baby boomers surviving the big D, Sarah and Paul were among the oldest people in our new economy. Decades of living each day outdoors hid their age until moments like this reminded me how fortunate we were to still have David's parents in our lives.

"The media will be reporting the ambush of a mixed U.S. consulting and military leadership group at the Asunción airport overnight. No one knows who is responsible for that action." Paul's face lost elasticity giving him the look of a general facing battle. "That's all we know, or at least all the DOE will say." Shakiness started in my upper legs, a forgotten reaction to extreme danger. "The DOE sent Milan and one of their executives to tell me before news stories are released."

A chair whirled on its casters as Paul pushed it aside on his way to where I stood. His arms folded around me, blocking the morning sun with well-worn cotton over well-developed muscles. I closed my eyes in the safety he offered. We leaned on each other in silence.

"So he's alive?" A father's voice mixed defiance and doubt, not unlike David's challenging the Bureau's therapist about treating Phoebe's night terrors.

"No one said anything else." My lips quivered, and I brought one fisted hand to my mouth. "He has to be alive." On Paul's chest I let tears fall even as I released my fingers to stretch my own arms around his body. "We need to tell Sarah and the children before one of them hears the morning news."

"If you've told me all you know, I'll talk with Sarah." He brushed a hand down my back as we moved apart. "If you want to wait, we'll join you and the kids."

"What am I going to tell them, Paul? Watching Phoebe these past two nights already has me worried. David's her rock of strength."

"You're wrong about that. She worships David, but she leans on you. You're the one she wants when the night is bad. You're the one she calls mother, and there's no role more sacred."

Family breakfast would be served in twenty-five minutes—sleepy boys, Phoebe reading at the table, Sarah drinking strong coffee. "Paul, there are two more things I need to tell you." I took a deep breath before touching the first painful topic. "Milan is legal guardian for Phoebe and Noah. If David . . ." I faltered, looked to the floor for words before telling David's father hard information about our world. "The way Bureau protocol works for children of intellectuals, legal guardianship is usually not held by their parents. Because of Tia's instability, protocol ruled."

"Phoebe doesn't need to know that."

A horse-drawn wagon carried laborers to produce gardens on the far edge of Ashwood where a single farmer had tried to make a living. Potatoes grew right up to a small yard area remaining around his two-bedroom house. "You're right, but I'm trying to tell you that if anything happened to David, Phoebe and Noah could become wards of the Bureau."

I had no magic bullet to change this reality. Paul now knew one of our secret burdens.

"David and I explored every possible legal action to break the contract that was signed before the kids were conceived. No one is willing to take on the case." I drew in a breath, saw Paul's unwillingness to accept that his grandchildren could be taken away. "No one," I repeated. "Milan assured me he expects everything to remain unchanged." I didn't tell him about the temporary waiver. "Sometimes it's uncomfortable to remember that, beyond being a friend, Milan represents the Bureau's interests."

"Well, let's take him at his word." Paul, on his way to the door, stopped. "What else?"

The words came out like the impatient question of an action-oriented man already thinking of the immediate task of breaking the news to his beloved Sarah.

"Andrew Smithson is my biological son."

He blew air through his nose and made an undecipherable sound before speaking. "Goddamn if timing isn't everything. Three kids who need you now and an orphan boy dropped into our house with a whole different set of needs. When does he arrive?"

I didn't respond immediately, struggling with surprisingly defensive emotions raised by Paul's tone. Just yesterday he and David encouraged me to open our home to Andrew regardless of the boy's DNA. Today the reality of this child, my son, sounded like a burden to the family. "Not until next week." I moved from my window view. "I don't want to tell the children about Andrew today. Maybe we'll know David is safe soon, and we can focus on my son's arrival."

I hadn't had my wits about me to seek access to the child's files. Andrew might have any assortment of metro behaviors, might detest estate dwellers, carry a personal weapon. Clarissa had kept him safe so I hoped he would be a good kid. I'd have years to learn his face, his characteristics, his dreams. If only David could be here.

"I love David so much that I can't imagine him in such danger." I bit my lip, held it between my teeth, knowing that losing David would be deeper and more painful than my first experience as a widow. "I know life goes on, but this life is one we built."

"Hold on, Annie. This is my son. He'll find a way to get back to you." My father-in-law and friend returned to my side. "You two are the best matched of all our boys and their wives. Inviting us into your lives made Sarah about as happy as she has been since the depression. Don't ever doubt that you and all the children are as much Regans as David." He gave me a squeeze. "We're family."

My father-in-law was more of a rookie in experiencing the loss of immediate family in an unnatural order. The families of David's siblings owned land that served as the Regan home address for seven generations. My family and first spouse shared wall space in a Minneapolis mausoleum.

For Paul, family still implied the sweet trail of genetics. I saw family as a fluid collection of people bound by emotion and experience and expectation—like Magda and Lao and the children who grew up at Ashwood. David and I, with our children, created a core family, but as a survivor I let my love grow beyond those with a common last name.

Paul held open my office door, placed a roughened hand under my elbow, and escorted me from the office building with the kindness of an older generation. We supported each other as we walked through the windowed passage, speaking quietly and projecting hopeful thoughts into the thin information we knew about David's disappearance as if practicing what to say to Sarah, Phoebe, Noah, and John.

I saw the boys, faces freshly washed and dressed for the day, lounging in our family quarters. Before they could see me, I snuck past the door to the kitchen to my old friend.

"Terrell, could I talk with you for a second? Maybe in your office?"

Morning meal preparation stumbled along, workers not used to Terrell's methods. Sarah, who knew the team and the kitchen, was absent. He wiped his hands as he followed me to his office.

"I know what you're going to say about David. The DOE hasn't shut me out of their employee communications yet and I read about the ambush in the morning briefing report. When I saw that transport leave, I figured they came with bad news." He folded his arms across his chest, but the softness around his eyes told me of his empathy. "How you doing?"

"I've known far better days. We're trying not to get ahead of ourselves."

"I remember your wedding out where the kitchen gardens are now. He built you a rocking chair as a surprise and made you sit in it while he filled a plate at the buffet. That's how I guessed you were pregnant."

Stories of shared history make my world a little brighter—when you lose all the people who know all the special stories about the big and little times of your life, having others build new memories is a gift.

"This is going to be rough." I hung my head, rubbed at my nose. "I can't fall apart. I have to talk with the kids." He gave my back a small rub. "Can you hold family breakfast until I buzz you?"

"Phoebe's out reading next to the porch," he said. "I haven't seen your boys."

"They're hanging out in our quarters. They wait there for David or me before breakfast." I thought ahead to change my morning schedule to be there for the kids. "Thanks, Terrell."

Our girl sat in a porch rocker, slippered feet pushing herself back and forth as her eyes traveled down her reading tablet. Not even the creak of floorboards brought her head up.

"Morning, sweetie," I said as if this morning was the same as the past ninety days of summer. "I love watching you read out here where the flowers smell so good." She raised her head, eyes telling me some other place and story still held her mind. A hair clip held back curls. "I need to talk with you and your brothers before breakfast, so turn off your reader and walk with me."

"It's Daddy." Voice quivered around the most important word of her vocabulary. "I couldn't find him when I dreamed last night."

I took one hand, held it in both of mine as we walked. "You've been on the same wavelength so long."

"Is he dead?" The question should never come from a young child's mouth.

"Ambushed. That's all we know."

"Oh, Mommy." Thin but strong arms circled my waist. "Oh, Mommy."

"We have to think positive thoughts, Phoebe. Don't let your mind race ahead." Lowering my head, I kissed the top of hers. Birdsong marked the time as morning, early worker sounds carried from the production areas, conversation bits could be heard as day laborers left the dining building. I rocked Phoebe in my arms, connected to David through another living, breathing human who also loved him. "The boys need to be told before they hear the news from somewhere else."

Terrell moved a worker aside as Phoebe led us through the kitchen. She held my arm across her shoulders so we walked in awkward unison.

None of the family joked about our son John's extra sensory perception. Sarah suggested he inherited the gift from my Native American great-grandmother. I dreaded what the Bureau of Human Capital Management might want from our boy when they discovered his gift during mandated assessments.

Our youngest child waited at the door to our family gathering room, his six-year-old face still and pale under a light summer tan. Noah stood slightly behind, favorite stuffed dog in one hand. "What's happened to Daddy?" John asked. "How will he get home?"

My hand slid away from Phoebe as she rushed to embrace John. "Johnny knows Dad's all right," she cried. "You wonderful brother."

Shrugging her off, he came to me. "What's happened to Daddy?" he asked again, this time tearfully, the eyes he inherited from David latching to mine before he tucked his head into my ribs. Noah followed. I didn't know the answer. Phoebe joined us, and my arms stretched to surround her.

"I'll tell you what I know," I promised. "Right now that isn't much. Daddy was in a group ambushed by people in Paraguay. Do you know what *ambushed* means?" Two boys nodded. "Our government is working really hard to find Daddy and bring him home."

"I'm going to go find him," Noah said. "I'll call the transport driver, and he'll take me to Paraguay and we'll find him."

"That's stupid," Phoebe said.

"Shhh, Phoebe," I stopped the childish disagreement. "Noah doesn't know geography yet. After breakfast you can show him where to find South America." I gave each head a kiss. "First we have to eat breakfast. We have to live each day just like Daddy is away on a business trip and we're waiting for him to come back." Three worried faces suggested skepticism. "I'm not saying we aren't scared. But we need to keep ourselves strong and healthy so we can be ready to step up and do whatever we're asked to do when Daddy comes home."

Antwone knocked on the door. "Ms. Anne, there is a media person at the front door. Wants to talk with you." His eyes stayed focused on Phoebe, a little girl known for a big smile, who now had tears sliding down her face. "She says she's got history with Director David, Ms. Anne. And she might know something about something happening where he's gone?"

"Send her to the main entrance of the DOE building." From the days after Tia's death I learned never to face media without a DOE spokesperson. Still curious, Antwone left.

I kept my arms around the kids while I notified Lao of a media person who made it through our security gate. His voice told me she wasn't the only attempt. David was a big DOE consultant name. There would be curiosity about his disappearance. At that moment, three young people were my priority, not media management.

"Let's blow our noses, wash our hands, and go to breakfast. I think Grandma and Grandpa will want to be with us." Noah stayed close while John and Phoebe pulled away. "One more thing. There will be news stories about Paraguay until after Daddy comes home. If any adults from outside Ashwood ask you about this situation, say nothing." They stayed quiet, kids learning more about life in the government fishbowl. "Talk to your grandparents or me any time you hear anything or you feel worried or scared." I smoothed Phoebe's hair then pulled them all close one more time. "I love you. We'll show everyone how we stay together as a family."

Walking to breakfast, I could only hope I told them the truth.

Chapter Twelve

Terrell messaged me when news of the Paraguay ambush broke on local outlets while the kids and I ate breakfast. The very first story focused on David, our family, and his involvement with Ashwood. Before dishes were cleared, more reporters and citizen journalists crowded Ashwood's gates and jammed our communications.

Only familiar day laborers from Lakeville or Northfield were hired in the morning market as Lao increased security on the estate. Magda and I stood on the residence's long porch and looked at vegetable beds waiting for harvest, orchards just weeks away from picking.

"You should be glad Lao was far away from kids when our communications system went down. I've never heard him use that kind of language. Of course he had a backup ready in five minutes." I couldn't smile, not even at this rare Lao behavior. Magda put a hand on my shoulder. "Hopefully our regular laborers won't accept news source bribes." She removed her hand and pulled her hat back up on her head. "The helicopters are unnerving. Why can't they leave you alone?"

"Because we've become media du jour. Maybe tomorrow something bad will happen in Texas and the ambush will be of no interest." With land transportation still a luxury, I wondered who could afford the half dozen helicopters buzzing overhead. "I need to keep my kids under cover while those devils are out."

"You have bigger things to worry about than filling seasonal vacancies, so stop thinking about it." She brushed away a bug. "I have two estates willing to barter for lower combine fees in exchange for a day or two of sending people to Ashwood." Magda began moving away. "That worked in the past."

"I forgot we did that." I sighed, worried about what surprises today might hold. "If you need to do some premium pay or referral bonuses, do it." As she walked down the steps I wished there was such an easy solution to free David.

The management team showed up at my office for our daily operations meeting after staffing assignments had been completed. Because I forgot to suggest they meet without me, I listened to their words, but couldn't focus on anything. David's locked office door screamed that all was not right. I gave up. "If you all wouldn't mind, I need a few hours for myself."

They left, respectful of a request I seldom made. I sat at my desk, staring at David's door on the east wall of the building.

"General Manager Hartford." A familiar voice came through my communication earpiece. "Are you able to talk?"

"Yes, Milan." I closed my office door with the push of a button. "I am alone."

"How are you doing, Anne?"

"Not great. The morning has been tough, and you know about the media frenzy outside our gates. We're in security mode when we need extra hands for harvest." I stopped, knowing that Milan truly wanted to know how I felt, not a lot of facts. "I'll be honest with you. David's parents and our kids are coping, but I'm angry as hell that David was sent into this situation, confused about what this country is doing in Paraguay, and scared."

"Scared of what?"

"You can guess. Beyond David's safety, I'm scared to death that should something awful happen, our family could be torn apart." I swallowed, took a deep breath. "I've lost one entire family in my life and I can't bear to think of that happening again. These are our children at risk. You're a father. You must understand."

Silence. Sharing my greatest fear generated nothing from Milan, the man who held legal power over David's children. Not even my legal adoption of Phoebe and Noah after our marriage broke the government's contract.

"Talk to me, Milan." A small quiver weakened my voice. "Why isn't there someone in a position like yours out there standing up for Andrew Smithson? How broad is your legal guardianship?"

"What makes you think Andrew's aunt really wanted to give him to you?" Milan answered. "She and her husband were unable to have children. He did take illegal actions with the boy's legacy funds, but the full story is that he hid the money so that they could buy safe transport to England and raise Andrew where the older boy is living." I heard him tapping on a surface, typically a signal that Milan had a more serious topic to discuss.

"Don't fixate on the Smithsons, Anne." Milan began his transition. "Your decision to adopt Phoebe and Noah doesn't displace my assigned guardianship, but it is important in planning their future should David not live until they reach legal majority. I just can't offer absolute assurance to you that they'll remain permanently on Ashwood if David dies." He coughed, a summer air-conditioning kind of sound. "Actually, I'm calling to talk about the children."

"Can this wait?"

"There's another news story connected to David that might be surfacing in the coming days."

Silence now filled my side of the communication. "Yes," I finally answered.

"The *Times* has been investigating possible irregularities in the government surrogates program. As you discovered when you learned Andrew's story, not everything was under tight control in the early days." His voice slowed. Chills prickled through my back as we headed toward some piece of information I knew would be beyond my belief. "What the *Times* will report is that fertilized eggs of a small group of intellectual couples were not destroyed as promised, but were implanted in additional surrogates. Those offspring are being raised by a select group of senior agency and bureau leaders across the government."

"Are you telling me David and Tia have more children?"

"At least a half dozen."

"How long have you known this?"

He didn't hesitate. "In some ways I guess I've known since some of them were born. That would be the only explanation why I'm legal guardian to a fragmented group of kids scattered across the country."

"Milan, I can't believe this. What about the legal rights of the parents?" My voice rose in pitch while lowering in volume.

"There were some in the early Bureau of Human Capital Management who thought the United States needed to build a generation of geniuses in order to answer future customers of our products." His calmness didn't settle me. "Some argued it was irresponsible as a government to limit our next generation of bright thinkers by listening to young intellectuals focused on the size of their own families." He paused. "If you remove ethical questions, there is logic in the thinking."

"Finally ethics is mentioned."

"Today, we have leaders uncomfortable with the way surrogates were used."

We were both quiet. I felt the body blows of this day's news tip my natural optimism.

"People in the Median Party?" I gave him no time to respond. "Where are these children, Milan? I would think the courts will say David has the right to know where his biological children, incubated from embryos he never agreed to give away, live today."

By his quiet, I knew that someone had approached the courts with that question. "Where are his children?"

"I can't answer, Anne. You have no legal claim to that knowledge."

"Does Phoebe have a right to know this information in the absence of her father? What about Paul and Sarah?"

"Neither of us is prepared to have this discussion right now." Milan's tone changed from confiding to directing. "I wanted you to know so you can prepare David's family. Media is already camping at Ashwood to cover the Paraguay situation, but some might be waiting for this story to break open."

"How do I 'explain' this to our children? They've only had six hours to understand that their dad is missing and in danger." Carefully, to not make any telltale sounds, I put my head on the edge of my desk, thought about sitting under it and hiding from Jega and all the other DOE faces in the outer office. "Milan, is there any new information about David?"

"Nothing." His voice softened. "The United States is still unraveling who staged the ambush. Six groups have claimed responsibility. Patience, Anne."

"I'm thinking of taking the children to South Dakota for time with their cousins on the Regan ranch." The thought just came into my mind. "Any problem with clearing that travel?"

"It's not a good idea now, Anne."

His answer was logical. Ashwood could provide protection from the media. Suddenly I realized Phoebe and Noah could become public personalities. "Can you tell me how many other couples had their genetic materials used without permission? Are we talking a hundred couples or a thousand?"

When Milan hesitated, I stopped breathing and hoped for an immense number. "About a dozen couples, all DOE."

"Why feature the Regans?"

"Tia was the brightest scientist in this country at the time." He didn't mention that under her brilliance ran deep instability, drug use, insecurity. "Her story is one of the more interesting ones."

"My children could be exposed to the world." I stood, used my limited authority as a successful estate business director to issue an order. "You have to protect these kids. Milan, you know Phoebe's night terrors have become worse these past months. Do what you can."

"We're doing our best." He coughed again. "I thought the cover would blow off this story years ago. A few highly positioned individuals have lost their jobs already. More will follow."

Twice I stubbed toes as I walked back to the main residence to find Sarah and Paul. My feet dragged, my muscles fired slower than usual, and I knew I had taken the last stress I could take for the day. I headed for the kitchen, not for food, but to find Terrell.

I found him in the midst of workers. They wore summer garb—girls allowed to choose sleeveless dresses in the house or shorts and light shirts. Continuing a Tia tradition, all the workers' clothing was in bright colors. Terrell wore his chef clothes to impress the crew during these first days.

"Have a few minutes, Terrell?" I asked after he finished giving one worker instructions.

"Always, Ms. Anne." He wiped his hands on a towel tucked into his pants. "And I have iced tea plus fresh biscuits with honey." Before I could respond, a large, cool glass was in my hand, and he walked alongside me with a plate of food. "You look done in and I don't remember seeing you show up for lunch."

"Milan called." Terrell tucked his free hand under my elbow, led me around corners I know better than anyone in this house.

Somehow in his first day he managed to move a few things around in the cook's office and bring back an old overstuffed chair I liked. "I thought we moved this to storage because a foot was wobbly." I sat in the chair tentatively. It did not rock to one side.

He raised an eyebrow and sat down as well. "Friends made sure that chair was waiting here this morning. I haven't had the chance to find out who brought it in, and now I know they also took time to do some repairs." With a smile he pulled the plate of biscuits back toward himself. "Maybe I better set these aside?"

I didn't intend to cry. My generation of women learned to be more like men with emotions, but the events of these two days had pushed me so far beyond a sense of control or personal safety that I let tears happen. My father once told me I cried prettier than anyone he'd ever known and suggested I use tears carefully or a future husband would fall apart. These weren't pretty tears. These tears formed rapidly and rolled down my face without a single sob.

"How about you use my towel," Terrell suggested as he removed the iced tea glass from my hand and put the linen in its place. "I don't know what Milan had to say about David. I have a few calls in with past associates who know people though. We'll find what these DOE contact people don't even know."

"There's another story about to be published." My voice, already low, sunk with the effort to talk through the emotion. "Terrell, I can't believe what I'm going to tell you, but I thought if I tried telling you I could find the words to tell David's parents."

"They found him?" Terrell's thin, beautiful brown face leaned in toward me.

"No, nothing to do with Paraguay." I gulped down air. "A reporter's been working on a story about a practice within the Bureau of not destroying genetic materials of a small subset of intellectuals, including David and Tia. Surrogates carried those babies, which were placed with high officials."

"My God." He sat back. "Unbelievable. Between learning that you are actually Andrew's mother and this story, the surrogate program sounds like something out of a sci-fi book. People are going to get all riled up about that program again." He rubbed one hand over his face, looked at me. "So Phoebe and Noah have a brother or sister?"

"Six brothers or sisters."

His amazement showed me how the public would read this story. Surrogacy, practiced to protect the working productivity of female intellectuals, still repulsed many citizens. This story would create a wicked storm of publicity when regular women were required to have a regional permit to carry a child.

"The reporter has names of a dozen couples whose fertilized eggs were used. That's all I know." My tears were done. I placed the towel across my knees and pulled the iced tea glass back from Terrell's desk. "I trusted the Bureau integrity and promises of protection."

"What about your kids?" Terrell's soft spot for young people, and particularly Phoebe, sounded in the gentle tone of his question.

"They could be thrilled to know they have siblings, or deeply confused. This could affect their entire sense of identity." I swallowed tea, realized how dehydrated I had become. "Phoebe's night terrors are bad already. I wish we could have a real ongoing relationship with a therapist right now."

"I can help with that." A therapist before the big *D*, Terrell had been a good resource for working with troubled kids who came to Ashwood. "I have a few friends who are still licensed to work in pediatric therapy. They'd work with Phoebe for cash instead of government allocations."

"You're suggesting we barter for therapy?" My thoughts jumped to some bureaucrat throwing those words at me in a custody battle for Phoebe.

"These are good practitioners. They use a strict clinical review process. You'd be surprised how busy the private practice is for non-Bureau therapists." Terrell leaned back in his chair. "Lots of people interested in keeping their files out of the government systems. I'll make sure they have recommendations from the right kind of places."

"I trust you, Terrell."

"Don't forget I also held that girl when she was just days old." Bringing his body forward, he touched my knee. "My first concern may be you, but Ms. Phoebe's state of mind is a close second. Let me make a few inquiries."

"Do you think I should tell the kids about Andrew Smithson at the same time as this news?" I drained my iced tea while thinking through my own question. "I feel like doling out so much difficult news might raise general anxiety."

Terrell shook his head just once. "You and David have raised those kids in as stable a home as is possible in this world. They got to learn to take bumps in the road. Talk about brothers and sisters and lay it all out for them. Be calm, stay with the facts."

We both stood. Work and kids and David's parents waited for us. Suddenly I remembered my early days at Ashwood when Terrell and I limited discussions in this office to work because of DOE listening devices.

"Lao negotiated a deal with the DOE years ago about their invasion of our privacy," I volunteered. "He developed a fairly sophisticated method for sweeping the residence. I think your office is a safe zone."

Laughing, a big warm sound in the day, Terrell opened the door. "Well, at least it has been safe since about forty-five minutes ago when we did a search," he said. "Found a nice little DOE device and two Bureau snoops." We stepped into the hall. "Do you think I'd talk about family matters in an unsecured place?"

I decided not to be sidetracked by the perpetual distraction of listening devices in our private residence. The DOE and Bureau showed equally irritating curiosity about Ashwood's conversations, perhaps heightened by our direct employment of managers.

"It's so great to have you back," I said. Through the dining room I could see Sarah sitting in a rocking chair, knitting needles in hand, her eyes focused on a tree branch outside a nearby window.

David told me his mother gave up her promising career in agribusiness to marry Paul, the South Dakota rancher's son she met at a football party in St. Paul. A classic blond Scandinavian woman, she aged into a beautiful grandmother with thick silver hair, gray-blue eyes, and a complexion marked only by deep laugh lines and the lightest crow's-feet.

"How are you doing?" I stopped to ask her, dreading what I had to do next.

"Your friend Terrell is a great guy," she said and rested the knitting in her lap. "He and I always had interesting talks years ago when I called to ask what you could use from our farm. Watching him with the workers is just wonderful. I don't know if he'll need much of my help."

Her response didn't answer my question, true to Sarah's discomfort with talking about herself. "I guess I was doing all right until the kids headed into afternoon school." She sighed. "It's just a lot better for me to stay busy and not think about David. What about you?"

"I wish there was something I could do," I answered. "If the DOE doesn't have more to say in a few hours, I'm going to start calling everyone on my Washington, D.C., contact list."

"Paul said the same thing. He already sent a few messages to folks we've supported over the years." Sarah turned her head back toward the window and something I did not see outside. "I pray. I'm an old-fashioned Catholic who still puts the safety of those I love in God's hands. I've been trying to find just the right words to capture what I want to ask." I saw a small smile pass across her lips. "Not that the right words are necessary, because God already knows what is in my heart." She turned back to me. "You do lead a lovely Sunday prayer service, Anne, but I'm not sure you really find much comfort in faith."

From my grandmother's rosary beads on my mother's dresser to my years singing Lutheran chapel services at St. Olaf College, religion and faith were wedded. The big *D* challenged not my belief in God, but certainly my loyalty to established churches. I never fought leading the Bureau's required nondenominational weekly prayer service, but I would not let the kids under my care be forced to attend church in the community without their parents' permission.

"Maybe religion had been dumbed down by the time I was growing up." I wanted to sit at her feet, lean my head against her knee, and be a daughter who might give and receive comfort. Moving closer, I knelt, then sat back on my feet. "Sarah, Milan called to give us advance notice of a breaking news story about the government implanting fertilized eggs from a small group of intellectuals into surrogates without the knowledge of the couples. David and Tia were part of that group."

Sarah's eyes widened and lines deepened on her forehead. "What are you saying, Anne? Does this mean that their children are being raised by strangers?" The knitting dropped from her hands and her lap.

Picking up her needles and yarn, I answered gently, thinking how I would feel. "Yes, that's what Milan said. Six children."

"Have you told Paul?" Sarah's body remained still, no more rocking. Gentle grandma disappeared from her eyes. "This is unforgivable. I would say unbelievable, but too much has happened in this country in the past decade. Of course we want to know where these children are living and try to bring them here." Sitting upright in the rocker, she held its armrests. "Imagine, six more grandchildren. What wealth for this family to have so many little people to carry on our name."

Surprised by both her excitement and her intention to seek out the children, I shifted back to my knees and prepared to rise. "I intended to tell you together," I said. "I thought you might be upset."

"I can't really get my mind around this," she said. "Our son has been poorly used by our government merely because he is bright. Our other sons' lives, and their children's lives, are so much easier. If Paul and I must take legal action to bring these children home, then we will do so." One hand came to her head. "You won't mind a few more kids running around the house?"

"Sarah, we don't know how old these children are or what kind of lives they have now. They may be perfectly happy." She frowned as I spoke. "I've been worried about how our children might feel and how you would react."

"Let's find Paul. I think this might give him some hope." She stood, took my arm. "God wouldn't make us aware of these children if David wasn't returning to be their father."

We made our way to the business offices, me worried about Sarah's sudden overt religious comments. A quiet person in our household of extroverts, she had a practical sense of running the household operations that made Ashwood a training site for estate matrons. Her business sense couldn't be shaken. This response left me concerned that the day had affected her too deeply.

I asked Paul to step out of a discussion with field team leaders and the three of us made our way to my office. Sarah moved close to Paul as I shut the door.

"Paul, Anne had the most amazing call from Milan this afternoon." I watched my mother-in-law's strange behavior. She seemed eager to share Milan's story, as if the existence of these six children restored joy to our world. "Some awful government people felt free to implant David and Tia's embryos in surrogate mothers without David's knowledge. Now there's going to be a story in the news." Paul's face fell into the stoic image of this morning. Sarah noticed, and her voice became soothing. "Milan wanted us to know we have six more grandchildren out there somewhere."

Paul looked my way, clearly not as pleased as Sarah. "Tell me what he said, Anne."

Sliding to the floor, closing my eyes and pretending the world didn't exist wasn't an option. I quickly shared the gist of Milan's comments and my concerns about how our children might take the news and how to protect them from media exposure.

"Damn it. Nothing, absolutely nothing is sacred to those people in Washington, D.C." He stepped away from Sarah, deep red staining his cheeks and nose and forehead. "Why are you so fired up about this, Sarah?" He looked my way. "Any chance this is a government smoke screen to stir up a lot of interest and take the focus off South America?"

Neither of us attempted to answer Paul's question. Sarah may have been caught off guard by her husband's response.

"Sounds like a goddamn awful situation that this family shouldn't have to be thrown into," Paul said. "As if Phoebe and Noah and John don't have enough to think about. Now we have to walk into a touchy discussion of human reproduction and how it is that their father doesn't know where all his children live."

"Hon, they live on a good-size farm. The process of making a baby is hardly a mystery." Sarah touched Paul's arm. "I think we have an opportunity to distract them from worrying about David by telling them that we will be looking for these children. That we want to bring their brothers and sisters together."

Part of me wanted to ask Sarah how she would acquire transportation credits to visit each of these children, pay the legal fees that would certainly build as assigned parents fought losing their children, feed six more hungry young people when Ashwood's supplies could not support our current family and staff. Another part of me knew I had to conserve my energy for the fights that were mine—finding David, keeping our children safe, welcoming Andrew, and managing Ashwood. I had nothing else to give.

"Is that what you want, Anne?" Paul asked.

"No." How I would have liked to end the conversation and walk away, but they both looked rather surprised at my quick response. "Here's what I want—to tell as few facts as possible to my kids about the whole surrogate system. I'll start with Andrew coming here to live with us, then talk about possible media coverage about other children living with other parents who could be their brothers and sisters." I stopped, checked for their agreement and continued without it. "Then I need to go over security and protecting our privacy." Paul began to nod. "They need to know only the facts that children can understand—what it means to us as a family, and what to do to keep ourselves safe from the media."

My mother-in-law wanted to interrupt, but I continued. "I'm sorry, Sarah, but to go further and conjure up the possibility of more brothers and sisters living here would be taking this further than six- and seven-year-olds can absorb."

Through my window I could see children walking to the greenhouses and wondered how the afternoon had passed with so little accomplished. Sarah also saw the workers, and the rhythm of so many days settled on her. "I should get over to the classrooms for homework drills," she said and rose. "Paul, perhaps you and I should talk to Anne's friend about what we can do as grandparents in David's absence. And I respect Anne's wishes." She walked to the door. "I'll see you all at dinner."

As Sarah closed the door, I wondered if her behavior sprung from a different set of maternal instincts than mine.

"You might think your mother-in-law has gone off the deep end," Paul said. "The whole surrogacy program disturbs her. I don't think she's ever said much to you, because she loves you so much."

Paul grabbed the door. "Don't know if I should dig back into work, go be with Sarah, or jump on a horse and ride out to the Mississippi River banks to think." He bent to kiss the top of my head. "But you should go and be with your kids."

Chapter Thirteen

"Andrew is John's big brother, but he's no relation to you and me," Phoebe told Noah after my careful words about Andrew Smithson joining our family. "He's Mom's son by a stranger. You and I and John have the same Dad."

Many times I have sat down with children, and their Ashwood mentors, to share unpleasant news—a canceled home visit, an older sibling knifed at school, a runaway parent. I thought too much about how my three would react to the addition of Andrew, but couldn't predict their feelings about the surrogate scandal.

The boys thought a big brother joining our family was great in spite of Phoebe's mixed emotions. Her deciphering of bloodlines confused her brothers who were stuck on the fact that Andrew was joining our family because his known parents had passed away.

"So is he an orphan or not?" John asked. "That would be sad."

"He can't be an orphan. You have the same mother," Phoebe said, one small hand gesturing near John's face. "He's your older brother, but not really a Regan." I hugged my boy. "His father and the woman he thought was his mother have died, so he feels like an orphan. He had no reason to doubt that she was his mother, didn't know that she wasn't until a few days ago."

"How did that happen?" The beginnings of logic skills showed in many of John's questions. "How could you not know your mother?"

"It's complicated. The officials made a mistake." I waited for the small shrug that told me John had moved beyond the need for more information. "We're his second chance at being part of a family."

"Does he play soccer or baseball?" Noah asked a typical little-boy question, then followed it with a modern-day fear. "And if he lived in the city, will he carry a knife or be part of a bad gang?"

Phoebe frowned at the knife image. "You're sure Dad wants this boy to live here?"

"Yes, Dad and Grandpa want him to live with us." I ran my fingers over her curls, wondering why she had not shared her knowledge of Andrew with her brothers. "His aunt's apartment isn't in the gang areas of the cities and if he carries a knife, we'll take it away. That's an estate rule no one breaks." Noah and John appeared to lose interest in talking about Andrew. "He's a boy who needs family."

"Do you love him?" asked Phoebe.

"I haven't seen him since he was born, sweetie, but he is my son." I gave her a quick squeeze, removed a curly hair from my hand. "He is my son and I'm excited about getting to know him."

Her beautiful green eyes moved quickly across my face. Was she worried about Andrew taking some part of the love and attention now given to her and her brothers? I moved on to the second subject.

"So the three of you understand what a surrogate is? Phoebe nodded right away. John and Noah looked at each other. I recognized their discomfort and shrinking attention to this discussion. "A surrogate is a woman who carries a couple's baby in her womb before it's born. After the baby's born, the parents take it home. Phoebe and Noah were carried by surrogates. Right?"

Three children stared at me.

"There was a mistake made by the government agency that watches over the surrogate program. Some babies were carried by surrogates and put into people's homes who actually have different parents." Noah looked at his hand. John's forehead wrinkled. "Some of those children are the brothers and sisters of Noah and Phoebe."

"Are they all coming to live here, too?" John sought clarification in a polite voice. "How many kids will have to share a bedroom and desk?"

"Do they look like us and will you love them like us?"

I told myself that Phoebe's question could have been asked by any child before answering. "I don't know what they look like or where they live. I only know that they are alive." She nuzzled into my side with her head down so I couldn't read her emotions. "It's such a strange situation that I don't know how to say anything more. But the news media have a story that will be broadcast soon, so I wanted you to know this before you hear it from someone else."

Noah shrugged. "I don't think I understand? I think it's something big people should worry about." He looked at John. "We don't have space in our bedroom for more than Andrew."

"When Dad comes home, he'll know what to do," Phoebe added, then she moved away and picked up a book. The conversation closed. To lighten the mood, I suggested playing a game. Phoebe lost interest after a few minutes, picked up her book, and left.

The boys turned our game into a two-person match. I thought I was watching their play, but my eyes closed. Paul's gentle tapping on my shoulder woke me from my unexpected nap as the dinner music sounded. The boys were gone.

"Maybe you should let Sarah and me take Phoebe watch tonight? Don't know if anyone here has ever seen you sleep while the sun was still shining." He didn't smile. We'd been through a horrific day and there could be more of the same. "How did the kids respond?"

"I think Phoebe needs to know I'll still be here for her so I better pass on your offer. Thanks anyway." My eyes felt gritty, my brain not ready to kick into normal operation. "I don't know that the boys really understood the surrogate story. We'll see how they process everything."

"General Manager Hartford."

"Excuse me, Paul." I pointed to my earpiece. "I'll join you in the dining room." He walked away. I activated the call. "Yes?"

"This is Lars Peterson. Do you have a minute?"

"Is there information about David?"

"There is information about the ambush."

I could hear faint noise behind his voice, tried to place where he was. "Yes?"

"We can meet with you in the DOE offices in approximately twenty minutes."

Images of military officers in full dress uniform ringing the home doorbells at dead armed forces members' homes entered my thoughts and stuck. As a scientist and an intellectual, David carried officer classification in the civilian military division. The oxymoron of civilian military played in the popular media. In this society where government bundled everything in an elaborate interwoven hierarchy, I never gave a second thought to this minor title on David's large human capital file. I pushed away the dead soldiers thoughts, sure that, like John, I would know if David was not in our world.

"I'd like my father-in-law to join us." Like Sarah's earlier this afternoon, my eyes were attracted to the window without the slightest ability to focus on anything. I stood. "He's just sitting down for dinner, but we can be there in twenty minutes."

Peterson hesitated. "I don't think it is necessary to involve Mr. Regan."

"If it is bad news, tell me now." I managed to sound in control. "It's cruel to make me wait twenty minutes not knowing what's happening to David."

"Bring someone, if you please." I recognized the sound of a displeased bureaucrat. "And have your kitchen set up dinner for seven staff in the DOE building." The call ended.

His command to provide food, a precious commodity, marked pulling rank. Peterson could make the same demand anywhere and be accommodated. Concerned about Peterson's news, I walked to the kitchen.

Bowls and platters covered every surface as dinner service began. Workers moved about under Amber's supervision.

"Ms. Anne, is everything okay?" Her tone hinted that I looked unusual.

"Thanks, Amber. I hear you're doing a great job helping with the transition here. Where's Cook?"

She pointed to the kitchen's deep cooler. "Checking breakfast supplies."

In the cooler I stood with my back to the door, called his name.

"Good God, Anne, you surprised me." Terrell held blueberries in one hand. "What's wrong?"

"Can we talk in here?"

"Better we go to my office."

"I remember when the cooler was the safe place to talk."

Taking my elbow, he led us out of the cooler, bumped its door closed with his backside and handed the berries to a worker.

"Take a few breaths as we walk," he said so others wouldn't hear. "Do you need a drink? I've got hard stuff and cold water in my office."

"Water."

He closed the office door. I stayed on my feet.

"The DOE representative who was here with Milan this morning just called. He's coming with information about David." A quiver cut my words short. "And wants dinner for seven served in the DOE offices."

"And?"

"I asked him to tell me what he knew. He wouldn't answer."

My old friend's thick, strong cook's arms surrounded me. I leaned my head on his shoulder, felt his support. "You're already thinking the worst, Anne. There's lots of room between what we know and where you're thinking."

"I believe David's alive, but I need to hear that." The second half of my sentence turned into a plea instead of a statement. "Why is Peterson adding people? He must have some motive beyond cordoning us off from the media?"

He rubbed my back, not a gentle comforting gesture but a quick motion as if to invigorate an athlete preparing for competition. "In all my years working for the DOE, I learned never to guess what might be coming next. They are a bunch of wolves who tend to see the world divided into those who belong in the den and those who pose danger. Just got to stay in the right pack with those folks."

"Could you and I carry their dinner over to the offices, and then you stay for the meeting? Peterson knows I'm bringing Paul."

Turning away from me, Terrell opened a desk drawer and picked out a pen. He dismantled it as he spoke.

"Listen to me, Anne. The DOE doesn't like extra visitors in their meetings. Let Paul eat his dinner." Terrell slipped a thin, clear sliver from the pen's interior. He bent toward me. "Without David around, the DOE could get aggressive. It's important that you keep your stature when dealing with these guys. Show your strength." I let him slip a hand deep into the back of my summer-weight shirt. I trusted this man, knew whatever he was doing was for my safety. "They'll see Paul as a protector. You don't want that."

He patted the back of my bra with a gentling hand. "You are a highly successful, and visible, civilian businesswoman. Just treat them like an important client." He straightened. "You've got them over a barrel 'cause David isn't about to leave Ashwood for some other estate like a regular DOE director might be forced to do if the agency didn't like the managing matron."

I understood that he and Lao would monitor the meeting through the small device now enmeshed in my clothing.

"Want some water?" Twisting around me, he filled a glass.

"Thank you." He motioned for me to take a sip. I obeyed. "I don't want to be the one to carry all the bad news to Paul and Sarah."

"You shouldn't assume all is bad, Anne." He motioned for me to drink more. "You've managed this place through plenty of storms. That's why people, including your father-in-law, call you strong." Like a breeze in the midst of a still hot day, Terrell's voice brought me back to the moment. "Deal with this Peterson. Listen to what he has to say. And, as hard as this might be for you, I'd suggest you keep your own counsel around your pal Milan right now."

"Why do you say that, Terrell?" I finished the water, let him take the glass from my hand. "Do you know something?"

"Remember I played that dual employee role for a lot of years—cook for the Bureau and personal observer for the DOE. Never stood in the way of you and me having a good working relationship, but the higher up the castle wall a person climbs, the trickier it is to please two powers." Terrell checked the time. "Your friend is about as high on the ladder at the DOE as he can be with his other foot in the Bureau. He likes you as a person or he wouldn't be so available for matters far below his station."

"He wants what's best for the kids. That's what a guardian does."

"Just listen to Mr. Peterson and think what you want showing up in official files before you speak. This isn't a normal time, Anne." I knew by the way Terrell pulled at one ear that he was deadly serious.

I made my way to the DOE offices alone, walking outdoors. Dark clouds gathered in the sky, the first hint of rain in almost two weeks. Barn cats wandered across the yard, cows mooed in the closer field. David often stood in the yard after returning from his travels to breathe the air, a country man deep within. I tried to gather a deep breath for him, wished I could send it across continents to offer comfort.

An unfamiliar DOE guard and I moved through intricate lockdown security procedures. Inside, overcooled air raised goose bumps on my bare arms. I found a sweater in my office, made a cup of tea, and busied myself. The estate daily report looked stronger than I expected. In regular times, I would look across to David's office, and if the door stood open, I would tell him the good news. Tonight David's locked door felt like a bad omen, a barrier no amount of wishing or praying or positive thinking could cross. I tried to hold on to Terrell's pep talk as I buried myself in a backlog of mail.

That's how Peterson and Milan found me. They said nothing as they sat in the chairs in front of my desk. I thought of standing, moving us to the table, but I read by where they chose to sit that nothing really awful had happened and stayed still in my chair.

"Director Peterson, you didn't mention that Executive Milan would be accompanying you." I used the language of bureaucracy. Rank no longer intimidated me. "Who else are we feeding?"

Neither man responded. The atmosphere felt heavy as if a storm waited to break.

"Milan, I don't know if you heard that we have been able to attract Terrell back to manage all our on-estate food matters." I read in his eyes that this was news to him, perhaps distracting him from what was about to happen. "He will be supervising delivery of a light dinner for your crew any time, Mr. Peterson."

Bureaucratic gamesmanship crept into the meeting as I said, "I haven't asked him if he still has DOE staff clearance, but at least your guards won't have to create a totally new file for him." Peterson's left eyebrow barely moved upward as I displayed this bit of inside knowledge, and I knew I had stepped back into command from the state of shell-shocked wife.

"Anne, we have news from Paraguay and business to discuss." Milan spoke, Peterson watched. "If Ashwood has space, the DOE needs beds to station a handful of staff here for the duration. If not, they'll set up beds in the lower conference room."

"I could put two in the residence guest room and scatter the rest around our staff sleeping quarters."

"We prefer they be together in the residence." Peterson came close to demanding.

"Can't do it without disrupting rooms of workers." My voice remained calm. "I would think you'd want them within your secured quarters."

"We'll set up in the lower level. I believe there are full bathrooms off the lab space." Peterson settled back, looking as if this small decision made him winner of our first round.

"Are you going to trust our food or will this be one of those times when DOE provides its own?"

"Why would we be concerned about safety of food for a group of public information specialists?" Peterson flushed, realized he'd put cards on the table before the dealer called the game.

"If your staff will be working with the media, perhaps we should station them at the small building near the gate?" I saw Terrell push a wheeled cart into office central space. He looked my way, and I realized my guests had not closed the door as they entered. "I don't think that's what you want me here to discuss. Let's start with Paraguay." Terrell's movements slowed, and I suspected his timing had been prompted by monitoring of the conversation.

Milan reached from his chair to close the door. "Let's remember we're all on the same side as employees or contractors of the DOE." I heard a reprimand in his voice, a reminder that the DOE provided Ashwood with very generous financial support. "I understand your discomfort right now. I'd feel the same if my spouse was missing."

"Why haven't we located David?" I directed the question to Peterson, disappointed in Milan. "He has the latest tracking chip embedded. You must know where he is." I looked into his face. "You're hiding something."

Peterson stood. "We need assurance of your complete confidentiality." He held out a hand. "I need any listening devices you might be wearing."

I stood as well, took a chance that Lao had out-technologized the DOE's snooping ability. I removed my earpiece and held it out. "This is a business and family home, Director Peterson. We have little need for spyware although our staff sweeps plenty of bits and pieces of the stuff that get planted by government agencies on Ashwood and Giant Pines."

"Turn that off." Peterson pointed at my communication piece. "Nothing else?"

"You can wand me, if you wish." I answered his request and came out from behind my desk. "I assume your folks already cleaned my office before your arrival?"

Milan raised a hand. "I think we're ready to start." He lowered his hand, reached into a pocket, and withdrew a small electronic pad. "We do need you to sign this confidentiality agreement." I sat down as he extended the pad across my desk.

I read through the loosely constructed statement that read like the contract new estate professionals might be required to sign. The possibility of treason or perjury or deep legal liability faded on my second reading of the document which made no mention of the federal government or any of its agencies or bureaus. I read through it a third time, looking for the catch.

"Do you have a concern, Anne?" Milan's voice sounded like that of my confidant, the man who moved red tape or questioned my personal motives in many difficult points through the years. I looked up and saw kindness in his eyes.

"I don't really know what I'm signing. I'd like this to be reviewed by legal counsel."

"You have that right," Milan replied. "But I suggest we dispense with the document." He withdrew the pad. "I have no doubt you are a loyal citizen."

A small cheek motion showed Peterson's disapproval as he spoke. "We were not entirely forthcoming earlier. You, of course, would know that we are able to track the DOE chips in David's team and had an exact location when we spoke with you this morning."

"So, go and get them. That is the sole purpose of your tracking chips. What's the problem?" My response sounded unsophisticated, emotional. I gathered my thoughts. "There must be a reason you haven't taken action. Why don't you tell me more?"

Peterson tried to establish eye contact, but I wasn't ready to trust him. He gave up, settled in his chair, and started to speak in a low voice that demanded attention.

"The United States has had a military presence in Paraguay for decades to monitor terrorism activities. Not a lot of people think of the Middle East terror groups settling on this side of the world, but Paraguay has been their favorite stew pot for decades." He stopped. "Did David ever talk about this? Maybe he talked about the gas reserves project the Bolivian government stopped about five years ago? You must remember the time he and a team were airlifted back to a safe base?"

"Wasn't that a project with military security?" Intuition told me Peterson assumed a lot of pillow talk about our jobs. Stronger intuition suggested I couldn't begin to guess where this conversation was taking us. "There are many factors about work that David doesn't tell me."

The DOE man wanted to continue his exposition. "It is still critical to the future security of this nation that Paraguay be cleared of our enemies and that free access to the natural resources of Paraguay and its neighbors be maintained." I couldn't remember any Paraguay natural resources although I'd read about significant irrigation projects supporting development of agriculture in its dry, landlocked lands. Penfeller's threatened requisition of our harvesting equipment as a national security action began to make sense.

"The advisors put up no fight at the airport because they knew the 'ambush' was a U.S. military exercise." Milan jumped to what I wanted to know. "Not that the ambush squad wore U.S. military garb or identified themselves as such. Certain members of the advisory team were told about the ground action while they were in flight. David would have been one of those individuals."

"So he is safe with U.S. Army troops pretending to be terrorists?"

"Not exactly." Peterson stepped back into control. "The group consists of contracted operatives. It is critical that the Paraguay government appears to be connected to this action and these individuals."

"Let me understand." Words flowed through my brain, contradictory feelings of relief that David was safe then alarm that the allegiance of hired guns could be swayed by more of whatever they valued—money, influence, free rein. "The U.S. staged this ambush using merchant troops to embarrass the Paraguayan government about the true state of lawlessness in their country. And that will keep access to Bolivia's resources open?"

Peterson shook his head. "It isn't really important that you understand the nuances, General Manager Hartford. This is part of a significant military and diplomatic initiative. Your husband and his crew will be recognized as civilian heroes when they return home."

"But David holds an officer commission as well. Won't the media find that a contradiction?" I sat forward and leaned on my desk. This time I used the quiet, slow tones of a teacher demanding meticulous attention. "You can play whatever PR games you want, Director Peterson, as long as you do not compromise my husband's reputation or endanger our family." I paused. "Now, please give me a simple answer—is my husband safe?"

One, two, three seconds passed. I looked at my data pad and noticed it was six o'clock. Players would be warming up for Ashwood's Wednesday night softball game. Phoebe and Sarah would be sitting at the dining room table for another language proficiency review. And I waited another second for what appeared to be a difficult answer. I looked to Milan, ignoring Terrell's caution. "Is this a difficult question?"

Milan stayed quiet in his chair, hands resting on his legs. Peterson shifted position in the next chair, his arms folded across his chest.

"We'd like to believe that David and the team are safe," Milan said. "There have been a few communication glitches." He looked at Peterson who nodded, then continued. "Tracking chips indicate the DOE crew has been split up and taken deeper into the countryside than planned. There could be a good reason. But it is a deviation from plan."

"Someone has been in communication with this contractor's leaders to ask what's happening?" I guessed the answer but wanted to hear how Peterson might phrase it.

Milan continued to act as the spokesperson. "Nothing is as simple as we'd like it to be, Anne." He smiled, a small upward movement of his mouth accompanied by softness in his eyes. "We'll say there's nothing we know that would indicate David isn't safe, but neither Peterson nor I can give you an absolute answer."

I sat back, watched the two of them, not sure what to say. "Why are you here with a DOE crew?"

Milan sat back, looked in Peterson's direction. I did the same.

Peterson began speaking as if addressing a recalcitrant audience. "The buildup of American troops in Paraguay is raising questions domestically. The DOE is giving the army guys a chance to stay in the background by assuming responsibility for media management." He finally blinked, took a breath. "Which is why we are here. We need to put a face on the ambush. The Regan family—you, your children, and David's parents—provide the kind of story people can understand. Americans are in danger in Paraguay. Americans with kids and family right here in the Midwest. We'll issue news updates from Ashwood."

"Not my children." Looking to Milan, I jabbed my forefinger in the air. "You're their legal guardian. Tell this man that the Regan children will be left alone. My kids are scared their father will be hurt, confused about a news story about having more siblings, and will be absorbing a new brother in days." I paused. "You will leave them alone."

"I forgot you were a patriot surrogate, General Manager Hartford." Peterson's voice told me he had already thought of ways to connect that phrase with David's elite intellectual status. "Did I also hear you are expecting a second child of David's?"

Milan and I looked at each other, mirroring surprise.

"You have that wrong," I said. "Real wrong. You must have snooped in the wrong person's medical record."

"In eight months no one will care that it was a false alarm. The story will play well when added to Ashwood's family drama. Demonstrate the love of children you share with David. You will be a role model of the new private businesswoman balancing many demands."

"I want nothing to do with any of this deception." I controlled my voice. "None of it."

"General Manager Hartford, unless you want the estate's valuable combine collected by a national security requisition team tomorrow morning, you will cooperate."

"We did seek legal counsel on that matter," I answered, matching his icy tone. "That equipment is privately owned. We have been advised that Ashwood's equipment can be requisitioned only if there is still a clearly defined need after all machinery has been withdrawn from government-owned estates. I will fight you on this issue."

"But you don't have time to stage a fight," he responded. "You can file court papers today, but not before I have a flatbed here to load whatever Mr. Penfeller might like from your inventory. By the time the courts review your request tomorrow, your equipment will be at the Twin Cities air force base loaded on a cargo jet." His voice dropped. "The air force can be terribly efficient in times of a national emergency. Like this one." He paused. "Private legal counsel privilege is trumped by national security needs. Check your Homeland Security provisions."

I worked in the DOE office building at David's request and hadn't seen the possibility of this day—when the DOE would call in payback for its largesse. They planned to control our family to protect David without really assuring me they had the power even to locate him.

Outside the window our lands quieted for the night. Through the small window column next to my office door I could see the dinner trays assembled by Terrell. I tried to find my way out of this situation, to find ways to negotiate a resolution, to accept what had to be done to keep David safe and Ashwood intact. Anger fueled circular thoughts. So deeply enmeshed in the United States government on a daily basis, I understood I was had even as I rebelled at the blatant manipulation of my civil rights and my fellow citizens' integrity.

"Milan, what can you tell me?" From him I hoped for empathy. "At the least, we need to spare the children." My hands wanted to extend across the table, but I remained still in this high-stake negotiations. "Think of how Phoebe, Noah, John," I hesitated briefly, "and Andrew could suffer."

Bureau protocol demanded absolute shielding of the children of intellectual elites. These vulnerable government investments had attracted kidnappers demanding king-size ransoms. "Surely, you don't intend to expose David and Tia's children and risk their safety?"

Peterson shifted in his chair. "Why don't we fill our dinner plates and sit at your table to work out the details?" He rose.

"I'd prefer to eat after we've come to an agreement about the children." I indicated he should sit. "Milan, you're the legal guardian of three of them. I assume you would be the person who would bear the legal ramifications of abusing their rights."

We locked eyes across the desk, the man who reported to two bosses and the woman who mothered two families. Milan trusted my instincts and motivation every time his guardian approval was required. I trusted him to make decisions with both heart and mind engaged.

Milan blinked first, rolled his eyes down as if contemplating the age spots on his hands. He turned his body in the chair, faced Peterson. "According to the intellectual elite surrogacy laws, I cannot approve any activity that might place the three children under my guardianship in the public media. Phoebe, Noah, and Andrew are protected under law."

"Change it, Milan." Peterson spoke as if the discussion had been finished. "Your authority might trump mine in the DOE, but the U.S. military is not going to accept that some soft-heart HCM Bureau legality is valid in a situation threatening national security."

Standing, Milan walked to a wall and leaned against it. I understood that he disliked Peterson from this gesture by a man known for his courtesy toward everyone. "Peterson, you are forgetting that you are the only one who is declaring that this a national security situation. If that were the case, the U.S. military would not be turning over media relations to a crew of young people from the DOE." He rolled his shoulders, turned his head to one side, and then straightened. "You get me directives from Commander Broadline through my supervisor, then we'll talk. Until I have that directive, stay away from the kids."

"So that leaves me with David's wife, the second son, and his parents?" I heard a new approach in Peterson's voice and knew that the directive would not be sought. I also heard of higher vulnerability for John.

"We treat all our children the same. You hurt John, and Noah will be affected and Phoebe will respond like an angry mother lion."

My guests appeared distracted by Milan breaking Peterson's authority. I tossed my concern toward Milan while he appeared to be in control. "We are in a very delicate place with them right now. Milan, I ask you to protect all David's children."

"Peterson, nothing happens involving any of the children without clearance from me." Milan, used to commanding, gave the order without fanfare. "Now let's eat."

Terrell had provided an attractive summer dinner—Caesar salad with cold diced chicken, fresh fruit, and oven-warm rolls. Estate food, while simple, trumped what most people could buy or prepare in the city.

"If we could wrap this up in a half hour," I said as we carried our plates to my office table, "I need to be with my kids at bedtime tonight. We have had the most difficult day. I wish you brought news about David that could make us sleep easier tonight, but that's not the case."

At the table Peterson ran through a list of support needs his people required, ranging from housekeeping to meals to additional electrical outlets. His ignorance of the general state of our economy surprised me.

"When you demanded twenty-four-hour kitchen support for up to fifteen people, were you aware that there are developing food shortages? You are increasing our daily diners by twenty-five percent and think we can provide meat and produce on demand?" Little beyond Peterson's request for three kinds of fruit, a hot and a cold meat, and fresh baked goods every six hours stayed in my mind. "Because the feds increased agricultural product quotas, I am feeding our morning crew oatmeal with fruit every other day instead of eggs and dairy products."

Milan stopped eating. Peterson continued, the sound of lettuce crunching between his teeth could be heard when I ran out of steam.

"The DOE will provide its own canteen service within two days," Milan said. "Is the estate able to meet the DOE electrical and water requirements?"

"Listen, Milan," Peterson said, fork still in hand. "Power and water are plentiful on this estate because of a DOE water reclamation plant and a DOE electrical grid system. I'm not negotiating those."

I shrugged as Milan looked my way. "We hold our own. As long as your crew keeps a reasonable showering schedule, I'm sure water will hold." Peterson nodded. "If you can bring a solar generator for backup, please do. What systems will your crew be running?"

"Increased security and a communication and media center with ability to transmit audio and video beginning with an interview tomorrow morning with you and your father-in-law about David's abduction." Peterson checked his data pad. "Looks like we'll need the two of you to report at five-thirty for makeup and hair."

The late September evening sky suggested we'd been at this discussion too long. Little outside sound penetrated the DOE offices. "I'll bring Paul up to speed on your plan," I said, wondering when I could find time or strength to do that.

"What Mr. Regan needs to know is that a communication hub is being established at Ashwood to manage media interest in this unfortunate situation and that we want to give the media a glimpse into how the ambush is affecting your family." Peterson placed his hand in a strange, spiderlike position on the table. "You do understand that everything else we talked about in this room is confidential and may not be discussed outside?"

"You've made your point." I rose and picked up my dinner tray. "Now I need to spend time with my family." At the door I stopped. "Perhaps I could ask the two of you to move to the small conference room so I can lock my door?" It was a symbolic question since DOE security staff could open any space in the building. Milan and Peterson stood.

Light flowed from David's office, unnerving me. I set my tray in a bin and moved toward the light. A young woman with the most astonishing violet eyes stopped me.

"I'm Anne Hartford, David's wife," I said as if that should earn me entrance into the place where he and I spent many hours. "I just want to see his desk."

"Is there something specific you are looking for, General Manager Hartford?" Her voice held Blue Mountain smokiness.

My husband, I wanted to whisper, I'm looking for my husband. "No," I responded. "We often work together at his table and I miss seeing inside his office from my desk."

"I understand." She looked behind me where Peterson and Milan waited. "I'll be interviewing you here in the morning, so why don't we plan where we will sit?" Her hand, gentle on my arm, exerted more strength than I expected.

The first time David showed me this office, he told me he never felt like he was really home until he unlocked its door. That all changed as our family made the residence his haven. On a top shelf his high school baseball cap kept company with a photo of Joe Mauer signed in 2011. Pictures of the kids, of me, of his parents' South Dakota ranch clustered above his work surface. I knew where he hid a dish of chocolate caramels, where he kept his favorite pen, how the seat of his chair held the imprint of his butt, how to shake the upper desk drawer when it stuck.

"I know who you are, but I didn't introduce myself." High cheekbones and thick, coarse hair hinted at native people heritage. "Tabitha Sweetwater." She tipped her head forward, engaging me with those beautiful eyes as she straightened her neck. "I'm a media specialist for DOE and will be spending time with your family." Her voice, warm and comforting, suggested she could be a great best friend. "I'm looking forward to getting to know all of you. If you'd consider including me in a meal, I'd find the kind of insights viewers appreciate and it would help me better present your family's interests."

"Thank you, I'll consider that." I breathed in, expecting to find the essence of my husband in the purified air.

"You should wear your hair down for the interview," she offered. "With those big brown eyes, viewers will fall in love with you. I know you have an important job running this big place, but what viewers want to see is the beautiful wife of a missing intellectual. We want them to like you."

Looking around David's space one more time, I knew I needed my kids. "Have a good evening, Tabitha. I've got to get back to the residence."

"I understand. You could bring your little girl with you in the morning. Even if she's not dressed for the day. She's a beauty."

"You'll need to rethink that, Tabitha. The kids are legally off camera."

Slender brows rose above her eyes. I knew she wanted to know more, far more than I would ever share with a government-hired media personality. "Good night," I said and left for the residence.

Chapter Fourteen

MEMORIES MADE ME FEEL LONELY AS I WALKED between the DOE building and our residence. David encouraging Phoebe and Amber as they learned to ride bikes here, the boys' laughs while playing catch with him, a rainy afternoon when we ate Noah's birthday picnic dinner on a blanket spread over slate tiles. Fearing for his life fueled my anger at the manipulation of this strange man who claimed to be concerned about keeping us safe.

Young workers' voices practicing a foreign language or reading out loud or reciting memorized lists from geography lessons played in the background while I debated whether I wanted to talk with Paul or calm myself with my kids. I headed for our family quarters.

"Will Dad be home tomorrow?" Noah scrambled to his feet for a hug when he saw me. Phoebe, sitting cross-legged on the floor with John, raised her head, two worry creases showing on her forehead.

I wrapped my arms around Noah, kissed his hair. "No, even if the soldiers found him tonight, he wouldn't be home for a few days." I released him. "We have to be patient."

"Why weren't you at dinner? Grandma waited for a long time before she let us start without you."

"Business. Cook Terrell knew I couldn't be with you. Didn't someone tell Grandma?"

Phoebe answered. "Cook came out and talked with Grandpa, but nobody would tell us what was happening. We were afraid those people came to tell you something bad."

Three worried faces looked to me for reassurance. I made a decision. "There's nothing new. I think it would be helpful to spend tonight together." Phoebe slipped a hand into mine. "Do you agree?" No hesitation sounded in any of their voices. "Since Daddy and I have the biggest room, we'll stay there."

"Will you read to us? Maybe that old Harry Potter book?" John's words came slowly. I ran a hand over his head, felt feverish warmth.

I pulled him closer. "Do you feel all right?"

"I have a headache." He pulled away.

"Grandma says he's worried himself sick," Noah volunteered.

"All of you get ready for bed and bring your things to my room in a half hour." I checked for time, not sure if I'd sent them off to change hours early. It was eight. "I have to talk with Grandma and Grandpa, then Terrell. I'll ask him to help me make us a bedtime snack."

They left with no whooping or hustle. Children were resilient, but not immune, to frightening events. I found Paul and Sarah in their quarters, talking about the day. Paul stood and pulled a chair closer to theirs.

"What's the government doing here?" I knew by his voice that he expected to hear that David was dead.

"There's really no news. The tracking chips are still working and soldiers are looking for David and the others." Sarah's face released some of her worry as I spoke. "We've been designated a communication hub for the DOE and the military. The good news is that they are assigning security to keep the media from hounding us. The bad news is that they expect us to become part of the public face of this situation."

Paul's reaction was quick and true to his personality. "Tell them to go to hell. They don't own David or us or this estate."

I tried for a smile. "I'm afraid I tried that and they played some very tough hardball. Let's put it this way—if we want to keep our farm implements safe from requisition, we'll cooperate within a limited parameter."

"Holy damn. They can't put us in that position. This shit-for-brains idiot wants to pull our business apart." He pounded on his knee with a closed fist. "Goddamn it. He has absolutely no legal foot to stand on."

"I know, Paul, but he threatened to confiscate first and let the courts rule later." My voice stayed steady even though my body felt dirt-tired. "There are too many estates and farms relying on our equipment to play chicken with these people." I leaned back in the chair, slumped for comfort. "I've been around the block so many times already that I know they'll do what they threatened. Milan was here and helped negotiate."

"Would you like a cup of tea?" Sarah asked. "You look terrible." She tried to smile. "Like us."

"No thank you. I just needed to tell you what I learned before I check in with Terrell. Then the kids and I are going to close our door and stay together for the night." I rose and walked over to give each of them a hug and a kiss. "Paul, you and I are going to be interviewed in the morning. Five-thirty in the DOE offices. Can you do that?"

"I'll know better in the morning."

"Well, we'll start without you if you don't choose to come. Don't do anything that makes you uncomfortable." I started for the door. "Try to sleep tonight. I'm so thankful you're here." Sitting side by side, Paul's arm resting on Sarah's, they were the picture of what I hoped for our future. "I love you."

Chapter Fifteen

Lao waited with Terrell in the kitchen. Following their hand directions, we left the residence for a walk outside.

"I only have a few minutes. The kids are waiting for me for bed." The soft silence of day's end on a farm surrounded us. "What did you hear?"

"Everything." Lao looked straight ahead as he walked. "This is a big problem."

"You could both be in trouble if Peterson gets wind of the listening device." I saw their heads bob in agreement. "I think the worst is over. You need to remove it."

"I'm not so sure," Lao replied. "With your friend Milan out of sight, this Peterson could be devious." In the gathering dark, I saw Terrell nod in agreement.

"But if we're caught?" I paused. "What could happen to us?"

"Don't worry about that, Anne. You should be thinking about keeping your family together, about your son coming home, about Ashwood. Lao will worry about defending your right to protection." Terrell put an arm around my shoulder. "Let us take care of this one."

"These look like threads," Lao handed me a brown envelope not much larger than my thumb. "Weave them into your clothes. They'll dissolve in the wash so don't worry about removing them."

Transports and a satellite dish parked near the DOE building. My office windows remained dark, but lights shone out other windows.

"Sounds like our visitors will be bringing their own meals and need kitchen space," Terrell said in a more casual tone. "How did that happen?"

"I blew up when I read their request for restaurant-style service for up to fifteen people a day. Obviously the DOE doesn't understand that the food growing on this place isn't entirely at our disposal." We walked in easy strides back toward the residence. "Will their cook cause problems in the kitchen?"

"Everything is a problem in the kitchen at this time of summer, but their lead food person seems reasonable." Terrell coughed and laughed at the same time. "If I were younger, I'd hope she was reasonable in other ways."

I stopped walking and turned to face my friends. "I have a feeling something is under the surface with you two and I don't know how much to ask."

"Don't ask anything," Lao answered. "We're doing our jobs."

"Now let's get you back to your kids," Terrell said. "Those boys will probably hog the snack I put together so I hid one in my pocket." He held out my favorite small filled pastry treat. "How about you turn off your mind for a few minutes and enjoy that, the company of two fine men, and this breeze. Maybe the heat will break."

They filled our last few minutes with small talk about the evening's softball game. I nibbled and listened. Their advice was good, and I disciplined my mind to turn off the problems of the day by the time I opened our bedroom door.

The king-size bed David and I shared easily accommodated three small children and their assorted stuffed animals and personal blankets. Phoebe and I took turns reading from a chapter of an old children's favorite, *Harry Potter and the Sorcerer's Stone*, then turned off the light. Sleep came quickly for them. I wondered if Terrell spiked their milk or if children's minds more naturally calmed when their bodies demand rest.

Surrounded by their small noises, I thought about David before dozing off. I woke during the night, feeling someone watching me. On the other side of the bed Phoebe lay propped up on one arm. She put a finger to her lips and pointed at John.

"Listen," she whispered.

In his sleep he perfectly recited lines from what we had read hours earlier. "Hogwarts School of Witchcraft and Wizardry" came clearly from his lips.

Phoebe muffled a giggle. "Weird," she whispered, then lowered her arm and settled back on the pillow. In a few minutes I heard her breathing slow. John quieted. I wanted to stretch my arms across the bed like a road block barring the world access to my children's innocence. How would Andrew Smithson fit into the world of these tightly knit siblings?

The files sent by Milan had images of Andrew at school, playing soccer, singing in a boys' choir. I thought I could see my mother's round brown eyes under arched brows. His face was more oval than round, like hers and mine. But I had no idea how he moved, or spoke. I hoped he would accept Phoebe's fierce mothering if she offered it. I hoped he might become a big brother to make her path easier if she was willing. I prayed David would be here to share his masculine wisdom with my boy.

I pushed at my pillow, trying to find a cool spot, as a few tears slid down my face. A skeptical Christian, I found myself negotiating with God for David's return and Andrew's happiness. My grandmother always cautioned me to be careful what I asked from God. I tried to be concise with my petitions, which became fuzzier as I fell asleep.

Chapter Sixteen

Tangled sheets, stuffed animals, and a set of skinny boy arms made waking up more interesting at four forty-five. I dressed, spent a few extra minutes in front of the bathroom mirror, then headed to the kitchen. Ashwood's residence halls rested in the quiet of the early morning.

"No one makes coffee like this," I commented as Terrell passed a full mug my way. "Maybe the real flavor of the coffee is in the company."

He shook his head, but smiled. "I made sure the communications crew had a good breakfast, and you need the same." Terrell removed a plate from the warming oven, lifted off its cover, and placed it on the counter in front of me. "Eat up. Who knows what Thursday will bring."

"They want me in makeup in ten minutes." Even as I spoke, I reached for a fork. "Has Paul been in yet?" Scrambled eggs, rich with herbs and cream, tasted better than Jeremiah's best.

"Haven't seen your father-in-law." He gestured toward my plate. "Good enough to make you look more like your healthy self?"

"Food can't fix what's wrong now."

"Well, I'm going to do my best to keep this family strong physically." He sipped his own coffee, leaned back on a counter. "How did the family bed work out?"

"The kids, including Phoebe, slept well. I might invite them back for one more night." I put down my fork. "I need to go. Thank you for everything."

Paul never showed for makeup call. He remained missing when a technician settled Tabitha across from me at David's office table. As the sun began filling windows, I disagreed with Peterson's crew about displaying pictures of the kids during the interview. The room felt strange with Tabitha reading her data pad while the crew treated me like a prop. Coffee and scrambled eggs churned as I fought an urge to flee. A small stopwatch moved toward an on-air signal.

"We're bringing you the first interview with Anne Hartford, wife of David Regan, the internationally respected United States scientist ambushed in Paraguay while leading a prestigious consulting team. The ambush took place on the tarmac of a private airport near the Asunción National Research Center." Tabitha turned toward me. "Anne, how are you and your children and David's parents holding up these past thirty hours?"

Before I spoke I thought I saw coolness in her violet eyes and realized that everyone involved in this broadcast, except me, knew a big moment would happen. I tensed, held my emotions intact, and kept my response short.

"We're very fortunate that David's parents live with us so we can support each other." I paused. "Until we know David is safe, we're all anxious."

"You must know that your husband's job might include risk. Isn't it true that his first wife, Tia Weisberg Regan, was killed while on assignment in Romania? How do their children feel with their remaining parent in danger?"

I looked into Tabitha's face, couldn't tell if she knew that Tia died in an alley during a drug deal gone bad, that everyone involved with Tia's last months of life expected just such an end. I didn't know how the DOE covered the dirty reality of Tia's death, but understood it was important for the kids that I uphold the fabricated truth.

"Most of David's work poses little risk beyond travel, so we don't worry when he has to be gone." I avoided talking about the children. "It's true Tia Regan died in service to our country."

"What do your children want to know about their father?"

"That he is okay and when he'll be home." I paused. "They are young and know nothing about world politics."

"You might not know that overnight three of the team were rescued from a small town about a hundred miles from the airport. Early information suggests they were held by Paraguayan military troops and were found bound and injured." She looked up, a facade of empathy not successfully hiding curiosity. "What will you tell the children this morning? Little Phoebe, Noah, and John?"

I hated her and hoped the children were still asleep. "This is the first I've heard of these developments. I can't really respond until we've been briefed on the situation." My right hand covered my wedding band under the table as I thought of David. "We all have high hopes that David and the entire crew are safe. They all carry U.S. government identity tracking chips so this rescue shouldn't be so very difficult."

"And if your husband doesn't return? What would happen to your family and to this beautiful, privately held estate?"

"My attention right now is focused on doing what I can to bring my husband home safely and to keep my family strong until that time. Ashwood, while it is our home, is also a business with a great management team." Weariness filled my voice. "David is at the heart of Ashwood, but isn't involved with the business of the estate." I looked toward the camera, away from her pert face. "We all want him home."

"This is Tabitha Sweetwater with Anne Hartford, the wife of David Regan." She reached over to pat my arm. "We'll be here with the entire Regan family as this story unfolds." She held her pose for as long as the camera person indicated, then abruptly sat back.

I removed a small microphone from my shirt, stood, and pushed my way to the door through furnishings that had been shoved aside. No one tried to stop me. Through the outer office, the hall to our residence, the central hall of Ashwood, I walked alone with newfound fear that David might not come home. Before Paul and Sarah asked questions, I needed to find answers of my own.

"Lao." Tapping my earpiece, I called my security specialist. "Where can we talk?"

"Meet me outside the estate offices."

Terrell joined me when I moved through the kitchen, giving my shoulder a quick squeeze. We walked out of the residence. Day laborers moved into the dining hall for food and then their assignments. I noticed the lack of humidity, a cooler feel to the morning.

"Did you watch?"

He nodded. "You did well—strong and caring and intelligent." Brushing a finger across his lips, Terrell began talking about a day laborer with strong kitchen experience who arrived on the first transport. I stumbled on the gravel path, not really listening to his words as my mind and emotions battled over what I could do to influence David's situation. Terrell steadied me.

Lao waited outside Ashwood's business office, a lightweight jacket held in one hand. "You look a bit cool in this fresh air." He placed it over my shoulders, then made a gesture directing me to slip into the jacket.

I knew better than to question Lao and not only put my arms into the sleeves, but also pulled up the zipper. Lao and Terrell stayed quiet until the zipper reached its end.

"This way." Lao led us to the back entrance. I reached for the door handle. He shook his head and pointed ahead to one of the stables. Terrell and I followed. Lao picked up a jumpsuit like those worn by the stable workers, held it out to me, and opened a door into a decent-size square room I always assumed was a small storage closet. He mouthed, "Take off your outer clothes."

Twenty-four hours since Peterson and Milan brought me news of my husband's ambush and I stood in an unknown room on my own estate stripping out of the clothes Peterson's makeup crew had brushed down, the strap someone tucked back into my shirt. Lao would tell me what they had attached, would offer protection. From whom?

Terrell waved me out of the changing area, extended a garbage can for my clothes—the light teal shirt David brought me from Spain, a new camisole trimmed with lace by Sarah, my comfortable brown pants. I said nothing, but stored these losses with the anger that began during Tabitha Sweetwater's surprise news. We moved back into the hidden room. Lao pulled out a chair, waved me to sit. I followed his direction, silence continued. From behind, Lao tipped my head, began moving his fingers through my hair. He pulled, whistled into a clear thread, and then broke it in two.

"All clear." Lao patted my shoulder. "They planted two listening devices on you during the makeup and hair time this morning. Don't let their technicians near you again."

"Why would they do that?"

"They could suspect you're wearing a thread." Terrell kept his deep voice low. "Peterson didn't believe you yesterday. Maybe he didn't feel he could call your bluff with Milan in the room."

"Or Peterson might want to trap you in unpatriotic conversation." Lao added his thoughts without emotion. "We have closed all outsiders' access to the estate offices. Do regular work in the office set aside for you there.

Any confidential conversations or communications are best held in this room. Carry your own food and drink everywhere on the estate."

"Prisoner in my own home," I said. "I have only one priority today—anything that can be done to find David." The words stated what I wanted to do, but I had no idea where to be helpful. For someone used to making things happen, I felt inadequate at a most important time. "Any suggestions about how to start?"

Lao leaned against the edge of a small table that used to be in the school building. "There may not be anything you can do, Anne." He pursed his lips, a rare sign of discomfort. I knew he had information that might be difficult for me. "The military contractors are obviously working as double agents. The larger ambushed group, including David, was split into three small cells during the night. Two of those cells have been traced. Our real military lost contact with the third cell." He crossed his hands over his chest. "David is one of five people in that group."

"What about their DOE tracing chips?" I think I always knew the DOE placed more confidence in their technology than it could deliver, like believing a simple handkerchief could stop a pandemic.

"It's only a small bit of metal and wire, Anne. Removed from a body, it can be crushed with the heel of a shoe."

Would mercenary soldiers use sanitary procedures as they removed chips from their captives? I closed my eyes, thinking about David experiencing such brutality. The chip had been injected deep in his shoulder muscle. I opened my eyes, terribly frightened.

"This is all my source could share." Lao stood almost statuelike with only his eyes actively assessing my response. "Don't think too much, Anne. We don't know anything else."

"I'll call Milan." The only person I knew high enough in any government branch to possibly have influence over Peterson's crew. "I want to talk to him about this morning."

"Do that, Anne, but in my opinion, he will be relatively ineffective in dealing with this situation." Lao pulled up a chair. "Call Milan. I'm sure he watched the interview. Tell him about the listening threads. Ask for the DOE crew to be shut down. But don't be surprised if he can't help. Ask him what he knows, but don't volunteer what I just told you." He paused. "Then make your own decisions."

We sat in silence. I felt a sense of isolation.

Terrell looked at his communication wristband. "I've got to get back to the kitchen and I think Paul is eager to talk with you. He feels bad about letting you face Ms. Tabitha alone."

"I've been monitoring your communications. You have a number of messages being held," Lao said to me. "The one with most immediate concern is a change in Andrew's arrival schedule to this afternoon. His aunt starts work at the Mayo Clinic tomorrow."

Dropping my head for a second, I took a deep breath, let go of the plan to huddle through another night with my children. I straightened my back. "He couldn't arrive at a worse time. Imagine walking into this family crisis. I wanted it to be so different." I stopped, aware that there could be a far worse time. Denied tears thickened my words. "At least Clarissa found work."

"We'll move a bed and storage unit into the boys' room this morning." Lao checked his wristband once more. "Let's get you out of here so you can join the kids for breakfast."

Paul and Sarah welcomed me to the table where the kids were reenacting John's sleep talking. I noticed Paul's eyes take in the laborer's jumpsuit and shrugged.

"Sorry my stubbornness put you in that she-witch's crosshairs," Paul said with his face turned from the kids. "Won't happen again." He passed berries my way. "Terrell tells me Lao's made a few changes to where we'll do business while the Peterson squad uses the DOE building. I'm part of your daily escort team. I think the kids used to say 'we've got your back.'"

The children's restlessness and everyone's clean bowls gave me little time to respond to news of my informal bodyguards. I had to share news of Andrew's arrival.

"Phoebe, Noah, John, I need your attention for a few minutes." They looked my way and I saw a night of good sleep had restored their energy and optimism. "Because Andrew's aunt must start her new job tomorrow, he will be joining us this afternoon."

"Will he be in school today?" Thankfully, Phoebe's voice was just that of a curious child. "I could be his classroom buddy until he learns his way around."

"That's my girl," I said. "As long as you aren't distracted from exam preparation."

"Did you hear anything about Dad?" John's question took me away from Andrew and brought silence to the table.

On the way to breakfast I thought through how to tell them the little I knew from Tabitha's interview. "The good news is that some of the crew was found overnight. They are all right. But Dad wasn't in that group."

Our younger son analyzed what I said. "Is that okay or bad?"

Wishing I had the blessing of his ignorance, I told a partial truth. "It's good to know our soldiers found some of the DOE team, but not much has changed in what we know about Dad."

He slid from his chair, came to my side, and leaned there. "Why are you wearing those clothes?"

"I backed into something outside and messed up my shirt and pants." I elaborated on my lie. "Just another John-like walking into a goopy piece of equipment the DOE folks moved into the office building. It was embarrassing."

"If Andrew is really my brother, will he get into messy stuff like you and me?" he asked. "And will Dad adopt him?"

"I am his birth mother." I put my arm around John's sturdy body. "Remember what we talked about—how I was a surrogate and didn't know he was my baby." All the kids nodded although I knew their understanding was very skeletal.

"Do you love him?" Phoebe and Noah sat still as John asked a question I thought I'd answered yesterday.

"Before he was born, I loved him." I gave a quick squeeze to one of the sons I knew I loved. "And that's something to build on. That kind of love doesn't disappear. We'll all find ways to love Andrew."

The chime for morning lessons sounded. I drew John close and kissed his cheek. Phoebe gave me a hug and Noah smiled like his father. David's easy grin on his young son's face brought me close to tears again, but I forced myself to return the smile. "You all have a good morning."

"Pick up your plates and take them to the kitchen." Sarah's regular morning instruction started the day, offered the kids stability in the midst of uncertainty. I piled my things on the stack she gathered and watched her walk with Phoebe from the room.

"I didn't believe that story about your clothes." Paul's calloused hands rested on the table. "Want to talk about what really happened?"

What I wanted meant nothing. I couldn't tell Paul much with the threat of listening threads that could gather words. "It's a long story," I said. "I'll tell you when this is all over. Now I have a few calls to make on behalf of David, and then I hope to spend the rest of the day with the kids, including Andrew."

Paul's initial offer to help Andrew adjust wasn't repeated. I knew he was struggling with the emotions of David's situation. "I am excited about meeting Andrew." I managed a small smile. "I think he physically takes after my mother's family."

He leaned back in his chair. "Must be a woman thing, that looking for family traits in each child. Sarah's always talking about which grandchild has somebody's eyes or nose or mouth or whatever." Arms folded across his chest. "I have a few calls of my own to make about David. Some time ago David gave me a couple of names to contact if we needed help. Can't think of a better time to call in those favors."

"Lao has set up a safe communication room you should use when you make those contacts." David hadn't told me the names of the emergency contacts he'd left with Paul, but I had a short list I intended to call as well. "I can't say why Lao felt that was necessary, but I'd like you to respect his decision. Check with him."

"Maybe I'll take care of that now." Paul stood. "You should get back into your own clothes before your son arrives," he said gently. "After all, he thinks you own the place, not milk the cows." His signature wrinkle of the nose let us both smile.

I not only took off the jumpsuit, but also showered as if I could wash away the morning. While I dressed I thought about calling Milan and realized that if he could do anything he would already be in action. With Milan, Paul, Lao, and Terrell making contacts, I called Andrew's teachers to talk through his orientation. While they told me their plans, I jotted down two or three names I would try to call about David. After they finished, I closed my eyes and prayed.

Chapter Seventeen

The transport bringing Andrew to Ashwood arrived almost forty minutes late. I sat on a bench near the visitors' gate with nothing on my mind but wondering about this unknown son, how he would change our lives, and what he might need. Standing just inside the gate, I watched the transport driver exchange documents with our security person before unloading Andrew plus a pack, a big suitcase, and one box.

I knew I shouldn't crowd his entry by rushing toward him at that moment. He looked straight ahead, inserting his fingers into the security scanner, thanked the guard who helped moved his things through the gate, then stopped as it closed behind him. Andrew took his first steps up our path with determination, like he expected to travel the distance to the front door alone. I remembered that feeling, but this newest resident had a mother to meet him and a sprawling, stucco-covered building to call home.

He didn't see me as he moved like a city kid, showing no apparent curiosity about this new place. Or maybe he looked ahead straight ahead because there was no landing place behind him. I wanted to call someone to take his things and leave him walk unburdened, but I knew that most of the kids walking through this gate were threatened by separation from what they carried in of the past.

"Andrew." Unable to wait for my first touch, I approached him after his fourth step. "I'm Anne Hartford. I spoke with your aunt a few minutes ago and promised I'd be sure you knew that she is thinking of you." I held out my hand. "I also told her that she is welcome to visit or stay with us any time. The bigger our family becomes, the stronger we all can be." Auburn highlights in his dark hair captured the late morning sun, bringing painful thoughts of whether my mother ever saw my brother just like this. Would I remember this moment throughout our lives? "I want to welcome you here and hope you make Ashwood your home."

Standing still, carrying his things, he looked not at me, but at our surroundings. "My aunt said you own all this. That can't be right."

His comment didn't hit me as odd coming from a child of intellectuals who lived in comfortable settings, but seldom owned real estate. "Your aunt is right. Ashwood started as a government estate, but I have owned it for a little over seven years." I held out a hand. "Let me carry one of your bags."

"This one isn't too heavy." With a small grunt he transferred the suitcase, which weighed as much as a three-year-old child, to my hand.

"We can carry the box together. When do the rest of your belongings arrive?"

"This is it." He increased the space between us. "We didn't pack my winter stuff because nothing fit. My aunt sold my coat and stuff to the consignment store." We walked another three steps in silence. "The suitcase is heavy because of my books."

"You're right about it being heavy," I acknowledged but wondered where all the furnishings of his parents' home might be stored. "Are you hungry?"

Andrew turned intense dark eyes to me. I recognized the look of food deprivation, almost as if the body rations energy and sends an alarm to all the senses to use only what is necessary.

"Terrell held lunch for you. Remember, on estates we don't worry as much about food." I offered information to comfort this boy who wouldn't have known real hunger before his father's death. "We might eat things you don't care for like fish or oatmeal or lots of vegetables, but Terrell has a way with food."

"We only need to eat to feed our bodies," Andrew said with a note of disapproval. "My father ate too much and was flabby. My mother thought he'd fail his physical requirements."

"You won't find overweight people here unless they are inexperienced day laborers. We're very physically active. Do you like sports?" He nodded, turned his head my way in a first genuine connection. "There are soccer games late every afternoon until we have too much snow to keep the field clear. Thanks to my husband, David, we have softball competition from April through September. Some people cross-country ski and snowshoe in the fields in the winter. Any of those fit you?"

"Yes ma'am." He shifted his back pack. "I'd like to get on a soccer team."

"Great, I'll let Lao know. He runs our soccer schedule." We moved in silence until I opened another subject. "After you eat, our first priority is introducing you to Teacher Jason." I looked for some reaction to my mentioning school. Andrew walked forward, now watching his feet. "He may be the best estate head of school in the nation." Still no response. "Your tests and records show you are a bright student." Andrew's head came up, and he looked toward the residence. "The school building is just southwest of the residence." His eyes followed my pointing finger.

"I'll do my best, ma'am."

"I trust your word." We walked the final yards to Ashwood's kitchen entrance. "I thought we'd go in this way because this is how we all tend to go in and out of the residence. The kitchen is a pretty informal area except during meal prep. You can stop in any time for fruit or something to drink."

"You don't have to be so nice." He sounded like the survivor kid he had become. "I'm not a soft intellectual kid anymore. I learned to be self-sufficient. I'll just pack myself some food in the morning."

"No, Andrew, you'll join everyone for three meals a day. That's what our family does."

"What am I supposed to call you, ma'am?"

"How about if you start with Anne?" I saw his head nod. "I have a lot of titles. Most of the workers call me Manager Anne. Some of the adult laborers call me Ms. Anne. Phoebe and Noah have always called me Mom because they were infants when their biological mother passed away." We were almost to the house. "What did you call your parents?"

"Father and Mother."

His shoulders were so close; I put my right hand on the one closest to me. "I'm glad you're here, Andrew." Emotion thickened my voice. "We're in the middle of a difficult time and you know about those." He didn't move away. "Your arrival fills in a hole in my heart."

We walked a few steps together. I stored the feel of him and the sweetness of this moment for when the getting to know each other process became rough. I opened the residence's back door and gestured for him to go in first. "Welcome to your new home, Andrew Smithson."

"Come on in, son, and let me help you with that box." Paul extended a hand and smiled. "I'm Paul Regan, Anne's father-in-law and grandpa to the Regan clan. If you'd like to call me Paul, but treat me like a grandfather, I would be honored." He hefted Andrew's box, then relieved me of the suitcase. "Cook Terrell has the makings for a good sandwich on the counter.

Introduce yourself to him, grab some food, and I'll see that these things get to your room."

Andrew followed Paul's directions with visible respect and a humble attitude. I felt Terrell assess our similarities, saw surprise in the way his eyebrows raised, and knew the boy would be recognized as mine. My friend looked my way, let his droopy eye close into a wink. "Well, Andrew, I first heard about you when Phoebe was days old. She was born a few weeks before your birthday and your mother felt sad remembering the little time she had with you."

"My mom said she loved you before you were born," John's deep little boy voice in the kitchen surprised me. "I'm your real brother, John. If you need help with anything here, you can ask me." He extended a hand. "We're going to share a room with Noah, my other brother. He can be your other brother, too."

"Why aren't you in classes?" I asked, trying not to look at Terrell in case we both laughed out loud.

"I couldn't pay attention because I saw Andrew walking with you." My matter-of-fact kid was honest. "Teacher let me go." His eyes moved from Andrew to me, them back to his new brother. "And, I'm hungry. I think I forgot to eat enough lunch 'cause we talked so much about you."

Terrell's laugh, so low and rich that children always responded, answered John's indirect food request. "I have enough to feed at least two boys. Go show Andrew where to wash up and how to get back to the kitchen. You two can eat at the counter."

Andrew didn't look back as John led him from the kitchen. I turned to Terrell.

"Still the Ashwood I love," he said. "Never have to worry about feeling alone. You going to sit with the boys? I got iced tea and a few cookies waiting." While he spoke, he set plates on the breakfast bar he insisted we build years ago. "By the way, anyone who sees that boy next to you is going to know you're related." He shook his head. "Amazing how genetics works."

"Thank you. For everything." My wristband pulsed and I read the message. "Damn, it's Peterson. I need to meet him in my office."

Paul, returning with the boys, reminded me of Lao's directions that I not be alone with the man.

"Is Dad all right?" John's easygoing befriending of Andrew slipped. "Isn't Mr. Peterson the one with news about Dad?"

"He might have news, or he might want to talk about the DOE crew working here." I rubbed his back lightly. "You two eat your snack. If I'm not back in twenty minutes, could you introduce Andrew to Teacher Jason?"

"This is the way it is around here," John said to Andrew. "She's busy during the days, but we have family time at night. When my dad isn't traveling, he eats breakfast and lunch with us. You'll like him."

Paul and I hurried through the residence and office building passage. Rain clouds had begun to gather over Ashwood's distant fields. Good news for the farm, but superstitiously I hoped they were not forewarning me of difficult news. Catholics like my mother or Sarah might have made a small sign of the cross. My right hand twitched at the thought of that long-ago comfort gesture.

The DOE guard stopped us, made Paul answer questions that I understood to discourage my father-in-law from entering the offices. But I would follow Lao's direction that I not meet Peterson alone. I tapped Milan's code into my wristband. When he didn't respond, I gave him open access to the conversation about to take place.

"You've done your job," I told the guard. "You've known Paul to have absolute access for all the years you've worked in this building. Your son plays on the soccer team my father-in-law coaches, so don't treat him like a stranger."

"New rules, Manager Anne." The woman kept her eyes low.

"This is still my property that the DOE rents." I gave her a small smile because our sons played together. "Please don't make this any more difficult a time than it is for my family."

"You have my thoughts and prayers, Manager Anne," she said. The door opened. "They're waiting for you in Director David's office."

"What the hell's going on?" Paul kept his voice low. "I thought these guys were here to make sure the media were kept at bay and to take care of you. Now I wonder whose side they are on?"

Not being part of my earlier conversation with Peterson and Milan, Paul didn't know whose side the players lined up on. "It does feel awkward," I said to provide an answer without real substance.

As soon as we entered, I headed to my office, relieved to see the door was still closed. They may have tampered once more with the lock David had installed, but for the moment all appeared normal.

Paul trailed behind me on my way to David's office where Peterson waited at David's conference table. I noticed that more pictures were in different places, and a pitcher of water with unfamiliar glasses stood on a tray on the edge of the desk where David kept work reports. All the subtle changes irritated me while signaling more challenges coming from this man.

"You didn't need to disrupt Mr. Regan's work, Manager Hartford." Peterson rose from a chair. "I merely wanted to update you in person."

"It is more efficient for both of us to hear your update at the same time." I remained standing. "And I prefer that you work in a visitor's office or conference room. David will not appreciate the disruption of his things. Is it DOE practice to go through their directors' work space within days of any interruption of their normal activities? Have your staff ruffled through David's things when we vacationed away from Ashwood?"

The man flushed, perhaps flustered at my words, or irritated at my willingness to challenge his poor decisions.

"Maybe you thought you could find information in David's office to help you locate him?" I stopped, stepped back into the hall. "I won't meet with you in there, nor will I ever sit down at that conference table with Ms. Sweetwater." Paul stepped aside as I moved toward my office. "We'll use my table."

They followed me. I placed my hand on my door, felt the security system hesitate before the door opened. Nothing looked out of place, but now I knew my space had been searched and probably bugged.

"Hopefully your crew didn't upset the estate files," I said as I pulled out my chair at the table. "You see, the scanner had a bit of a hiccup at the door—a signal to me that there has been another breach."

"We've gotten off on the wrong foot, Manager Anne." Peterson looked at me with eyes like deep Great Lakes winter water, dark and blue. "I apologize. I may have taken liberties with these offices assuming they operate like most DOE-owned facilities."

"Mr. Peterson, you know this is now leased space on privately-owned land. The DOE has played a supporting role in Ashwood's success and I am appreciative. Let's not get into boundary issues. I only ask respect as you work with us."

Paul sat. Peterson continued to stand.

"Sit down, Mr. Peterson." My fear of what he might tell us about that small third group of ambushed Americans gentled my voice. "We are eager to hear what you know about David." I tried to sort out what Lao told me from what I knew through the morning interview. "The last I know is that only the group including David is still missing in Paraguay." Like a hungry animal watching food carried by another, Paul's eyes followed Peterson's moves. "Please, sit and talk with us."

He pulled out a chair and lowered himself as if sitting might corral him in an unwanted position. Paul leaned back; I stayed upright with elbows resting on the table. Outside clouds thickened suggesting a sudden rain storm's arrival. Andrew might have to wait a day to find a soccer game. Paul fidgeted.

"There have been developments," Peterson began. He spoke like the manager of a troubled company trying to maintain face while offering false comfort to investors. I concentrated on maintaining my own calm and strength.

"As you mentioned, the ambushers split the group, and American military personnel rescued most of our team within the last twenty-four hours." I nodded. Paul did not respond. "The remaining individuals were divided into two groups."

Peterson paused. I wondered if he needed to restructure what he said because Paul did not know the full story, or if the presence of another man in the room changed his style. "We located one group, but David is among three DOE staff still missing."

"Use that damn tracking chip and find him. I can't believe the U.S. military can't just resolve this and bring my son home." Paul, brother of a marine and son of a Vietnam vet, grew impatient with the bureaucratic verbal dancing. "This should have been over yesterday. Who's in charge?"

Before Peterson responded, Lao's words came to mind. "Paul, the tracking chip is only technology." Speaking to my father-in-law, I kept my voice low. "These individuals could remove the chips. Is that what you're going to tell us, Mr. Peterson?"

I appeared to sidetrack Peterson's presentation. If I had not asked him specifically to sit with us, the hands positioned palm down on his chair might have propelled him back to his feet to deliver the rest of this carefully worded update.

"Yes, the tracking chips of those missing were removed." I closed my eyes, feeling again a sense of nausea in response to David's pain. "We found those chips alongside the bodies of two other DOE crew."

The next few minutes of conversation barely penetrated my terrible fear about David's safety. I wondered if Paul's intensity was response to knowing that two crew members had been killed. Paul's voice, while strident, also sounded like an old man demanding the impossible.

"Where is that site?" Paul now leaned forward, so close to Peterson that he could grab him. I don't think I could have held Paul back if he had tried. "What country is holding David?"

"Personnel on the ground tell us David is being held by Paraguayan military within the country's borders."

I closed my eyes, understanding through all of Peterson's bravado that the Paraguayan situation had spiraled with no one now in control.

"It's a stinking small country. Heat-seeking technology can find these people faster than you can drive back to the Cities." Like a commander himself, Paul directed the conversation. "I want a complete report from a military representative within the next half hour. Anne and I will wait here."

"Mr. Regan, I do represent both the DOE and the U.S. military. Like your son, I carry dual titles. I will answer your questions."

"Then start talking. What is the U.S. government doing to find David?"

"This is a very delicate diplomatic situation, Mr. Regan." Peterson stood. "I'm sorry, but I can't tell you any more."

"Sit down, Mr. Peterson." I opened my eyes and saw Paul push back Peterson's chair with a foot. "Let me tell you what I learned from someone I know very high in the State Department. Whatever organization you represent bungled a stupid staged event in Paraguay that has now resulted in two deaths and endangers my son. Someone in your chain of command hired the wrong people to embarrass a shitty small country's corrupt government. People are aware that you're here to blackmail Anne and build a media frenzy to disrupt the Median Party's foreign relations agenda."

Paul coughed. Peterson, sitting away from the table, waited for the coughing to stop before standing. I feared he might put hands on Paul and stood as well.

"Your source fed you a mix of truth and political speculation, Mr. Regan." His words were as powerful as a sharpshooter's bullets. "Your interference in this top-security mission is unpatriotic and threatens our efforts. I am placing you under house arrest until this situation is resolved."

"Under whose authority?" Paul sputtered. "Who sent you here, Peterson?"

"No more, Mr. Regan." Peterson touched his hand toward a small holster I hadn't noticed. I put up my hands, tried to find a way through this insanity by turning the discussion back to Ashwood, to what I knew.

"I don't understand what just happened, but locking Paul up will place immeasurable stress on my family and this whole estate." The conversation felt crazy and Peterson's continued handling of the gun horrifying. "Paul is needed by all of us as we struggle with my husband's absence. Ashwood and many neighboring estates are relying on Paul for a successful grain harvest. You said you were here to keep us safe, not cause us harm."

"Manager Hartford, we will keep this man within this building for as long as needed. We will provide food and a comfortable place for him to sleep. He can work on estate matters from one of those guest offices you mentioned." Peterson's voice dropped to a growl. "But, he will not leave this building unless he is accompanied by a guard approved by me." He held out his hand. "Give me your communication band."

Paul rose, approached Peterson. I attempted to move between them. "Give the band to me," I interjected. "His calls are from family and estate staff. If you won't let Paul use his communicator, then I will take it."

My office door was opened by a stocky middle-aged man who stood at attention.

Peterson jerked his head toward Paul. "House arrest for the duration."

"Before you leave, what is being done to rescue my husband?"

"Everything possible," he said and left.

"Mr. Regan, if you will come with me, I'll show you where you can work." Peterson's guard stood at Paul's side.

My father-in-law began to bluster. I held a finger to my lips. "I'll get this straightened out, Paul. It's best if we just work this through the right channels. You'll be okay in the guest office. You've worked in there before."

He offered me his wristband. The guard stood at attention. I looked around my office, at what had become a gulag center on Ashwood's land.

"I'm glad you heard the truth, Anne," Paul offered. "Work this through the channels as you said. You know I was arrested for civil disobedience in protest of that whole Iraq mess, but I've never been called dangerous to my country." His voice quivered. He cleared his throat, coughed. "Government idiots spend all their time kissing ass and scheming and don't have a clue what it is like to be a regular American."

We walked out of my office together, past members of Peterson's team in the middle of a disagreement. I tried to eavesdrop on what they said and heard the name "John" and the word "kid" both mentioned. They hushed. Paul began giving me small instructions about for our staff.

"Paul, you've worked out of this space." The color in his face alarmed me so I lowered my voice, touched his arm. "You can tell people directly what needs to be done." Lights turned on as we entered the office. "As long as you remember that everything might be monitored, you can have exactly the same communications from this office data pad as from your wristband."

"Can you bring Sarah over later?" Heading for the only window in the room, Paul looked outside. "Rain. That's great, we could use an inch or so." He turned back to me. "I need her to know I'm all right."

"No problem." I tried the data pad and checked drawers for basic supplies. "Anything else we can bring for reading or work?"

"When I've cooled down I'll figure that out. Maybe Sarah can pack a bag with pajamas and my shaving stuff and clean clothes."

"Sure thing, Paul." I rested my head against his chest as we hugged, heard his heart beating fast. "Could you just relax for a few minutes? David's new football magazine is out in the family folders zone. Sit and read."

"Don't worry about me. You get back to your boys. I think Andrew is a keeper."

Chapter Eighteen

BIG GOVERNMENT COULD BE GOOD IF YOU BECOME homeless and found yourself transported to a place like Ashwood through workforce assignment. Parents with a sick child could be thankful for a medical system controlled by bureaucrats, not corporate executives. For those living in the urban gang communities, no government would ever be as expansive as the societal problems demanded. But no citizen was a match for people in authority who threatened home and family with no explanation offered beyond maintaining national security.

"General Manager Hartford." I recognized Jega's voice behind me. "You are not allowed to exit through those doors."

I turned around to face David's bodyguard. She stood at attention, dressed for the first time in my memory in military garb. The frozen features of a soldier during inspection replaced the warm, rounded face and friendly eyes of the woman who shared our offices every day. The fierce protector of David, the person willing to put herself in danger to keep him safe, appeared to be deployed against me.

"What's this about, Jega? I'm just going to walk down the path back to the residence. I need fresh air before talking with David's mother."

"Colonel Peterson has established a secured perimeter for this building, ma'am." Jega gazed somewhere near my left ear. "No unauthorized individuals may enter or exit through these doors."

"He better make sure someone waters David's roses." A stupid statement in the midst of Peterson's assault on my family, but the harsh words I wanted to spew had nothing to do with Jega. "You want us to use only the glass walkway?"

"That's the directions we've been given, ma'am."

"I appreciate the situation you are in, Jega." I turned before she had to reply and walked back through the building, now aware of desks that had been moved and extra lighting.

For years in my life, fear could hold me captive—fear of being homeless, of being hungry, of losing my loved ones. Peterson nearly pushed me back to that place, but the insult of barring me from leaving through the front door and walking through David's roses stirred my emotions one more time, bringing up deep anger that covered the fears.

I headed for the estate office building and found staff inside moving around as if this were any normal day. Lao sat in a chair in the office kept for my use. He held up a small, clicking device. "You're clean and the office is also. We can talk here."

I closed the door and leaned against it. "I only have a minute. You heard everything." Not waiting for an answer, I continued. "So now Paul's under arrest for the unpatriotic action of asking a friend within the government for the truth. I'm so angry I think I could physically kick Peterson's ass off the estate if I channeled all my emotion into one foot." I paced the small room. "We're all virtually under house arrest the way the that man is operating."

"Milan heard your conversation." Lao sat forward on his chair, gray streaks in his black hair reminding me of our history.

"Here's Paul's communication wristband. It's ridiculous that Peterson didn't just have someone block Paul's contacts." I handed Paul's band to Lao, noticing how it was tattered on one side. "Something isn't right about this whole setup—the ambush, fake military action, choice of Ashwood as a communications center. None of this makes sense."

Lao and I received a communiqué from Milan at the same time. "Sit tight. Bureau friends in DOE guard. Resolution of all within week."

Lao showed no surprise as he asked. "You think you can hold on for a week?"

"If I knew David would return safely, I'd hold on for that long. Peterson fingered a gun while talking with Paul, but I don't think he'd hurt any of us." I tried to adopt Lao's calm demeanor as I turned our discussion to Paul's absence. "We need Paul in the fields these next weeks to supervise harvest—not just here, but on the estates under contract for use of our equipment and labor. How do we negotiate for Paul's daytime release?"

"Take a step back, Anne. If Peterson is carrying a weapon, he's acting under military guidelines. Your communications is still open for Milan's people to make note of that change." He paused, perhaps for DOE or Bureau listeners on my communications to seek clarification, then followed my thoughts about Paul's status. "We could offer to pay for a DOE agent to trail Paul throughout the day."

"If it could be that easy, consider the budget approved." Anger and fear mixed together, I wanted action. "Paul will be safer every moment we can keep him out of that building. Isn't that right?" Lao nodded, once. "Would we be taking any risks if Sarah spends nights with Paul in the office?" The erratic beat of Paul's heart under my ear still caused me concern. "Is there some way we can generate a medical need to have her there as a monitor during the nights?"

"You have mentioned that your father-in-law has complained lately about shortness of breath." Lao checked his communicator then spoke. "We had to reschedule a meeting because he had a consult with the regional medical unit."

"David told me that Paul had a number of little health issues that were exacerbated by the heat and pollen, but not to be concerned." I accepted David's explanation of why Paul stayed in the house one hot afternoon instead of traveling to Giant Pines. I would never take my father-in-law for granted again.

"Consistent with what Paul told me, but let's see if Sarah can be with him. She'll lower his anxiety." His words came out slowly. "We'll do what we can to monitor her while she's in the DOE building. I'll talk to her about how to take care of herself, but I don't think Peterson would threaten her. He's more interested in getting at you."

Magda, carrying leaf bits and garden dust on her clothes, joined us. "Do either of you know where I can find Paul? I have Little Creek's field manager here to talk over harvest schedules. It's not like Paul to miss a meeting."

"Close the door," I said. "We need to operate without Paul the rest of today and maybe for a few days. He is being held by the DOE folks for stirring up information they would rather be kept confidential. That's all I can say."

"Freakin' mother of God. Are those folks all crazy?" When I first arrived at Ashwood, Magda would have cursed in a colorful mixture of Romanian and English, regardless of the age of others present. "That man is about the most loyal American in this whole estate region. Some of the workers call him Uncle Sam reborn. These people got their heads so far up their asses they only see the world through their own putrid guts."

Putrid became a favorite Magda word after spending significant time with a traveling British agronomist. She used it to describe everything from smelly shoes to rainy weather, usually to break tension. There was nothing joking about her response to Paul's absence.

"You can conference with Paul." I looked toward Lao for agreement. "He's in the DOE building extra office. Just don't let the Little Creek people know what's going on. Make up some excuse about why he can't meet face to face."

"Not a problem." She pulled a twig from her shirt. "I look like a mess, but that's what this guy gets for showing up early. Not that I would clean up much for another field manager." She lowered her voice. "You holding up okay, Anne? We haven't had time to talk."

"Yeah, I'm doing okay."

Being Magda, she changed emotions quickly. "By the way, that Andrew is a good-looking kid." She pulled her hand back to pick at other greenery on her shirt. "Just like the lady I saw walking with him. No one with eyes would doubt that kid came from you." When Magda slowed enough to smile, she raised smiles in others. "Got to go."

"I should do the same," Lao said. "And you need to talk with Sarah."

Before I did that, I called Peterson to make the case for allowing Sarah to spend nights with Paul. He needed no persuasion. His voice implied he had little interest in his prisoner. My request to have Paul in the fields during the coming weeks also met little resistance. I held back on suggesting how Paul might be monitored by the DOE. The whole conversation lasted two minutes and made me wonder if Peterson regretted his hasty arrest.

I checked on Andrew on my way to our residence and saw him working his way through a set of assessments with a tutor. He didn't notice me in the classroom building, but I noticed the stiffness of his back and hoped he was not so stressed that his performance suffered. They reached a stopping point. The tutor pointed my way so I joined them.

"Not giving Andrew even a few hours to observe?" I kept my voice light as I addressed the tutor who was one of Phoebe's favorite school people. "I had a minute and wanted to be sure Andrew is comfortable."

"I asked if we could do some quizzes, Anne." Andrew said the last word with caution. "I missed a bunch of school while my aunt and I looked for work, and didn't want to just sit around here without my own assignments." His voice lowered. "If that's okay?"

"Couldn't be better, Andrew." I wanted to ruffle my hand through his hair. Instead I gave his shoulder a gentle squeeze. "You've had a difficult day, so don't push yourself too hard." He looked into my face for a second. "I'll see you at dinner."

Two seasonal laborers walked out the kitchen door as I approached, signaling the end of another day of preserving newly harvested produce. According to Terrell, Sarah really managed stocking the food shelves with little direction from our past cook. The two of them sat on stools at the long kitchen counter where windows looked out to the busy area we called the estate courtyard. With an old paper notebook and a data pad, they were reviewing food inventories.

"Your Andrew seemed to fit in well with Noah and John," Sarah said as she patted the seat next to her. Twenty-four hours into our crisis, sadness dimmed her cheerful nature. "He's a good-looking boy."

I hugged her, remembered how my mother never got over my brother's death, and I hoped she would be spared that pain. She felt smaller in my arms, more vulnerable, and I wondered about whether sending her into the DOE building was safe. "Thank you both for helping to make him feel welcome."

She patted my back, then pulled away. "Of course, he's welcome, Annie. He's going to do just fine with the children. David will love him."

Terrell passed a bowl of thin apple slices my way. "You didn't eat much at lunch today." I remembered his amazing cobblers and wondered if these were left over from making dessert for dinner. "That boy has a lot of sadness in his eyes," he said. "His aunt did the best she could, but I think there's some hurting there." Straightening his spine, Terrell stretched his shoulders. "It's probably been a while since he's had anybody that excited about seeing him walk in the door."

Through the years I'd learned to trust Terrell's insights. I pushed the dish back on the counter. "He just told me that he missed school while they looked for work. He's asked one of the tutors to start assessments so he could start studying."

"Got to like that." Terrell winded my way. "I offered him an afternoon of hanging out here, but he seemed excited about going to school with John."

"I actually came to talk with Sarah about our meeting with Mr. Peterson."

"I already spoke with Paul. Maybe five minutes before you walked in." She shut the notebook, clipped her pen to its edge. "Thought I might bring him dinner then stay with him for the night." She reached over and brushed hair from my face, a mother's soothing gesture. "I also know that the news wasn't good about David." I could see tears in the corners of her eyes. "Are you going to tell the children? About the chips and those two crew found dead?"

The way Sarah and Terrell looked at me, I knew this was what they were discussing before I arrived. "I'll tell them just enough so they aren't surprised if other kids talk. But I don't want them to be more anxious."

"And what about you?" Emotion choked Sarah's voice. "How are you?"

"Pretty much in the same place as you, Sarah." In the comfort of these two, I let my shoulders lower, uncurled my fingers from my palms, and felt the fear and sadness. "Lao wants to talk with you about how to take care of yourself when you're in the DOE building tonight. Make sure to do exactly what he says. We need you here in the morning. I love you and Paul."

"Why don't the two of you sit out on the porch for a few minutes," Terrell suggested. "We're going to have kids in here looking for snacks. I'll load yours up and send them to sit with you."

Magda joined us for dinner to fill Paul's vacant seat at the family table. Phoebe and Andrew continued a conversation obviously started in school about the language proficiency exam and his experience taking the same test. The boys spoke with Magda about picking apples. I had no appetite, just listened to the kids, observed Andrew, and thought about David.

"You would like us to take Andrew on a tour of Ashwood after dinner?" Magda asked me as others finished eating. "You need time to talk with the others?"

"Can't I stay?" With the ability of a kid to hear adults' quiet conversation in the midst of other noises, Andrew began to build his place in the family. "I know how it feels when your parents are in trouble."

I began to love my son in more than an abstract sense. Terrell's observation that Andrew carried sadness gave me reason to look into his eyes, see the shadowy depths that defined his world.

Raising my voice to gather the others into our conversation, I said, "Magda suggested we show Andrew some of Ashwood before dark. We can talk out in the orchard."

"Are you going to tell us anything upsetting?" Phoebe asked. Magda put a hand on the back of Phoebe's chair. "With Daddy missing and everything else, I can't study." Tears accompanied her words and worry.

"Honey, you've only missed two days. We're in a bit of rough water here." I dreaded the night ahead, thought I should keep her with me.

"Teacher Jason said you're the best-prepped student he's known," Andrew pointed out. "You got to stay loose." Phoebe paid attention, didn't shake her head or look away.

"Mom, tell us about Daddy now." John spoke.

Noah added "Please."

This was parenting, no planning allowed. I pushed my untouched plate away. "Okay, pull your chairs closer. Boys, come next to me so I don't have to talk across the table." They moved, pulled chairs to my side. Andrew stayed, now a part of our family worry.

I almost lost courage as I looked into their faces. My own fears of losing David, of having our children taken away, of moving through the future as a single parent held calm words captive in a throat closed tight. Magda tilted her head, a frown forming above her eyes. I faked a cough, reached for my glass of water. Fear slid over their faces—eyelids lowering, lips closing, the suggestion of creases forming on foreheads.

Water caught in my throat. I coughed and remembered the worst days when a clean glass of clear water became unreachable because I couldn't pay our utilities. My family would never sink to that level of life. Never.

"More of the DOE crew was rescued last night in Paraguay and two died. But Dad is still missing." Phoebe stared at me, Noah looked at his hands, and John leaned closer. "His identity chip isn't working, so the military have to use other ways to find Dad and the other two." I kept my voice confident, gentle, and strong. "The best people are searching. That's what I know. Dad will do everything he can to come home."

Noah put his head on his arms.

"Where's Grandpa?" John asked.

"He's staying in the DOE office building for a while. Grandma is going to sleep there with him." How to tell them the rest of the story ran through my thoughts.

"Is he helping them find Dad?" Phoebe gave me space for a half-truth.

"Mr. Peterson would like Grandpa closer while they look for Dad. So Grandpa is going to work real hard—be out in the fields during the day and in the DOE building at night." How to explain the DOE guard came easily. "The DOE will have someone with him so Mr. Peterson knows where to find Grandpa at all times."

They accepted the story. Magda widened her eyes as I spun partially true stories.

"I'm scared." Phoebe sat back in her chair, broke the family circle. "What if they can't find Dad and he's hurt and can't escape. What if . . ."

"My Dad said you gotta walk one step at a time," Andrew cut in. "I'll study with you for the exam." He looked at Phoebe till her head came up. "We'll pile up good news for when your dad gets home."

So Andrew pegged his place among the children as a wise child. I offered thanks to whichever parent nurtured his thoughtfulness.

Tears stayed in Phoebe's eyes, but she calmed. Our daughter understood striving for achievement. I suspected in the future these two would compete hard for honors and recognition, but that night Phoebe treated Andrew as an ally.

"Thank you, Andrew. That's great advice," I said. "Let's take a walk, then do homework."

"Phoebe, we can do drills while we walk," Andrew volunteered.

"Sounds like I should get out of the way." Magda stood and gathered plates. Her company usually gave me time to relax, to be an adult without responsibilities an arm long, but that wasn't to be tonight.

As they strolled the orchard path along Ashwood's eastern and then southern walls, Andrew and Phoebe spoke Spanish, French, and Arabic to each other. The young boys stayed close for a short time before childish energy brought on a surge of running and horseplay. I stored the sight and sound of this walk for a future time when David and I would walk again through these trees, talk about our day and our kids and the future. I pulled a Cortland apple from a low branch, cleaned it against my pants, and bit into its crisp surface. From the smell of rotting fallen fruit to yellowing grass, the dry heat of the last week was taking a toll. We needed rain soon. I dropped the apple, left it.

Rounding my foursome back to the residence, I felt as if eyes followed us. All four of us visited the boys' room to see Andrew's bed and belongings.

I sent the kids to the family quarters to finish schoolwork, considered visiting Paul and Sarah in the DOE office building, and instead headed to the kitchen. I thought I needed a drink and turned toward the water dispenser. Each step took extreme energy on legs that moved as if deep mud sucked at my shoes. I faltered as the remaining dinner cleanup workers' voices became louder and the room stuffy.

I heard someone gasp an instant before I reached for the counter when lightness claimed my head and my legs gave up the effort of walking. "I feel..."

Perhaps I should have called for help instead of merely describing my sudden weakness. People used to being in charge are often poor judges of their own condition. Thankfully, strong hands made it to my side and eased my final descent as the world went black.

Terrell's voice issuing directions brought me back to the moment. I rested against his shoulder, felt nauseous and embarrassed. "I'm all right," I said, projecting a wobbly voice through rubbery lips. "I don't know what happened."

"And we don't know what happened either so you just stay where you are," Terrell said. "I got you, and you're staying right where you are until I decide something else."

With Terrell back on the estate, my medical responsibilities fell to second-in-command, followed by Magda, then Sarah. No one at Ashwood ever had as powerful a natural knack for handling these matters as Terrell. He almost delivered John when labor came early.

"Please help me to a chair in case one of my kids comes in." His arms tightened as I put my hands on the floor, readying to push myself up. "Terrell, I can't let them see me."

"I know, Annie. I'll let you get up when I think you won't fall back down." I felt his hold switch to support. Amber knelt down next to us, offered me a glass of water. My hand trembled as I reached. She helped steady the glass as I sipped.

"Thank you." I moved myself away from Terrell's support, closed my eyes when the effort surprised me. But I stayed upright on my own. Amber put the glass on the floor, then sent the remaining workers off to their studies with directions not to mention "Ms. Anne's accident." Silence filled the kitchen, an oddity during this hour.

"I'd like to get you to your room," Terrell said. "If that's not possible, you're going to lie on the floor in my office, with your feet up. Will I have your cooperation?"

"Yes."

He brushed hair from my forehead while I regained my strength. "I think you're plain tuckered out and not eating," he said. "Food and early bed."

"The kids, Terrell. The boys are excited about sharing their room with Andrew, but I can't leave Phoebe alone."

"I hear you haven't had a real night's sleep in weeks 'cause of Phoebe's terrors. We'll take care of her tonight. You got to trust somebody with that girl."

Amber returned to us in the rather tight space between the serving counter and the drinks station. "How can I help?" she asked, her voice softened.

"I'm feeling better," I said and pushed myself to stand. Except for a slow churn in my stomach, nothing much happened. "Cook thinks I need help getting to my room, and he's the expert."

On the way to standing, I saw a large platter had fallen down with me. Terrell made it possible for me to get to my feet with some dignity. Amber kept me balanced on my feet as he brushed stoneware bits from my clothes. I wobbled my way out of the kitchen between them with a quick stop at Terrell's office for him to grab a medical kit. Closing my bedroom door, I sat on our bed in a cold sweat.

Amber found my pajamas, turned her back as I changed. She picked up my clothes and opened the door for Terrell, then stayed in the room to witness Terrell conducting a medical assessment.

"You're not pregnant, your blood sugar is fine, and your heart is strong." Terrell spoke as he repacked the kit. "So we're going to call this fatigue compounded by stress. And, you are going to sleep tonight without an alarm in the morning."

"I have to be available for the five-thirty makeup call."

"Nope. I'm the medical officer on this estate and I say that's not going to happen." Terrell turned to Amber. "Am, please get Ms. Anne a glass of water." She left for the bathroom. "I'll call Sarah and they can interview Paul if they want a family member. Amber will sleep with Phoebe, and we'll get Sarah or Magda if needed."

"Can we keep this out of the med reports? I don't want Peterson to broadcast it to the world."

"I got two weeks until the monthly report is due." He shook out a sedative. "If you're cooperative and take this little pill with this nice glass of water, I think we can avoid a remote medical consult." He held out the tablet. "We're going to monitor how you're doing for the next few days to be sure nothing more serious is going on."

"I really shouldn't take that, Terrell."

"That's not an option."

One tiny pink pill was the reason I slept through Phoebe's screaming and why she knocked poor Amber against a wall before walking out of the residence without ever waking up. Because of that pill, my daughter's small pajama-clad form was captured in the front courtyard on video by Peterson's team.

Chapter Nineteen

"Ms. Anne. Wake up. Ms. Anne"

From somewhere near my bed I heard a young girl's voice, high with fear yet ragged as if it had been pushed through a mush-filled mouth. Terrell's little pink pill suppressed my natural response, made me think about how to open my eyes or pull on a robe. "Is Phoebe all right?" I asked into the night.

"She's outside. Through the front doors." Before I could focus, I recognized the voice as Amber's and heard tears under the words, maybe pain. "I couldn't stop her. I'm so sorry."

"Get Terrell." I grabbed my wristband, pressed Lao's icon. "Phoebe's in the estate," I said as I stumbled toward my bedroom door. "She's sleepwalking. We need help. Now."

"Magda's got her." Lao spoke so quietly I had to hold the communicator wristband to my ear. "Go back to bed, Anne. Phoebe's right here."

"Where are you? I can't believe I slept through her call."

"Stay where you are, Anne."

"Amber is hurt." Through the haze I saw blood dripping from her nose, down one hand and arm. "She needs attention. In my bedroom." I grabbed a towel from a drawer, handed it to her. "Sit down, Amber. Here." Gently I pushed her to the floor, guided her to hold the towel. "Keep your head level." I moved away, steadying myself with a hand against the wall. "Someone will be here in a minute, I have to go to Phoebe."

She tried to stop me, but I was stronger than a twelve-year-old. Even in my muddled sense of awareness, the open front door jangled my alarms. From the steps I heard my vulnerable Phoebe crying for her father.

I rushed down the wide slate steps and through a small garden of carpet roses. Maybe the medication made me unstable on my feet and I stumbled, fell to one knee on the gravel drive. On the other side, in Ashwood's courtyard, Magda stood with her arms around Phoebe. I waved Magda side, already offering comforting words for Phoebe. Magda stepped aside with reluctance. I took my child in shaky arms, held her close, dried her tears with my shirt.

"Sweet one." I rocked with her in the cool Minnesota fall night air. Her shoulders stiffened with dream anxiety yet remained almost flaccid like a newborn baby not knowing how to use muscle and bone. I rubbed her back, and as she awoke the cold, damp gravel underfoot registered in her mind that we were not in her room.

"Mom." The whispered word settled us back where the world felt safer. Terrell appeared, dropped a blanket around her shoulders then gathered her up in his arms. "Where is Daddy?"

"He's away, Phoeb." I walked next to Terrell, kept one of her hands tucked into mine. Magda fell into step next to me, placed her arm around my waist. Looped together we might have looked like Dorothy and her trio returning from the Land of Oz. In the distance I heard men's voices exchanging heated words, some kind of commotion. But, the moment was devoted to calming Phoebe, returning her to safety, helping her find sleep.

"Put her in my room, Terrell." My teeth chattered, my feet now felt the cold and stinging bruises. "I think I cut my toe on the garden rocks?"

"Keep your hands off me, you estate jerk." A stranger's words carried across the dark courtyard. "You can't mess with the DOE." I missed a step as I turned toward the voice.

"Keep walking, Anne." Magda spoke close to my ear. "Lao has everything under control. Her arm pushed me forward. Phoebe's hand pulled mine. Up the steps we climbed, into the open foyer. Magda closed the door, pressed the security pad.

"Your grandma's waiting in your room with dry pajamas, Phoebe," Terrell said. I nodded as he spoke, gave Phoebe's hand a squeeze.

"She'll help you change, then we'll go back to sleep," I added. "Just give me a few minutes."

"We need your mom right now, Phoebe," Terrell interrupted. "You'll be okay with your grandma, little one?" She released my hand; her head dipping against his shoulder in the first stage of drifting back to sleep and away from whatever drove her outdoors.

Magda walked with me to my room, cleaned out a nasty scrape, and folded back the bed.

"Why wasn't Sarah with Paul?" Some parts of yesterday stood clear in my sleep-dazed memory. "Do we need to get Phoebe?"

"Sarah said something about sleeping on a cot in a small space with a big snoring man that made her own bed look attractive. She'll stay with Phoebe. You need to be a good manager and get some sleep." Gently, but with strength, she pushed me against my pillow. " Anne, you'll need to have your head together in the morning."

Before she dropped the blanket over my shoulders, we both noticed a spot of Amber's dried blood on my hand. "My God, how's Amber? I left her here with a towel."

"She's in the kitchen waiting for Terrell. Let me clean that off."

"I can do it. Please go check on Amber."

"Lady, you got to let others take care of a few people and get back to sleep." She wiped my hand and arm with the same brisk action I used on my children. "There. Now go back to sleep. Believe me, we need you at your best in a few hours."

Chapter Twenty

The little pink pill still slowed down my whole morning routine when I forced myself out of bed at the regular time. In the kitchen, Terrell looked a whole lot more alert than I felt. I reached for light switches, dimmed the main fixture.

"Sit down. You look like death warmed over." He pushed a mug of coffee my way. "We need to talk."

"What's happened?" David sprang first to mind, then Paul.

"The yelling you heard as we walked in with Phoebe during the night was Lao confronting a DOE crew member who happened to be out shooting moonlight footage. I don't know why. He caught Phoebe on film the moment she walked out the residence door."

Coffee dribbled down my chin. I extended my neck over the counter while I swiped at the fluid with my fingers.

Terrell handed me a towel. "I filed a complete health assessment report last night about your fainting, so it's on record that you were under my medical supervision, which included administration of a sleeping aid." He leaned over to wipe a droplet from my neck. "Your concern about Phoebe's sleeping arrangement is included, along with steps we took to assure her safety."

Putting the mug down on the counter, I let the potential for disaster erase the feel of hot coffee on my skin. "How bad do I look in that film?"

"It appears that you are either on drugs or drunk—the fall, the pitch of your voice, a general lack of awareness." He handed me a glass of juice. "Drink this and don't ask questions." I complied. "I was amazed that Amber was able to wake you, that you took care of her bloody nose and made your way outside. Young Phoebe has a determined mom watching out for her." He took the juice glass from me. "There is nothing, and I mean nothing, stronger I could have administered. You should have been out cold for at least eight hours."

The sleeping medication hangover began to lift. Terrell held up a hand and shook his head slightly. Two workers entered the kitchen. He asked them questions about the laborers' dining room and sent them away.

Milan's protection gave me some assurance that this event would pass. But I also knew such images lived long beyond a single day and could be altered or used for many reasons. I rose.

"Where you going?" Terrell asked.

"I want to be sure Paul was left alone overnight, then I'm going to my temporary office to send Milan a note. He needs to know about the security issue last night from me." Terrell's manner suggested I had not grasped the big picture of Phoebe's nighttime walk.

"Paul is fine." Terrell held up one hand. "Sarah stayed with Phoebe and the rest of the night was quiet. Dr. Frances, the therapist we discussed, arrives after lunch to begin work with Phoebe. I cleared that with Milan, who should be arriving soon."

"Tell me what I'm missing. When did you speak with Milan?"

"When he called about an hour after Magda put you back to bed. After Milan spoke with Peterson."

"Milan called you?" I tried to return to my chair. Terrell put a hand on my elbow and led me out of the kitchen.

In the hall he spoke again, his voice so low I leaned his way to catch the words. "Lao redirected all your communications to his reception after you went to bed last night. I thought you wouldn't be able to respond to messages. Lao spoke with Milan first."

Our footsteps took us nowhere. My irritation with Lao impeded my ability to read where our conversation traveled.

"Anne, Milan is on his way because Peterson filed a letter of concern about the parenting of Phoebe and Noah in the absence of their father." I stopped, and he pulled me forward. I shrugged his hand away. "As their legal guardian, Milan must be with the kids within twenty-four hours of the filing."

"This is a horrible mistake." A sense of purpose jolted through emotion and replaced my early hypothetical worry about losing the children. Letters of concern permited the Bureau to immediately remove gifted offspring from their caretakers.

"Damn right." In the light of Ashwood's foyer I could see fatigue in Terrell's dark eyes. "Lao's been up all night piecing house security images to document what happened. Milan understands there are shenanigans involved, but a letter of concern doesn't get lifted easily. I told Lao we'd meet in your estate office." He activated the front door security pad.

"How did Phoebe get out this door?" I rapped a hand against the solid red surface. "She's not cleared for nighttime passage from any outside door. A security alarm should have sounded." My mind wanted to stay away from what brought Milan to Ashwood and grabbed at the security break. "Since residence security is automatically activated each night, someone played with the system to make this possible."

My friend stopped me with a gentle slide of his foot into the back of my sandal. "Anne, listen to me. There are bigger powers than Milan pulling strings. You and I know that Lao checked every angle of last night's security. He probably knows how that door was able to open." I waited, impatient to secure my hold on the children. "But a formal investigation has to take place regardless of Lao's discoveries. Bureau protocols dropped into place at four forty-five this morning."

Regular day laborers greeted us, and a few stopped to express concern about David's fate. No one knew the coming days could challenge what I held almost dearer than my beloved—our children. He would have voiced the same priority. For both of us, nothing meant more than keeping the children secure and thriving. We had plans ready to execute to protect them from almost all the threats we thought our family might face. Almost.

Only one overnight staff member was at work in the estate offices this Friday morning. Mai, a favorite local woman who preferred nights in order to be able to care for elderly parents, easily did the work of two during the typically quiet down time. More important, she executed overnight commodity trades with brilliant strategy.

"Odd activity in the South American markets," Mai said as we walked past her workstation. "We got the best price I've ever seen for our excess corn and snagged energy futures at rock bottom."

Normally I'd stay to ask questions about the markets, but not today. She noticed Terrell and assessed him in the way of a single woman sighting an attractive man. He appeared oblivious as he hurried me beyond my office to a conference room.

Lao pulled out a chair for me. Breakfast waited on the table. Terrell passed fruit and yogurt in my direction. We settled with small talk about Mia's trading comments. Lao set up his data pad.

"I've collapsed the security files so Milan will be able to see all that happened from the time Anne fainted through 5:00 a.m. this morning. Magda uncovered a few facts while taking care of Amber's nose. There's definitely a conspiracy in place to discredit Anne."

I watched the images as Lao spoke. My faint in the kitchen passed quickly including my concern about Phoebe's care. I became riveted by Antwone sitting against a wall in the hall near Phoebe's room long after workers' lights out. Terrell and I watched him blindside Amber outside Phoebe's room, first tripping her, then swiftly kicking at her face. When Phoebe walked toward my door, eyes open wide but unseeing, he turned her toward the central hall and urged her forward with a menacing side-to-side swaying motion. She ran, and slapped at the front door, which opened. She never touched the security pad, never turned the door handle.

Simultaneous images caught Amber, face bleeding, following them. She was in pain, maybe shock, and crying as she turned back to my room. I averted my eyes as the hall camera caught my zombielike ragged rush through the residence, flight out the door and tumble in the garden.

"Security's been broached, Lao." Words I never had to say. "Somebody inside the estate set us up, hoping Phoebe would have a sleepwalking episode." I sat back, piecing together words about Antwone.

"Antwone and I had a bit of a rough encounter the day Clarisse Smithson arrived. I reacted to more of his cocky street kid behavior." Terrell made a small noise in his throat. "It wasn't a big deal, but I know he was resentful."

Lao looked thoughtful, but remained quiet. Terrell responded.

"He's a kid with a knack for self-promotion," he said. "Bent my ear with stories about all the chores he could do better or faster, but doesn't seem to really do much. Knows how to talk a good game." Terrell crossed his right ankle over his left thigh. "Jeremiah may have turned a blind eye to the kid's laziness, but I've been keeping Mr. Antwone busy. He may be clever, but I'm not so sure he's real smart."

"Regardless, Antwone could not disarm Ashwood's security," Lao interjected. "Someone hacked our code so that door could be opened without a retinal check or thumbprint after the evening lockdown." He turned the data pad back toward himself. "We found the hacker's work, which appears to have originated yesterday from the only data pad on the estate with capability to work behind the firewalls of both the DOE and Ashwood—the one in Anne's office."

"I locked my office, but someone was in there before my meeting with Peterson yesterday. Peterson admitted taking what he called liberties with my office." I paused. "You have that admission on file." Lao agreed. "So we have a fairly strong case to connect Peterson's people to what happened last night."

"No doubt, Anne." Lao added nothing more.

"You're concerned about security right now." I waited. "That's why you look so worried?" David nicknamed Lao "Ashwood's Dragon" because of his willingness to go extremes to keep Ashwood and our people safe.

Lao stood, pushed in his chair, leaned against a wall. Terrell and I watched his every movement. "Milan is bringing security experts with him today. I've already spoken with their leader."

He licked his lips, stuck his hands in his pants pockets. "I'm confident they'll find everything in order. What I am concerned about, Anne, is how you are going to hold up under the child guardian protocols while Milan does a formal investigation. Particularly with what we have learned about Mr. Peterson."

Ashwood's Dragon sent a fireball into the room. "Mr. Peterson has no DOE connection."

"He told us that when he said he a military appointment similar to David's." I crossed my arms over my chest instead of fidgeting with my wedding band.

"That wasn't exactly true, Anne." Lao came back to the table, but didn't sit. "Captain Peterson is head of an elite section of Special Forces. He's been deeply involved in Paraguay operations for almost two decades. My inside source found a trail that suggests this is Peterson's last opportunity for success before he faces reassignment to a desk job." Lao stopped. "He likes to play psychological games with civilians. In fact, he's known as a head job himself. Very unstable."

In this windowless room, I could see nothing of the world David and I had built as a couple. Not the flower gardens we planted for relaxation, not the shop where he and Paul did woodworking projects, not swing sets for all the kids. I could only visualize the faces of four young children I loved, vulnerable to a man without controls.

"So what do we do?" I uncrossed my arms and stretched out for the data pad as if to write a list of our thoughts.

"You do nothing." Lao, himself a military vet, issued the command. "You do everything Milan asks and concentrate on your children and getting Ashwood through harvest." The look he directed my way was powerful, a leader ready to do battle against another acknowledged leader. "Make sure there is no questioning of your actions."

"Are you suggesting I not talk about Peterson's cover with Milan?"

"You definitely should discuss this with Milan, but know that he is working on levels you and I must not question."

Terrell stood as well. "I've got to get back to the kitchen. Milan will be here in about fifteen minutes."

"That gives me time for breakfast with the kids."

Terrell and Lao looked at each other before Lao said, "Sarah is in charge of the children until Milan's assigned guardian ad litem arrives."

Chapter Twenty-One

With these two men I could be plain Anne Hartford. I let seconds escape as I put my hands over my head, scratched at my scalp while my mind skittered over what had to be accepted—our children were not really ours. Except for John. David and I thought of John as Ashwood's only truly free child, all the way from the natural blending of our DNA to the absence of government directives over his daily life.

"I'm sorry, Anne," Terrell said, breaking the silence. "I followed medical guidelines last night, but I accept responsibility for how this developed."

"Don't go there, either of you." Bringing my hands back to rest in my lap, I sat very upright. "If you want to get all analytical, Antwone brought me a glass of iced tea from the kitchen as the others had dessert last night. I may have fainted because of something put in my tea. We could follow a lot of blind alleys looking for the answer to how this ball started rolling, but I think Lao's discovery about Captain Peterson's history is all we need."

One small dot of coffee stained my shirt collar. I rubbed at it out of habit. They watched and I felt self-conscious.

"Well, I had better get over to the residence for breakfast while my mother-in-law, who does love me, is in charge of my children. From what I remember of studying the guardian protocols, I will have open access to the kids as long as there are no claims of mental instability or potential for physical harm." I looked to Terrell.

He shrugged. "Sounds logical, but this isn't my area of expertise, Anne. We're all going to walk carefully as the investigation goes on."

"Let's get started," I said as I stood. "I'll walk over with you. Tell me more about Dr. Frances."

"You're going to like her." We left the conference room, walked back through the offices. "She's older than you, completed her training before the D, did a pediatric clinical internship at Morgan Stanley Children's Hospital in New York, and has managed to practice both within the Bureau and independently."

"Sounds impressive, but tell me what you think of her as a person, Terrell."

"Rock solid. Blessed with deep insight and the love of kids and people who love kids. Not all clinical types like parents and teachers." He pushed open the outside door and waved me out first. "Frances will want to work with you as well as with Phoebe."

"Understood. How did Milan respond to hiring outside the Bureau's short list?"

"He wants to clear up Peterson's concern quickly for the kids' sake and Frances is well respected." Terrell waved to a worker, then yawned. "Hard to miss a night's sleep." Another yawn formed. "By the way, did I tell you she's damn expensive and we'll be housing her for a couple of weeks? Milan approved both, but I'm not sure whose budget gets hit."

Amber, looking tired and uncomfortable with a swollen nose, directed final breakfast logistics in the kitchen. On another day, when my actions weren't under investigation, my arms would have held the child. "Executive Milan wants to meet with me now, Cook Terrell. Is it all right if I go?"

As the surprise that Milan was at Ashwood without contacting me passed, I thought how intimidating such a request was for a worker. "He's a kind man, Amber," I said to assure her. "Did you want someone to walk over with you?"

"He said I shouldn't talk with anyone about last night."

"Go on," Terrell handed her a towel. "Wipe your hands first. He's in the estate office building."

"Before you go, Amber, thank you for coming to get me last night." I touched her arm. "I'm so sorry you were hurt. Terrell, can you spare Amber for the day? I'm sure you didn't sleep well."

"Cook suggested that, but I would rather be here." She wiped her hands, touched fingers under one eye. "My mom once had a shiner that lasted for a month. I didn't know how much that could hurt."

Terrell and I did not look at each other. I did gently hug her, remembered the scars we found on her back when, at five years of age, she was the newest worker at Ashwood. I promised myself I would look into extending permanent legal protection over her.

She walked across the courtyard, head down. "How did you know where Milan was located?" I asked Terrell over my shoulder. "Was he already in the building when we were talking?"

"Don't worry about the small details, Annie." He gave directions to a boy loading the dishwasher, and I fretted about what I wouldn't know in the coming days. "Go say hello to the kids. Have a cup of tea. Avoid more caffeine until this evening or the antidote I administered might set your nerves jangling."

I left the kitchen, checked my appearance in a hall mirror. For my kids' sake I shook off tight shoulders and concentrated on walking into the dining room with my normal energy and confidence.

Andrew spoke with Sarah and the boys at our family table. Phoebe looked lost in thought until she saw me and pushed her chair back to run to me for a hug.

She smelled of soap and shampoo, her curls damp against my shirt. My arms tightened around her skinny body as I bent to kiss her head. I remembered the first time I kissed her in the dark of the old nursery and promised to keep her safe as long as I remained at Ashwood. She stepped back.

"You have coffee on your shirt, Mom."

Circles under her eyes would tell teachers of her difficult night. Of course, it was possible the entire story of the courtyard drama had spread around the estate.

"It was a tough night, sweetie, and I started the day in too much of a hurry." We walked back to the table. "Since you're the second person to notice that spot, I better change my shirt. Good thing I wasn't interviewed this morning or the whole country would know I spill things."

The boys giggled. I kissed Noah and John, wanted to at least squeeze Andrew's shoulder but knew he needed time before such intimacy. I sat in the empty chair at his side. "I hope you slept well your first night and these two didn't keep you up?"

One shoulder rose, then fell. He finished chewing a toast crust. "Sleeping in a bed again felt good. I shared a room with my older brother so John and Noah were no big deal."

"Where did you sleep at your aunt's?" Already comfortable with Andrew, Noah wanted to know about this new friend and stepbrother.

"On the floor. We found an inflatable mattress, but it always leaked so I just made myself a place to crash out of blankets and a rug." He looked at me quickly, then picked up another slice of toast. "It was okay."

"That's your fourth piece of toast," Phoebe observed. "You must really be hungry this morning."

Andrew flushed.

"Andrew and his aunt didn't always have enough food," I offered, watching how the information settled on Phoebe. "Believe me, it takes a few weeks if you've been really hungry to get your body back in balance." I took the liberty of extending my arm around the back of Andrew's chair. "That's doubly hard when you're growing. So Andrew should eat as his body needs."

Sarah sipped her beloved morning coffee. As always, she appeared tidy and ready to work, except for her eyes which carried a mixture of fatigue, worry, sorrow. We glanced at each other over the table. Starting this morning I was almost as powerless as Sarah to change what was wrong.

"Will we go hungry this winter, Mom?" John's question surprised both Sarah and me. All our children stopped eating or drinking. "Cook Jeremiah told some workers that our cellars were empty and we might have a hungry winter."

"Well, he was wrong," Sarah answered. "And your mom sent him away. Cook Terrell is working hard to make sure we have more food than we need in storage. We have been canning and preserving food for hours every day and have plans for big, wonderful greenhouse crops."

"I heard Cook Jeremiah was stealing," Phoebe said, "and the police took him away."

Sarah looked to me for a response. "None of that really matters, Phoeb. Estate gossip can stretch truth pretty far." I poured myself a glass of water, decided to pass on eating. "There's no new information about Dad, but we have other important things to talk about this morning."

Around the table I sensed weariness in this constant flow of bad news. The kids looked wary, even Andrew.

"Is this about last night?" asked Phoebe. "About me sleepwalking outside?"

"Yes it is, dear." Sarah's blunt answer surprised me.

"I'm not sure I agree with Grandma, Phoeb." Sarah gave me a cool look across the table, a look I don't think I'd seen before. "There was a security breach last night which allowed you to walk out the front door. Because of everything else happening, Executive Milan had to call for a special review, which includes bringing in a person to stay with us during the process."

Sarah's cool look disappeared. "I didn't have all the information and mispoke. I'm sorry."

I knew Sarah wouldn't hurt Phoebe's feelings intentionally, but that meant nothing when my daughter put her head on her arms on the tabletop and began sobbing. Sarah rose from her chair, but stopped as I put my hand up. Putting aside the whole letter of concern investigation, I acted as Phoebe's mother and drew her close.

"I wish I was dead," she whispered so only I could hear. "If Daddy's dead, I want to be with him." Her crying intensified.

Few words from my stepdaughter could frighten me more. I wanted to cry with her, to strap her to my chest and hold her safe until the world calmed, to fight demons or angels on her behalf.

"Sarah, maybe you can take the others outside." I gestured above Phoebe's head. "Please."

They hesitated, three young boys, frightened and fascinated by Phoebe's intense despair. When they left, the room felt larger, too impersonal. So I carefully lifted Phoebe from her chair and sat us on the floor, where I could cradle her long little-girl body into my own. I rocked with her, smoothing her hair and making the kind of small gentling sounds that often broke her terrors at night. As her sobs quieted, her body relaxed. I leaned against a table leg.

"Listen to me, Phoebe." I vowed to protect Tia's daughter, called the child my own, and hoped my heart and mind could lead us to stable ground. "You are a beautiful, wonderful person, exactly the kind of person this world needs. Nothing has happened that should make you feel so very bad." I kissed her head, wiped tears from her cheeks and chin with my shirt. "Your biological mom asked me to take care of you and Daddy. All of you are the very, very best parts of my life. If you ever—and I mean ever—feel like life is too difficult, please come to me."

"If they take me away from you, I'll die." Her voice, so childish and small, still sounded firm. "I don't want to be like the kids who come here all alone and have to sleep in a dorm with strangers."

"Phoeb, I believe Dad is alive and will be back." I assessed what I had said, knew I wasn't lying. "I don't have the odd feeling I remember when my family members passed away." She settled, listened for comfort but also for truth. "I'm worried about Dad, really worried. But I don't feel like I want to crawl out of my skin."

"You wouldn't make that up?" She began to sit upright, to draw away even while she pulled at my shirt to wipe more tears from her face.

"No." I leaned toward her, gave her free use of the shirt. "I'm worried about keeping you healthy and eradicating those night terrors. I don't like Executive Milan's legal guardianship right now when Dad isn't present. But, in my bones I believe that Dad will be back."

"Will he take us away from you? Me and Noah? And will Andrew get to stay with you?"

She was almost eight, a wise child with genius intelligence and keen perception. From experience, I knew I had to careful if I blurred the truth.

"I honestly don't think so, Phoeb. But you and I have to be very serious about what happens over these next days or weeks." She shook her head, not understanding. "This is part of something big that is controlled by powerful people. I can't predict what might happen. You and I and the boys and Grandma might get scared at times."

"What about Grandpa?"

"Even Grandpa gets a little scared." One foot wiggled. "There's something special you and I need to talk about. Terrell has found a therapist to help us understand what causes your bad nights." She pulled away more. I kept her anchored with an arm. "Her name is Dr. Frances and she arrives today and will stay with us for some time. I think this is better than having long-distance sessions with a counselor."

"I want to sleep with you tonight."

"I don't know. We'll have to see what Dr. Frances thinks." I didn't tell her there would also be someone else who might want to approve her request.

"Maybe I can sleep in the boys' room so I'm not alone."

My girl moved from the brink of fear to problem solving. Her spine unfolded, her eyes engaged with mine. "I think you should talk with Dr. Frances about that right away."

She looked down. "I'm sorry about last night," she said gently, quietly.

The demons I vowed to fight crowded near us. "There's no need for you to apologize. When you're asleep, you're not responsible for what you dream." She played with a loose thread on her shirt, head still down. "Phoebs, I'm sorry I didn't hear you last night."

"You always hear me." Her head came up, a look of surprise in her eyes.

"Last night I was kind of sick and Terrell gave me something to help me sleep. It was really hard to wake up when Amber came for me—kind of like trying to wake you up. But I got to you."

With her mother's ability to experience several emotions at once, Phoebe put her arms around my shoulders. "Poor Mom," she whispered. "Who's taking care of you?"

"Don't you worry about that, kiddo. You know that Magda and Lao and Terrell and Grandma and Grandpa are all here."

"Mom, don't you think it's weird that Mr. Peterson might know where Dad is and won't let Grandpa be with us? It's like only women and children are left in the fort. Like a weird war story."

"That's a big thought, sweetie."

Phoebe left my side and stood. She waited for me to get to my feet, and held my hand as we left the room.

Chapter Twenty-Two

Milan's request to meet arrived as Phoebe and I headed to her room. I helped her wash her face, walked her to school, then joined Milan in my estate offices. I wore the same shirt with its spot of coffee and messy residue of Phoebe's tears, breakfast jam, and snot.

Compared to the DOE's formality, my small space in this building had more feminine accents with soft yellow walls and clear finished wood furniture. Overnight someone had lined my windowsill with potted plants.

Milan appeared out of synch in this room. Glasses on top of his balding head, he stretched his legs while he rubbed his eyes. Barely past eight o'clock and the day promised more challenges. Neither of us offered a greeting, Milan merely began what might be a difficult discussion.

"You look like you had a really rough night and the morning hasn't been much kinder." He lowered his glasses back into position, one of the only Bureau officials to wear traditional corrective lenses. "Anne, you don't deserve this, and I think it's going to get rough." His left hand wandered across his chin as he stifled a small yawn. "I never expected to be summoned with a letter of concern about the Regan children when the doorbell rang at four thirty this morning. Even my wife was quite upset and told me to offer any support she can provide."

"Your wife is a sweetheart, Milan." Normally a small joke might follow my statement, but we were far outside normal boundaries. "Talk to me."

"The children, and anyone else who needs to know, will be told we are taking special precautions because of the media stories. I've viewed Lao's files, interviewed Amber and Antwone. Clearly Phoebe's walk outside was encouraged to create a crisis that could be recorded by Peterson's crew." He stuck one index finger behind the lens to rub again at his left eye. "I'm not beyond thinking Peterson hoped this would distract attention from an internal review of his activities. That said, I am legally bound to follow strict protocol related to Phoebe and Noah."

I stayed with Milan's explanation of the investigation process for ten minutes and felt relief that Hajar, a former junior teacher in Ashwood's school, had been asked to serve as the ad litem guardian. I hired her when her disastrous first posting disappeared. We enjoyed talking about teaching and books and sparkling wines before she left for graduate school.

From where I sat the residence's summer kitchen gardens were distracting when Milan returned to Ashwood's financial responsibilities. Young workers picked vegetables under the early morning sun. Andrew could have been among those children if Clarissa had not been persistent. Only a week ago I doubted her story.

"Anne, I need you to listen. I was talking about Hajar."

I turned my attention back to Milan. "I'm sorry. I do appreciate all you are doing. Hajar is a terrific defender of children." He didn't respond. "My kids might not remember her, but many of our long-term employees and workers won't ask questions about why she's here."

"True." His head bobbed as he appeared to weigh his next words. "You need to keep Ashwood steady until I can move Peterson out of the DOE building and off the estate. Jurisdictions are intricate, so while Peterson misrepresented himself to a couple of critical people, it may take time to unravel who takes responsibility for managing him."

Living in a country dependent on a large, controlling government meant little surprised citizens about interagency issues. Branches of the government didn't willingly share data, fought over duplicate resources, evaded difficult decisions. All those inefficiencies meant Ashwood needed Counselor Joel Santos to navigate official requirements and a private attorney to keep pushing issues.

"I don't know what about us attracts Peterson." Tired of this distraction, I wanted to be in my regular office with my husband working at his desk. "I'm sure Lao told you that Peterson's people have twice cracked the double security coding on my DOE office. They've rifled through everything in that building."

Antwone moved past the windows, dragging a small wagon filled with empty produce boxes. Milan and I watched the boy.

He broke our quiet first. "As of this morning Bureau and DOE authorized security have been added to Ashwood's regular staff. I don't want you or the children leaving Ashwood without prior clearance. Phoebe's language exam will happen at some future date. In the outside world, the surrogate story is growing." Without a twinge of malice, he added, "A number of people in high places are preparing to step down."

Political fallout was insignificant to me at this moment. My children were worried about their father, their grandfather, the disruptions at Ashwood. Phoebe might be relieved about the rescheduled exam, or she could be further stressed.

"Milan, Paul's release would make a world of difference to all of us. Isn't there some way to make that happen?" Phoebe's comment about leaving the women and children on their own resurfaced. "There is a sense of vulnerability in the residence—a question of who might disappear next."

"Your father-in-law managed to communicate with someone higher up the ladder than I would think possible for a South Dakota rancher." Milan laughed, a small sound. "Got to hand it to Paul. He called one of the two or three people who can ultimately hold those above Peterson accountable. I can't say more, but Paul will be released. Maybe tomorrow."

"Will Paul be safe another twenty-four hours? Peterson's people have weapons."

"We're planning for the best outcome."

Bushels of tomatoes stood around the garden's edge. Antwone circled back without gathering filled containers. Sarah watched the boy, but offered no direction. When he sat down in the wagon, one of Magda's work leaders approached.

"That boy will need to go home until he can be fully assessed for a different assignment," Milan said when he saw that my attention had been distracted. "Unless someone here wants to take on a special project."

I didn't know what brought Antowne into the estate system—an overextended family, a single parent, a home in the roughest of neighborhoods. A kid was never sent back to that environment without careful consideration.

"I trust your decision," I said. Milan shrugged. "We've sent three or four kids away out of the hundreds assigned here, and I don't see how we can work with Antwone's needs."

"Your harvest reports look strong."

The change in subject came abruptly, not normal in conversations with Milan.

"True." I thought he wanted to speak about something else. "Now, if we can hire temporary labor to bring in the remaining crops, we will meet the increased government quotas plus have a nice grain surplus to take to market."

"And what about estate food reserves?"

"You know where we were a week ago." I fidgeted, becoming irritated with his avoidance of some issue. "Terrell and Sarah are doing a fantastic job of making use of everything that's coming in from the gardens and greenhouses." Milan continued looking out the window, probably not listening. "What's on your mind?"

He shook his head, just once. "Nothing specific." His left thumb rubbed back and forth over the inside of his fingertips, a habit I knew indicated thoughts I might not hear. "This investigation is a big deal, Anne. Peterson is no small fish in Special Forces. He's been demoted because of a number of serious missteps, but no one has actually been able to strip his command." His eyes stayed focused on mine. "I'll be honest, I'm worried about David's safety and your family's security. Few cross-agency issues are handled this high in the Pentagon. This guy is trouble."

"Thank you for your honesty." Milan never exaggerated. His concerns would be based on facts and knowledge of politics. His worry deepened my fears. "How long can you stay?" I hoped he would make this one of those times he stayed through the evening. "The children miss a full dinner table."

"I'd like to join you and the kids." He pushed back from my desk. "Maybe early dinner, after I meet with Terrell's hotshot psychiatrist. I should get out of your office so you can get some work done. I think the new property tax formulas were released this morning." He rose, gestured toward the door. "Why don't you say hello to Dr. Frances with me?"

My daughter's new therapist waited in the reception area. She appeared to be a few years older than I—a short, rounded woman in severe black clothes with ivory-colored skin, closely-cropped gray hair and eyes the color of a copper rich stream. She rose as we walked in and met us in the middle of the space. We all bowed.

"Beautiful estate, Manager Anne. Terrell didn't exaggerate when he described Ashwood." Frances had a surprising, beautiful feminine voice with just a touch of Georgia twang. "And you must be Senior Executive Milan. Thank you for bending the regs to allow me to work with the Regan family."

"Your credentials speak for themselves, Dr. Frances." Milan waved her toward our conference room. "You'll have time to become acquainted with Anne, but my time is limited. So let's you and I get started."

Alone in my office, I rested in my desk chair and thought about David—just closed my eyes and imagined him sitting with me. He wore sandals, his thin feet always looking slightly unreal when they were exposed in warm weather. His pants were wrinkled, the effect of long travel. I knew his hands would be in his pants pockets, or holding the arms of the chair, a silver wedding band on his left ring finger. But I couldn't picture his face. The thoughtful look of discussions about our children, the serious concentration he gave to Ashwood, the kindness others saw—not one expression formed fully in my memory. I opened my eyes, experienced doubt about his safety, and a dull realization that I might lead this family on my own.

So I focused on the present, on reports and mail and Ashwood. I apologized to David for turning my mind to work but knew this is what he would want. Wheat, barley, and soybean harvesting were ahead of schedule because of dry weather. We were on target for meeting our government quota as well as meeting our own milling requirements. The first of the corn would be coming in the next week and Paul projected a better than average crop.

Abundant fish and poultry stock would allow us to place more on the open market than in previous years. Paul recommended expanding our dairy operation, a potential battleground with Magda who thought milking detracted labor from the greenhouses. Our winter discussions would be interesting.

New tax forms were indeed in the day's correspondence. Rough calculations suggested a significant increase in our property taxes. In some odd bureaucratic logic, the Bureau of Human Capital Management also announced a placement fee to be paid by employers accepting trainees in all worker and laborer classifications. Blocked by law from hiring any other trainees or child workers, I struggled with understanding the logic beyond a government grown so large that fees popped up every quarter to support mandated programs.

Correspondence from the Council of the Urban Youth Initiative formalized Ashwood's exemption from the program in deference to the

DOE gifted-student grant. I searched for confirmation of the DOE grant and saw we would accept students with the start of the next academic grading period. Our school would be self-funded for another year.

Notice of rescheduling Phoebe's language proficiency exam also appeared. Keeping Phoebe calm for this one silly measure of her future potential faded. She would be eight when the exams were next scheduled in January, still one of the younger children tested.

For the first time since his arrival, I had access to Andrew's Bureau academic and testing records. Clarissa Smithson's portrayal of Andrew as a not bright enough intellectual elite offspring bothered me. Children of professional citizens weren't tested and scrutinized like the intellectual elite, but also missed opportunities to attend the best schools.

Nothing in Andrew's file justified Clarissa's belief. His early testing profile resembled Noah's with high potential in math and foreign languages. He was among the youngest students across the nation to pass the language proficiency exam. Except for poor grades in the months following his father's death, my son certainly held his own among his peers.

Chapter Twenty-Three

Instead of looking forward to the distraction of our kids during that lunch that day, I steeled myself for what could be awkward with Noah and Phoebe eating their meal with Hajar. Sarah stayed in the kitchen to supervise production of the morning's harvest. I hoped to hide my distress by asking Terrell for a picnic lunch that John, Andrew, and I could eat outside.

Under a cluster of maple trees at the edge of the residence's courtyard, we sat with plates of sandwiches, cheese slices, fruit, and cookies. I studied their faces, noticed small similarities, as John asked questions about living in the city. With little experience of life outside the estates region, Noah and John believed the metro streets were filled with dangerous people and weapons.

Andrew's first sandwich disappeared faster than I thought possible. I watched him look at the platter. Without speaking, I pushed it his way. He bit into his second serving more slowly. I suspected he might never have tasted homemade strawberry jam.

"The boys can't wait until they are able to spend a few nights in Minneapolis." I took control of the conversation to give Andrew opportunity to talk about himself. "I'm more curious about how your first morning of classes felt?"

"Okay."

"Teacher Jason says Andrew can probably speak any language at all, like Chinese."

"John, we should hear about the morning from Andrew."

"Sorry, Mom." John grabbed apple slices. "I bet this isn't like city schools."

Andrew swallowed milk, licked his lips. "Ashwood is more like the Philadelphia gifted school. I didn't do well in the Minneapolis gifted school after I moved." He offered no excuses, no mention of losing his father or his home. He just stated a fact and reached for fruit.

"I was a teacher, so each week the kids and I review learning plans. Sometimes I can be helpful with homework. And you should feel free to ask any of the teachers for help right away. Don't wait until you're lost."

Andrew nodded as he finished his apple. "Thanks. I'm pretty responsible."

"My dad does homework checks." John chimed in.

"Okay." Andrew offered the word without enthusiasm. "Whatever you want."

"You need a few days to settle in. Then you and I and Teacher Jason will talk about your learning program." I moved cookies across the table, pleased to see both boys' hands extend. "Maybe the beginning of next week?"

With young child curiosity, John stopped eating as Andrew examined the sugar cookie in his hands but didn't respond to my question. Never meaning to make our newest family member uncomfortable, I impulsively stretched an arm around his shoulders.

"We'll take it one day at a time." I wanted to feel him lean into my arm, but was satisfied that he did not pull away or stiffen. "My lesson planning for the rest of the day is that you should eat two cookies." I eased my arm away. "And I give you full permission to tell your little brother to back off if he asks too many questions."

"I can do that, Anne." Andrew picked out a second cookie. John giggled.

"Let's get the two of you back to work." I piled them with empty plates. "We're lucky to have an all-day school that meets gifted kids' needs so you don't have to do remote learning." David and I committed personal resources to keep the program acceptable to the Bureau so Phoebe and Noah could be educated at Ashwood."

We carried everything back to the kitchen. With the boys returning to school and Phoebe with Dr. Frances, I spent a long afternoon alone, even taking an uncomfortable nap at my temporary desk. Tired of reports and quiet, I visited the greenhouses, fields, gardens, and barns. Eventually Milan paged me for a meeting with Hajar to go over the ad litem requirements. Milan was kind, but the restrictions on my parental decisions for Phoebe and Noah were fixed in Bureau protocol.

Milan, Hajar, and Dr. Frances joined us for dinner that evening, requiring a larger table. I asked Teacher Jason to fill in the last chair, yet even with his positive energy, our family's stress showed in subdued conversation and quiet children.

Hajar had become a strong woman with a kind smile and a dry sense of humor who could talk to the children about life in Miami, New York, and Paris. She spoke French with Andrew and Phoebe, admired an art project by John, and found a way to thaw Noah's cool behavior.

Our children loved having Milan in residence, treating him like an uncle willing to appreciate their childish stories. Tonight they talked about the past twenty-four hours. Andrew answered questions politely, but didn't volunteer information. John and Noah became anxious when Sarah left to prepare for an evening with Paul.

The doctor remained aloof throughout dinner. From where I sat I could watch her observe our family, and she could watch me. We both looked like we had worked a long day.

"Mom, Dr. Frances told me that I'm not going to take the language exam next week," Phoebe lobbed across the table. "Why didn't you tell me?"

Silence followed the question. The children looked my way, Noah and John showing the normal apprehension that can develop when a sibling challenges a parent." Andrew absorbed the exchange. The doctor looked interested.

"I made that decision, Phoebe," Milan volunteered. "I want all of you to stay on Ashwood for the next weeks."

Phoebe drew herself up, spine straight and tall for a mere seven-year-old. She put one hand flat on the table, appeared to be thinking. All eyes watched.

"It's just that there are a lot of new adults here," she said. Her voice, while friendly and informative, held a wary note. "There's always lots of gossip on the estate." She nodded toward her brothers. "Noah and John and I expect to hear about important things through our parents." A smile and a dimple appeared. Raising her hand from the table, she smoothed back hair dangling in her eyes. "With everything so upside down, we need to hear things from our Mom."

Noah and John nodded in agreement.

"No offense." Phoebe settled back in her chair. "You're all very nice people. We're just a bit traumatized."

Adult faces remained frozen.

"Anne," started Andrew, "has been really straight with me. This whole guardian thing shouldn't have been started just 'cause of a last night. My father would have said that was kicking the dog because the horse ran away."

"I do apologize, Phoebe." Dr. Frances kept her comments brief. "I thought you knew of the decision. I would not mean to dishonor your mom."

Hajar led us out of the discussion. "No one wants to come between you and your mom, kids." Her tone showed respect for their concern. "We adults will have to be more careful about coordinating our actions. You're right, Andrew, about Ms. Anne. She is straight with others."

The kids' posture eased. "Do you think Cook Terrell might have real dessert tonight because we have visitors?" Noah asked. "And it's been a hard day. Real dessert might give us energy to finish our school work."

"Maybe we could take dessert to Grandpa?" John cut through our small laughter.

"Let me check with DOE security. If they agree, we'll do that," I suggested. "We'll eat it in my big office." Stepping into the hall, I sent a request to Peterson's people, waited for fifteen minutes without an answer. Rejoining the family group I pulled Milan aside to tell him about the delay and my plan to walk over. Aware I was going against Lao's earlier warnings not to face Peterson alone, I activated an open channel on my wrist communicator en route.

At the DOE entrance, I punched my code into the security register. A guard, another stranger, watched. He put me through all clearance processes available in our small facility from simple questions to an iris scan, a finger-prick blood test, and a complete wand scan. Eventually the door slid open.

Inside every light was lit, strictly against energy conservation practice when the sun still provided decent lighting. At least thirty people crammed the compact space, with additional data pads set up on tabletops and counters. Peterson sat behind my desk. Like Alice in Wonderland falling down the rabbit hole, I made my way through the chaotic scene to the place that had my sanctuary, the first office in my life that had a name plaque on the door and a chair built for my comfort.

"What difference a day makes, Colonel Peterson." I didn't stop at the door, but walked straight into the room. "From a small communications team managing DOE-related information about the disappearance of David's team to something much grander." He ignored me. I rested my hands on the back of a visitor's chair, remembered choosing the wood with David, felt strengthened by that memory. "I would think a tall man like you might fit another chair and desk better than mine."

"Manager Hartford, if you have nothing important to say, I'm busy." Peterson still didn't look up. "Do you want your husband back, or your office kept tidy?" At this point he raised his head, cool eyes looking quickly beyond me. Dismissed my presence.

"Tell me what your people are doing in this building." Milan's counsel slipped beneath my anger.

"If this is about the having-dessert-with-grandpa question, you can see children don't belong here." He pulled his head slightly to one side as if communicating with two women who approached my office door. "If you want to speak with Paul, you can be escorted to the lower level, where he is currently restricted."

"This is my office." And I'm used to being acknowledged, I wanted to add.

He pulled an unfamiliar pair of glasses from the top drawer of my desk, put them on while looking at me. "The U.S. government requirements supersede a small property owner's whine."

"Perhaps in your squad you feel powerful enough to speak disrespectfully to others. I am not part of your squad. I am a significant property owner in the state of Minnesota." I closed the office door, activated a special lock David designed. "By now you must know we have figured out who you are and have some questions about whether you should be anywhere near Ashwood." As his head came up, I regretted letting my frustration override Milan's warnings.

Peterson pressed a button on his communication wristband in response. The two women moved toward the door.

"You can share a room with your father-in-law," Peterson said as he stood. He pushed me aside, twisted the handle. The door did not open. He twisted it again, pulled at the handle.

The latch served as a prototype for the handle of our main residence safe room. Although I was now locked inside my office with the enemy, the simple device also gave me a few minutes of delay.

"Christ sake," he muttered as he continued working at the lock. "You won't smile when you lose those kids."

"I can assure you I'm not smiling now, Captain Peterson." I stood back a distance from the energy he wasted on the door handle. "It has been a horrible eighteen hours since someone sabotaged our residence's security system and a member of your team was apprehended outside our door with a camera in the middle of the night. Unless you are a parent you have no idea of the stress my children are under because of your actions. Believe me, no one is smiling."

He turned, looked past me, and moved toward the guest chair's partner. His large hands settled around the back. He raised it, began a small backward swing. Somehow my right hand caught one of the chair's legs and we struggled. With a thrust, Peterson shoved the chair legs into my chest, and I fell backward like a lioness warded away from escape.

As I dropped toward the floor I saw the chair crash through the half-windowed interior wall. My head cracked against the side of my solid oak conference table before I landed on one elbow then bounced to my back. The sounds of glass shattering and people screeching deadened the sound of head smacking wood. Loud security alarms blared, would continue to blare until circuits in the window casement were deactivated. I believed Lao's team would be here in minutes and stayed quiet.

"Security," Peterson bellowed. "Get in here and take her downstairs to hold with the other prisoner." The door remained unopened. "Crawl in through this window. Quit gawking."

I heard a man yell for something to cover the window's jagged glass edge. With my desk running along the inside half wall, jumping from outside the office to inside meant walking on sensitive data transmission equipment that was already compromised. I remained still, forcing Peterson's man to assess the impact of my fall before finding a way to transport me out of the office.

"Turn off the damn alarms." Peterson came close, extended a hand. He turned his head and yelled louder. "I want that alarm off in five seconds." Looking back my way, he bent far enough for his hand to come within inches of mine. "On your feet."

Pictures of civil disobedience came to mind. Peterson could have his people carry me across the office, through the window frame. Angry, frightened, my chest beginning to ache, I decided to not move.

"Captain, we need you in debrief." A young male voice projected from the outer office. "Code yellow, sir."

"Whatever fantasy you have in your mind about causing a delay, add that you could be responsible for your husband's death if I am not able to answer that call." Peterson's voice now sounded as rough as loose gravel in a wood box. "Don't be a fool, woman."

Behind his words alarms still blared, lights began a rhythmic flashing. If Peterson's team had not destroyed the building's security system, Lao knew the tricks needed to gain access. I chose not to believe Peterson's threat about David. We were in a standoff.

One of Peterson's men stepped onto my desk, cracked the frame of my family photo, and broke my heart with the snap of that inexpensive twenty-year-old item bought at a discount store as a gift for my mother. I rolled to my side, surprised at the pain in my chest.

"Once I'm out, move her." Peterson turned, speaking into his communication device, stepped on the remaining visitor chair and then the desk, and jumped over the jagged window edging. The man in camouflage approached, eyes with as much warmth as ball bearings.

Years of practicing karate with Lao were about to be tested as I prepared to kick up with one foot into the man's groin. I waited for him to reach my side, to bend toward me. I brought my leg up, my foot engaging with its soft target. I prepared to roll away. He grabbed my ankle, held me suspended, dragged me out from under the table. With my energy centered in the core of my body, I twisted. He turned my ankle sharply. For the first time I screamed, not voluntarily.

"Ready to move on your own?" he asked in a nasal-dominated voice out of sync with the combat clothes and overdeveloped body.

"Let go of my foot." My voice came out hoarse. The sentence ended with a groan. He released and stepped back, this time out of my reach. I slowly managed the downward movement of my leg, knew as I tried aligning my foot that I was injured. As he watched, I sat up. My ankle would not support my weight, so I maneuvered onto my knees and hands. "I can't get up on my own."

He extended his forearm, strong as a steel beam and almost as inhuman. "You're bleeding," he said, pointing toward my chest with his chin.

"Your captain hit me with a chair." I made it to my feet, a beaten captive in the place designed to keep me safe. "Who are you people?"

"We're here to keep the nation safe. Sometimes civilians don't understand." He swept a hand toward my head. I flinched, tried to duck. "You have glass in your hair. Stand still."

Closing my eyes, I let him ruffle my hair, but brought up my arm as his hands moved lower. "I'll do that myself," I said. From the reception area a half dozen of Peterson's people looked into the office. Their faces told me all were not comfortable with the sight of a United States resident, on her own land, experiencing rough treatment. Bits of safety glass fell while I patted myself. As I tried to step forward, everything from my toes to leg throbbed. "Oh, man, I think you broke my ankle." In my head a buzzy feeling began eating at my balance.

The man with arms of steel picked me up, making a small sound of exertion, somewhat more careful in front of an audience. He carried me to the window, passed me to another uniformed man. "If you put an arm around my neck, you'll be more comfortable," my new carrier said politely as if he were transporting an accident victim.

"My chest hurts." The feeling of last night's blackout returned. I fought to stay conscious.

"She needs medical evaluation," he called to his peers.

"Just dump me in the passageway. Be reasonable." I thought how frightened the children would be when I hobbled into the residence.

"Downstairs."

How much more frightened they would be when I didn't return at all.

"Tell me why you're placing me under arrest. I'm entitled to know that."

"I'm just following orders, ma'am."

Each step jarred my chest. My dangling injured ankle banged against my other foot. I waited for Lao or Milan or someone to stop Peterson. When we reached the lower level, he placed me on a chair. Another chair was shoved across the tile for my foot. Paul came out of an office.

"Annie." His voice rumbled under the alarms. He muscled Peterson's Special Forces man aside. "Annie, what have they done to you?"

His beloved face provided temporary comfort, a false sense of protection against the man upstairs. "I guess I slowed down Captain Peterson," I said. "The guy who did this to my ankle told me sometimes civilians don't understand what has to be done to keep the nation safe."

"You're bleeding."

"Peterson hit me in the chest with a chair leg and I crashed into my oak table." I didn't sugarcoat the truth with Paul, knew my father-in-law to be tougher than just about anyone. "I can't walk on it." I swallowed a low groan and blew air out my nose.

"Get her medical attention." Paul bellowed. "The cook is fully trained. Bring Terrell here."

"He's not cleared in this perimeter, sir," my carrier said. "We'll take care of necessary treatment." He stepped away. "I need to return to my post." He left, locking the door to the stairs.

Before his footsteps stopped, I activated my communication band, waited for Lao or someone to answer. Heard only a buzz. For the first time I knew the vulnerability of Ashwood without Lao's team.

Chapter Twenty-Four

"Sarah will arrive soon," Paul said as we sat alone in the office building basement. "Communications are down, but when I talked with her earlier she promised to be here around seven with decent food."

A half hour later, if I knew what to do, I would have volunteered to disarm the alarms myself. My foot and ankle showed the start of discoloration. The only cooling pack Paul found in a lab first aid box covered a very small section of the injury. My chest seared each time I took in a deep breath or tried to shift on the chair.

Aware that Peterson's people could be listening to our conversation, we talked about the day's happenings with me skirting the prior night's security breach and the arrivals of Dr. Frances and Hajar. While Paul reported news of the day's harvest, I forced myself to think beyond my injuries. His serious recital of acres and bushels meant nothing when I wanted to know what was happening in Lao's office.

Another half hour passed without Sarah. My head hurt, or maybe the pain was spread throughout my body and I chose to focus on the egg forming at the back of my skull. "Paul, I need to lie down," I said when the discomfort settled into a significant snare drum beat between my head and my toes. "Can you help me move?"

"Join your hands and put them around my neck." Paul bent toward me, wrapped his arms around my back, and helped me stand. "Let go, but lean on me." I listened, trusting his strength and wisdom. "No weight on that foot."

I hobbled next to him to an empty cot Peterson's people had placed in a darkened office. Easing into its wobbly bedding proved more difficult. Paul helped me settle then left and returned with a book and towel to elevate my foot.

"Sarah's not coming," I said. "We're truly prisoners. Of war, Peterson claimed."

"He's dangerous, and that isn't my amateur opinion."

"I don't think it's a coincidence that he is holding David and us captive."

"You could be right." Paul carefully pushed one hand through my hair, shook his head, his eyebrows drawn close together. "How's your head? Could be a concussion."

"I'm kind of worried about that. I feel nauseated, but my vision's okay."

"You should try to sleep."

"I'd rather you brought in a chair and talked with me."

Paul got down on his knees, a life of physical activity making the action still possible for a man his age. He hauled a folding chair out from under the cot and opened it. Even with the natural thickening of age, he still looked tall and lean, particularly to someone lying on her side on a low surface. "Assholes said they'd have someone down here to look at you over an hour ago. I'll try the communication system again," he grumbled.

As he walked out of sight, the room seemed to shrink. I wondered if Peterson would hesitate to kill two civilians while commanding his self-made war. I had experienced starvation, assault, loss, but never had I been a prisoner. In Peterson's cat-and-mouse games, Paul and I were small animals running in a stainless steel cage. I pressed my wristband and bit my lip to hold back tears as the screen remained dark.

"Don't think too much," Paul said as he walked back into the room. "They're blocking our systems. The one advantage we have is that everyone in the residence knows exactly where we are." He didn't sit down, instead folded up the chair.

"I'm going to move the other cot in here for the night if you don't mind. Sarah and I tried to sleep that way last night." He left again, the light dimming even more.

In the near dark, Paul returned. He dropped blankets and a pillow near me and set up his cot. The space, designed as a small office, accommodated the two cots with barely enough room to stand.

"Paul, I'm sorry, but before we settle, could you help me get to the bathroom?" Independent to the bone, I floundered to get up without his assistance, but Paul lifted the bedding and had me on my feet as if I were a grandchild. "Thanks, I'm sorry about all of this."

"Nothing to be sorry about. Best we get moving before the lights go out," he said close to my ear. "Didn't David tell me you get spooked by the dark?"

"I'm embarrassed to admit it." Both feet on the floor, I exhaled. "I may as well tell you that if they shut down the air circulation system, I'll get claustrophobic, too." His strong arms steadied me.

"I found this cane in a workstation." Paul slipped the curved wooden head into my hand. "Lean on me and see if it helps."

"There was a visiting geologist here last year who had a broken foot. Thank God he left this," I said as I embraced the satisfying feel of a potential weapon. I left the bathroom door open for light as I awkwardly used the toilet and then washed up. Leaning against a hallway wall, I waited for Paul to have time in the washroom. The lights continued dimming. My new cane displayed bands of illuminating material.

Keeping my action out of sight of monitors while I waited for Paul, I pressed my wristband. An emergency code appeared and then faded. I rapped near the bathroom door with the cane.

"Give me a minute," Paul answered. Leaning against the wall, I turned my wrist only enough to see if the code would return. When the code flashed, I felt connected to the outside world. "Do you need to get back in here?" he asked as he emerged.

"Sorry," I said. "I'm jumpy." He put an arm around my waist and I twisted closer than necessary in order to give him view of my band's screen.

"Move back, Annie, or I'll mash your other foot," Paul growled, but nodded slightly as he directed us back to the room with two cots. "You could turn the lights up, you knuckleheads," he said to unseen monitors. We moved cautiously past office furniture. Paul picked up a water bottle from one desk.

Settling in the cot's mesh sling in the dark, bruises stiffening, was even more difficult this time. I swallowed a small yelp while I rolled into the most bearable position. Paul elevated my foot, drew up the blanket. The lights went out. "Let's put your cane where you can see it." He turned the light strip upward.

In the blackened space I listened to Paul settle himself, saw the faint shape of my father-in-law's head on a pillow near mine. Under my blanket I pressed at my communication band, heard nothing. Paul's hand touched mine as I lifted the blanket, hoping for the tiny brightness of lit letters.

"Sarah has always prayed in the dark. Says she finds peace doing that." Paul's hand gently held mine. "Me, I find I can walk the fields behind my closed eyelids and really see what needs to be done in the morning. Without all the visuals and voices, it's like the soil can show itself." His calloused fingers made a small dome above my palm. "What are you thinking about, Annie?"

"David." I worried about the children, about Sarah, about what Peterson might do in the morning, but David held my thoughts. "I wonder where he is, how he is."

"Let's hope he's as comfortable as we are. If he was here, nobody could hold him back from dealing with Peterson."

"I keep thinking about how much pain he felt when they removed his tracking chip and how easy infection might start in the jungle." Tears threatened. I swallowed. We were both quiet. "I'm not giving up hope that he will come back. But I know life will go on if he doesn't return and that's what scares the hell out of me."

I heard people speak of entering a zombie-like state when they experienced losing a loved one. I wasn't that lucky when my first husband passed and have memories of sitting on the floor through long nights, holding his beloved navy sweater as if it could warm my cold arms. I remember feeling like part of my future was thrown into history. When I arrived at Ashwood, I was a person almost without emotion—more of an automaton, not a zombie.

Paul's voice, soft as the fur on a puppy's head and thick as spring syrup, whispered across the distance. "How bad is that ankle?"

His question, asked with such emotion, caught me by surprise. "Probably as bad as yours when you slipped off the porch. Not that I wouldn't appreciate ice and a few aspirin, but this isn't the absolute worst pain I've felt."

"What would that be?" Emotion back in control, I thought Paul might be pushing conversation as a distraction.

Do I tell my father-in-law about the awful trauma of long-ago sexual assault or do I steer to more commonly understood injuries? "David told you about how I had ribs broken in that transport explosion. This chest bruise is kind of like that. It hurts when I move or breathe."

"When David was a little boy, he got too close to the wrong side of a cow that was in for milking. I saw her hoof go up and grabbed for the kid." Paul made a small snorting sound. "Took one to the side of my neck. Thought I was going die there. That was pain."

"Well, we could talk about giving birth, if you want to swap pain stories."

He laughed, short and not like the great guffaws Paul often let roll. "You women always drag out childbirth. Got to say I wouldn't want to try it."

"I wonder what the kids are doing." I peeked at my communication band again, saw the number eight show, then disappear. Sarah would be putting the children to bed. Phoebe would be nervous, suspicious about my absence. Noah and John might be frightened. And Andrew might be worried about losing this home if another parent disappeared.

"Sometimes it helps Sarah relax if I hum." Paul cleared his throat. "Would you like that?"

The thought made me smile. Paul's choice of songs might include country-westerns from thirty years earlier or random melodies drawn from worship services. I'd heard him calm the kids, quiet himself while he was working on equipment, fill the air as he walked a field. Gently I squeezed his hand, then extracted mine to be able to shift on the cot. "If you'd like to hum, go ahead."

He pulled his hand back across the narrow space between us, rolled to his back, and cleared his throat. I couldn't name the song he butchered, but his bass tones did have a comforting effect.

I rested one hand over the communication band on my other wrist, not mentioning the pulses that signified Lao's people were trying to break through the firewall installed by the Peterson crew. Four quick pulses followed by a long vibration, an emergency code queried if I was safe. Under the cover, I pressed the answer key three times, three quick jabs, signaling that we needed help.

Lights came on in the outer hall.

"Food or water for either of you?" The young man who had carried me down the stairs appeared with a jug of water and sandwiches. "We won't be down again until after the morning broadcast."

We blinked at him, vulnerable as fish out of water, stranded on our cots.

"I gotta have your wristband, General Manager Hartford." He approached my side. "And the captain wants you in separate rooms." He extended a hand toward me. I worked at the band's latch. One part of his mission complete, he turned to Paul. "I'll move your things, sir."

"I can't leave my daughter-in-law alone. She requires medical attention. That ankle means she can't get up on her own." Paul rolled to his side, then stood easily.

Our visitor looked puzzled at Paul's protest. He lifted the blanket up over my feet, saw the swelling.

"My chest is bothering me more," I volunteered. "Hurts to move, even hurts when I breathe."

"I'll see what I can do." He dropped the blanket. "Let me help you up for your meal."

I waved him away. "I ate a large dinner with my children."

"You have to eat." He bent down, his arms extended as if to scoop me up. "The lights are going off after I leave, so this is your opportunity."

Paul approached, stood close to the man's side. "Leave her be. Neither of us needs food or water right now."

Our captor's representative straightened. "I can't take that upstairs with me. Captain Peterson gave very clear directions that you were to eat."

"Remind the captain that he's on a farm," Paul said, "and we're fond of that old expression that you can lead a horse to water, but you can't make it drink."

"You'll sleep better if you eat at least a few bites." The young man delivered these words with a stillness that suggested caution.

"Take the tray and get out of here." Paul picked up the tray, shoved it into the guard's chest.

Biceps showing through snug fabric, he accepted the tray, then put it down on a work surface. "I have to relocate one of you, sir. Perhaps we should help General Manager Hartford to the restroom and move the cots."

"Not going to happen." Paul folded his arms over his chest, stood close to the guard. "My daughter-in-law needs medical care and assistance. She could have a concussion from cracking her head on that conference table. Medical protocol says observation for the first twelve hours." He swayed onto his heels. "I'm not medically trained, but I've cared for a few guys with concussions in my days."

"Paul, we can't send this soldier upstairs with none of his mission accomplished." I propped myself up as far as possible. "A helping hand to the restroom is fine. But Paul is right that I need someone close tonight. I'm a bit nauseated and dizzy. If you move that cot, my father-in-law will drag it back after you leave."

I accepted the strength of the guard's arm to stand up, then hobbled at his side to the bathroom. Once I was finished, I splashed water onto my face and looked into the mirror as I dried my hands. Except for a pale face, all looked normal from the neck up. I patted my head to feel the bump, pulled down my T-shirt to inspect the ugly abrasion and bruising below my breastbone. If we got out of here, I wanted revenge. I opened the door.

Paul and the guard stood talking about South Dakota, the young man speaking animatedly about his parents' place near Brookings and his days at South Dakota State University before he joined the Marines.

"I'll let you help her back while I use the facilities," Paul said. He made an odd hand motion, like smoothing a blanket over a child, that the guard could not see. I took it to mean I should fuss, delay my helper.

The jolt of pain accompanying a purposeful stumble nearly brought me to my knees. "Holy crap," I muttered, now fully aware that the ankle bone was connected to a lot of other bones and tendons and nerves and muscles. My hand tightened on the guard's arm. He held steady, waited until I could take another step.

"No pain meds down here?" He looked toward the empty lab. "I thought labs always had good first aid kits."

"That's where we found the small cold pack. My father-in-law raided the pain meds last night for his arthritis." We took a few more steps, me holding onto his arm as if I was an old woman walking on ice. "I'm worried about the pain when I breathe." I touched my shirt above the bruise, "This needs more attention than my ankle."

With strong but gentle hands, the young man helped me lower myself back to the cot. He moved the pillow, grabbed Paul's blanket, and rolled it to fill the space to keep my foot elevated.

"I'll report on that bruise upstairs, ma'am. I think it is more painful than physically threatening, but I'm sure it makes moving uncomfortable."

"If you'd like to feel my head, Paul is right that I hit it hard against the table." I closed my eyes. "Maybe that's why I feel so disoriented." The lie slipped out easily. "I didn't even think of concussion."

"You didn't tell me you were disoriented." Paul waited at the door. "I'm not leaving this room." He wiped his hands down his pants leg. "Changed my mind and had one of those sandwiches. Heavy on the mayo."

Not happy, the guard carried the tray with him. Paul sat on the edge of his cot and the lights went off. Anxiety tweaked my mind as I lost sight of him.

"Want me to start humming again?" Paul asked with a teasing tone.

"No, thanks." I closed my eyes against the darkness. Sarah would go silent at such times and we knew she dug into her deep spiritual belief for comfort. Because her faith was so organic, we gave her free rein to share with our kids, even asked her to lead the state-mandated weekly spiritual sessions now and then. But rock-solid belief in God was a part of Sarah's natural goodness. My own spirituality shattered during the depression and redeveloped in a fractured set of beliefs that teetered between knowing that God existed and wondering why God treated people so inhumanely.

In the darkness, with fear surpassing pain, I remembered Sarah's simple prayers for strength, for patience, for wisdom. This basement space could withstand tornados, operate independently of the estate power grid, maintain structural integrity under insane conditions. Paul and I would not escape. So I prayed for the safety of my children and my husband. I tacked on one for Paul and me to find strength to outlast Peterson's siege. And under those prayers for help, I remembered to add words of thanksgiving for all David and I had built in these Ashwood years.

Paul thrashed around on his side of the room, the creaking of his cot breaking my meditation. The smell of warm ham added to the odors of two bodies in a space never ventilated for sleeping adults. I thought the sandwich had passed through Paul's system quickly, wondered if they fed him tainted meat.

"Sorry, Annie," Paul whispered. I sensed him leaning across the space between our cots. "When I tucked that sandwich down my pants I didn't think ahead to where I'd put it after that guy left. I think it's laced with something. We'll have it tested when we get out of here."

"You're a wonderful optimist," I whispered back.

From the sounds I knew Paul was climbing out of his cot. "So are you, Annie my dear, so are you. I got to find someplace to stash this thing." He stood. "Be brave," he said just inches from my head. "I'll be back in a minute. If I don't come back, send out the dogs."

For an older man, Paul moved with impressive silence through the white noise now filling the lower level. I fought anxiety by counting backwards from one thousand.

"I'm here," he said, leaning close as I finished the three hundreds. "Doing okay?"

"You're a wonderful man," I answered.

He moved his cot closer to mine then settled, this time for the night. I felt the love as he extended a hand over my arm. Near tears, I thanked God for Paul. Over a decade ago I sat through the longest night waiting for my mother to take her last breath. Through ten hours of nighttime labor I struggled for Andrew to be born. But held in this place with no light or clock or glimpse into the other world, I prepared to experience what could be the worse night of my life.

Chapter Twenty-Five

MY SCREAMS WOKE US UP SOMETIME DURING what I wanted to think of as the tail end of night. My sleep consisted of a mixture of pain, fear, and dreams of Phoebe searching through ashes for her parents. My fear of the dark seemed like the lesser evil than the dreadful emotions unleashed during my sleep.

Paul's hand applied a calming pressure on my arm. I listened for his breathing and slowed mine to meet his rhythm.

"Do you need to use the bathroom?" His voice sounded thick, coated with slumber. "Would it help you settle if we walked around?"

"In the dark?"

"It's not absolutely black in the labs." Paul spoke slowly, the voice of a man who drank coffee sixteen hours a day. "A few still have active equipment with monitor lights. I even know where we can find a clock."

"Okay." Almost any place beyond our small, dark quarters sounded attractive. I tried extending my legs, started with the injured left ankle. Anticipating stiffness, I pushed myself upright and felt pain move through my body like a steel ball in an old arcade game, lighting nerve endings up and down my spine. My foot jammed against his cot.

"Paul." His name came out in a wavy, weak squeak. "I'm not doing very well."

"Sit still." The suggestion was easy to follow. "You're lucky I'm seventy, not eighty, or I'd never be able to get my body out of this damn bed." I heard much creaking from the cot as Paul moved.

The hand that touched my arm was strong, but too small to be my father-in-law's. "Shhh, Anne" sounded as I blurted "Paul" out loud. Another hand came over my mouth. A familiar scent of Ashwood-made soap reached my nose even as my lips prepared to separate and bite the unknown skin. "It's Lao, Annie-Panny."

The code Lao and I put into place years ago sounded like music. Paul stumbled across us as he bent downward. Hearing wasn't his strongest sense. "What the hell," he growled.

I pulled him close to my face, "Lao's here, Paul."

His hand extended as Lao's arm came up to showing an active communication device.

"I'll be damned," Paul whispered. "Answer to Sarah's prayers."

Lao, crouched on the floor, updated his team. We stayed quiet, barely breathing, until he gathered us in a tight circle.

"Can you crawl, Anne?" he whispered. "Can you pull yourself across the floor on your arms?"

To get out of the building I would make my body do anything. "I'll manage," I said.

"We've deactivated lower sensors throughout this level giving us three feet from the floor for movement."

His hands moved across my back, and down my ribs as he talked. "We'll head for a dead-end ventilation trunk that leads to the residence." I flinched as he touched a tender area near my waist. "I'm going to put a numbing patch here. You'll move easier."

I heard the slightest swish of packaging removed and then felt gentle hands pat my back.

"How is your chest? Need another patch? Don't be a hero. We'll need to move fast."

"Open it and I'll put it in place." My hands shook, but the patch stuck. Lao wound a wristband on Paul, then one on me, and tied light rope around our waists. My lower-back pain began easing. I wondered what kind of medical patches we stocked at Ashwood.

"I will go first, then Anne, then Paul. Stay flat, move carefully. Turn left as we leave this room. Crawl toward the first lab station. Paul, you know that place?" Paul whispered yes. "In that station, under the long wall table, there is a panel. I'll open it, then we'll crawl through. Anne first, me last."

Paul and Lao helped me to the floor. Muscles protested, my lower back clenched in a spasm, but the rope tightened as Lao crawled ahead. On the flats of my arms, hands in fists, I moved. My left ankle was like an anchor and I tried holding it slightly off the floor. Keeping up with Lao's steady pace demanded concentration. The warmth of Paul's breath hovered over my heels.

The rope went slack. I stopped. Lao tugged. I moved forward cautiously. "There are turns ahead. Hold my foot." He started forward, I grabbed at his foot, felt Paul touch my good ankle. In the dark, I sensed Lao's changes of direction, tried to stay aligned.

David and I once played a child version of Dungeons and Dragons in this space with the kids. John fearlessly hid anywhere his little body fit. Phoebe always wanted to be the one searching. While I concentrated on Lao's movements, I tried to remember that game to place where we crawled. Suddenly I recognized the odd chemical smell Jason and I encountered when we explored this space as a possible study hall. Long tables were bolted to the wall some thirty feet ahead. Small lights glimmering in active stations.

Lao stopped. I heard the sound of a metal grate being moved. He tugged on the rope and I crawled alongside him. With one hand, he tapped at my wristband. With the other, he removed the rope around my waist.

"You first into the vent." Lao spoke into my ear, his voice light and fast like the sound of a bug's wings. "The space is two feet high and three feet wide. You will slide feet first for a distance. Do not make any sounds. People are waiting to catch you at the bottom."

"How much of a fall, Lao?" My hand searched for his arm, for his strength.

"Stop thinking. Just do." Awkwardly I squirmed into position. He gave directions while helping me lift off the floor. "Hold your hands over your stomach."

Air of a different temperature cooled my bare feet. I hesitated and then obeyed Lao's command to not think, but to trust that this small, enclosed shaft would lead to freedom. I slid myself into the black hole, and suddenly the metal tilted downward and I shot toward an unknown landing.

Eyes closed, silent, I felt metal tear my clothes and nick my arm. My feet sank into a cushion, bad ankle forgotten with the overall jolting impact. Hands grabbed my arms, tumbled me from a giant bin of bedding, and eased me to the floor.

I blinked in the dim light, saw a half dozen uniformed marines. One protected the entrance to this space, others focused on the chute. I drew back against a wall, one hand protecting my chest, thoughts racing through everything that happened since hearing the voice I trusted to be Lao. No one else knew of my brother's childhood teasing name. We were either saved or doomed.

Paul landed with a grunt. I watched as the troops dumped him to the floor, with speed and care. Lao shot through the same space, an acrobat following two amateurs.

"You two." A tall female marine gestured our way to the landing box. "We need you back in here." Paul and one of our rescuers offered me assistance. "It's tight. Lie on your sides, close together." Adrenalin dominated reluctant muscles as I rose from the floor. Arms lifted me without words, set me down gently. I flopped onto my right side, swollen ankle resting on top. Paul followed, lowering himself behind me in classic spooning position. "We're going to put a lid on this box, then wheel it out of the building and across a drive. Stay quiet." She extended a cloth toward me. "Your right elbow is bleeding."

Paul grabbed the cloth, wrapped it around a nasty cut. "You're not going to squeeze Lao in here?" he joked.

She smiled. "We need him elsewhere." More blankets were tucked around our sides. "Don't look so scared, Manager Hartford," she said as they finished. "The worst is over for you."

They lowered the lid, encasing us in blackness. I closed my eyes, but the panic was too strong. "I can't breathe," I called and kicked the box.

Two marines lifted the lid. Dim light flowed back in.

"I can't breathe in here."

"You can breathe, Annie." Lao spoke from the side. "I will punch a hole here so you can have light, but there is air coming into the box through the sides." He poked a sharp tool through the container near my face. "Just fifteen minutes, Anne. Stay cool." The lid was lowered again.

Eyes closed, I felt Paul's arm loop over my side. Hating my weakness, I forced myself to think we were not in a coffin, but tucked into a large crib. The distraction lasted seconds until we began moving and the bedding absorbed only a minimal amount of the pulling and shifting. Once the box was settled on a wheeled vehicle, we swayed with its forward motion.

I knew Ashwood's buildings better than the contents of my dresser drawers. Twice a year Lao and I inspected every storage zone, production building, and tunneled walkway. The box carried us along a straight path before we were lifted and carried down a short flight of stairs. I bet myself we would see the residence laundry and sewing room when the crate opened. I was wrong.

Strong arms helped us out into the residence's lower-level food storage area. Coolers and freezers hummed, shelving for canned goods stood partially filled with this fall's harvest. Dr. Frances leaned against one wall, our residence medical bags at her feet. Terrell waited next to her. Two chairs, blankets, and a small table had been brought into the room. My legs quivered as I stood.

"Who smells like bad ham and mayo?" Terrell asked as he wrapped his arm around my waist.

"Me." Paul reached into his pants, pulled out a mashed sandwich. "Peterson's guy was so insistent we eat these that I got suspicious. You might want to test it."

"Paul, you're some man. The marines stage a magnificent rescue and you can't pass up bringing a sandwich home," Terrell joked. "Give that sandwich to the doctor while I help Annie."

Many chuckled in the room. Dr. Frances opened our medical kit, pulled on gloves, and extended a sterile container toward Paul for his sandwich. I noticed blood drip from the side of his hand. He noticed my attention. "Someone should have told the construction crew who installed that vent to cover screw ends so that people don't get hurt when they're sliding out of a building." He held his hand up to show the doctor his injury. "Is there something in the kit to cover this before Annie faints?"

"I'm fine." I forced strength into my voice. "Take care of Paul first." He tried to defer. "This is a time when age takes precedence, Paul." Dr. Frances turned from me.

"Are the children okay?" I asked, watching as she attached monitors to Paul's chest.

"Sarah and Hajar settled them for the night, Annie." Terrell wrapped a blanket around me. "Dr. Frances helped Phoebe with a little medication to take the edge off a possible anxiety attack. Your girl is sleeping with her grandma."

"I don't have the slightest idea what time it is."

"It's four-forty-five on Saturday morning." Lao pointed at his communication band and I remembered he had snapped one on my wrist. I felt for mine under the blanket. "You and Paul will stay here until the head of this squadron gives clearance. Ashwood is under military command."

Paul turned from Dr. Frances. "What will that do to the grain harvest?"

"We'll worry about that in the morning." Lao spoke with respectful authority.

Military command of Ashwood consumed my thoughts. It was unclear to me how these marines related to Peterson's marines. Were they here to protect us or extend his tyranny into our home? I watched Dr. Frances's actions, aware she could be working on any side in this curious situation.

My blanket dropped and as Terrell bent to pick it up, I leaned close. "Do my medical assessment."

He caught my insecurity, gestured toward the doctor. "That woman was the love of my life when neither of us knew where we'd find our next meal. She's good through and through." Dr. Frances's head popped up. "Don't you worry," he said and squeezed my shoulder.

He held the blanket for my privacy as Dr. Frances ran health monitor tests then examined my bruised chest. "A couple of inches lower and Captain Peterson would have a murder on his hands," she reported. She pressed forcibly near the site, deep discomfort breaking through Lao's pain patch. "Let's do a diagnostic image, but I think this is a deep tissue injury with a nasty laceration that needs sutures. There'll be a scar."

"It won't be my first." Her hands covered the rest of my chest and back. "Did you think you'd be practicing this kind of medicine when you studied psychiatry?" I asked in a clumsy effort to establish connection.

"Did you want to become a business manager when you went through student teaching?" Weariness gave her words an edge. "I'm better at my specialty for the years of delivering babies and taking care of people's bodies." She knelt. "Give me your injured foot." I extended my left leg in her direction. She twisted my foot one direction and then the other, felt along the muscles and tendons, stretched it toward her. "Bad sprain. Fairly high. Something to bring down the swelling is about all that can be done. Kind of a bully bruise."

Clammy sweat formed on my forehead as each bruised area responded to manipulation. "What's your assessment?" I lifted a shaky hand to wipe drops away.

"Let's start at the top." She handed me a wash cloth as she stood up, extended one hand and pulled down a finger with her other hand as she ran through her exam results. "Bad bump on the top of the head with your eyes having some difficulty following a light, which suggests a concussion. Probably give you headaches for some days. You'll need to curtail activities and give your brain time to heal." I knew the cautions about concussions, worried about being sidelined.

"We talked about the chest. You may have hyperextended your neck when you fell." She took a breath. "Deep muscle bruising in the lower back with spasms. Pain patches, hot packs for that. And that ankle." Leaning her head to one side, she slowed her voice. "Elevation and cold or hot packs for a few days. Ten to fourteen days of meds for pain and swelling. We'll go over all this again when you're ready, but the bottom line is there shouldn't be any long-term issues. Just a few painful weeks. Lots of rest."

Another doctor might have smiled. Dr. Frances finished with her diagnostic inventory and began recording the data. I fumbled with my shirt, my hands too shaky to manage fastners.

"Let me take care of that laceration before you bother with the shirt," she said, watching me while tapping on a datapad. "Your mother-in-law packed fresh clothes." I heard Terrell sharing the same information with Paul, who worried about leaving his favorite field boots back in the DOE basement.

Dr. Frances worked in silence. Looking beyond her head at Ashwood's produce coolers, I did the talking. "What can you tell me about Phoebe? I worried about her all night."

A needle jabbed under my chest skin with a slight burn then numbing. She turned to the medical kit, withdrew antiseptics and a butterfly suture. Quickly she cleaned the site and applied sutures.

"We'll talk when there's quiet." Now I felt gentleness in her hands. "You've had a rough twenty-four hours. Let me help you clean up before you put on fresh things. I'm going to give you both something to help you get a few hours of sleep." She held a number of tablets my way. "Anti-inflammatory, painkiller, and an anti-anxiety pill. We're not going to risk a true sleep aid with the military on site."

Marines rolled in the portable beds we used for sick bay. I took the pills I recognized, held the anxiety med, let her wipe me with a warm washcloth then help me dress.

"Is there's any news about David?" The doctor shrugged. "Before I rest I want a complete report on what's happening." I looked for Lao. "Would someone find Lao?"

"Marine Lieutenant Kapur, General Manager Hartford." A medium-tall man with overly developed biceps stepped forward. "Ma'am, we are off communications at this time to avoid information interception. I speak for the unified command."

Kapur had eyes like undiluted coffee and hair a shade darker. He wore his authority well, his voice projecting respect, intelligence, even kindness. It wasn't how Kapur carried himself that made me nervous. Taking advantage of the painkillers in my bloodstream, I sat as tall as I could and tried not to act like a prisoner in my beloved home.

"Thank you, Corporal Kapur." We looked into each other's faces. Used to an environment filled with managers closer to their forties and kids under university age, I was surprised by his young twenty-something appearance. "You don't need to stand so formally."

He shifted his stance, kept his hands behind his back. "Thank you, General Manager. Marines are closing in on the group holding Senior Research Director Regan and the remaining members of his team. There has been visual confirmation that they are alive."

"Hallelujah," Paul yelled and clapped his hands. "They're going to bring him home, Annie." He stopped walking the perimeter of the room to come over and give me a gentle hug, very gentle. He and Terrell exchanged high fives. I wondered about their naiveté, about how they could jump to the most optimistic conclusion when Kapur said nothing about David's health or the difficulties of rescuing him.

"What do you know about their condition?" In a clean room with all my injuries treated, I thought about David's possible wounds. "Did they look like they were moving on their own?"

"We have no specifics." I recognized bureaucratic-speak. "The three were sitting against trees and eating." He lowered his chin, his eyes made more readable from where I sat. "They wore military camouflage and were chained together."

They were being fed, they were resting. I stored away the positives. "Thank you. Now, please tell me what's happening on Ashwood."

"You'll have to trust us, General Manager Hartford." Kapur's posture became stiff once more. "This is an internal military operation unfortunately involving Ashwood. Chief Engineer Lao is operating under our orders as civilian representative for the estate. None of your family or staff are in danger."

"I disagree, Lieutenant Kapur." I managed to stand. "Look at me. Captain Peterson is waging a rogue operation from our offices. He and his troops are willing to endanger civilians."

He tipped his head. "You have the apologies of our commander. Full restitution will be made when this operation is completed."

"Lieutenant Kapur, you speak from a sense of military honor, but I don't think you can begin to calculate full restitution for a little girl who has been traumatized by her father's absence or for my husband who has spent days in captivity." I kept my hands quiet, my voice calm. "I assume the U.S. government will offer compensation to repair our property and cover medical care. But how will we restore our children's trust in this government?"

Members of Kapur's small squad stood with eyes focused on the wall behind me. They were like a poster of all that was admirable about the marines. "General Manager Hartford, your record is that of exemplary citizen known for supporting the U.S. government through very difficult times. I'm sure you are an excellent parent who will demonstrate the same for your children."

I guessed he wasn't a parent. He was early in his career and life experience. I had no quarrel with his loyalties, just the mess he represented.

"Does this operation involve our Giant Pines location?"

"No." He was back on tactical grounds. "We have a small patrol squad on that site as a precaution."

"Then I want my entire family evacuated to Giant Pines with generous security for the duration of this military operation. I want them out of here in a half hour and I want to see them leave." I turned to Paul. "Jack has space at Giant Pines. Do you agree?"

"That's an excellent idea. And I'd like to be with them," Paul added.

"Perhaps Dr. Frances has an opinion," I said.

"It wouldn't hurt to move the kids," she responded. "But let them wake up at their normal time. They'll need to know that you are safe and that they will be safe."

"Well, Lieutenant Kapur, could you run that proposal to your commander?" He considered, then gestured for one of his troops. I wanted to sit, but not while I negotiated control of our home. Kapur gave quick directions to the chosen man then sent him away.

"Sit." Dr. Frances touched my arm and gestured toward the chair. "It's painful to watch you stand on that ankle." Even the bare wood of a folding chair felt comfortable. Terrell cobbled together an assortment of crates and rugs to elevate my foot, wrapped a cold pack around the worst of the bruising. The doctor spoke to us as our guard watched from across the room. Paul rested on one of the beds, his face pale with fatigue. "Is there a place the children could be kept safe here if Giant Pines isn't an option?" she asked.

"Ashwood has a safe room," I said. "There's one at Giant Pines as well. Phoebe doesn't do well with our annual twenty-four-hour drills in it."

"I think you understand your daughter." Dr. Frances rubbed at her neck. "Terrell, you didn't say anything about how exciting estate life might be."

"Seems to me like this kind of excitement happens in a seven-year cycle around here," he answered. "I got to get upstairs for breakfast prep." He waved at us. "You and Paul stay out of the coolers. I'll bring you real food. Get some sleep."

I leaned my head back, careful to avoid the bump from last night's fall. "Hard to believe we were all sitting at dinner about twelve hours ago. Is Milan still here?"

She lifted her shoulders. "We stayed at the table with the kids until Lao sent for him. I didn't see him after that."

My eyes felt grainy, my head heavy. "It's generally pretty peaceful here. Believe me."

"I'm going to repack the medical kit. You should rest. That's what people do when they have a concussion."

I watched Dr. Frances reassemble portable monitors and take inventory of used disposable goods. Marines wandered in and out of the cooler. Paul, relaxed under his covers, fell asleep within minutes. I remained sitting.

"You didn't take all those meds, did you?" Her question carried no reprimand. "Your medical record shows no pharmaceuticals beyond vitamins, so I'll warn you that if you kept the anti-anxiety pill, don't take it unless you're ready to sleep."

"If I hadn't taken a sleeping aid that night, things might be different. I'll sleep when I know all my kids and our home are safe."

Dr. Frances shrugged, snapped a last packet shut. "We're all survivors, General Manager. We may have different ways to stay ahead of the flood."

She pulled one bag over her shoulder. "I'm here to help keep your family and its members intact. Terrell, who is one of your staunchest friends, was clear about that goal when we negotiated this arrangement." Her eyes surveyed the storage unit. "We'll get the rest of these things upstairs later. I'll tell all your children that you're banged up but will be fine."

After she left, I sat in the chair with my head leaning against a wall, too tense to really relax and too uncomfortable to walk off that tension. Almost two hours had passed since our escape. Military action was taking place on our estate and I was out of the information chain. Would our laborers be able to work in the fields, our kids have breakfast and go to school. The small details were less stressful than wondering if armed vehicles filled the courtyard or the awful possibility of innocent people being caught in this action.

Lieutenant Kapur returned to the cooler, appeared surprised to find me awake. "I know I'm supposed to be asleep in that other bed, but you can understand why I'm eager to go upstairs. Could we speak?"

He moved like a warrior, smoothly and quickly. "We should hear back soon."

"I'm asking for access to watch the estate monitors, not engage in communications. If you don't want me to feel like a prisoner in my home, then I need to see what's happening." He seemed unmoved by my request. "Corporal, I want to see my kids."

Kapur's runner returned. "The family evacuation request will be honored, sir." Neither looked my way.

"I hope that gives you some peace of mind, General Manager Hartford. I am needed outside. Corporals Smith and Rodriquez will remain on watch here." He prepared to leave. Briefly his eyes and voice gentled. "I trust you will be reunited in time to tuck your children into bed tonight." Nodding to Smith and Rodriquez, they stepped outside the room, closed the door.

I thought he was too optimistic. Paul remained asleep. I unlocked the security system cabinet and adjusted the screens to survey what could be seen of early morning. As images changed, I saw military transports parked among estate vehicles in an attempt to maintain a low profile. I watched Magda walking the outdoor vegetable garden acres with her partner, arms thrown open in broad gestures across the plants ready for harvest. Sarah appeared alone in the front sitting area, head bent. On another screen, Terrell directed house workers through a routine breakfast prep. Phoebe, dressed for the day, wandered into the kitchen as the screen changed.

I turned away, remembering the early days of the first pandemic when teachers and students were told to stay home. Watching twenty-four-hour news coverage obsessed me. Film of empty grocery stores and parks implied something menacing, still I watched. Ashwood's security screens went blank. Lost between memories and the present, I startled.

I pulled at the door handle to check with our guards about the system failure. At first the handle refused to move. I worked it hard. The tumblers moved, the handle slid, and the door opened. Paul's breathing hitched into a snoring sound.

Cautiously I hobbled out, unsure how the guards would respond. In the hall, lights flickered, turned to weak yellow as I looked past empty chairs. Weak yellow dimmed to a glow just a shade brighter than a child's nightlight. I knew the power grid drill, began counting to forty-five while returning to my father-in-law.

"Paul, wake up." I shook his shoulder. A great shuddery sound came from his mouth. My count passed thirty. Our emergency generator system would target this room for early power restoration. "Paul, please wake up."

"Where are we?" His voice told of decades of interrupted sleep for all the reasons a family and farm might throw into the dark of night. "Annie, are you okay?"

"Something is happening to the power grid. We need to find the kids."

He pushed himself upright, appearing refreshed on an hour of sleep. "I'm coming with you. Let's take our marines."

"The guards are gone." The large storage room began to shrink as darkness filled its corners.

"How long have the lights been down?" He stood, stretched his back, crunching and cracking exaggerated in the hard-surfaced room.

"Over sixty seconds." My eyes adjusted to the near dark. "There's some power holding in the system, or the generators should have kicked into operation." I took his hand, led him toward the door. "On the other hand, the security screens blanked out."

"Did the kids leave for Giant Pines?"

"I saw Phoebe in the kitchen before the system shut down."

Fully awakened with this news, he shook off my hand and moved ahead. "I can be upstairs faster than you with that ankle. Is your wristband working?"

I held up my arm so he could see the lit inactive button. "Do you think Kapur was trying to keep us safe or quiet?" I asked.

"Doesn't matter now, Annie." Paul stepped into the hall first. "I think the marine's plan went off-kilter. I'm going upstairs and will send someone to help you. It might be time to send you and the kids to the safe room."

Chapter Twenty-Six

The hitch of Paul's left foot from an arthritic kneecap, the flat-footed way his shoes hit the floor didn't slow him as he scurried away. Even with a cane and sense of urgency I moved at only a fraction of my normal speed. Somehow a grandfather a few days shy of turning seventy managed two steps at a time up the stairs. I climbed like a toddler having to step with both feet on each tread.

Long before I reached the top step, I heard John questioning Paul, and Phoebe shushing Noah. Terrell said "safe room" in the distance, stopping my advance. I waited on the seventh step from the top, one finger to my lips, ready to greet my children. John ran down first, his face a montage of surprise, joy, fear, and discipline. He almost stumbled, his arms held open while obeying my sealed lips. Andrew came next, one hand holding Noah's.

Terrell followed, a hand extended back to Phoebe. He didn't smile, just pointed down the stairs. I carefully turned and led the group, obediently silent, back toward the food storage room, then through a cooler, hoping Terrell would call all clear. I worked the unique lock and opened our safe room, waiting for a reprieve.

The children tumbled past me into the sixteen-by-sixteen secure space. "You, too, Annie," Terrell directed. "Lao was clear you got to be safe, too."

I turned away from the children, kept my voice low. "Tell me what's happening."

"All our systems went off grid about five minutes before Captain Peterson launched crazy stuff at the residence." Terrell began to turn away. "Too much to talk about right now. Lao's taking no chances with these kids and you."

Noah held on to my left hand, fear draining his face of color. "What about Grandpa Paul and Grandma Sarah?"

"They'll be fine, Noah." Terrell began to ease out of the room. "I got to get back. You stay here until we give the all clear. Who has the communications band?"

Andrew held up his wrist. "Looks like we've got one that works," I said. I grabbed at Terrell's shirt. "You've got to tell me something."

"If we knew, I'd tell you. We got the day started as normal as possible and sent most of the house kids out to help in the gardens. But when the power grid got funny, the commander ordered the family into safety. Put laborers and workers on buses and got them out of here. Paul and Sarah stayed. Couldn't get them to move."

He loosened my hand, gave me a hug. "I think they pulled the alarm too fast, but nobody wants anything to happen to you all." He bowed his head. "Andrew and Phoebe, help your mother. She's not in the best shape. Now I'm getting out of here and you close the door. I promise good eats when you get back upstairs."

I wanted him to stay with us, or at least give us one of his slow winks. But all I saw was his back as he sprinted through the cooler space. The door closed, air kicked in and lights glowed.

Phoebe threw herself against my chest, against the butterfly sutures holding my torn flesh together and the surrounding swelling. "Easy, sweetie," I said through gritted teeth. "I've got a nasty bruise right about there." I kept one arm looped over her shoulders. "We'll be okay."

"I wish Grandma and Grandpa were with us." Her frightened voice became wispy.

"Can you tell us what happened last night, Anne?" Andrew asked. "And what does Cook Terrell mean when he said you're not in good shape?"

"Let me sit down." I looked around the room. "Noah, can you unfold a chair for me?" As he pulled a chair from its storage rack I took the time to look at each child, wondering how their morning had played out before the call to send us into safety. "Thank you." I hugged him at my side, leaned on him just a bit as I lowered myself into the chair. "If you want chairs, each grab one and we'll talk. Stay near me and away from the door."

Andrew handed each child a chair, stayed back as they positioned themselves, Noah and John to my left, Phoebe on my right. He set up next to Phoebe, his chair completing our circle.

"Maybe Dr. Frances told you that I'm banged up. She says I'll be as good as new in a couple of weeks. All the same, you can understand if I'm cranky. Lots of me hurts. And I have to use this cane. Not cool."

The little boys' shoulders lowered on my poor attempt at tempting their smiles. "Look at me the next time you're think of climbing too high in a tree and stop. This boot really slows me down." Still no lightness in their faces. "We're all here and we're safe. Just like we've practiced."

"But Dad's not here and Andrew's never practiced with us," Noah said. "Should we show him how to use the toilet and where the water and food are stored?"

"My family has one of these, too." Andrew's voice faltered. "Had one."

"Maybe, if we're in here for a long time, you might tell us about your family?" Phoebe's request let me know she was finding a way to deal with her fears. "Stuff you liked to do with your parents."

Our girl at her best, I thought, and wished for many reasons that David was with us. "I'm sure Andrew appreciates our interest, Phoebe, but he'll tell us stories when he's ready." I pulled together a smile, something we never had to practice in our annual safe room exercises. "I do have news about Dad." The air system became louder than the children's breathing. "The people looking for Dad saw him and two people sitting under a tree and eating."

Phoebe's head drooped and tears fell. I leaned her way and welcomed her weight against my shoulder. "This is the best news we've heard." My voice fell.

"John and I pray for him every night," Noah said. "And we prayed for you and Grandpa last night. We were really scared when you didn't come back."

Beautiful dark eyes from his father's family were the highlight of Noah's face. I thought about how David once told me that Tia was the only female scientist in their government group willing to consider marriage to a rather plain lab rat. At the time I was talking to a married man and couldn't tell him that anyone with his dark eyes would never be considered plain.

"Thank you, Noah." I hesitated, trying to form a safe description for the kids about last night. "Grandpa and Lao and Milan discovered that the people using the DOE offices were not operating with authority of the U.S. government." All watched me. "Captain Peterson became angry when I challenged his right to be at Ashwood."

"But our soldiers aren't supposed to hurt us, Mom." John, my logical son, sat still. "Then other soldiers came to protect us. How do we know the good soldiers from the bad?"

Phoebe, with her intelligence, would be exempted from mandatory military or domestic service. Hopefully, the boys would be able to contribute years of domestic volunteer work instead of going into the armed services. I couldn't know their futures, didn't want to say anything that might change their unbiased minds.

"Sometimes people make bad decisions, and when those people are leaders that can cause big problems." I knew their attention would wander soon, so I cut this lesson short. "The marines who report to Captain Peterson have to follow his orders. So they think they're doing what is right to protect the United States because they trust him. But Captain Peterson is disobeying his leaders."

"But did soldiers hurt you or did Captain Peterson hurt you?" John puzzled.

"That's not important, John." I patted his knee. "I'd like to get our monitors set up. Could you three show Andrew around this space?"

"It's just like the one at my old house."

"Humor me, Andrew, and could I have the communication band?" I stood, wondered how long the pain medication would hold. He handed the wristband to me and I made my way across the room to a security station wired into the safe room's dedicated energy cell.

The cabinet opened with a scan of my iris. Three simple monitors came on. Inside the residence all appeared quiet with Terrell and Sarah working in the kitchen with a dozen other people. That screen changed to show an empty hallway outside the storage rooms. In the outside view, Magda waved to a smaller transport leaving Ashwood's courtyard.

The DOE building interior resembled an old black-and-white movie of urban espionage. The complete disconnect between the quiet in Ashwood's residence and a real battle taking place in our offices stopped me, then accelerated my heart rate.

I moved so the children would not be able to see uniformed people using tasers, or maybe real guns, on other uniformed people. I stared for seconds at what might have been a dead body outside my shattered office window, at the beginning of a blaze from somewhere near the coffee area. In the extraordinary quiet of the safe room, I closed the monitor station, took a breath, and turned. Four children, digesting what their unready eyes had seen, moved close.

"We have to watch, Mom." Phoebe approached, hands extended. "That fight is going on in Dad's office."

"But he's not there. We're not going to watch, Phoebe." I backed against the monitor box. "I'll check it in few minutes, but we're not going to watch that fight." I activated the communication band, signaling for Lao, needing information.

While I waited, I shepherded the kids back to their chairs, spending extra seconds smoothing hair or touching an arm.

"Anne." Sounding winded, Lao's voice gave me a half second of a secure feeling. "What do you need?"

"An update of any kind." I walked away from the kids' circle, as far away as the room allowed and turned toward a storage shelf that doubled as a sleeping bunk. "I saw action in the DOE building, but I don't understand."

"The marines shutting down one of their own who went rogue."

"And the fire. That building can't sustain fire damage. David's work archives."

"Trust me, it was a small fire. I'm monitoring everything. Should be about over." He turned away briefly, speaking to someone else. "Hold tight, Anne. I have to manage logistics. We'll be in touch."

"Lao, can't we return to the residence?"

"Negative. Not until all is clear."

I opened the security box again, using my body to block the kids' view. Gardens and yards were empty. Inside the residence, quiet ruled. I couldn't understand what I saw in the office building, felt emotional at the destruction and possible deaths. I closed it down once more, returned to our chairs.

"Andrew, would you be strong and help distract us by telling us a story or two about your family?" His frown indicated confusion or reluctance. "Or maybe about your favorite school."

"What do you want to know?" His voice quivered, a nearly eleven-year-old boy in a scary situation.

"We'd love anything you'd be willing to tell us. What your cook made for breakfast. How was your bedroom arranged. What you like about your big brother."

Looking down at his leg, Andrew spoke low, running words together. "My brother and I shared a room until he went to school in England. He's seven years older than me and was born during our father's first marriage. So we're half-brothers."

"Like you and John," Phoebe offered.

"Yeah, I guess so." Andrew looked up. John sat on the edge of his chair, hands under his legs. "Anyway, when Timothy went to England, I got the whole room to myself." He paused. "We lived in Philadelphia where estates are just old homes with a few greenhouses and a small barn for chickens and cows. I never saw a place as big as this before."

"What about school?" Phoebe's favorite activity. "Didn't you have your own school?"

"No, we were picked up by a transport. I started when I was three. Really long days Monday through Friday and a half day on Saturday for stuff like music." Noah made a monster face. Andrew nodded before continuing. "It was hard, but because my parents were like yours, I didn't have a choice."

His voice strengthened and I noticed how well he told his story. "I liked the mornings our cook made fried apples for breakfast with scrapple. That's a kind of special sausage. I didn't talk with the workers very much 'cause they had classes at night and I had homework. Lots of homework."

"Did you have a dog?" John asked with sincere interest. "We asked for a dog for Christmas."

Andrew shook his head. "No dog. But I had fish and we had house cats to hunt mice. It was a very old house. My father hated living in an old place. He would have liked this place." The last words were said softly and made me think what a topsy-turvy world the government threw in place. Its most valued citizens received prime housing. Some of those people those loved wood and windows and hated the energy-efficient concrete and steel residences they were assigned, while those who wanted high-rise glass-window views lived in Victorian comfort.

My band vibrated. These four kids watched me raise my arm. "Anne, here."

"If you're watching the monitors, we're moving everyone still here into air-filtered buildings because an unknown device placed near the DOE building is spewing a cloudy substance. Good news is that Peterson and his troops are under arrest." Lao's military training sounded in his brisk tone. "Military experts are out testing the emission and searching the grounds."

"Is everyone safe?" I walked while we talked, wished for my earbud communicator instead of the wristband that provided no buffer for the kids from Lao's information.

"Yes." Voices filled in behind Lao. "We'll talk later."

My left foot's swelling now extended from my arch through my calf, but I tried to move quickly away from the kids. "Andrew, if you could continue," I said over my shoulder. "Maybe tell John and Noah and Phoebe about your favorite foods or books. I don't want any of you to turn around to watch the monitor." Phoebe, always a firstborn, protested and rose from her chair.

"Sit down, Phoebe." She stood tall, then pushed aside her chair to follow me. "Please, I don't have time to discuss this with you. Just do what I asked." She hesitated. "Please, Phoebe." I kept my pace, a hand now on the security setup. She returned to her seat, put her head in her lap, cried.

The first monitor showed the dining area crowded with a small group of adults gathered behind fire doors and breathing filtered air. "Grandma and Grandpa are in the dining room," I reported back to the kids. Outside, the empty courtyard with closed building doors looked both eerie and calm.

The DOE building camera scanned destruction, two inert bodies, marines standing at guard at its entrances. External weather shutters installed during a recent energy project, closed in some areas. Before closing the station, I broke open the safe room's earpiece communicator and placed it in my ear to follow estate conversations.

Being plugged in to Lao's actions this way calmed me. I returned to the kids. "We have playing cards if you'd like to do something." Noah opened the small stock of books and games. "Phoebs, we're going to be okay." I sat next to her. "Want to huggle?" She moved close at the use of a babyhood word. "When we get upstairs, I will need a nap. Interested?"

"We just got up, Mom," she reminded me.

"You lucky girl," I teased. She stayed at my side.

Chapter Twenty-Seven

THE BOYS SLID OVER A BOX TO USE AS A TABLE and we played a few hands of Crazy Eights. Noah suggested some other game that involved sitting on the floor, and they were gone. Through the earpiece, I followed Lao's identification of the haze as an eye irritant that dissipated with the start of light drizzle.

One hour after invoking the filtered air protocol, Lao gave an all clear call for the rest of the estate. The buses could return and work resumed. By two hours into our evacuation, playing games ceased to amuse the kids. The boys built towers with the cards. Phoebe made up stories about the structures, her voice often raised to a level not easy to tolerate in a metal and concrete space. John found a safe room instruction manual and sat on the floor next to me to read.

By eleven o'clock, after four hours in isolation, hearing nothing about us in Lao's communication with estate security, I became irritated. Visual monitors implied that everyone outside once again moved freely.

"Anne, you're getting impatient?" I heard fatigue in Lao's voice. "You have not been forgotten."

"I trust you, but unless the estate is still under military control, decisions should be running through me." I heard Paul in the background, maybe Milan. "If there's no specific threat, we're leaving the safe room."

There followed a blur of voices. "I'll meet you in the hall," Lao said. "Is there anything you need?"

"An ankle support once we're upstairs and something mild for the discomfort." I gave the okay sign to the kids as I spoke. "The kids are ready for lunch and a piece of fruit with a nutrition bar would be great for me. I want to see the DOE building damage."

"We'll talk about that," he responded.

"If there is a security risk fine. Don't be protecting me from unpleasant. We'll be out of here in about three minutes."

Under Andrew's direction, the kids cleaned up cards and books and chairs. I shut down the security station. "Ready?" I asked as I initiated opening of the sealed door. The younger ones ran ahead. Andrew stayed at my side.

"Do you need a shoulder?" he asked as if his were tall enough to fit under my arm.

"No, but you're kind to offer. If you stay near, that would be a comfort."

Together we hurried to freedom. Lao met Noah and John. "I hear you kids are hungry," he said. "Cook Terrell is ready for you in the kitchen." They hesitated, waited for me. "Your mom and I have business to discuss. Go ahead."

"Do you have news about Dad?" Phoebe held her brothers back. "Mom said the soldiers saw him. Is he rescued?"

Lao shook his head. "Nothing new, Phoebe. Now go to the kitchen." Andrew hesitated. "You, too." Lao put a hand on Andrew's arm. "Life at Ashwood is actually calm. Enjoy lunch."

As they clattered up the steps, Lao turned to me. "A full military investigation has already begun in the office building. They need twenty-four hours. It is better you stay away."

"Are we allowed to access the building?"

"You and I have access."

"How many died in there?"

"That isn't important, Anne."

"Everything connected to Ashwood is important to me, Lao." I began walking, upset by what felt like my right-hand security person usurping authority. "I want to see the DOE building. Then we can do an update in the estate offices."

This third walk down the long basement hallway zapped my energy. I paused to rest.

"We tucked the wheelchair in the supply room. Want me to get it, Annie? I can push you up the delivery ramp."

Looking out a window at gray skies, David came to mind, maybe walking under the midday Paraguayan sun with a wounded shoulder. We had reason to believe he would come home. Now I wondered how this time apart would affect our future.

"Annie."

"Thanks for the offer. I think I better get used to moving slowly." I leaned on the cane and stepped forward on my good foot. "Just stay by my side."

Patiently Lao did that. He talked to me about how well staff managed the evacuation and Sarah's tears as she and Paul refused to leave Ashwood. We made it to the steps. He climbed behind me, offering words of encouragement. At the top I moved out of his way, leaned against a wall, and rested.

"Let's get you to the kitchen for a drink and someone to rewrap that ankle." He put a hand in the small of my back and steered me to the right, away from the DOE building. I accepted the suggestion.

Terrell waited for us at the kitchen's entrance. "We need about ten minutes," he said to Lao, then helped me to his office and closed the door.

"Put your foot on that low table." Terrell gathered supplies. "You got a choice of low-, medium-, or heavy-duty pain medication. How alert do you want to be for the next three hours?"

"I'm just looking to take the edge off," I replied. "I don't want to feel drugged."

He selected an inhaler, cracked off the tip. "Lean back and exhale. Breath deep on three." He shook the small container. "One, two, three." He shook the container once more, inserted the inhaler in my other nostril. "Again. One, two, three."

"This pad will take down some of the swelling." Terrell wound a thin disposable patch the size of a sheet of legal paper over my heel and ankle before he replaced the wrapping and strapped on a walking boot. "I want you here after dinner for a rewrap and concussion check." Each layer of treatment brought more physical comfort.

"Thanks, Terrell, for everything since you returned."

"Before you go, you listen to me, Anne." He handed me a glass of water from the crockery jug behind his desk. "You think you've seen bad stuff. I'm not discounting what you've been through back in the Depression. But I pretty much know you've never seen anything like what's happened in that building."

"Part of the destruction happened because Peterson got angry at me. Remember? I saw the monitors. I think I'm prepared." He held his large hands tight between his knees, his eyes appeared to focus somewhere beyond the room. "I've stepped over a corpse, Terrell. We've just never had reason to talk about the guy who died in the hallway of the boardinghouse where I lived."

His attention returned to the moment. "Fresh dead in your own surroundings is different," he said. "You'll know what I mean." He stood, extended a hand. "I'm coming with you. Lao's got plenty to do and you will need a friend."

"Terrell, I can't cover my eyes when life gets ugly and expect others to do the hard work."

"No, Anne Hartford can't do that." He took off his cook's coat, stuffed two washcloths in his pants pocket. "Let's go. Amber's in charge. I didn't expect to change your mind."

The residence felt calm as Lao, Terrell, and I walked through its main halls. My kids sat with their friends eating lunch. I avoided eye contact with Sarah and Paul, not to be distracted from this responsibility and not wanting my father-in-law involved. I realized I hadn't eaten anything this day. I suspected that would be good.

"First, tell me why Peterson chose Ashwood," I said to Lao as we walked. "I understand he was a rogue military leader, but that doesn't explain the campaign against us—David's assignment to the Paraguay group, the combine requisition, the command post, and the home invasion."

"Don't know." My clumsy motion slowed our progress. "You and I will have an early dinner with Milan to debrief." We turned a corner into the hallway to the DOE building. "Anne, nothing has been cleared from the building. The military investigation is underway so we will be escorted. Do not touch anything." He squared his shoulders, put his hand through my arm. "Ready?"

I nodded. We approached a temporary security checkpoint, were required to suit up in protective clothing and boots. Terrell bent to help slide everything over my ankle brace. Lao convinced the guard to access Terrell's records for permission to enter as a medic attending me. Before the door opened, we slipped on masks and gloves. I left my cane at the door.

I half listened as the guard gave final instructions. My mind focused on constructing a hasty repair plan for the building. If we could find competent laborers, I wanted the work started the minute the military left. Perhaps by the end of the week I could settle back in my office with its views of David's desk and our orchards. I reminded myself where I saw the photo of my parents on the floor of my office as Peterson's goon carried me away. The last photo taken of my father before he died.

The door opened slowly, a great gush of smells and sounds filling my senses.

"My God." My utterance exited in a hybrid of anguish and prayer as the monitor's small and poorly lit images now surrounded us in real life. Lingering smoke, a variety of chemical smells, and the odor of human bodies mingled in a most unpleasant soup. I stepped forward too quickly for my boot brace, stumbled toward a pile of sodden cushions that used to cover a lovely restored upholstered sofa presented to us by Magda when I was pregnant with John. Our babies all napped on that sofa.

"Easy, Annie," Terrell murmured as he helped me step over what was now trash. "Look down and be careful where you put your feet."

Looking around, I could see glass from all six inside office windows covered the floor, not sparkling as one might expect, but dirtied from smoke and water. And blood splatter. Building windows, bulletproof, remained intact except in my office, where the outer wall no longer existed. Sadness dulled my senses as I surveyed my beloved haven.

From the window cavity I forced myself to assess the rest of my office. The large conference table was shattered with bits of chairs tossed about. And next to the rubble Peterson's body sat upright against the long inside wall. His eyes remained open as if he were staring at my desk, a number of flowerlike red spots dotted his upper body. Blood spatter stained the wall, the calm green paint Phoebe and I chose just last spring mocked by mayhem. I turned, saw another man's body face down near the reception area's coffee table.

"Are these the only fatalities?" Unconsciously my hand reached for the strength of Lao and he stood by my side. "What about the lower level?"

"There are only two." I focused intensely on his words. Perhaps Terrell had been right and I should have stayed away. "The lower level sustained water and smoke damage." He covered my hand with his own. "The DOE is sending a team to test for hazardous material leakage from the labs. We can't go down there, and we shredded the monitors' connections before we pulled you and Paul out."

We moved no further. "When will the investigation be done?" I asked because no question really made sense in this chaos.

"General Manager Hartford." Behind a full face mask I recognized a DOE representative who dealt with us on property management issues, a nice guy in an agency of seasoned bureaucrats. He tipped his head in greeting. "Chief Engineer Lao. I'm Peter Jones, DOE property management services director. I'm sorry this is the reason I am visiting Ashwood."

"It's good to see a familiar face," I responded.

He moved aside, reopening my view of the offices. "A transport just arrived to remove the bodies, and I understand the military is leaving two investigators to work with our team to assess the damage."

I pointed to people in David's office and asked who they represented.

"Members of the DOE data recovery unit, General Manager Hartford. They're inventorying Director Regan's work-related materials."

Fortunately David maintained personal files on a private system Lao managed for our use and we were careful about keeping paper documents in a safe in our bedroom. Ashwood documents, early drafts of a book he was writing on intellectual public service, and plans for the business he hoped to develop when he was free from his contract remained confidential. "Are you emptying his office?"

"I believe that would be premature," Peter said.

Terrell stepped forward to offer food for the crew, and the three men talked. I pulled away from Lao, once again surveyed the offices. If hazardous materials were found, I knew DOE would condemn the structure. I thought of my first discussions with David in this space, of the day his first wife sat here and asked me to consider him as a future partner.

"If I make a list of items in my office that I would like removed, can that be handled?" I broke into their conversation. "There's a picture of my parents and brother that I last saw under the desk." Peter's deep-brown eyes showed empathy. "It would mean a lot to me. There's also a dark wood frame with three pencil drawings of our children that David gave me for my birthday. I can't replace those items."

"Let me ask one of the staff." Jones moved faster than I thought a big man in a hazmat suit could in this mess of overturned furniture and death.

"I'll be in here with a recovery team tomorrow, Anne," Lao said. "Make a list for me."

"I'll be in here as well." I didn't wait for his approval. "Peterson kicked that picture of my family before he hit me with the chair. It's important."

Terrell cleared his throat. All three of us lost so much during the big D that neither man questioned my request. "Cleanup of this place is going to be tricky," he said as he gently turned me away from the bodies.

"I don't think it is going to be put back together." Breathing hot, wretched-smelling air through my mask began to turn my stomach. "After Peter comes back I need to leave." I turned a quarter of the way toward the back office area. "How did it happen that Ashwood, our home, has become a place where two people died so violently?"

My friends could not answer, didn't even try. I now stood with my back to my office, felt Peterson's dead eyes on me.

"General Manager Hartford, the investigators did a quick wipe down on these and want you to have them." A DOE person handed me the pictures. "They might need some professional restoration, but they can be saved."

My voice thickened and I couldn't say a simple thank you. I nodded my head, bit my lips together.

"It's okay," Peter said. "I'll be here for a few days."

"Thank you. Please call me Anne," I choked out.

He tipped his head and excused himself.

"Want me to carry those?" Terrell lifted the pictures from my hands. "Let's get out of here."

Chapter Twenty-Eight

As gentle as a parent stripping away a child's wet snowsuit, Terrell removed my protective garb and booties. Neither hot chocolate or warm blankets could touch the cold that made me shiver. Chaos and darkness now existed within the sanctuary of Ashwood.

"You gonna talk about what we just saw?" Terrell asked as we walked the hallway back to our residence. "What's brewing in your head?"

"I'm not going to talk about anything right now. I'm going to carry these pictures to my room, look at my injuries, and take a shower." Terrell walked protectively on one side, Lao behind him. Creating distance from the damaged building demanded the fastest steps I could take. "Then I'd like to piece together what the hell has happened in our home." The steadiness of my voice created a facade of control I didn't feel. An odd, murky set of odors settled in my nose and throat.

"Not that we shouldn't have that talk," Lao replied, "but I thought the doctor suggested that you rest."

"I'm counting four hours sitting on a folding chair in the safe room as rest." My steady voice broke as I grabbed for another breath while I kept up with the men. "Could we slow down? I only have one good foot."

"I need about thirty minutes to file reports," Lao said as he walked away from us to the exterior door. "Call me when you are ready, and we'll meet in the estate offices if you can walk there." He waved and went out into the September afternoon.

"I think I need fresh air," I decided. "Thank you for taking time to stand by my side, Terrell." I nodded toward my pictures. "If you could take those back to your office, I'll pick them up later. I'm going outside before I take a shower."

The short distance from the front door to the kitchen's side entrance convinced me I did need lunch and a rest. Like the shadow of an eagle's wide wingspan, calm once more covered the residence. Sarah and Paul drank black coffee at an empty lunch table, kids bumped into each other as they left for classes. Voices carried faintly from the kitchen area.

"Andrew," I called to him just as my younger kids turned a corner.

He looked my way, concern changing his face from typical youngster to frightened person. We met in the middle of a hallway.

"I wanted to say that you've been a trouper since you arrived. You've helped the little boys tremendously." I put one hand on his shoulder with a light touch, gave him space to reject my contact. "I'm sorry this has been so difficult. I'm looking forward to having happier times with you."

I wish I could rewind the security tape to show his wonderful smile to David, to Paul, to whoever was interested in Andrew's adaptation to Ashwood.

"My aunt said you were the best person to help me and Ashwood would be a good place to live until college." He looked at his feet for a few seconds, then really looked at my face. "I don't want to muck this up. But I don't feel right just living here. I'll earn my keep."

His shoulder felt substantial under the summer-weight shirt. He was a few years away from his teens, not a little boy. "Andrew, you're my son and having you here is a great, unexpected gift. You don't have to earn your keep." I bent to look into his eyes. "I want all the best for you."

He nodded, the kind of action kids do when they don't fully understand adult words.

"We can't replace life with your family, but there are a whole bunch of people here ready to make those years until college go well. We all want you to have a shot at your dreams."

I saw his shoulders twitch, then relax. "Can I call you Annie?" he asked.

"Certainly. It's a name only family and really close friends use."

"That's what Terrell said." The moment broke. "I'll be late for science."

"Go ahead."

He moved fast on long legs, maybe the same way his father ran. I made a note to research the Smithsons, starting with Clarissa. Perhaps there could be a role for her at Ashwood so my son could grow up with both halves of his family.

"Anne, do you have a minute?" Hajar came from behind me.

"If we walk to the kitchen. It has been a long time since I ate last night." She joined me. "Well, in spite of our military insanity, what do you think of Ashwood?"

"Jason is such a gifted educator. He should be teaching teachers," she replied. "But he'll never leave here." She put her hands together, forming a temple with her fingers. "I wanted to be the one to tell you that the letter of concern has been revoked. That means I'm leaving."

"Stay with us for a few days. Tell your supervisor that you want to observe Jason." I held out a hand to her. "I'd love to find out what's going on in your life."

Holding out her right arm, she pointed to a slim silver bracelet. "This is what's going on. I'm heading to North Carolina in a few weeks to marry a wonderful man. The bracelet is a family heirloom. And I have a new assignment near Chapel Hill."

"Congrats, Hajar." News of weddings between people who found each other had become more common as society distanced itself from the years of Bureau-arranged marriages. "How old are you?"

"Thirty-three," she replied and leaned toward me. "I'm three months pregnant," she said quietly. "We are so pleased."

"Double congrats." We hugged. "Do you really need to leave?"

"Mohsen and I filed for our marriage license months ago and have been waiting for our mothers to plan a party." She raised her shoulders, shrugged. "I need to get back to help. I wish I could stay longer."

She had more to say. "Before I go, I must tell you that your children are treasures. Phoebe is an exceptionally bright child, and all your boys have great potential. I noticed John has not been tested for the offspring program. I'll request that he be considered."

"We'd rather not have him have that classification." I said nothing about our intention to keep John out of the government's data bank to preserve some of his freedom as an adult. "What do you think of Andrew?"

"Andrew will do well here. I don't know why his education got derailed." Hajar paused, appeared to think. "There is something in his file about having a strong father but a distant mother."

"That sounds like what he has told me."

"Well, that gives you lots of room to mother him." She tipped her head. "Good?"

"Yes, good." We hugged, knowing it could be the last time. With regionalization of employment and travel, we might never see each other again. I wished her luck and encouraged her to stay in touch.

Workers on release from school for the day stood by every available counter space and table in the kitchen, cleaning or preparing fruits and vegetables for canning. Sarah moved from group to group. My conversation with Magda about harvesting Ashwood's kitchen gardens felt like a memory of a long-ago past. Light vertigo slowed my walk through the activity.

"Ms. Anne, Terrell had us put a lunch plate aside for you." Amber stood at my side. "Would you like us to bring food and iced tea to the dining room?"

Knowing her as well as I knew my own children, I was touched by deep emotions when I saw her bruised face. "You and I are both in kind of bad shape. How are you doing?"

"Okay. Cook has been really kind."

"I insist you find a good book, take your dinner, and go read. No work tonight." She protested. "Amber, I miss our weekly walks and talks. If you're willing to walk slowly, we should start again in the next few days." The first subject would be my interest in offering her legal protection to stay at Ashwood until she turned eighteen. The possibility of the Bureau reassigning her and taking her from Jason's school had no upside for her.

"I'd like that."

"Me too." I moved away. "About your question, a tray would be great, but in the small dining room. Thanks, Amber." I hobbled through the kitchen to the quiet of the small space and elevated my foot. David consumed my thoughts. He had been seen. They were feeding him. He would have a beard showing, his skin would be the golden color of a kid who grew up on a farm. I knew his strength and determination. I wanted him home.

I pushed the tray aside, hungry but unable to escape the awful murky odor that followed us from the DOE building. I lowered my foot from its resting place on another chair and placed my head on my arms on the table to stretch my lower back. Through my crossed arms I stared at the tiled floor, a color David chose to brighten the small room. The past twenty-four hours catching up with my body, I closed my eyes and fell asleep.

"Mom." A deep childish voice squawked next to me. "Mom, wake up."

"John, is something wrong?" My words blurred into one sleepy sound. A younger, uninjured woman's spine might have remained limber after sleeping bent over a table. My back, my chest, and all the other bruises made the simple movement toward sitting upright a struggle.

"I got the highest score in the whole state on the flying plane puzzle test." David and I had no idea where little boy John got his manly voice. He bent his head to look into my face as I straightened. "Are you all right, Mom?"

"Fine, honey." The final stretch of spine brought more normal alignment. "Let me give you a hug. The flying plane puzzle is a really big deal." My lunch tray had disappeared.

His head settled on my shoulder, a comfortable place, and I landed a small kiss on his coarse dark hair. "Grandpa Paul is in bed. Grandma Sarah says seventy-year-old men can't take this much physical abuse." Stepping away, he looked to me with a visual request for assurance that Grandpa and I would be okay.

"He hasn't slept well for a few nights so he probably needs a long nap. Grandpa's birthday is in a couple of days." John adored birthdays—his, anyone in the family, worker kids, favorite adults, the house cats. "Do we have cards and table decorations?"

"Grandpa wants to wait until Dad is home." He stood on one foot, balancing against the table with fingers. "Does that mean he doesn't even want one card?" Uncertainty wrinkled across his forehead. "Isn't seventy a big deal?"

"You're right. Why don't you organize your brothers and sister to make a few small things, and we'll hold off on a big party until later." Suddenly I wished David's brothers could leave their farms to wait with us for his return. I resented the scarcity of resources that made travel such a luxury for regular folks while bureaucrats buzzed around in private transports.

John's face lightened. "Mr. Milan gave me a high five about the puzzle prize." Those unique arched eyebrows went higher. "And, he sent me to tell you he'd like to meet you in your office in twenty minutes."

"Nice to mention that now, goofball." I wouldn't attempt to stand until John left.

"Oh, and Phoebe said she likes Dr. Frances and invited me to have a snack with them. Got to go." He turned and hurried out to the lure of food. I called Milan to move our meeting back ten more minutes, then hobbled to clean up and put on clothes that didn't smell like the DOE building.

Making my way down our residence's front steps, I stopped to enjoy the soft warmth of a late summer afternoon. The air smelled of a ripening orchard and cut grass. Looking toward the DOE building, I saw a large hazardous materials trailer, suggesting demolition had been ordered.

Staff members smiled as I walked through Ashwood's office building. I concentrated on moving as normally as possible to assure them that the estate was on track. One or two expressed pleasure about the news of David having been sighted.

In my office, Milan greeted me with a quick, gentle hug. "Last night was one of the longest in my life. I thought there was a significant possibility we would lose you and Paul," he said. Every age-related wrinkle on his face added to an overall tired appearance. "You look a lot better than I expected from Dr. Frances's report. Sit down. Do you need to elevate your foot?"

"Thank you, and that would be helpful. Maybe I should have thought about a dose of meds when I freshened up." From my chair at the small conference table, I could almost reach headache tablets stored in the desk. Milan caught my look. "If you don't mind, I think there's a small container of generic stuff right up front in that drawer."

Two mild tablets chased down by cool water did nothing for tension that kept me anticipating the next invasion of bad news, threatening action, fear. I carefully placed the glass back on a coaster made by Phoebe as a Mother's Day present. "What do you know about David?"

His silence slowed my breathing, made a second sip of cool water taste like juice from moldy field grass. He shook his head as he said, "Nothing new in the last twelve hours."

That was the time passed since Paul and I first sat in the food storage room, rescued and dazed. Half a day gone with no progress. I lowered my eyes, pushed a water droplet around the table's glass top. Silence became the language of my office as I thought about David, about what I should ask, about how tired I felt. "Milan, what is happening to my family?"

In a behavior I knew represented stress, Milan rose to pace the office, stopping here and there to adjust a blind or straighten a light shade. With one foot carefully elevated and the start of a killer concussion headache, I had patience to wait for Milan's explanation.

He stopped walking, leaned back against a window ledge. "Two stories come together—the rare reality that sometimes bureaucracies think they can hide their troubled leaders instead of removing them and the oldest reason for a man to seek revenge," he said. I settled back in my chair.

"I'll start with the personal side. Peterson had the affair of his life with a young science student from New York studying at the University of

Michigan. Her family managed to hold on to some part of their comfortable life during the early depression so she had money for dinner out, for good wine, for travel with him. He was a campus military instructor, almost ten years older, didn't expect to fall in love with a nineteen-year-old girl."

"Peterson was involved with Tia?"

"Even as a young woman, Tia discarded men when she wanted something new. Peterson may have been obsessed with her, but she was always obsessed with having a good time." Milan reached for the water, poured himself a glass, closed his eyes while he drank. He twirled the glass, made the ice cubes clink. "As much as possible, Peterson managed posts within a hundred miles or so of Tia. There are pictures of them together when she worked on her doctorate at MIT. They would have had a very enviable life at the time—he earned decent money in the Marines, she had her family trust and graduate stipend. Think of how you were living in the city fifteen years ago—worried about keeping a rented room and eating one meal a day."

Muscle spasms danced through my lower back. I shifted in my chair, tried to lower my foot to the floor. He watched, moved the chair from under my foot with flawless timing.

"Tia's been dead seven years."

"The night of the security breach, he expressed interest in having Phoebe transferred to his guardianship and assigned to his family home." With a long swallow, Milan emptied his glass. "If you weren't on painkillers, I'd pour us something with alcohol." He sat around the table from me. "Peterson apparently believed that if David Regan had not won Tia's attention and affection, the Marines would have approved his marriage to her. The investigators found correspondence between the two of them right up to the day she died. Let's say Peterson became convinced David should be punished for her death."

"Peterson was insane." My hand touched the edge of a butterfly suture under my shirt. "I thought he might kill me last night. And what about the man who twisted my ankle?"

"Peterson's right-hand aide. A man with his own devils."

I knew basically good people sometimes did bad things in order to feed their kids. I saw it happen on the street, had my bag taken at knifepoint. But I never met a person who injured others for pleasure like Peterson's aide. My ten minutes in his control moved evil from an abstract concept to concrete reality.

"Peterson and two other officers did receive directions to cause an incident in Paraguay. As David told you, there was no reason for him to be part of the group."

Sitting hurt, walking hurt, standing hurt. None of that mattered as I wondered if Peterson's command of the Paraguay ambush might extend beyond his own death. If nothing would bring an end to Peterson's influence until David was also dead. I attempted to straighten my spine and wondered if knowing the answer to that question would be helpful. Milan sighed, the sound that comes before difficult words. I stopped searching for physical comfort to bring emotional relief.

"When his aide came to us with the proposal to set up a communications base here as well as staff a security patrol, the Bureau thought it would provide your family and Ashwood comfort and safety. No one could know, Peterson hoped to create chaos—the kids living elsewhere, you dead, the business destroyed."

"Will David be rescued?" After I asked the question, I looked out the window at the large agricultural operation my South Dakota farm-boy husband loved. Ashwood, where child workers could use late-afternoon free time to play games or sit on the screen porch of the school building and study. One of his spare-time projects, a swing set built for kids and adults, attracted two teenagers. The girl wore her hair as short as possible. The boy also wore a close buzz style. "You're not answering, Milan. You're always honest with me."

"Peterson didn't leave a coherent communications trail, so military investigators are piecing together data about the mercenaries who are involved. It's true that the U.S. is in Paraguay because of government corruption with terrorists and mercenaries steering the ship. That makes the search challenging." He leaned toward me. "Keep your hopes up. When this story leaks, heads will roll in some high levels of the military establishment."

"Is your job secure?"

"Don't worry about that, Annie. I think I'm signed on to parts of this job for life."

My chest bruise ached, an irony I kept to myself. "Let's keep this part of the conversation private. Hope is so much easier to live with than doubt."

"With the expanding media circus, I've changed my mind about your taking the family to South Dakota for a break. If Lao can provide security, you should go."

"You're not a farmer, Milan. This is almost the worst time of the year for a crisis or a getaway." I paused. "I'd like Paul to be evaluated by a good geriatric specialist. If he and Sarah want a getaway, send them. I don't want the kids separated from school and friends."

"I agree Paul is tired. I can have those arrangements made tomorrow." Milan made a note, looked up. "How worried are you about him?"

"Moderately. He carries a lot of responsibility here and is taking David's absence hard. When he's stressed, he's started to rub his chest and his breathing sounds labored."

I checked the time. "Terrell and Lao are expecting us for dinner in twenty minutes. Strange to think that yesterday we introduced Hajar and Dr. Frances to the kids over dinner."

Milan didn't smile. "You're a strong person, Anne. Four kids, two grandparents, dozens of employees, and the extended community rely on you to make good decisions and you don't let them down. While the Bureau had no reason to know of Peterson's intentions, we accept responsibility for putting you through hell."

When the government was flush with money, such statements often preceded offers of cash. Ashwood experienced interruption of its business and would file for compensation to cover our losses and expenses. I wanted my husband and our life, not cash.

"So what now, Anne?"

"I get a good night's sleep, wake up tomorrow, probably hurting like hell, and hope for a more normal day." Putting my hands on the table, I remembered Dr. Frances's mission at Ashwood. "I'll concentrate on Phoebe's situation and spend time with Andrew. Maybe Dr. Frances could help all of the family process the trauma of the past week."

"I was hoping you'd say you would follow the doctor's direction and sit in a chair and let your head heal."

A knock sounded at the door before I replied. Amber and a second worker waited with a dinner cart.

"Cook Terrell thought you'd do better eating here than walking back to the dining room." She bowed to Milan and greeted him by name, then set up the table with baked chicken, fresh garden vegetables, warm biscuits.

"Amber, Cook says your injuries will take time to heal. Make sure you are better than Ms. Anne about following his directions. He'll know when you're ready to return to a full schedule." He smiled. "And Teacher Jason tells me you are very good with languages," Milan continued. "Korean, French, Spanish—quite impressive."

"Ms. Anne started that all," Amber said, blushing a beautiful rose under her warm brown skin. "She said every worker at Ashwood would have a mentor, and my first mentor was Nurse Kim. When I was little, she would talk to me in Korean or French every day. I like the way languages are put together."

What I remember of Nurse Kim was how she presented me with my first true management challenge—neutralizing the personal agenda of a staff member. As a distraction, I assigned her responsibility for mentoring a five-year-old Amber, who was having problems learning to read.

Milan spoke to Amber in French. She answered, her eyes brightening. Their conversation continued. I closed my eyes, the heaviness of Peterson's hatred fitting my shoulders like an old, old winter coat.

"We've put Ms. Anne to sleep," Milan said softly.

"No, I was just thinking about how cute Amber was as a little girl." I smiled her way. "Now that I've embarrassed you, we'll let you go. Please thank Cook Terrell."

Cheeks once again pink, Amber departed.

"When everything slows down, if that girl is interested, I want to adopt her. Or at the least apply for legal guardianship." Milan listened. "We adore her. She's smart and has potential if she can stay in a good school with supportive people. I don't know if I can remove her from the worker class, but I'd like to." Talking about the future felt good, hopeful. "Of course I need to speak to David, but he knows how I feel."

"I gave you the name of an adoption lawyer. Give him a call."

Chapter Twenty-Nine

Lao brought the smell of a sun-warmed day to our dinner gathering, and I wondered how to replace the freedom of outdoor running until my ankle healed. He looked tired as he exchanged logistics information with Milan about the need to move the hazmat trailers. We served ourselves, unfolded napkins, began our meal before beginning business talk.

"The military's investigative team cleared out earlier than we expected, and there is agreement about unacceptable chemical contamination of the building. It needs to come down as soon as possible." Lao offered the information with no inflection in his voice, as if talking about demolishing an old field shed.

"DOE has absolute authority to make that decision." I spoke as the estate owner even though the plan broke my heart. "But, our contract does require them to rebuild, and we have the right to approve the replacement design."

"Do you want them to rebuild?" Milan's question surprised me.

"David has almost three years left in his DOE contract. If he can't work from here, he'll have to spend significant time in the city." Once he came home, I wasn't ready to risk having him away. "They deeded the building to us last year, and we had long-term plans for its use. In the short-term, the DOE gifted student group will require lab space."

"I agree with Anne," Lao added. "We use their conference rooms, our school uses labs, and having Anne based in that building frees up this office. From an engineering perspective, Ashwood truly benefits from DOE's technology projects."

Remembering my conversation with Terrell days earlier, I brought a few negatives to the discussion. "On the other hand, we feed extra people, which will be an issue if food supplies become tighter. There is also the DOE affection for planting listening devices. How often do we sweep for bugs, Lao?"

"At least once a week. But don't forget that we find as many Bureau devices in the residence."

Milan blew a small laugh out through his nose. "Jeremiah, the cook you fired, was on Peterson's extended payroll. And in turn, Jeremiah taught Antwone a few tricks. I think with both of them gone, you'll find less government listening at Ashwood."

"Did you know about Jeremiah and Antwone?" From the creases above Lao's eyes and the tight line of his mouth, I suspected Milan's information was news. Lao shook his head.

"It would be nearly impossible for an outsider to worm into the military expenses system to track down payments made to Jeremiah," Milan volunteered. "Unless you looked for Feed Our Souls Kitchen and knew Jeremiah's friend created that front for a handful of illegal activities." He saw Lao frown. "Don't fire your intelligence mole, Lao. I stumbled on the information at a Twin Cities benefit event."

The food on my plate, a precious commodity, no longer held appeal as the precarious safety of my family was uncovered. Jeremiah, who had fed us each day and managed our food sources, collected pay from a madman bent on destroying my husband.

"You'll receive a copy of the investigation report, Anne." Milan speared a cherry tomato. "When does the DOE want to move on demolition?"

"In three days."

Lao's words began a string of questions in my mind. "What's the hurry? Could they wait until we're through with harvesting the orchards?"

"There is a possibility the building could explode." Lao waited for me to ask another question, continued when I stayed quiet. "A team has begun packing what can be saved. Anything in the basement needs to be destroyed. There is also a contamination issue in the empty office next to yours, Anne, so they recommend we not save any of the furniture from either space."

Tears formed in my eyes as Lao spoke. David and his father built or refinished each piece of my furniture.

"I want to pack my office." I meant the words.

"It's in the hands of the hazmat folks, Anne. Maybe tonight we can garb you up to supervise one of their people."

"Any impact on Ashwood operations during demolition?" Milan reached over to cover my hand with his while planning moved forward.

"The walkway from the residence is being sealed right now." Lao took out his data pad. "Everyone needs to be off the premises when the building comes down in case of airborne particles, so we'll transport workers, staff and family members to Giant Pines. Before that happens, the demo crew will build a dome-type barrier over the building."

"Who's packing David's things?" I wanted to sit in his chair once more, look at the shelves he built and his favorite collection of old sci-fi books.

"DOE's taken care of anything related to them. Anything remaining will be handled by the same crew that packs the rest of the building." Lao sat back. "It makes me nervous to think such strong contaminants have been in the lower level of a building so close to the residence and school. I insisted that they notify us of such dangers in the future."

"Did they say when they would start rebuilding?" I knew the answer would be tied to David's return. From the minute pressing together of Lao's lips before he answered, I guessed the suggested date.

"That's difficult to establish right now," he offered. "Soil testing needs to be conducted and infrastructure examined for integrity." His words slowed. "Assuming no problems, probably two to three months."

Before my emotions crashed, before tears flowed, I struggled to find a way to complete what we had to accomplish. "Include me in discussions with the DOE property folks, Lao." I sighed. "Let's give the demo crew as much time as we can. Take everyone to Giant Pines for a barbecue and campout. The kids can sleep on the floors or in tents. Anyone who wants to stay should be able to do that, but I'd like Sarah and Paul to be with my kids. Put Jason's team in charge of fun."

It might have been admiration in Milan's eyes when I looked across the table. I prefer to think he was surprised that I could be the manager at such a bleak moment, and not that he wondered if I was in complete denial. I needed to be alone. "Lao, maybe I could ask you to work that plan?"

"Sure, Anne." His eyes followed my slow rise from the chair. "Need help?"

"Just air and time to think," I said. "Milan, do we need to talk business?"

"We've set the clock back forty-eight hours, Anne. You're in charge, the kids are back under your care. I return to the city tonight assuming you will prepare a thorough report of the present and anticipated expenses incurred because of this episode." He rose. "Do let me walk you back to the residence."

"Thanks. Lao, let me know when I can get into my office. I'll supervise packing of my space and David's personal things." He stood up as well. "And thank you for steering the estate during these past days."

Minnesota September evenings feel so different from the same time of day in August or July. The air cools quicker, the sun drifts toward its resting place with purpose, leaving no doubt of moving into a time when everything must be harvested, covered, protected from the Minnesota cold. Leaves change color, each variety taking center stage with rare vibrancy for a few days. David's favorite time of year, I thought. This time I let the tears begin.

Milan guided me away from the residence, the curious children, the anxious family. We walked over already cooling earth toward a pond dug to balance the earth's elements around our home. We sat on a bench built early in the summer by David and our boys. The whole family looked forward to planting a new garden in the fall. David developed a landscaping plan, which I hadn't seen before he left. For all that might be lost, I placed my head in my hands and cried.

Chapter Thirty

When I was a girl, POSTTRAUMATIC STRESS DISORDER became a widely used diagnosis to explain irregular behavior of discharged soldiers, abused women, children raised in war. The big D dropped millions of us into unbelievably horrible situations, and we stopped talking about the long-term psychological impact. We had survived and walked the earth hoping nothing as awful would ever happen again.

I cried and scrambled to find emotional balance. Milan sat close, his arm across the back of the bench, and told me what he admired about David and our kids. I listened until I could manage a steadier voice. We agreed that there was hope David would return. If the worst happened, Milan promised he would personally bring the message to Ashwood.

Needing to return to the cities, Milan offered to help me to the dining room. Paul and Sarah led the dinner conversation. Their chairs appeared closer than normal, and I saw Sarah's hand resting on Paul's leg. Dr. Frances sat between the younger boys and laughed at one of John's knock-knock jokes. Everyone looked tired.

"Mom." Phoebe jumped from her chair and ran my way for a hug. I noticed Dr. Frances watching my daughter's movement but didn't mind. Phoebe's head rested near my chest wound, her hands touching at the top of the bruise on my back. This was the way parenting happened—love was offered and accepted and sometimes hit touchy spots.

"I'll have a cookie," I said as the boys dragged a chair to the table for me. Sarah put one of Terrell's best sugar cookies on a plate and moved it in my direction. With so many heavy topics on our minds, I wanted to steer us to a normal activity, one without emotion. "If anyone needs help with homework, I'm all yours. Anyone?"

"We don't have any," Andrew said. "Teacher Jason said we should relax after all that stuff this morning."

"Could we have a game night?" Noah made the suggestion while shoulder-bumping John.

"That sounds like a great idea, and I bet even your grandpa might be easy to beat tonight." Paul scuffawed and the boys chuckled. "I'll play until I get paged to pack our things in the DOE building." They would be sad about the building's demolition, but had to be told. "It has to be taken down because it is very damaged."

"We'll help you pack," Phoebe stated, as if she were in charge. "We don't need to play games."

"Thanks, sweetie, but there are contaminants in the building so only adults can enter. We have to wear special clothes."

John said what many at the table thought. "What will Dad think when he gets home and his stuff is all in boxes?"

Sarah's eyes brightened with tears. I dug deep to stay confident for the kids. "Dad probably knows exactly what bad chemicals were used in the lab and will explain it all to us. He and I will both be sad because we have special family memories of each of you connected to those offices." I looked toward Andrew. "Even you. The last conversation David and Paul and I had in my office was about you joining our family."

Paul winked at Andrew. "That's right. Pretty exciting conversation."

"But where will Dad work?" Phoebe's hands, clenched into small fists, pounded the table.

"We're talking with the DOE about new construction. Dad will have an office." The half-truth slipped into the conversation as a hopeful statement.

I stopped talking, picked up my cookie, and took a bite. Around the table stories about the building began to flow—crayon drawings on walls, baby spit-up on a chair, sitting for the portraits in my office. Everyone shared their memories until Sarah suggested moving to our family quarters.

"If we could take a minute, General Manager Hartford." Dr. Frances walked next to me. "Maybe we can talk in the front room."

"I'd like to be with the kids right now." The world felt a bit blurry and I could name a handful of reasons. "Maybe in the morning?"

Her eyes opened wider at my response. "That's the perfect answer. We'll talk in the morning."

Hoping my voice remained steady, I tried to bring her closer to our family emotionally "If you're comfortable with this, please feel free to call me Anne."

She smiled at me and we walked into the room filled with children who all needed an early bedtime after a crazy day. John invited Andrew, Sarah, and me to play cards. Crazy Eights reigned as the favorite game. Phoebe cornered the doctor, obviously a new best friend, for a game of building stick towers. I convinced Paul, a consummate card game winner, to take my place when Lao called.

My stiffened back and aching ankle suggested what life might become in two or three decades as I limped outside for the walk to the DOE front door. David had insisted on painting it red to match our residence. Star-filled skies above Ashwood reminded me of how fortunate he and I were to live this life. Lao talked about plans for making the Giant Pines a rare evening of relaxation during the crush of harvest. My thoughts were ahead of us, in the damaged building, with David.

In a tent next to the entrance, cleaning crew members helped us into protective clothing, complete this time with respirators. My cane, too difficult to swaddle in disposable protective wrap, stayed outside, so I moved even more awkwardly into the building. Much had been cleaned and removed since the military's early wrap-up. Our damaged sofa was gone, along with the rubble that had covered the waiting area and coffee station. Two conference rooms stood bare.

"We've sanitized the rest of your pictures, General Manager Hartford." My guide could have been male or female, a thin-faced, short-haired young person. "We're doing a quick sanitation on everything going into boxes from the offices, then those boxes will be run through additional cleansing at our plant. You'll have access to everything in about two weeks."

"You've done so much more than I expected." My respirator added weight, rested on a tender muscle. I wanted to tell my helper that we liked to place dried flowers in the outer office to add an outdoor scent to the DOE's filtered air, but I saved this androgynous individual from such a feminine emotional tidbit. "Which office should we start on?"

"Well, we actually have most things out of Director David's space."

"Tell me your name? We're going to be working together."

"It's Fran." My helper smiled. "My parents named me after an old friend of the family."

I looked to Lao, finding this situation funnier than it should be. His dark eyes, like those of a parent in church, suggested I stay on task.

"Okay, Fran." Government protocol wouldn't allow this person to use my first name unless we became informal friends, so I didn't offer. "Let's look at David's office."

Every drawer in his oak credenza had disappeared. Workers on six-foot ladders passed books to others to be placed in a metal apparatus that sounded like a vacuum. The spines were scanned, then the books were placed in lined boxes. I watched as they finished one box and placed an inventory list on its side. A stack of boxes stood outside his office door, each marked with specific shelf identification: kids' artwork, photo, baseball hat, coffee mug, toy tractors.

Industrial lighting overwashed the rooms with harsh brightness. My husband, who loved natural light by day and soft illumination at night, was as removed from his office as the Paraguayan jungles.

"Maybe we could work on my office." I turned away. Lao moved aside, engaged in discussion with the site manager. While I walked the distance between our offices, I reminded myself that these people were doing their job with efficiency and competence and had no reason to add compassion to a tight time line.

My conference table pieces now lay piled against one wall, four intact chairs shoved aside. The visitor chair Peterson smashed through the window had disappeared, as had its mate. My legs began shaking and I knew I could not sit at my desk and have the stain of Peterson's blood on the wall fill my sight each time I looked up.

"Lao was right." I turned away. "You should finish this. I'll just hold up your work."

"It's no problem, General Manager Hartford. I'll stay here and help." I appreciated the kindness in Fran's voice but knew I needed to leave.

"I'm sorry if you made special accommodations for me, but I really can't do this, Fran." Turning with me, the cleaning staff member followed me out and helped me remove the protective gear.

The night felt cool, as if October was closer than the calendar showed. Hobbling alone back to my family, I reminded myself that this was only a building, not our life. I originally arrived at Ashwood with everything I possessed in my mother's old suitcase and two boxes. Having built a new life, I'd not leave my home the same way.

Chapter Thirty-One

Our family quarters were dark and quiet when I arrived. Finally I followed Dr. Frances's advice about rest. Ignoring medical protocols, I medicated myself with the strongest pain medicine in our bathroom kit plus a sleeping aid, put on my pajamas, and turned out the lights. Finding a comfortable position in our bed took as many minutes as the little yellow pill required to drag me into sleep.

My mind traveled far and wide through a tornado of the last days' experiences. At three, back muscle spasms woke me. I waited in the dark for something bad to happen. At four o'clock I put my good foot to the floor, then my swollen one, hobbled to David's small coffeemaker and started a mug brewing while I showered. Five minutes under a hot water spray couldn't steam away my stiffness. Dressed in soft clothes, I began Sunday. During harvest, it was almost like every other day in the week except for a morning devotions hour and closed school building.

With our bedroom curtains pulled aside, I watched dawn break the darkness. Sitting at David's desk, I turned on my data pad to review yesterday's production reports and mail. The DOE offered a temporary lab trailer if we remained willing to participate in their gifted student program. I responded enthusiastically and forwarded a copy of the plan to Jason and Lao.

A picture of Tia and David at a long-ago holiday party accompanied the morning news' expanded story of the government's surrogate program scandal. Dancing around defamation laws, the reporters implied that Tia, while brilliant, was unstable and not the best DNA source for children to be raised by unassuming strangers. Videos of three of the Regan surrogates, two girls and a boy all living in Chicago, were offered. The children, one a year older than Phoebe and two younger than Noah, shared physical features with our kids. Making the video public broke all Bureau security guidelines.

I read the story, angered by the fine line reporters were willing to walk in keeping facts straight while suggesting novel interpretations. No one in a senior position in the current White House could speak to how the surrogate program became corrupted or convince readers that this tampering might not still be in practice. At the end of the article, the reporter reminded readers of the ambush in Paraguay and wondered at the irony that the surrogate son of David's second wife recently came to live with the family. That an orphaned surrogate child had been forced on a woman who might soon be widowed and raising her husband's orphaned children. Without thinking of the time, I called Milan.

"You're lucky I have an early-morning flight, Anne." Milan, while he was awake, didn't sound like he was ready for business. "Something must be wrong."

"Have you read the morning news post? A second installation on the surrogate story that features David and Tia."

"Give me ten minutes and I'll call you back. We had an agreement that the second story would be held for next week." He disconnected.

I stayed at the desk, wondered how Sarah and Paul would deal with all the pain raised in this story—the insinuation of mental instability for Tia's offspring, the videos of the grandchildren they might never know, the closing paragraph with its mention of me as a widow. My coffee went cold as the morning light gained meager strength. Milan called back.

"Anne, I've read the article. The series is meant to embarrass the secretary of Welfare, the executive directors of the Bureau of Human Capital Management, and the president, whose husband spent his career in the Bureau." Irritation played under his voice. "We've taken the only action we can and shut down the video segments." He coughed, a morning tendency I've sat through during years of early calls.

"I'm keeping our kids close to the residence. We've posted specific signage forbidding photographing residents, workers, and all staff." I already felt tired, wanting just one day to begin without drama. "I suspect this story is big enough to attract photographers to Ashwood for pictures of our kids."

"Tell Sarah and Paul that I'm sorry."

"What they want to ask about is why you didn't tell them about these children." He didn't respond. "I think they feel betrayed that they haven't heard this from you."

"Anne, my official responsibility is to the children, not to the Regan family." Again the cough.

"To Sarah and Paul, the children *are* the family." My quiet time for the day was over. Long-ago unethical decisions of people in power now threw us into the uncharted legal grounds of this scandal. "They would like all six of these kids brought to Ashwood and might well engage counsel to press their interest."

"In David's absence?"

"Perhaps because of David's absence." Someone knocked at my door. "Because they believe this is what he will want and because they want to hold on to anything that reminds them of their son. I have to go."

"I'll be in touch."

Paul waited in the hall, a big man made even larger with anger. "Turn on your data pad. There's a story."

"I've read it, Paul. I talked with Milan. There isn't anything the government can do."

"Fine friend. He's legal guardian for David's children and hides them from us. Doesn't even have the decency to let you and David know any of this until it can't be hidden. He's a snake."

I eased Paul into our room, closed the door before the whole estate heard his words through gossip. "How is Sarah?"

"She's making plans for where they'll sleep when we get them here. I'm thinking maybe we should take all of our grandkids to South Dakota and the ranch. Life is simpler there. Not so much pressure, not all of this crisis."

"Sit with me for a few minutes, help me think through talking with the kids."

He shook his head, ready for action, not talking. "Isn't that why your friend sent the doctor here? Talk with her, then have her tell Sarah and me what she's figured out."

"Milan did not send Dr. Frances here. Terrell made the arrangements on our behalf." The generally patient, wise Paul left as emotionally tight as I'd ever seen him. I followed, steered off into the kitchen. Dr. Frances sat at the counter, on the stool where I usually sat, talking with Terrell. They both turned.

"You've read the news," she said. Terrell stood up, offered me his stool.

"Yes." I waved Terrell back to his seat. "Paul and Sarah are overwhelmed. I'm so angry about everything in the past week, I can't even think straight."

"How do you do your best thinking?" I thought her lips looked different, her eyes softer. Terrell moved away, touched her knee first.

"Usually on my own, but if you don't mind moving slowly, I would appreciate company outside."

She slid from the stool. "Lead the way."

Terrell handed me a travel mug of coffee, a half sandwich, and two tablets. "Better you take these here with a glass of water and eat that sandwich as you walk."

So, like a child, I stood next to the counter and took my medicine. "By the way, when you conduct the next medical audit, I'm guilty of self-medicating."

"We'll take care of that. I want to rebandage that ankle, then you can take a walk."

Dr. Frances and I slipped on yard coats. My feet wanted to move fast, to trot or run, but even a rough hobble taxed my strength. I led the doctor around the front of the residence, glanced at the DOE building, where a crew already readied for demolition. We headed to the orchard, where the smell of sun-ripened apples mixed with the overly sweet stink of fallen fruit rotting in tall grass. The bees would be busy when the sun truly rose, but in the half-light of early morning all was still. Bunnies dashed out ahead of us. Across the near silence, sounds from the livestock could be heard.

"Phoebe says walking here with you is one of her favorite activities."

The comment made me smile. "There was an old orchard here that David and I decided to restore the first year we were married. We are both tree lovers, but every estate investment must support food production and jobs." I breathed in, held the sweet air in my lungs. "We planted hundreds of fruit trees where we could see the growth from our offices."

"How do you feel about the story referring to you as a possible widow?"

"It's not just about how I feel. You do understand that, if David dies, the Bureau could determine that Phoebe and Noah should be raised elsewhere? I'm afraid of losing my kids."

"You are a powerful influence in your stepdaughter's life." Dr. Frances walked like an experienced country hiker, not needing to watch her feet on the uneven ground. "Your resiliency and steadiness give her an important sense of stability. And your sense of humor encourages her to be a child. Phoebe needs you."

I slowed, relieved to hear this clear declaration. "It's become a bit more complex because of how Paul and Sarah are responding to this story. If David doesn't return, they want legal custody of all his biological children." I slowed to sip coffee. "There has been a lot of pressure on our business to increase production, pay more taxes, and make all that happen with fewer resources. Paul works very hard and he isn't a young man. Because of all of that, they want to return to South Dakota."

"How does that make you feel?" She spoke softly.

"I think you can figure it out." I sipped again, took a few bites of the sandwich, then threw the rest down for the birds. "I know they have no real understanding of how the Bureau managed these gifted kids' futures."

Grackles filled the air around us with their edgy heckling. Something about these black winged creatures frightened John as a baby and still made him nervous. They circled near the edge of the trees, possibly fixated on a mouse. I understood their victim's feelings too well.

"David has never spoken with his parents about the legal requirements we must meet in education, testing, and developmental activities to keep Phoebe and Noah with us." Rough ground snagged my support boot, making me stumble. Dr. Frances reached for my elbow, steadied me.

"Anne, don't underestimate what your parents-in-law know. They've done a bit of their own research over the years. For example, Sarah told me you pay a handsome salary for Teacher Jason to keep her grandchildren at home."

"But she can't really understand how the Bureau plans to manage these kids' adult lives and keep them as intellectual employees." A large rabbit dashed ahead on our path. "We just act like parents and hope for some major change before Phoebe and Noah grow up."

"You're sensitive to Sarah's feelings about surrogacy. Why?"

"How do you think a woman who gave up her career to raise five boys on an isolated ranch would respond to a government program requiring a woman to have her tubes tied and allow her babies to be carried by a surrogate?" I took a wrong step again and my ankle twisted. "Damn." Distant sounds of machinery and animals and voices drifted through the trees, a life I never sought. "They didn't have to make the tough personal decisions our generation made to pull this country out of the depression. Financial stuff changed on the ranch, but not freedom. They don't want to know the hard fact that their surrogate grandchildren are not truly free citizens."

I tossed most of my coffee in a high arc into the grass. The air was warming, the sun showing beautiful fruit nearly ready for harvest. "It stinks. David and Tia got a good education, comfortable housing, and generous compensation but lost the most fundamental rights of human beings—choosing their own mates and raising their own babies."

"Everyone sacrificed to bring the United States back to stability." Logical tenacity appeared to be Dr. Frances's strength. "You wanted to be a teacher, I wanted to do research, Terrell wanted to be a therapist. This is what happens when countries tank."

"I'm fine making those sacrifices for myself—but not for the next generation. Our rights weren't taken away before we were born. Our DNA wasn't manipulated to make us supposedly superior individuals." I stopped. "Let's go back. My ankle's not quite up to another half mile."

We turned around, walked in silence. "Dr. Frances, I am grateful for how my life developed, but it's hard to set my mind at peace with what might be expected of our children." Grackles flew up in front of us. Dr. Frances startled.

"I feel betrayed by somebody." I wandered into sharing thoughts I never felt free to speak before. "The government did a bang-up job hauling this country out of the depression. Somehow I thought if my generation worked really hard, our kids would have a life more like what we knew before this all happened."

Dr. Frances stood at my side, her face warmed by the sun. She toed an apple, bent to pick it up. "This one looks good," she said. "You're not alone with those sentiments." She wiped the apple on her jacket. "So back to what to tell the children. I'll be with you, but you know how to speak from the heart. They know the basic story already."

"And how do I comfort Phoebe, who will read that last paragraph about the possibility of being an orphaned surrogate child?"

"With love, Anne." A breeze rustled tree branches around us. The grackles gone, birds sang in the trees. "You can only assure her that there are people here who love her. No promises about her father. She's not as fragile as you think and she needs honesty."

With that opening, Dr. Frances began to speak about Phoebe's night terrors. "You know Phoebe is a genius. But she's still a little girl. I'm working with her to help her manage her intellect. On a very basic level, she is also very creative, with no outlet for her artistic side. So she and I are starting a quilt project this afternoon—fun activity in no way connected to academics, although she'll use all her math skills without knowing it. Right now she needs to make things with her hands."

"Like David. You know about his woodworking."

"About time someone mentions that she is her father's child as well as her mother's. Yes, like David." The doctor nodded. "How are you doing now?"

We left the orchard, heading back to Ashwood's morning bustle. I realized that my complaints about the country's direction could only be made by someone whose life had improved significantly, that most of the folks working at Ashwood still faced a daily struggle to feed their kids.

"I'm going to take everything one day at a time for a few weeks," I answered. "Today is going to be difficult."

Chapter Thirty-Two

THE CHILDREN LISTENED AS I TALKED ABOUT the morning news story. Noah and John asked age-appropriate questions about their siblings. Perhaps the ease of Andrew's arrival led them to think their grandparents and mom could easily spread love and attention over six more kids. Phoebe read through the story as I answered the boys.

"News writers like to be mean." She cut off Noah's theory that Teacher Jason would have to hire more teachers if all the Regan kids attended our school. "They just like to make people feel bad." She waved a hand in my direction. "How can they call us all orphans when people saw Dad *and* we have a mother?"

"I know he's coming home." John whispered. "I know it, but he could be hurt." His chin quivered. "He's coming home." I kissed the top of his head, felt hair as coarse as David's under my lips.

In a quiet moment, they each processed our discussion, and then acted like kids as they chose to put absolute trust in John's sense that their father would come home. Sarah and Paul sat by silently, their morning anger not entirely spent.

"Mom, maybe we should get a dog now instead of waiting until Christmas," our youngest child suggested. "At night it could sleep with Phoebe so she doesn't have bad dreams, and it could chase writers away when we're in school."

"Grandma says we need a distraction," Noah added. "If we got a dog today, we could teach it tricks to surprise Dad."

Paul smiled. "We'll do it," he announced without looking my way. "Not a big dog, but some nice smallish mutt that needs a home. I have one in mind." He remembered to show political sensitivity. "Your mother is right that pets are a luxury as long as there are hungry people, but we'll figure out a way to make this happen."

I sat with my kids during the morning devotions service. Sarah's words flowed past me as my mind wandered. Andrew and Phoebe joined a crew gathering vegetables from the kitchen gardens and the young boys brought their weekly lesson plans to me for review. By lunch, my head hurt more than my ankle and I rested for a few hours. After a quiet dinner, Paul and Sarah asked me to their quarters.

Their sitting room was my first room at Ashwood. The view of meadow and trees still made me pause. They named a wingback chair near the windows "the Annie seat." Tall-stem glasses waited next to a bottle of white wine. I gave Sarah a small kiss on the cheek, turned down a glass from Paul because of my medications.

"We've decided to pull together an organization of families caught up in this awful surrogacy program," Sarah started. "I don't mean to be critical of what you and all the surrogate mothers did. You were quite selfless." She looked at Paul. "We have a friend who is a lawyer in Washington, D.C., quite a powerful lawyer, and he has agreed to help us challenge the Bureau of Human Capital Management's right to control the lives of these children."

Paul stood next to her chair. "We don't expect you to get involved. You have a very full plate. This is a Regan family issue."

"A few days ago you were telling me that the two of you called me a Regan." I tried to smile.

"Dear girl, Paul didn't mean anything." Apology and love thickened Sarah's voice. "We will be wherever you and the children need us to be as your family."

Paul moved behind my chair, put his hands on my shoulders. "You're a part of our lives, Anne Hartford Regan. I should have chosen my words more carefully. As blood relatives of these kids, we have legal rights that you can't claim. That's all I meant. We're doing this for all David's biological children born through surrogacy. Sarah and I would like to think you could be the best mother for all of them. With our involvement."

For a moment the thought of ten children ranging in age from five to ten reminded me of one summer as a Montessori teacher's aide and the crazy level of activity generated by so many bright students. Paul and Sarah were chasing a pipe dream in challenging the Bureau, but it was theirs to do.

"Shouldn't you wait for David to return?" Sarah looked at Paul for an answer to my question. "Isn't this his decision as their biological father?"

"We thought of that, but Sarah feels timing is critical—to call media attention to the rights of the biological families while the story is fresh and politicians want to restore voters' confidence. Do you think anyone would have voted for our current president if they knew her husband was one of the architects of the surrogacy contract?"

Deep in South Dakota, the ranching Regans were spared from the worst of the big D. I knew David spared them the pressure he encountered—economic and patriotic—to accept the chains that accompanied his life. "What sounded right a decade ago might not make sense today. It was a pretty desperate time."

"Well, that's the point, Anne." Paul spoke as if he'd said these very things a number of times today. "Times change. There is a body of court decisions protecting grandparents' rights in divorces, unmarried couples' offspring, abandoned children. So now it's time to look at the rights of biological families of surrogates. Because Tia died without family, our case will be the easiest to file."

For fifteen minutes Paul covered the key legal questions identified by their lawyers. He walked the room, a confident man on a critical mission. Sarah, ever more tired and pale as the days stretched without David's return, added her insights. I kept quiet about what I knew of the surrogate contracts, and they didn't ask for copies of the legal challenges David and I had filed in our early marriage on behalf of the kids. When Paul began to repeat himself, I reminded them that I promised to spend the evening with my kids. We were able to laugh at Paul's rhetoric and separate with a prayer that Paul's birthday would bring good news about David.

Passing the dining room, I saw Amber and John decorating Paul's chair at the breakfast table. Birthdays never passed without notice if kids were present. Monday, the family sang to Paul at breakfast, then honored his wish to hold real celebration until David returned home.

Against Lao's advice, I didn't join the Giant Pines' outing, but stayed behind to witness demolition of the DOE building. The crew helped me dress in protective clothing. I stood respectfully quiet as our little piece of the earth shook for less than a minute and deflated the domed structure. Together Lao, the crew's chief engineer, and I toured the residence for any signs of damage caused by the implosion. A giant old mirror in our public gathering room had slipped from its brackets and cracked, a light in the dining room lost one shade, and a new crack showed in the foyer.

For the very first time, I slept absolutely alone in the residence, not one child worker or staff person or family member filling its space with sounds.

Unfettered from the DOE building, Ashwood seemed smaller, yet more dominant on the estate's horizon.

Within a few days, life settled back into its regular patterns. The kids chose to talk about David as if he were away on a long business trip. Sarah and I convinced Paul to take a day trip into Rochester for a checkup at the Mayo Clinic. He balked at time away from harvest and their "Stolen Children" class action campaign. Percy Slaxhill, the lawyer handling the case pro bono, grabbed media attention within a week of the original media story, holding a news conference with only one exhibit—a chart displaying the differences between annual income of the couples raising the stolen surrogate children and the earnings of their biological parents. He managed to paint a picture that implied the babies were given to individuals who were not merely powerful, but also extreme wealthy. Washington, D.C., reeled as names were attached to the chart. Milan was right. Heads would tumble.

Fourteen days went past with no new information about David. My ankle improved, the bruising on my chest began fading to yellow with traces of red and purple, my back calmed. Phoebe slept through the nights as her quilt project flourished. I found it harder to find rest.

October began with the final push in the fields, orchard, and gardens. Our harvest broke records, yet left us with less reserves after meeting the increased government quotas. Terrell, Magda, and I debated what to send to market and what to put in Ashwood's storage.

Andrew marked his one-month anniversary at Ashwood with a bad bout of homesickness for his parents' house. He and I sat at the pond's edge and I listened to a young boy's emotional basket of stories as frogs jumped and squirrels sprang lightly from tree to tree. We both wore multiple layers of clothes, the sun no longer able to keep us warm. I knew I loved my son, felt so grateful that Milan had brought him to our home.

Almost at the end of the sixth week, Milan called during the dead of night to give me the news that David and two associates had been rescued. All three men were weak and fighting infections. At three-thirty in the morning I pulled on a robe and ran to my in-laws' room to share the news. Together we gathered the children for celebration and prayer. Soon no one in the residence slept as the Regan kids raised their voices in wild joy. The new puppy, Rufus, peed on the floor. We all laughed. Laughing was once again easy.

Chapter Thirty-Three

When we could speak with David, the nightmare came to an end. He was alive, each of us heard his voice and felt connected. He heard about Rufus, spoke with Andrew, wished Paul a belated happy birthday. Each time I spoke with him in the next few days, I kept news from Ashwood light.

Arrangements were made for me to fly to Washington, D.C., to be with David. Strapped into a surplus seat in a military transport, I settled into my thoughts. The constant engine drone distanced me from my daily world, fueled my apprehension about how Paraguay might have changed David. Civilians moved down the walkway first. I hung back, looking through the windows for a first sight of my husband before he could see me.

David stood alone and I rushed to him, no children outpacing me, no bags slowing me. We were like many couples reunited after one of them has been to war—incredibly happy to feel our arms filled with the other's warmth, yet cautious about how our experiences might stop us from moving further. He was gaunt and favored the shoulder where the DOE chip used to lie so his arms no longer folded around me with the same easy fit. With limited foreknowledge, we avoided touching in certain ways even in this first greeting.

"I've been waiting for this minute," he said into my ear as we stood at the Andrews Airbase. "Sometimes at night I'd try to remember the smell of your shampoo." Like our new puppy, David sniffed my hair. Tears and giggles came together as I rested against his chest. "What? What? Tell me why you're laughing."

"David, right now it feels so good to feel you that my smile turned into a laugh." His arms tightened. He didn't join in my lightheartedness. "My God, I've been so worried about you." His arms tightened, and I inhaled the scent of his favorite soap.

"When they told me the chip had been removed I worried about how an open wound would heal in the jungle." I turned my head against his shirt.

"I thought about you at the oddest times, like when we had applesauce cookies or when John had hiccups. And the nights were the worst."

He kissed me, a rare public display of affection. Our military escort politely indicated that we needed to move into a waiting limousine. David eased himself in with a new stiffness of motion. There would be time to talk about what had happened, what had changed. For these few minutes we were like newlyweds on the way from church to reception, sitting hand in hand and watching a world unaware of how our world had evolved.

I hadn't been back to D.C. since completing estate management training. "I miss this place," I said as we drove across the Potomac. "Wouldn't it be great to take the kids here or to New York City or to see mountains?"

"You're talking to a man who spends half of his time away from home, Anne. Flying means work for me." He squeezed my hand, but his voice sounded grouchy. "Anyway, it will be soon enough when the Bureau begins sending Phoebe to education sessions all over the country."

We would need to uncover the new sensitive topics we had each developed, like my fear of home invasion and the growing rift between Paul and me about Milan. I dreaded discovering David's new forbidden subjects.

"I'm in therapy of various sorts from nine to noon, work for a couple of hours in early afternoon, then take a nap by doctor's orders." His fingers played with mine on the seat. "I hope you'll be all right on your own?"

"I lived here for years, David. This is kind of a homecoming. No one I know is still here to look up, but I can't wait to visit the Smithsonian, the Mall, the Capitol. One of my favorite neighborhood places is still open, and I'd like to take you there for breakfast or dinner." The transport pulled into the JW Marriott near the White House. The penniless estate matron trainee wandering D.C. never aspired to staying in a place this posh.

"Nothing but the best for DOE staffers held captive for over a month in the jungle," David quipped. "We have a suite on the seventh floor with a sliver of a view of the White House."

The limo door opened. I stepped out into the Southern autumn air, so different from the coolness settling over Ashwood. These were the streets I wandered when I was pregnant with Andrew. Pedestrians wore the uniforms of their offices, with few in simple civilian garb like us. David eased out, straightened his back with care, and moved to the doors. No time wasted between the safety of the vehicle and the security of the building. No opportunity for ambush.

How odd to see the luggage David carried from Ashwood on a rack in the hotel room perfectly intact. I emptied my bag as he watched from an easy chair between two corner windows. The silence felt comfortable, yet our experiences made us different from the people who kissed good-bye in September.

"I heard the DOE building is down." David's statement caught my thought, found me unprepared to answer neutrally. "The investigators believed Peterson brought in restricted chemicals to contaminate the building."

If he read the report, David knew about the blood on my office wall and the dead men in our work space. "They were good at cleaning small things and creating an organized storage system." If I closed my eyes, I could still see the empty offices, damaged furniture, broken windows. "Everything else is gone."

"They'll rebuild. Supposed to start this week." He rubbed his chin, moving around a scab. "You and Lao made smart changes in their design." David watched as I left to place my toiletries in the bathroom, and his eyes followed as I came back into the main room. "I'm off international travel for eighteen months. I had to take a cut in pay for that agreement."

"I'm relieved." I sat on the ottoman, rested my hand on his leg.

"How are you doing, Anne? Let me see your wounds."

"There isn't much to see."

"Come on, Annie, I want to see what that bastard did to you," he commanded.

"There's not much to see. The bruising is faded." The room felt airless, his face immobile. "We'll move on, David."

"Or die trying." David shrugged with a slight hitch near his shoulders, a motion of his body I didn't know.

"We should order lunch."

"Why don't we find someplace nearby? It's a nice day."

"Let me do this my way today."

We stayed in and ate spinach salad with almonds and chicken. We ordered wine instead of tea. Washington, D.C., moved about its normal business seven stories below while David told me about the ambush, the long hike into the jungle, the confusion of his captors. At times he'd point to a scar or a bruise and tell me its story. In the late afternoon, he finished.

"I need to sleep," he said abruptly. "Probably better if I do this alone. Please don't go away." He walked around the room, turned on every light, and opened the blinds. While he napped I sent assuring messages to Paul and Sarah and tended to business as a distraction. Our luncheon wine dulled my worries, but not enough.

Later a special dinner of lobster and filet was set up for us in our suite on a table with linens and candles. We decided to dress up. I pinned my hair high on my head, glad my natural auburn color still had shine, wore make-up and a midnight blue dress he liked. My city look, the kids would say. While we waited for dinner, we spoke about our kids' adjustment to Andrew and life in general at Ashwood. I shared pictures and stories.

"Tell me about my parents' Stolen Children campaign." David leaned back in his chair, ginger ale filling his wine glass. Chardonnay, not a good label, gave me an artificial sense of well-being.

"So you know about the scandal?"

"I was briefed during the return flight. Damn rude shock. Are you getting pressure from the Bureau to have the case dropped?" He leaned forward, picked up a roll. "I've been called by four highly placed DOE officials. And I'm supposed to be off-limits."

"Did you understand that the issue is about mismanagement of the entire surrogate program—from what happened to surrogates like me to stealing embryos like yours?" His eyes narrowed, suggesting I was bringing a new perspective to the story. "You didn't say how you feel about all of this."

He stopped buttering a roll. "Betrayed. Knowing my children were taken and hidden from me definitely changes how I approach life and this job." Like his father, David threw off powerful energy as he spoke about these children.

"It's been difficult talking to our kids about this—first I had to explain Andrew's arrival, and then the media story about the embryos began. We may be the only couple caught in both parts of the Bureau's fiasco." I sensed a lack of empathy when I mentioned Andrew and suspected David felt reparation had been made with returning my son. "If it wasn't for his parents' deaths, Andrew would be as stolen from me as your children. And I carried him for an entire pregnancy," I added. "It might seem like all has been made right, but I feel deeply mistreated."

As if weeks of isolation now placed David on his own emotional island, his thoughts and words focused on his feelings.

"No one will tell me anything about my three children who were not covered in the investigative report. I don't know where they live or what they look like. All I've been told is that there are four boys and two girls, all enrolled in the gifted offspring program." He licked his lips, shook his head. "I wish to God they had normal intelligence and were not of interest to the fucking Bureau of Human Capital Management."

"David, your father blames Milan for the cover-up." Creases above his right eye suggested I missed a step. "Milan says he was not aware that all the children he guardians were Regan offspring until he was notified that an investigative journalist had started working on the story. He had suspicions as the children began developing similar physical features, but nothing else. Your parents won't believe him, called him a complete phony."

He whistled low. "You believe Milan?" I nodded. "I think you're right. He's saved our butts and intervened on Phoebe's behalf more than once. I think he's got our family's well-being at heart. Especially when it involves you or Phoebe."

I reached out to touch his hand. "No one from the Bureau has talked with me, and I have no legal rights as far as the six Regan children. Your parents felt they needed to start action on behalf of their rights as grandparents." He didn't respond to my touch. I sat back.

David pulled back his hand, copied my action and sat tall in this chair. "You and I are meeting with a public relations and media consultant tomorrow. I intend to be in the middle of the legal activity." He picked up his glass. "Agreed?"

"I'll totally support you with the understanding that I want what's best for the kids." I spoke softly, aware that David might find my words disloyal. "They could be with terrific parents and have very good lives that this lawsuit would change." He closed his eyes. I hoped he didn't close his ears. He didn't challenge what I said, so I continued. "If I could be sure we were looking out for the children, not just for what we adults want, then I'm with you all. Horrific wrongs were done to all of us. I just can't universally accept that the kids would be better off at this age becoming part of their biological families and living with people they've never met along with a gang of other traumatized kids."

David's lips curved into a small smile, an almost sad acknowledgment that what I said was true. "You've always understood kids. I don't want to hurt anyone either." His hand moved back and forth across the table edge. "But I do want my kids to know who they really are and to be compensated for what was done to them. Maybe they could be released from gifted-offspring work commitments or given the opportunity to become active members of their biological families."

His words sounded exploratory while his face remained assertive. "I don't know what should be done, but I won't let the government decide that without my rights also being acknowledged."

"The oldest kids involved are older than Andrew—almost twelve years old. I'll support the lawsuit only if we protect their rights." I held up my glass as if to salute our common interest. "But I warn you that right now your father and mother are on the romantic road, with the goal of having all their grandchildren brought together for your mother's seventieth birthday party on the family ranch in South Dakota."

He raised his glass and we clinked hotel stemware. He put his down, rose, and took my glass away. "I want us to have a baby, Annie. A free child like John who won't be part of all this educational and institutional bullshit. Maybe two."

He pulled me to my feet. "Let's make our second free child now." We left lobster and candles as he led the way to the bedroom. I felt conflicted, desiring David but anxious about the aura of power he exuded. He closed the door, locked it from within, and turned to me like a man afraid of losing what was standing beyond his hands.

David ignored the pins that would loosen my hair and pulled at my dress. He used no words, wanted me naked faster than the dress would fall, was on top of me. I struggled at first, then accepted his passion and tried to meet his rhythm. He climaxed quickly, a low groan filling the room.

His arms spread on either side of my head, his face lowered to the bed. I lay trapped under his body, still in my dress, one foot dangling off the bed. His weight, a familiar quilt in our regular lovemaking, became heavy in this odd mating experience. David rolled away, pulled me next to his body, him lying on his injured shoulder. Within five minutes I heard the normal deep breathing of his sleep. Candles still burned in the other room. I had no inclination to sleep.

David gave a muffled protest as I eased out of his hold. He turned on me, eyes wide open. "No," he said and rolled us over.

"No," I echoed. "Give us some time." He backed off. I relaxed. "Just sleep. I need to clean up, wash off my makeup."

He mumbled something and rolled back to his side, eyes closing while his body remained tight. Moving carefully from the bed, I removed my dress, hung it in the closet, pulled on the hotel bathrobe. In the living room I turned off the lights, picked up my dinner plate, and sat at the window, where I stared at the city while I finished my meal.

When his sleep moved into a second hour, I showered and put on comfortable clothes before curling up on the uncomfortable hotel sofa to think about how our individual experiences of captivity might change our relationship. Around ten I stored the extra dinner rolls and fruit in my suitcase and called room service to have the table removed. I thought of sitting in the hotel lobby to watch those with social engagements wander in and out. While I finished the wine, my thoughts became caught on how life might have been had we lived here—where we would work and live, where the children would attend school.

I fell asleep on the sofa, like a child watching out the front window for Santa. After twelve I awoke and returned to the bedroom. David slept on the floor wrapped in blankets and a sheet from the bed, back against a wall. The surface wounds I thought well-healed showed me nothing of my husband's real injuries. I made myself a nest of pillows on the king-size bed, covered myself with the bathrobe, and ever so gently rocked myself to sleep.

Chapter Thirty-Four

The road to emotional recovery has fewer milestones than a healing cut, even one that's deeply infected. The next day, David and I worked with the publicist comfortably, as we had worked with other projects in the past. Tia may have fought the hijacking of her babies just on the principle that someone stole her property. David entered the fight as a father deeply concerned about the abuse of his children's rights.

Our evening turned hellish. David wouldn't eat, walked our suite incessantly as a storm developed. The sky darkened and large raindrops splattered on our window. At seven o'clock, he insisted I join him behind the locked bedroom door. He undressed, stalked me around the room until we called it a night. Once again he made love to me with a rhythm that I couldn't join. I slept with him in his floor nest.

On the fourth night, as his medications began to take effect, we stayed in bed, awake, my arms tight around his tensed body. I returned home on the fifth day after wandering Washington alone by day and managing David's ever-changing mental landscape by night.

Four weeks passed before David called me back to accompany him home. He took public transport to the airport to meet me. We spent a day in the city, visiting the White House and eating at a seafood restaurant. The next morning we boarded a DOE-chartered flight to Minnesota. Sweat formed on David's forehead as the plane landed. He hesitated as the door opened. But he walked off on his own, one hand in mine.

He'd left alone on a warm September day and he returned with me on a cloudy, cold November afternoon. He tired quickly as the kids' excitement rolled along and the puppy barked and his parents waited for their turn to feel David's arms around their shoulders. Only I knew that David's Pentagon therapist had contracted with Dr. Frances to stay at Ashwood and add him to her private clients.

Shortly before Thanksgiving, we held a small birthday party for both Paul and Phoebe. That morning David and I found his father sitting on the wooden foyer bench. Since the estate invasion, he always looked tired. This year I insisted he take the fields' quiet season as a time of rest. He chose to use his energy to further the Stolen Children cause. Finding us together, Paul began to complain.

"Our attorney wants to be released. His law firm doesn't know if they can afford to run without his billable time for the next two to three years." Paul sighed, then coughed. "Some of our group may not be alive to see this thing resolved, and our grandchildren aren't getting younger. What the hell is it going to take to shake sense into these bureaucratic idiots?"

"We knew that this could take years of court filings," I said as I sat down next to him. "What's upset you this morning?"

"I woke up feeling old. I woke up and realized I'd never know what all my grandchildren look like. I don't care if they don't ever see this old puss of mine, but it eats at me that I wouldn't recognize them on the street. It just got me down."

"You two find Sarah and wait in our family quarters." I stood. "Don't you dare go into the dining room or kitchen or you'll wreck the birthday surprises." I went to find holographic images Milan sent months earlier with strict confidentiality provisions. The little red-haired girl would surprise all of them. I hoped they would understand that these were six unique individuals, not rubber-stamped Regans.

David and his parents waited, totally unprepared for what I carried. "Paul, I know how you feel about Milan, but he took a significant risk to share something with me. Nothing about what you are going to see can ever be discussed outside this room. Do I have your word?"

Paul blustered about Milan and not wanting to give his word to a government lackey, now too frequent a tirade. "It's simple, Paul. Either you play by the rules or I go back to my office."

"Shut up, old man. I want to see what Annie has," Sarah said. Paul sat down.

They accepted the confidentiality agreement with their thumbprints. I handed over the holograms-six snippets from the lives of six youngsters living in five very different households around the country. The tears and exclamations that followed sounded like a family welcoming a newborn home. Everyone, including Paul and David, hypothesizing about these children's futures based on less than two minutes of images.

Sarah finally stood, hugged me. "You dear, dear daughter. This is Paul's greatest birthday gift. How smart you were to hold these for just the right time."

"I don't want to give them back," Paul said. "Let me keep them in our room for a few days."

As stubborn and crafty as my father-in-law proved himself in this battle with the Bureau, I couldn't take that risk. I held out my hands. David handed the storage cube with the six images to me.

"Actually, I think I'm the one who is the most thrilled," he said. "When I asked Annie to support my involvement with this lawsuit, she pointed out that this needed to be about what is best for these kids. I didn't want to understand what she was saying." He paused. "But it is worth a hell of a lot to see that their lives look good. Not that I'm ready to give up fighting to be part of their lives, but I feel assured that Milan is exerting a good influence and that they are doing well."

"Before I leave to put these away, I have one more thing to say." Paul looked like he wanted to disagree with David. Sarah had tears in her eyes. They all listened to me with different threads of thought coloring their receptivity. "This needs to be kept among this group of adults for at least the next month." Sarah's sadness appeared to lift, and she jostled Paul's arm. "I'm pregnant."

Chapter Thirty-Five

ASHWOOD SLID INTO THE HOLIDAY SEASON with less food in our storage than we had hoped as the Department of Agriculture ordered all agricultural units to release additional product for export. We were compensated for the lost inventory, but we needed the food. Inflation raged through the marketplace, pushing the price of sugar, spices and grain-based product beyond many households. We were frugal, grateful for the small grain-milling operation built at the insistence of Terrell. He and Sarah returned to reviewing depression recipes. I tried not to worry through this phase of managing Ashwood.

"It's like old times, Annie," Terrell commented as we finalized menus, including the estate's traditional Thanksgiving basket distribution and holiday buffet. "Only in our first year we had unexpected help from Milan and the Regan ranch. This year we have money, but I'm having to look farther than the Twin Cities to find products."

"Ironic that we can feed our people the finest meat and dairy products, even fresh produce, but it's so damn hard to find staples." Magda turned off her data pad. "Wish I could grow us sugar beets and spices. Thank God for last spring's record maple syrup collection. I'm going to research ways to distill better oils. We got to make Ashwood totally self-sufficient."

As usual when a government agency has wronged a civilian, the DOE poured money over us, as if a big bankroll could repair the damaged strands in our emotional fabric. Paul accepted compensation for his illegal incarceration and injuries, and dumped almost every dollar into the lawsuit. I settled quickly with the Pentagon to put the Peterson episode behind me. For the first time in my life, I invested some money in a careful portfolio of private businesses, betting that the country would return to a free market before our kids left home.

In honor of David's homecoming, the entire Regan family received invitations to Ashwood's Christmas celebration. Clarissa Smithson came to live with us at Ashwood as my personal assistant until after the baby's birth. Maybe the pregnancy tired me more easily, maybe the emotional hangover of September depleted my physical energy. I needed help and used the Pentagon settlement to pay for it.

With Thanksgiving three days away, Clarissa and I sat in my office looking over staffing reports. A handful of our workers would ride a special transport to the Twin Cities for home holiday visits, and three mothers were scheduled to visit their kids on the estate. Because of new greenhouse production, these small numbers caused ripples in staffing, which had been a heated discussion point at the management meeting that morning.

"Only a quarter of the child workers are going home this holiday season," Clarissa said as I explained our typical staffing. "That is so much lower than what the media report."

I sat back, admired her astute observation. Milan had been right when he encouraged me to reassess Clarissa. "It is the lowest number of kids going home since my first holiday here," I said. "The economy must be shaky when parents can't meet time or resources criteria for a home stay. I suspect there'll be more pressure to find work and housing space for kids by spring."

"It is extremely difficult for people to pull together a living." Her lips drew into a tense line. She sighed.

"Is that why you brought Andrew here?"

A rather quiet woman, Clarissa fidgeted with her pen, then looked my way without a shred of self-protection. "It is true that my husband funneled Andrew's funds to a foreign account. He daydreamed about our taking Andrew to Costa Rica. It was not only illegal but also stupid, like a lot of his other romantic dreams. We both had decent jobs and we lived in a secured neighborhood, but we never had enough money." Lines deepened around her mouth. "I was desperate when I appealed to Executive Director Milan. Absolutely desperate."

"You made the right decision, Clarissa. He's doing well here. Especially now that he can see you every day." I moved the conversation back to her responsibilities for the upcoming Regan gathering while my thoughts moved ahead to finding a permanent place for Andrew's aunt at Ashwood.

Gentle snow fell Thanksgiving morning, not enough to stick to surfaces for more than a few hours, but enough to create a holiday feeling. I gave myself a day off from Ashwood duties to be Mom. While our Thanksgiving meals would never look like the groaning-table feasts of my childhood, every person walking through the buffet had more than enough turkey and side dishes. Adults enjoyed regional wine or beer. We played games and sang and read out loud to each other. Some of the men and boys snuck off to watch sports, but the main attraction for the day was having downtime.

Clarissa and I finished buying Christmas presents, or end-of-the-year gifts for the non-Christians, during the week after Thanksgiving. I left her in charge of housing arrangements for the Regan crowd. I needed Sarah to put her energy behind kitchen holiday activities, but she and Paul remained obsessed with the Stolen Children campaign.

"I'd like to take the images of our kids with me next week to the lawyers," Paul told me as we left a management meeting. "I want to show them to a couple of our legal partners. They'll agree to Milan's terms."

"Paul, you agreed to keep those absolutely confidential. Not even tell others the images exist." Milan must have known Paul might talk, but still I made a mental note to forewarn my friend that information might be leaked. "No can do."

"But, Annie, those images are not yours to keep." Paul headed us down a road we'd been walking more frequently, drawing a distinction between the Regan children of David and Tia and those I mothered. "Those are my grandchildren."

"I'm not up for this discussion, Paul." Pregnancy hormones made me wickedly angry or slightly weepy as my blood sugar dropped about this time of morning. Today I just got angry, fed up with Paul's obsession. "You're drawing lines in this family—yours, mine and ours—that David and I don't like. Remember that I'm the one Phoebe and Noah call Mom." I tucked a shaking hand in my sweater pocket, upset by the frequency of my arguments with Paul. "Let the lawyers do their work. Government's slow movement will grind you down."

We stood close enough to touch, so close I could see thin red lines radiating across his cheeks under wind-dried skin. We shared the same space and air, but trod carefully on these grounds.

"I'm thinking I might need to step out of grains management. I'm seventy years old and these six kids mean more to me than filling production quotas for this government." He held his head high, a defiance I didn't expect. "Sarah loves what she's doing and one of us has to work to keep our government benefits intact."

"Can we talk about this after the holidays?"

He shook his head. "I want to tell the family over Christmas. I'm hoping a few will jump on board and be supportive of David's efforts to parent all his children."

"All right." I wanted to hug him and to feel those fatherly arms return the gesture. But Paul was too tightly wound. "I'm not going to look for a replacement until after the holidays." I pulled a handkerchief from one pocket and a small bag of dried fruit from another. "Sorry, I'm feeling shaky." I opened the bag, extended it toward him, and tried to smile. "Paul, you have to admit that we have a few things to celebrate this season."

His real nature showed itself with a grin. "Annie, you restore my optimism." His arms reached out to offer the hug I craved. "You need that dried stuff more than me."

Chapter Thirty-Six

December settled on Minnesota as if unsure of its direction. On the first day of the month seven inches of snow fell over twenty-four hours, putting an end to working outside in sweaters. Two days later rain fell intermittently for forty-eight hours, running down frozen paths, raising worries about icing. When the rain ended, temperatures bounced back into the forties.

The weather did no harm to Ashwood's greenhouses or livestock. Magda, Terrell, and I sat down with twenty days until Christmas to take stock of food supplies and estate greenhouse crops. We settled on a rotation of meatless and fish days to hold off butchering until January.

"We're better off than I expected," I commented. "Meals have more grains and eggs, but no one is complaining. Good go, Terrell."

He stretched, smiling as he lowered his hands from above his head. "I'm going to turn my kitchen over to Amber," he said. "That girl can come up with more suggestions about snazzy recipes than this old man. She should study estate management."

"Whatever Amber wants to study, she'll do well." Terrell, a key character witness in my process to adopt her, nodded as I spoke. Until the courts reached an agreement with Amber's mother, we kept the action under wraps at Ashwood.

"Good luck with attracting these kids to our jobs." Magda pulled on her jacket. "They think this is where they send people who can't do anything else." She slipped her data pad in a pocket. "Only three weeks until I'm in Europe."

"I'd like to spend a month away," I said. "Maybe I should plan on having this baby somewhere else, with a nice long recuperation. I think that was called maternity leave when we were young."

"The girls in the city still get eight weeks off." Magda put on gloves. "You're in the wrong profession, being an owner and all."

She left and Terrell hung back. "I've got some news just for you." He sat straighter in his chair. "Frances and I are planning to register our relationship in January."

I was off my chair and around the table for a hug.

"We'd like to apply for housing here if you have space."

"Of course, Terrell. But your news is mighty wonderful."

"I think this baby is the top story at Ashwood."

"Of course, but old news."

The pregnancy felt no different than my first two physically, but I was closer to forty than thirty. Emotionally I could not clarify how I felt—happy to have another child, yet uncomfortable with the circumstances of its conception. How odd to not use contraception for all those years and then become pregnant in Washington. David saw the timing of the pregnancy as a sign of a different future. I dreamt of a little girl with golden hair running through our orchards, a child of light.

During December David did a small amount of DOE work each day, but most of his time remained focused on recovery. Insomnia kept him walking the residence at night. His physical wounds healed, and he worked out every day to restore stability in his shoulder and flexibility in his back. Those who didn't know about the ambush would see a very healthy man.

"Dr. Frances says the pregnancy is going well." He looped his arm across my shoulders as we walked to our offices across the estate courtyard the day of Terrell's announcement. I felt like a college student walking to class. "What do you think?"

We bumped against each other by accident, and his arm slipped then resettled. "I feel fine. What scares me is thinking about how we secure a better future for our kids."

He turned, blocked our movement forward, his arm now enclosing my shoulders. "Annie, I've been in therapy for months to deal with Paraguay. My dad's working out his fears with dedication to a lawsuit that he hopes will bring control over his life." His arm tightened. "It's time we start paying attention to making you feel safe."

Over David's shoulder, I could see the resting orchards surrounding a very plain building we called our home. Ashwood's acres circled us on all sides, sounds from the roadway dampened by earth and rock and all we'd built—a safe, comfortable community of kids and adults moving ahead without fear of starving or freezing or violence. Until Peterson.

Small sleigh bells jingled across the courtyard, tied on the front door of the school building by one of the kids. Rufus raced across the distance directly toward me. David put a hand out to keep the growing puppy from jumping on my abdomen.

"Day by day I find it easier to put the Peterson experience in perspective, but I feel vulnerable." I couldn't look into David's face so I petted the dog's head, then started walking. "Some of that is natural for a pregnant woman." Rufus fell into step beside us. "I'd like to have some peaceful time, to get connected with this baby."

"Then let's work on those things—making you feeling safe, minimizing legal chatter and keeping you healthy." Just like a man to made a list and consider our worries solved. He opened the office building door, changed the subject as people looked up from their desks. "No criticism of Ashwood's offices, but I'm looking forward to the DOE building being finished."

Milan's voice called from my earpiece as we entered the building. "Anne, do you have time to talk about the Regan civil case?"

David's office door closed as I answered. "Sure. Let me close my office door. David and I just spoke about putting this aside until after the holidays."

He appeared on my desk screen, sitting in his home office. "Renovations at the Bureau so I'm working here for a few weeks." His voice dropped. "Driving my wife nuts."

"Remember, David and I are together almost twenty-four seven, so I can't empathize. I'd offer you an empty office here, but we're full up."

"This won't take long. By the way, congratulations on making production quotas during the last quarter. Your team held everything together during a difficult time." He smiled. "So Ashwood earns the top bonus award for its region."

"Milan, I'd rather have food supplies. If Terrell can find products, prices are higher almost daily. But, thanks, I'll distribute part of that bonus to our team." In fact I already had given bonuses to key staff members. "You mentioned the surrogate case?"

"I wanted to tell you this news first. You can tell David." He paused. "Your legal adoption of Phoebe and Noah makes the Regan kids unique in the surrogate scandal. The expert witness of Dr. Frances convinced Bureau officials to amend the original documents signed by Tia and David, and place permanent custody in your name should David die before Noah reaches nineteen years of age. Assuming both you and David are willing to sign the amendment, this removes Phoebe and Noah from one part of the class action suit." His look turned serious. "If David adopts Andrew, we might be able to extend the agreement."

The children's sketches saved from my old office hung next to my desk, and my eyes stayed there as I responded. "I would need to think about Clarissa's rights as well. Can we bring David in on this right now? It would give us peace of mind."

I called David to my office and watched his face while Milan went over the details of the proposed amendment. He pumped one fist in the air, his wedding band catching the light. "Send the papers to us and we'll sign." David gave Milan thumbs up. "We appreciate your work."

"I'll have copies sent to you and your legal counsel this afternoon." Milan punched into his desk data pad, then leaned into his camera. "I also want you both to know I'm doing what I can to keep a few kids and their parents out of what will be a very big storm. This will be the last we can speak of the case. All conversations with Bureau guardians of affected kids will to be scrubbed by investigators starting tonight."

I assumed our conversations were already stored somewhere and wondered why he made such a point of mentioning the listeners. "Milan, you and your wife are still planning on attending the holiday pageant December 22? We have workers who are hoping you two will read winter poems again."

"We wouldn't miss the pageant. And the reading is up to my wife. Whatever she says, we will do. As long as it doesn't include a costume." Normal for our conversations, he responded to another call and left abruptly.

"Excellent," David said in the quiet of my office. "Milan comes through for us." He stood, leaned over the table, and kissed the top of my head. "Let's enjoy what we have until after the holidays."

Six days before Christmas I spent a day in the Twin Cities to finish shopping, visit a private obstetrician, and have lunch with Milan. Based on how young people dressed on the streets, I guessed that we would have at least one worker return from home visits with only one wide strip of hair. Giant metal detectors as well as pat downs to stop knifings supposedly made shopping safer on some popular streets. Rumors of something called soft bomb hijacks could be heard in store lines.

I wore urban clothes, carried a hidden purse, and kept my eyes focused straight ahead. Everyone moved with a different energy on the sidewalks of Minneapolis. With packages in the transport and an uneventful doctor visit, I walked to a café for our lunch.

"You look great, Anne." Milan stood as I approached his table. "The cities always agree with you."

"This is where I expected to spend my life." I sat down, slipped off my jacket. "I didn't anticipate an estate would become my permanent address."

He lifted a hand to attract our waitperson. "We'll have a pot of your special tea while we read the menu." I nodded in agreement. "When do the Regans arrive?"

"December 23. Sarah is finally busy baking and reworking meal plans with Terrell." I sipped my tea. "I'm relieved one of David's parents is taking time away from the lawsuit."

In the café light, Milan looked different. Raised veins marked his hands, dark shadows circled his eyes. I wondered how old he was when I first met him and if we both showed the years.

"Annie, what do you want to do with the rest of your life?"

Milan's question dropped into our holiday luncheon as unexpectedly as if I had found Santa Claus suddenly sitting in the empty chair next to me.

"Why ask?" I waited for an answer. He continued to look at me, not speaking. "David has less than three years of DOE service remaining, and when Phoebe turns thirteen, her schooling could change how we live. I'm fairly content with my life."

He listened, poured his first tea, and sipped. I did the same, waiting for Milan to respond.

"I ask for two reasons. The more immediate is that there are two underperforming estates in the Ashwood region that I would like to discuss placing under contract with Hartford, Ltd., for management services. We'd leave the matrons in place, but have them report to you."

A waitperson approached and we ordered soup. Milan continued. "When the Bureau began, we had such high expectations for training a world-class workforce. But the farther we move from the economic depression, the less enthusiasm it seems people have for working hard or following an established plan."

"Inflation isn't helping," I suggested. "I remember feeling that no matter how hard I worked, I couldn't build any financial security. Don't you remember that?"

"The country's heading into a correction. We'll be fine by the end of the first quarter." Warm bread arrived. "Whether we're ready or not, the large international corporations are impatient for the resetting of the economies."

"You call it a correction, but people are going hungry. I think that's dangerous."

"You're right. We'll see change soon." His face became animated, not a word I'd usually connect with Milan. "More important, Annie, we want you to know there is always the possibility of a significant role for you in the Bureau. Maybe when Phoebe starts schooling off the estate, you might be ready for city living."

Four months ago I thought I knew what the future held for our family. Four months ago we planned for a small place in the city where someone would travel with Phoebe if she attended specialized secondary schooling. We didn't know our family would expand to include Andrew or a new child. David and I had not thought about the possibility of our dying before our children grew.

"You forget that Andrew might be our first to attend secondary gifted schooling." I smiled as I corrected Milan. I fidgeted with my wedding band for a few seconds, thought I might need to remove it in the next few months if my fingers swelled. "And, instead of a crew of kids all moving through schooling at the same rate, we will have a little one at home."

"Are you interested in the Bureau?"

Milan's calm question held layers of meaning. I thought of his life, of the confusing interagency reporting structures and intrigue, of the travel and possible round-the-clock phone calls, of all the conversations we had about when his job meant missing family events.

"I don't know, Milan. When I was a matron I wanted to be free of the layers of bureaucracy pulling me so many ways. As a private business owner, I'm always aware of my responsibilities. While I have the joy of living where I work, I carry a twenty-four-hour load like you." I sipped tea as I thought how to respond. "So I haven't thought about what I might do next." I put down my cup. "Retire?"

Milan laughed, a small sound that held little delight. "I think that word only describes what happens to outdated technology. Remember when our grandparents retired from jobs to garden and travel and be with their families?" One eyebrow rose. "Did you ever think you'd never stop working? That the American dream would change this much?"

Looking around the room, I found my memories of the time before the depression were vague—a mash of reality and film fantasy. The place where I had been a child didn't exist, and the cities where I wanted to live were far different than the places I knew as a young woman.

"Believe it or not, Milan, I just realized that what I really remember from all my life is just the past eight years—the Ashwood years."

ABOUT THE AUTHOR

Cynthia Kraack is the author of *Minnesota Cold*, a winner of the 2009 Northeastern Minnesota Book Award for Fiction, and *Ashwood*. *Harvesting Ashwood: Minnesota 2037* is the second book in the *Ashwood* trilogy. Cynthia is a graduate of the University of Southern Maine's Stonecoast M.F.A. program in Creative Writing and holds a graduate degree from the University of Minnesota as well as a bachelor's degree from Marquette University. Cynthia has published short stories and presented at a number of gatherings.

ACKNOWLEDGEMENTS

After my publisher, North Star Press of St. Cloud, Inc., the most heartfelt thanks go to my writing group for kind support and honest feedback. These terrific writers and friends deserve to be acknowledged by name: Roger Barr, Charles Locks, Loren Taylor, Paul Zerby, Terry Newby, and Pam Davis. Their insights and challenges push my work to a higher level.

I would also like to thank Lynn Marasco for her patient editing and guidance and Terrence Scott for another dramatic cover.

There are never enough opportunities to thank family and friends for all they add to my writing. Whether daily presence, late night talks, or the lure of lunch outside my office, these people allow the creative fire to stay alive. You have my love—Tom, Emily, Tim, Michelle, Pat, and Eric. For wisdom and endless love, I thank my father, Roman, and my mother-in-law, Helen. Ellen, you have a special place in my life, and I promise to put you in a future book. Thanks to my book club for expanding my horizons and the Dunker Dames for keeping my feet planted in the real world.